THE
UNGRATEFUL
DEAD

Also by Adam Simcox

The Dying Squad
The Generation Killer

THE UNGRATEFUL DEAD

ADAM SIMCOX

To Kirsty, Alfie and Oscar – easily my best trilogy.

First published in Great Britain in 2023 by Gollancz
an imprint of The Orion Publishing Group Ltd
Carmelite House, 50 Victoria Embankment
London EC4Y 0DZ

An Hachette UK Company

1 3 5 7 9 10 8 6 4 2

Copyright © Adam Simcox 2023

A CIP catalogue record for this book is
available from the British Library.

ISBN (Hardback) 978 1 473 23082 8
ISBN (eBook) 978 1 473 23081 1

Typeset by Input Data Services Ltd, Bridgwater, Somerset

Printed in Great Britain by Clays Ltd, Elcograph S.p.A.

www.gollancz.co.uk

Prologue

They came for us at night.

Not that night held any meaning any more. In our blackout bunker, time had ceased to justify itself as a concept. It was an elastic construct you knew existed, like air travel and elephants, but one you never personally experienced.

We were permitted one hour of light a day. This was a self-imposed diktat from my father, one my mother fought long and hard for. 'For the *texts*, my darling,' she would implore, her tone whispered, though no less urgent for it. 'Jacob must continue to learn the *texts*.'

'We know the texts by heart,' my father would always reply, jowls wobbling in fear as well as defeat. Finally, he relented, permitting a single flame for a single hour. We'd gather around it, my sister and I, her hair matted, her lips mute, making her mouldy bunny dance to the flame as I laid the book spine on my knees, my eyes squinting at the scratchy scrawl, my mouth whispering the words, my mother and father's eyes closed, their faces locked in rapture, their lips twitching soundlessly along as I read.

After an hour, my father would snuff out the flame between

v

finger, thumb and saliva and plunge us into darkness once more. He'd tell us of what was to come on the other side, the things we'd see and the glory that awaited us.

Then they came.

To begin with I thought it a dream, dead-float dozing as I was between waking and sleeping. Wood ruptured a few feet away from me, torchlight punching through a few seconds later. We shuffled backwards as a second beam of light invaded the room, painting belongings we hadn't seen properly for months in spiteful hues.

The men at the end of the light spluttered, spitting curses about the stench, and animals, and shit and piss. Their insults had not changed in the time we'd hidden away.

As they spilled into our sanctuary, I realised it had to be winter, such was the thickness of their coats. Torchlight slashed at us, barbed-wire beams lingering on our faces and groping our bodies.

'Is he there?' barked a voice.

Light blistered my eyes, my raised hand doing little to dissuade it.

'A man and woman,' another voice replied. 'A girl and boy.'

'Is he *there*?' the voice insisted.

I felt hands on me, prising my arms away from my face.

The smell of soured milk filled my nostrils. The musk of something curdled. A small grunt of satisfaction.

'He's there,' said the soldier.

Rough hands dragged me from a place I hated but that had until now sheltered us.

'Please,' said my father, '*please*. Let my son go. He's no good to you. Take us, but not him.'

What about Hennie? I wanted to say. *What about her? Is she not your daughter? Is she not your child?* It had always been like this.

I was the Crown Jewels of my father's eye, the justification for our existence. Earthly trifles were an indulgence. My sister was an indulgence.

My eyes fidgeted as we were dragged into the street, the black of the night a kaleidoscope of colours when set against what we'd been pulled from, the street lights crackling with aggression, poking at my skin, violating its pores, digging itself in.

A truck waited at the bottom of the street. The back of it bulged, flesh shapes pressing against its canvas hide. We all knew what it was for. We'd be together, at least. That meant something.

The soldiers yanked my family towards it, a hand on my back guiding me away.

'My son,' my father called out. 'Where are you taking him?'

A rifle butt answered. That was the way these men talked.

Hands spirited me away, firm but delicate, as if I were some sort of priceless antique the soldiers had liberated and didn't want to break.

'I want to go with my family,' I said to myself, to the soldiers, to God.

'No,' the soldier said. 'You don't.'

I asked where they were being taken, already knowing the answer. I wanted him to say it, though, this shaved warthog, this stumpy blob of flesh with a gun, wanted him to own the crime he was committing. Instead he said nothing, funnelling me towards an idling black Mercedes, its exhaust fumes warming themselves against the night air, a layer of frost caressing the vehicle's bonnet and roof.

A man stood on the car's running board. His trench coat was too well cut for him to be a soldier; it could have come from my father's own shop. Expensive-looking circular glasses perched themselves on his pointed, beak-like nose.

He smiled as we approached. No grimace was ever as terrifying.

'It's the one we seek?' he asked, looking past me.

Not him, 'it'.

The warthog soldier nodded, eager to please, or desperate not to displease. 'I've checked his papers. This is the boy.'

The man who wasn't a soldier nodded, reaching into his leather coat and withdrawing a silver cigarette case.

'Herr Himmler will be pleased.'

Minutes seemed like hours and days felt like decades. When we'd been hiding in our shelter, time had lost all meaning, but there had been tent poles to moor myself with. The hour of candle. A meal in the gloom. Habits. Traditions.

In the car, there was nothing. I would wake in a narcotic fog, permission slips of consciousness revealing the blur of a street lamp or the midday haze of fields rolling. I don't know how long we drove for. It could have been hours or days, but one thing was constant: the man in the back seat pressed himself against the window as if I were plague incarnate. The only time he moved was to inject me. I would feel the tip of the needle puncture my vein, narcotics flooding my system, dipping me under the haze.

Eventually the injections became less regular and something like clarity began to return. Trees flanked us, street lamps deserted us. Concrete absconded. *Where are you taking me?* I would ask, my speech slurred, my face dope-slack. The man simply looked away, as if such a question was nonsensical and not worthy of his time or mine.

Then it appeared.

The castle was a scar on the horizon's canvas. Three towers stood guard, the walls that kept them at arm's lengths so mighty it was as if concrete had been poured onto the sky to form them. Its appearance seemed to energise my travelling companion. He sat up straight, his left leg jiggling, pitched on the edge of his seat. 'How fortunate you are, boy. Wewelsburg is a place for the chosen few, not the filthy Jew. That a street rat like you should come here is perverse.'

It wasn't, though. Not when you considered what Wewelsburg was, what it represented, and who I was. When you considered that, Castle Wewelsburg and I were made for each other.

As we pulled up to the courtyard, the car juddering over the castle's blistered cobbles, a man stood waiting for us. He wore the uniform of Nazi royalty but not the bearing. There was a slovenly air to him. Receding greying hair stood up in clumps, and his untucked shirt climbed out from his pressed black britches. His face looked like it was squabbling with itself.

He opened the door, yanking me out without so much as a word of greeting. His gloved hands cupped my face, his shark-black eyes staring hungrily into mine. His leathery fingers creaked as he examined my skull, prodding and poking at it.

'Enough, Wiligut.'

A voice from behind my examiner rang around the courtyard, high-pitched and shrill. The man called Wiligut gave my head a final tap, as if trying to ascertain its hollowness, then stepped reluctantly aside.

My parents had sheltered my sister and myself from the worst of the Nazis' crimes, but there was no shielding a Jew from the likes of Heinrich Himmler. He loomed over everything, a pencil-moustached bogeyman whose existence demanded the end of ours. Hitler was reviled, but Himmler was feared; he was seen as the substance behind the Führer's bilious poison cloud. I never expected to meet him in real life, but real life, it seemed, intended for me to meet him.

He had a parched head, anorexic spectacles resting on a nose of skinny gristle, his face shorn of everything but the barest of features, like they were a luxury his genius didn't have time for. As he stood there waiting for me, the black castle loomed over him like it had been moulded to his exact specifications. I would later learn that it had.

Wiligut shoved me and I stumbled, my legs unconvinced, unpractised as they had become at walking.

Himmler frowned, reaching out a hand and taking my arm, preventing me from falling. 'Your manners do you few favours, Wiligut. Is that any way to treat a guest?'

'I prefer to think of him as a false prophet,' Wiligut replied. 'And will treat him as such.'

Himmler placed an arm around my shoulders, and my stomach lurched in response. 'You'll treat him well, because that's what I order.'

Wiligut trembled slightly, like his disgust was trying to escape.

Himmler crouched down in front of me, his mouth smiling, his eyes not. 'Your name is Jacob Block, is it not?'

I nodded. I saw little point in denying it. 'What do you want from me?'

He smiled.

'Everything.'

They watched as I ate. The act seemed like a betrayal of my family, but my body disagreed; it had received no sustenance for hours (days?), so when the casserole was placed in front of me, my hands moved of their own accord. I had devoured three mouthfuls before looking up to seek permission. Himmler smiled indulgently. Wiligut didn't try to hide his contempt.

'Do you know what we do here, Jacob?'

I shook my head.

'Perhaps you would like to explain it?' said Himmler, looking to the older man. 'Karl Wiligut here is the spiritual conscience of our movement. So much of what we've achieved – what you will help us to go on to achieve – is down to him.'

Wiligut peered into his glass of wine, a small smile on his lips. 'The credit belongs to you, Heinrich. My beliefs were there to be embraced by all – only you saw the truth of them.'

Himmler nodded towards me. 'Why don't you tell our young friend here the true history of the Fatherland? It is important, I think, for what comes next.'

Wiligut drank deeply, then replaced the glass on the table. He considered me with his coal-black eyes. 'What do you know of Atlantis?'

I knew little. I told him less.

'German culture – to which your Kike tribe has contributed precisely nothing – can be traced back to 228,000 BC,' he said. 'This was a time when the earth had three suns, and giants walked the sun-blasted earth. I myself am descended from the line of kings who ruled these lands.'

I chanced a look at Himmler, who was staring rapt at his apparent mentor.

'These lands were settled by the survivors of Atlantis, and my people were the best of these survivors, sages who were eventually driven into the wilderness by jealous rivals. In much the same way that your tribe seeks to drive out the true holders of the flame in our blessed country. I can read your mind, you see, little Jacob. It is a fetid, depraved thing, submerged in subterfuge and dishonesty.'

He's insane, I thought. He's either kidding me along, having a joke at my expense, or he's completely insane.

Himmler, though, hung on Wiligut's every word. I had no doubt he'd heard the diatribe on many occasions, but the expression on his face made it seem like he was hearing it for the first time. It was then, as Wiligut continued to rant about dwarves and dragons and telepathy, that I grew truly afraid. Not because I believed what he was saying, but because *he* believed it. And if he – and more importantly, Himmler – believed such ravings, then they would believe what was said about me.

Believe who I was, and what I was destined to become.

On the third day, they took me to the laboratory.

I'd been confined to my room, meals brought to me first thing in the morning and last thing at night, heaps of meat slopped onto plates of exquisite china, each meal feeling like my last. The helpings were so gargantuan when compared to the scraps I'd been used to in the shelter, I felt like a prize pig fattened for the cull. That a soldier sat with me, watching me devour every morsel, only strengthened that feeling.

There wasn't so much as a notebook in the room, so for hours I stared out at the castle's rolling grounds, a barrier of mist lingering at the perimeter, almost as if it were afraid of it. The world I'd left behind was unimaginable, the fate that was to befall my family unthinkable.

'They'll come for us eventually,' my father had said to me the evening before we locked down and hid away. 'It's inevitable. They'll come for us and they'll take us away, but if I can buy us a few weeks, then I will. Why, though, Jacob, will you not be scared when the jackboots finally sound?'

'Because of who I am,' I replied, 'and because of what I will go on to become when I die.'

'Quite right,' said my father, ruffling my hair despite his general distrust of affection. 'Your mother and I would prefer that you live a long and fruitful life before that blessed day, but if the Nazis have other plans, then so be it.'

He pressed a pill into my hand, closing my fist around it. 'I want you to promise me something, if we're taken. Swallow this tablet. Don't hesitate. Don't think about it. It will be painless. It will be quick. It will not be suicide, which would be punishable by the Almighty, but escape. Within five minutes you'll slip away, and paradise will await. Promise me, Jacob.'

I did. It's easy to say yes when no doesn't present itself as an option.

I turned the tablet over so many times, I knew every groove in it, every last grain and indentation. It had been easy to conceal from my captors, and it would be easier still to let it slip down my gullet on a flume of water. It was what my father wanted. What he'd ordered me to do.

I want you to smile when you take that tablet, boy. It will liberate you in a way the living world never will.

I sat on the bed, looking at the tablet, wondering whether that sort of liberation was what I truly wanted.

Then the door was rapped sharply, the handle turned, and my hand made the decision for me, stuffing the pill into the pocket of my trousers.

Himmler stood there, a suit bag in his hand and a leering grin on his face. 'I thought I'd bring you a uniform more appropriate. Your new life starts today, Jacob.'

He slid down the bag's zip, revealing what was inside.

'I won't wear it,' I said, the words out of my mouth before my brain could quarantine them.

The smile on Himmler's face slipped its leash. 'Yes,' he said, 'you will.'

He took a step towards me.

I swallowed, wishing it was to wash the suicide pill down.

Several moments later, I studied myself in the mirror.

I'd seen the uniform of the Hitler Youth before, of course. What had started as a niche concern quickly became aggressively mainstream, members strolling around the school yard like they owned the place, which they did. The star I was forced to wear on my breast made me the juiciest of targets for these thugs. The teachers stepped in to begin with, then didn't. When we were banned from attending school, it was a relief. Certainly, it was to my mother and father. They felt school interfered with my real studies.

What would they say now, if they could see me in my Youth uniform? Thick brown shirt, tie around my neck, swastika wrapped around my arm like a tourniquet?

Endure, is what they'd say. *This life is merely the prelude, an indulgence before your real life truly begins. Wear the uniform. Raise your arm and salute false gods. Take whatever name they give you.*

Tell them nothing.

Protect the Pen.

Part 1

Too Much Future

Chapter 1

Poor but sexy. That was how Ella's dad described Berlin.

Ella wasn't convinced. As far as she could see, poor had sold out long ago, and sexy had always been in the eye of the beholder.

Certainly there wasn't much sex appeal in front of her. SO36 was an embalmed vision of punk rock past. Real effort had gone into making the club look as run-down as possible; it was like an interior designer had asked Alexa to show them weaponised nostalgia, then followed the AI's designs to the letter.

Not that Ella cared particularly. Punk rock had always been her dad's thing (her grandad's too, if the old man's stories were to be believed), and she'd never begrudged him teasing the little hair he'd had left into a blue mohawk. She'd even refrained from taking the piss when he'd bought a new leather jacket then spent the best part of a week making it look like a frayed life partner. Just like everyone else here, he hadn't so much tried to recapture his East German youth as chloroform it.

No one really seemed to be old in society any more; there were kids like her, and there were old-timers in retirement homes waiting to die. Everyone else took a hammer to middle age and pounded it into a smear of youthful mush.

The support band finished their set and the crowd dispersed, making their way towards her vantage point at the bar. She drew a few curious glances, as she'd known she would; she was the youngest person here by about thirty years. It wasn't just her age, though. She was the spitting image of her dad, and half the people here would have known him. Liked him, too, because he'd been that sort of guy. Even his enemies still loved her papa.

Ella shivered, taking a slug of water and noting, not for the first time, the slightly odd atmosphere in the place, the distrustful glances exchanged between the old punks. 'When a city's gutted down the middle like Berlin was, the stitches sewing it back together don't always take,' her dad had told her. 'If elephants never forgot, old punks stubbornly refuse to; defections and perceived betrayals throb still in the city's veins.'

What she'd give to see him again.

That was what tonight was about. The chance to make that crazy dream a reality.

'I knew you'd come.'

She turned to see a punk slouching against the bar. She hadn't noticed him approach, but then in his game she supposed that was a virtue. Certainly it was impressive when you considered his size and general appearance. Green trench coat, a straggling apology of spiked hair. Just another ageing punk in a room full of them.

The difference was Klaus Weber's profession.

'How did you know I'd come?' Ella replied. '*I* didn't know I'd come.'

'Because you loved your dad. Because today would have been his birthday, and there was nowhere he loved more than this place.'

She looked around and shook her head. 'It's like a punk crypt. A fucking rock-and-roll theme park.'

Klaus laughed. 'So cynical. You're a punk, Ella. It's in your blood.'

She took another slug of water. 'Do you have them?'

He clasped his hands together. 'I have one. That's more than enough, believe me.'

'I'm no lightweight,' said Ella.

'This isn't coke or ket. This is a medical-grade drug that doesn't officially exist.'

'For something that doesn't exist, an awful lot of people seem to know about it.'

'An awful lot of people talk shit,' said Klaus. 'I'm the only supplier in the city. You wouldn't have a chance of buying from me if it wasn't for your dad.'

'Will it work? Will I see him?'

'It'll work all right. Whether you'll see him depends on whether he's here or not.'

'If he's going to be anywhere, he's going to be here,' said Ella. 'It was his favourite place in the world. How much?'

Klaus told her. Ella considered the amount daylight robbery.

She was bathed in the light of night, though, so she paid the money and took delivery of the bright pink pill.

She threw it down her throat, chasing it with a slug of water.

Now all she had to do was wait.

It was called Spook and if it was a party pill, the Day of the Dead festival was its spiritual home.

The rumours about it had started a couple of months ago. About how taking it allowed you to see the dead. You didn't split it, and you didn't take more than one. Ella had been cynical – since that girl blew up Tokyo, *everyone* claimed they could see the dead – but ultimately, curiosity had drowned her cynicism.

Desperation, too. It was a year to the day since her dad had died, which meant it was a year to the day that a big part of her had died, too. If this drug was legit, it meant she could see him again. Talk to him. Let him know how much she missed him. When she'd discovered his favourite band were playing at his favourite club on what would have been his sixtieth birthday, well, she'd seen it as a sign.

A murmur went up from the crowd, one that hinted that within minutes the lights would dip, the band would come on stage and the real world would be forgotten for a while. That appealed to Ella. The real world hadn't been working out so well for her lately. Her school grades were in the toilet, and her mum was constantly on her case. It was like her mum didn't miss her dad at all. Like all she could do was sweat the unimportant stuff.

She looked around the club. Everyone here was old, but they were pretty visibly not dead. They were supposed to glimmer, ghosts. That was what people who'd dropped Spook said on-line, anyway. Not much glimmer here, just manufactured dirt and grime.

The track pumping over the venue's speakers came to an end.

The lights dimmed.

Here we fucking go.

The band took the stage.

Colonel, the frontman and lead guitarist, stood, arms aloft, a returning general soaking up the acclaim of his grateful subjects. Ella could never quite make her mind up about Colonel – he was either the coolest dude around or one you wanted to beat to death – but her dad always said that was the point of a good frontman. You didn't want them to be like you. *You* were boring, and you came to gigs to escape boring.

Ella swallowed. Nothing doing with the pill, yet.

'We are the people!' Colonel bellowed into the microphone. 'We are the power!'

The chant was taken up by the crowd, who pressed in closer to the stage.

A techie handed Colonel a guitar. Feedback rang around the room.

The first chords were struck in fury.

Then it began to happen.

It was like Ella had something in the corner of her eye. A shimmering blur of light, just outside her range of sight. The more she squinted, the blurrier it got. Then it solidified a little.

There was someone on stage with the band who wasn't the band.

She could tell that by the way they glimmered. Couldn't tell much besides that, at least not yet, but it was like there was a hologram up there on stage. A glitchy-as-fuck one.

Ella's throat was dry. She lifted her bottle of beer, frowning when she realised it was empty. She needed another drink. That would settle her down a bit.

She backwards-shuffled towards the bar, her eyes fixed on the stage. The figure on it was gaining clarity by the second. Whoever it was, they were short.

No.

Could it be him? It was what the rumours always said, of course, but she'd never really believed them. She just liked the fact they were there to believe.

Where was her dad? She'd been so sure he'd be here. Instead, she'd got an urban myth.

She called out her dad's name, more in desperation than expectation.

People were looking at her strangely.

'What are you drinking?'

Ella turned reluctantly away from the stage, realising she'd backed all the way up to the bar.

She blinked.

This couldn't be real.

A man was standing behind the bar. He had an old Stones T-shirt on, a pair of beaten-looking grey jeans and a shock of flame-coloured hair teased into a blizzard of spikes. So far so punk, but he also glimmered. And that was where the horror began, not ended: his face was covered with green vines. One had popped clean through his eyeball. Others wound their way out of his mouth.

'What are you drinking?' the flame-coloured vine man asked again.

Ella staggered away, knocking into the gig-goers around her, drawing looks of irritation she didn't notice.

Her throat got drier. Felt like it was tightening, too.

She stumbled, her knees going, the floor coming. She smacked against it, hard. A mosh pit had formed in front of her. Most people hadn't noticed her fall, but a couple had. They had the same vines as the man at the bar. A woman with a mane of them flowing down her back. A man with them wound tightly round his fists like a boxing glove.

Half the man's face seemed to be missing.

Ella began to scream, and found that once she'd started, it was difficult to stop.

Chapter 2

'Theatre of Dreams. Theatre of shite, more like.'

'Very poetic,' said Megan, rolling her eyes.

Bits puffed out his chest proudly. 'Fucking Oscar Wilde, me.'

'Maybe, now he's dead.'

'No one's really dead,' said Bits. 'Look at me. 'Sides, I met the cunt in the Pen once.'

'No you didn't,' said Megan.

'Straight up. Mouthy bastard, Wilde. Mopey as fuck, too.'

'Well, he *was* dead. Has to put a cramp on your mood, that.'

'Bollocks. I'm a sunbeam.'

'You're a moron,' said Megan, 'but that's all right, because you're *my* moron.'

She swayed with the tram, allowing herself a small smile. On striking up this partnership with the dead-as-dead Bits, she'd perfected the trick of talking out of the corner of her mouth. She'd then realised it was a pointless skill to have in the modern age; all she needed to do was stick in a pair of headphones and it looked like she was chatting on the phone rather than to thin air.

She looked to her left, then right. The tram was packed full of United fans, most of them in stomach-clinging replica shirts. Not a flattering garment on runway models, let alone beery football supporters. Still, they weren't paying her any attention, which was a novelty. Her escape from the Generation Killer had lent her unwanted notoriety. She was used to double-takes in the street as people tried to work out where they knew her from.

She usually just told them she'd been on *Love Island*.

That she'd survived Elias, the aforementioned killer, was thanks to Bits. His partner, Joe Lazarus, too. Lazarus was missing as a result of that rescue, so when Bits had asked for her help in finding him, Megan had figured it was the least she could do. And in the course of that investigation, if she found out information on her own sketchy past – namely, just why it was she could see the dead, and how a grandfather she'd never known fitted into that – then all the better.

On cue, she picked at the barcode on the back of her hand, a skin comfort-blanket she didn't know she needed.

'Bad habit, that,' said Bits.

'I've had worse,' Megan replied, peering out of the window. Floodlights punched the sky as Old Trafford loomed on the horizon, a sight sufficient to ignite another round of chanting in the tram carriage. She noticed Bits twitch slightly. If she hadn't known what to look for, she'd have missed it, but she did, so she didn't.

'You need a gum hit?'

He shook his head. 'Had some of the gas and air back at the shelter, didn't I?'

'That was a couple of hours ago.'

'Need to ration it. Running low on supplies.'

'If you give it away to every Tom, Dick and poltergeist, it *will* run low.'

Bits sniffed. 'Can't keep it all for myself, can I? Not what the shelter's about.'

'The last person to run the shelter tortured then killed the spirits staying there,' said Megan. 'I think the mission state-ment's become muddied.'

'My job to clean it up, then. Seeing as it was the Pen that employed that person.'

Megan considered him. 'Tell me honestly: how much mem-ory gum do you have left?'

He looked away. 'Couple of days' worth. Three, with the gas and air.'

'Then you'll have to go back to the Pen?'

'If I can. Was tricky as fuck getting to the soil – can't imagine getting back's going to be much easier. Not even going to try, until I find Joe.'

'How do you know he's still around?'

'Because the bloke we're about to see reckons he met him a week ago.'

The bloke was known as Spooky Dave.

It was a nickname that suggested a character of whimsy and wonder, the sort of fellow who counted Halloween as his favourite holiday. That he was one of the hardest fuck-ers in Manchester had always amused Bits, when he'd been alive enough to be amused. Now he was dead, it merely in-trigued him.

He walked shoulder to shoulder with Megan as they climbed the steep concrete steps into the Stretford End's guts. He'd been to Manchester derbies when he'd been breathing, but that was when he'd had a season ticket for Maine Road: it had been inflatable bananas, E's and 5–1 thrashings in those days. He'd never set foot in United's ground before, and wasn't comfortable doing so now.

Still, a tingle prickled his spine as he was greeted by the vision of seventy-odd-thousand baying, yelling football fans. It was a sight he never thought he'd see again, and such a display of pure, unfiltered life was both wonderful and a raking reminder of what he'd lost.

Like your mate winning the lottery, he thought. You're pleased for him, but you're pissed off it didn't happen to you instead.

'Ever been to a football match before?' he asked Megan.

'Once,' she replied. 'An ex took me. I brought a book along, so it wasn't a complete waste of time.'

'Bet he loved that.'

'Split up at half-time, which was forty-five minutes too late.'

Bits shook his head. 'You're well high-maintenance.'

'Yeah, I'm a real princess. Where's the guy we're supposed to be meeting?'

Bits tore his attention from the on-pitch action, transferring it to the transfixed crowd. He knew they'd come out at the right entrance, but spotting Spooky Dave amongst this glut of humanity would still prove tricky.

Until it wasn't.

He pointed upwards. Megan followed his finger to ten rows above him.

'You've got to be fucking joking,' she said.

If he hadn't been so feared, Spooky Dave would have been catcalled at every United home game. As it was, the row above and below his didn't so much as look in his direction. A few hands were raised and lowered to shake when paying their respects, but these were season-ticket holders. The tourists, if they were caught staring at Dave and the empty row of seats next to him, were quickly encouraged by the regulars to avert their gaze down to the pitch. You didn't stare at Spooky Dave without a copper-bolted invitation, and usually not even then.

Fortunately for them, Bits did have such an invitation, and he was counting on Dave being intrigued enough by Megan, seeing as she shared his ability to see the dead, to give her a pass.

To the naked living eye, the ten seats next to Spooky Dave were empty. Those fans who sat below and above them would often complain of a cold, damp draught, one that went above the usual chilly winds football grounds 'enjoyed'. That was because the seats were anything but empty: Megan stared, fascinated, at the row of shimmering spirits that occupied them. Their milky eyes were focused with a laser-like intensity on the pitch, all of them wearing United shirts from different eras.

Ghostly football hooligans, she thought. I've seen it all now. Or rather, I haven't. I've only seen the tip of an insane fucking iceberg.

Spooky Dave gave the spirits a run for their money, looks-wise.

He'd eschewed the regulation replica shirt for a sharply cut navy shirt. A deepred turban sat on top of his head, and his long black beard was streaked with slivers of grey. Megan put him at sixty, but wouldn't have been surprised to discover he was fifteen years either side of that estimation.

He stood, arms crossed, surveying the action on the pitch impassively. Such an action would have normally brought a steward's request to sit down, but here the officials very pointedly looked in the other direction.

'You can see them, then.'

A voice deeper than she'd have expected. One that couched no fuckery.

She shuffled along the row to the left of the spirits, stopping when she was one (free) seat away from Dave. 'They're hard to miss.'

'Every other fucker in the ground has. Never met another like me, that could see the dead. Thought I was a freak.'

'If you are,' said Megan, 'then we're a couple of freaks to-gether.'

Because I mean it. And the more he sees what we've got in common, the more he'll trust me.

Or trust me as much as someone nicknamed 'Spooky' can.

'Curse it more times than I don't,' said Dave. 'Scared me shitless as a young'un.'

'Makes a liar of any adult that says there's no bogeyman in your wardrobe, or under your bed,' Megan replied. 'Because usually there is.'

'Normalised it all, didn't she? That Hanna girl and her video.' Dave's gaze was still on the pitch. 'Now half the world claims to see the dead. All it took was her nuking Tokyo.'

Megan nodded. 'Hate late-adopters. It's like when a band you've liked for ages gets famous without your permission.'

Spooky Dave finally tore his attention from the pitch and looked from Megan to Bits, who hovered a few feet back. 'What's a young girl like you hanging out with an old lag like that for?'

'Twenty-three when I got blown up,' Bits replied, puffing out his sparrow chest.

'City-centre bomb was decades ago,' Dave replied, 'so death must suit you.'

Megan nodded towards the spirits that sat alongside Dave, with their smorgasbord of United shirts. 'Are these people you knew?'

Dave nodded. 'My old foot soldiers. None of them passed over when they died. Seems to go that way sometimes, when they've been a wrong'un and met a vicious death.'

Megan stared at them closely. They were a motley crew. None of them looked like they'd gone quietly into the good night.

Ah. Now she realised how Bits had obtained this meeting.

'We've had a couple of these lads in the shelter.'

Spooky Dave nodded. 'Been dead a while, most of them. They get confused, except for when there's a match on; it's the only thing they really understand. Vines over their body. Elias, the bloke before, took care of them.'

Until he didn't, Megan didn't say.

'Now that your lad Bits here has taken over, he does the same thing for 'em. Gives them a bit of dignity. Cares for them. Doesn't go unnoticed by the likes of me.'

'Do what I can,' said Bits, shuffling, embarrassed. 'It's not much, but it's more than fuck-all.'

One of United's strikers blazed over the bar. Megan allowed for the *oooh* before saying: 'Bits reckons you've seen Joe Lazarus.'

'Right out with it. Good for you. Who's got time to fuck around?'

Not me, thought Megan. Not Joe, either.

The whistle blasted for half-time. Finally Dave gave her his full attention. 'Yeah, I've seen your ghost. Can always smell plod, dead or alive. He was with a German fella. Hans.'

'Was Hans dead?' asked Bits.

Dave shook his head. 'Alive, though someone should have told his complexion. Nasty-looking bastard.'

'How did the meeting come about?'

'They know I'm the main boy that deals with Berlin. Move a lot of gear from there to here. It's my main supply source.'

'Was Joe trying to arrest you?' said Bits, frowning.

'He's a fucking spirit,' Dave spat. 'How would that work? Nah, he was working with this Hans. They wanted to know if I'd been offered a drug called Spook.'

'Had you?' said Bits.

'I wouldn't touch that shit.'

'What does it do?' asked Megan.

'Word is you pop a pill, and it lets you see the dead, just like you and me can.'

15

She shook her head. 'That's got to be bollocks.'

'Why? There have to be more like us. What's to stop some mad scientist experimenting on them? Hop, skip and a jump to them being able to bottle it up and sell it to punters who want to experience the same thing.'

'But why would anyone want that?'

'You're a woman that asks a lot of questions,' Dave said.

'I'm a woman that needs a lot of answers,' Megan replied. 'Appreciate you don't have a reason in the world to give me them.'

He considered, then shrugged. 'Likes of me and you need to stick together. No other fucker'll have our back.'

'Why are people taking it, then?'

'Why's anyone take any drug? For the kick. For the thrill. It doesn't last for ever, and that Hanna lass, she got a lot of people curious. Started something with what happened in Tokyo. Pill only lasts a few hours, from what I hear. Fuck, *I'd* drop one if I couldn't see the dead.'

'This Spook something you sell, then?' asked Bits.

Dave shook his head. 'I said I didn't, cloth ears. Side-effects are brutal. Potent as fuck, and if you take more than one, you're dead. Not worth it. I'm old school. Like the classics. Know where I stand with coke and E's. This Spook muck? All bets are off.'

'You give Joe any info?' said Bits.

Dave shot him a look that could kill the dead. 'I'm no snitch. Plod's plod, whether it's breathing or not.'

Megan looked from Dave to Bits curiously.

'He doesn't count,' said Dave, 'because he's one of our own, no matter what his dead sheriff's badge says.'

'Did you get a sense of why Joe wanted to know about this drug?' she asked.

'Got the sense he was the junior partner. Hans was calling the shots.'

'What were their intentions, do you think? Did you get the impression they were trying to stop the supply of Spook, or seize it for themselves?'

'Joe wouldn't be interested in that tackle,' said Bits.

'What about Hans, though?' Megan replied.

'Got no more info on him,' said Dave. 'I know someone that might, though.' He nodded at Bits. 'Your Michelle.'

Bits swallowed, vertigo taking hold. 'What?'

'You used to knock around with her when you were still breathing. Right?'

He nodded.

'Well, her and her nephew have a bit of a rival concern going. Small-time enough not to put my nose out of joint, and they pay me the right respect. They flog anything new on the market. Road-test it. You want to find this Joe of yours, and this Spook drug he's chasing, that's where I'd start.'

Chapter 3

The guilty always had a certain look.

In Joe's experience, this look wasn't furtive; furtive was for rank amateurs. It wasn't shifty, either. No, the truly guilty had a sort of simmering rage that bubbled just underneath the surface. The naïve would see this as indignation at being wrongly accused, but Joe knew the truth: it was anger at being caught out. Frustration that someone had scraped away their lies to reveal the truth. If there was one thing he knew, it was that he was good at finding that truth, even if it was unpalatable.

Especially if it was unpalatable.

Take the man tied to the chair in front of him. He had guilt plastered all over his trust-fund face.

This was not a man used to being taken to task. This was not a man used to being disbelieved, and it made that man angry. He was trying to smuggle this anger through the door as outrage, but his eyes betrayed him. He knew something, and it was Joe's job to find out what exactly.

'Do you believe in ghosts, Luke?'

Well, his and his partner's job.

Hans emerged from the shadows. It was like he'd stumbled out of Aryan-master-race casting; a shock of blonde hair buzz-cut to within an inch of its life, a frame of billowing muscle and rippling sinew, and a cut-glass South African accent that screamed mercenary. A fighter, even when he was a lover.

His eyes were his most striking feature, though. There was a glassy, glimmering quality to them, like they'd been ripped from the ghost of a shark.

The man tied to the chair certainly seemed unsettled by them.

'I don't know who you think I am,' said Luke, 'but you're making a big mistake.'

Hans placed his hands behind his back. 'Wouldn't be the first time. Doubt it will be the last. Now, I asked you a question: do you believe in ghosts?'

Joe smiled to himself. This was always the best bit.

'No, I don't believe in ghosts,' Luke said, puffing himself up as much as one could when one was tied to a chair, 'because I'm not six years old.'

Hans smiled. 'More's the pity, right? Things are so much simpler when you're a kid. Adults like you and me, we're always so quick to dismiss them, but kids *see* things, man. The shit three-year-olds have told me, it'd turn your hair white. Way I see it, those little kiddies don't have overactive imaginations – they're just telling us what they see. Maybe there *are* monsters under the bed. Or ghosts.'

'Why don't you go and fuck a ghost,' Luke said, a sneer on his face, 'considering you love them so much?'

Joe saw the fear behind the sneer. Luke was scared.

He was right to be.

Hans took a step forward. 'Maybe I will. Maybe I'll let you watch. That your kick, Luke?' He looked behind him, straight at Joe. 'What do you think, Lazarus?'

'Who you talking to?' said Luke, straining to see past Hans.

Hans didn't reply, instead gifting Luke a small smile.

The sneer slipped from Luke's face. 'Since that Tokyo thing, everyone sees ghosts. It's pure bullshit, man.'

Hans nodded sadly. 'Ghosts have become a thing, a drug to be passed around that everyone wants to try. Thing is, me and my partner, we think you've been helping them see those ghosts. Or rather, selling the means to see them. I'm talking about Spook.'

Luke put the sneer back on, but Joe was of the opinion it didn't fit as well this time.

'Never heard of it.'

Hans sighed. 'I mean, at least sell us the lie. You've obviously heard of it. *Everyone's* heard of it. A good number of them have tried it. A drug that lets you see the dead? What's not to love?'

Luke curled his lip. 'Don't run in those circles.'

'You're a drug dealer, man.'

'Bullshit.'

Hans held his hands up. 'Now, normally my partner and I wouldn't care. Not under our remit, dealers, even high-end ones like you. And you *are* high-end, my friend. Politicians. Footballers. Film stars. You're quite the shining light, aren't you? Which makes me think you supply Spook, too. Why wouldn't you? It's the hottest ticket in town.'

Spray out enough shit, thought Joe, and some of it will stick.

Hans took a couple of steps forward, then crouched down in front of Luke.

'I'm going to give you a chance to tell us what you know about it. You're big-time, but you're not the main event. Tell us who the Spook supplier is, and we'll send you on your merry way.'

'Don't know who you are or where you're getting your information from,' said Luke. 'I work in finance. Sure, I've dabbled in the odd bit of coke now and again – they literally pay it as bonuses. I'm not a dealer, though. Why would I be? It'd be a pay cut.'

Hans shook his head like he'd just been told he had terminal cancer.

'Reason why I asked you whether you believed in ghosts? It's because you're about to meet one.'

I'm up, thought Joe.

They'd got this routine down well now, the old good cop/ dead cop. It was strange: in many ways the brutality he was about to hand out fitted him like a glove, but then in other ways it felt contrived and plain wrong. He supposed that was the problem with struggling to remember who you were: false narratives and conjured-up histories competed for the right to tell you your truth.

He approached Luke, his fists flexing. It required a little drama, this act; go in all guns blazing and you sucked the tension right out of it. You had to properly haunt the suspect first. Do it right, and you didn't even need to throw a punch.

Unless you wanted to. Joe found that he usually did.

Circling the suspected drug dealer, he blew on the back of his neck. Luke shivered.

'Cold in here, right? said Hans, smirking. 'That's the problem with abandoned warehouses: they're draughty.'

'That's it?' said Luke. 'A little breeze, and you expect me to believe in ghosts?'

Joe leaned closer, drew back his finger, then flicked the restrained man's ear. Luke cried out in surprise.

'That was your ear,' said Hans. 'Imagine what comes next.'

Luke tried to look behind him. 'I'm a commodities broker, you prick. I don't know anything about Spook.'

Hans looked directly at Joe and nodded.

Joe returned the nod, then kicked out with his foot, sending

Luke and the chair sprawling to the floor. A small smile played on his lips. Hard to deny that this was enjoyable.

Luke yelled with pain. 'Who's doing that?'

'He's about five ten, white as snow, and pissed off,' said Hans. 'Who's supplying you with Spook?'

'No one,' said Luke.

Joe didn't wait for the nod this time; he drew back his foot and launched it into Luke's ribs. Kicking him in the stomach would have driven the wind and words out of him; the ribs would keep him nicely motivated.

'Who supplies the Spook?' said Hans.

'No one,' said Luke, his eyes roving the room, his face contorted in pain.

This time Joe kneeled down, slamming a fist into Luke's nose. Bone crunched. Blood splattered, passing through Joe's formless form. His own blood was up, a murky red mist settling over him. He could do this all day. Part of him wanted to.

Luke began to cry, all bravado driven from him, leaving little but snot and fear. 'I've never used Spook. I've passed coke around a few times, that's all. Never even sold it. Don't need the money. Don't need the heat.'

Another kick to the ribs. Another scream of pain.

'My partner? He'll cut off your dick,' said Hans. 'He's strange like that, but who am I to judge? The guy's dead. Has to leave you with a couple of hang-ups.'

Joe grabbed Luke's crotch and began to squeeze.

'OK, OK,' Luke yelled. 'I'll tell you what I know.'

Of course you will. Joe kept a firm grip.

'Mean it when I say I'm no dealer,' said Luke, his eyes wild and watering. 'Mean it when I say I work in finance, too.'

'That's not what we heard,' said Hans. 'We heard you talked tall about Spook. Heard you take it. Heard you sell it.'

That's why you snatched me?' said Luke. 'That bitch Janey's been running her mouth?'

'Worry about *your* mouth, and your ability to continue talking out of it,' said Hans.

Luke slumped in his seat. 'I'm full of shit.'

Not exactly a revelation, that one, thought Joe.

'I was at a party. There was this musician called the Metronome or some bullshit. Real pretentious fuck. He was talking large about Spook, saying he uses it in his creative process. Talks to the ghosts of dead musicians.'

Joe and Hans exchanged a look. This was news to them. A coked-up exec trying to muscle in on the drug-de-jour made sense. It had felt like a solid lead. This? Not so much.

Although when you were dead, solid was hard to remember, let alone trust.

'And you thought you'd steal his story?' said Hans. 'Pass it off as your own to look the big man. What girl wouldn't go weak at the knees?'

Luke nodded mutely.

Joe released his hold, getting to his feet.

Another time-waster. Another one jumping on the Spook bandwagon. Maybe Luke would prove to be a cautionary tale, because it wasn't just the side-effects of Spook that were dangerous; it was the side-effects of boasting you'd taken it. When you wanted to get it off the streets as badly as Hans and Joe did, that could be extremely hazardous to your health.

'You never saw me today,' said Hans. 'You even think of telling anyone about this, my dead friend will come back for you and finish what he started.'

'What would I tell them?' said Luke. 'Some psycho and his ghost tortured me?'

Hans laughed. 'That's my boy.'

23

He nodded to Joe, and they started to walk towards the warehouse exit.

'Who are you people?' called out Luke. 'Who do you work for?'

Hans smiled, then looked back at him. 'We're the Dying Squad.'

The car was so sleek it was like it was part of the road. Joe had owned one like it when he'd been alive, he was sure of it. Not this exact model – this was a Mercedes so new it was as if had been ripped directly from the production line – but one similar. His motor hadn't had the tablet on the dashboard (the one with the high-definition map on it), or at least he didn't think it had. Who knew? Memory was a slippery fucker when you were alive; when you were dead, it was like it was soaked in hog fat.

Music leaked from the speakers either side of him. Glitchy beats that massaged his brain.

'You're very quiet, Lazarus.'

'I'm thinking about the case.'

'Well, that's what you're here for,' Hans said. 'For all the good that's done us.'

'We're at the beginning of the investigation,' said Joe. 'You can give me the end-of-year report when we crack it.'

'There is no *we*,' said Hans, 'not until you regain your memories.'

Joe shifted in his seat. 'I still don't see why you can't just tell me about my past.'

Hans looked upwards, like he was trying to strangle frustration in its crib. 'I have. Repeatedly. Hourly. It never sticks.'

Joe blinked. 'I'm sorry; memory loss is a condition of being dead. I'm frustrated at the situation, so I can't imagine what it's like for you.'

Hans took a breath, then looked at him. 'We've given you the important stuff. That you work for the Dying Squad, solving crimes the living police can't. That we have to take this Spook poison off the market. The rest has to come back to you naturally, otherwise they're just pre-packaged facts that belong to someone else.'

'If you say so.'

'*Lucia* says so,' said Hans, 'and she's a ninja when it comes to this sort of thing. Memory's a fragile thing and needs to be treated as such. Until you get those memories back, you're here to squeeze into the places I can't. Listen where I can't.'

'Think what you can't, too.'

Hans pursed his lips. 'Big words from a dead man.'

'No disrespect intended,' Joe said. 'This is your show.'

'You'd do well to remember that.' Hans indicated right and eased the car onto a mist-shrouded side street.

Joe studied his face, in particular his glassy black eyes. 'Do they hurt?'

Hans kept his eyes on the road. 'Do what hurt?'

'Your eyes. Optical implants, right? That's why you can see me.'

He tightened his grip on the steering wheel. 'Know how many times we've had this conversation?'

'I'm sorry,' said Joe. 'It's my memory. It's sketchy, you know?'

'Unfortunately, I do,' said Hans.

'It's more a process of observation,' Joe continued. 'The sheen of your eyes is different. They glimmer almost like mine.'

'You said the exact same thing three hours ago,' said Hans. 'I'm nothing like you. You got that?' His hand went to his coat.

Joe winced. He knew what that meant.

'Sure,' he said hurriedly. 'Didn't mean anything by it.'

'You said that three hours ago, too.'

Joe reached for his notepad. The word *Dragnet* was embossed on the cover. He ran his finger around the lettering. He didn't know why it brought him comfort, but it did.

He flipped the notebook open. Almost half the pages had been ripped from the front; their tatty stubs jutted out from the book's spine. On the twentieth or so page, the following was written, Joe assumed recently, such was the wetness of the ink:

My name is Joe Lazarus.

I'm dead.

I'm a detective.

I report to Hans Becker. He reports to Lucia Fischer.

We work for the Dying Squad, a special task force set up to solve crimes the regular police can't. We're authorised to use maximum force to achieve this.

I was knocked unconscious on my last assignment, bringing to justice a murderer called the Generation Killer. This affected my memory, but Lucia and Hans are helping me to get it back.

I'm to assist them on an investigation. A drug called Spook is circulating on the market.

Spook allows the living to see the dead. There have been several deaths linked to the drug. It seems to have a particularly bad effect on teenagers between the ages of thirteen and eighteen. It's our job to find the supplier of the drug and take him into custody.

'So we work for the police,' he said.

'We work independently of the police,' said Hans. 'Read on.'

Joe did.

We've just discovered that a musician called the Metronome is a confessed Spook user.

26

I'm to enter his recording studio and question him to find out the details of the dealer he buys Spook from. We then work our way up the drug dealer food chain to find the main supplier.

That was the last entry.

He closed the notebook, returning it to his pocket.

'Why are *we* hunting for the Spook dealer?' he asked. 'Why not the regular police?'

'Because we specialise in crimes of the uncanny,' said Hans, 'and so we're better placed than the police to understand the situation. Spook's too dangerous to be left to circulate as some sort of party drug. We have full dispensation to use any means necessary to bring these scumbags to justice.'

Joe nodded, closing his eyes and letting the music from the speakers soak into his unconscious. Some of the entries in his notebook rang true, particularly the Dying Squad bit.

Other bits, not so much. He owed Lucia and Hans a great deal – they were the first people he truly remembered, since the accident on the last case – but he struggled to feel a connection to them. There were others in the Squad he had a greater affinity with, he was sure of it, but when he tried to grasp for their names and faces, they ducked out of sight.

It was strange, but the more he listened to the music in the car, the more the fuzzy gauze over his brain lifted. He couldn't remember the time before the Manchester storm drain as such, but he could feel a certain clarity returning to his thoughts. A certain sense of regret, too, at the way he'd dealt with the suspect back there. The way he'd beaten him. The way he'd enjoyed it. He couldn't say for sure that wasn't the person he'd been, but the brutality he'd dispensed felt alien.

Maybe he was just kidding himself.

The music cut out.

Joe's eyes snapped open.

'We're here,' said Hans.

Hans had brought the car to a stop on Köthener Strasse, a street snugly situated in Kreuzberg. Joe could see an artfully preserved section of the Berlin Wall around 150 metres away. Slipping through the driver's side, he wandered over to it, Hans's eyes burning into his back. The Wall was covered in graffiti, some of it ancient, some of it altogether more recent. One piece was particularly striking: it featured a stencil of a white-haired girl. There was something familiar about her. Had he met her before? Or was it just that her image seemed to be everywhere in this city?

Text had been sprayed underneath: *JUST BECAUSE I DIED DOESN'T MEAN I'M DEAD.*

Amen, sister.

If creative magic could seep into bricks and mortar, nowhere was more drenched than Kreuzberg's Hansa Studios.

A grand stone building that had remained unravaged by the bombs of the Allies, the music house had recorded some of the greatest artists of the twentieth century. U2, Depeche Mode and REM had all graced its hallowed halls, but it was David Bowie the music fans came to pay pilgrimage to; the Thin White Duke had recorded *Heroes* there when he'd been a Berlin resident in the seventies. It was one of those places where musical magic crackled in the air, where musicians old and new came to be inspired, and to make magic of their own.

If ever a place has ghosts, Joe thought, it's here.

Not that he'd seen any yet. The lateness of the hour meant only the most skeleton of staff were present: a dozing re-ceptionist here, a covert cleaner there. The Metronome, the

Spook-using musician they had come to hunt down, was here, though; according to Hans, he'd made a big show of booking Studio 3 for a full calendar year. Joe supposed that made sense. When you were collaborating with ghosts, it must be difficult to get them to stick to production schedules.

Studio 3 was easy enough to find, tucked away on the ground floor. The plaque on the wall announced that the studio had previously been a cinema. It was difficult to explain, but there was an undoubted energy to the place; perhaps the rumours about the Metronome weren't bullshit after all. Perhaps there were spirits at Hansa he was drawing upon.

Then again, the bloke in question called himself the Metronome.

'What you have to understand is, I'm not in charge. They are. I'm, like, the least senior member of the group. I'm the tea boy. The water carrier. I'm just a conduit for these geniuses, these musical colossuses. They talk and I listen.'

Joe crouched at the back of the recording studio, position-ing himself behind a mighty-looking mixing desk. The Metronome sat behind a grand piano a few dozen feet away, holding court to a couple of teenage girls, while trembles of techno music played in the background. He was a cliché wrapped in a stereotype, with his black turtleneck sweater and chunky jet-black glasses. The guy positively reeked of pretension.

Joe guessed bullshit, too.

The Metronome linked his fingers together, leaning forward towards the girls. 'Bowie came to me first, of course. Two months ago to the day. It was my first time on Spook. It was like a religious experience. Within a few minutes of dropping a pill, I saw him sitting at this very piano. "Metronome," he said, "you're a genius. You're my natural heir. I wasn't comfortable in heaven, knowing I'd never had the chance to work with you. We have to put that right.'"

'Who's Bowie?' one of the girls said.

Joe wasn't sure whether she was joking or not.

'The second night, that's when Kurt Cobain showed up,' the Metronome continued, oblivious. 'The third, Florian from Kraftwerk entered the building. It was like a communion of creativity.'

This guy's so full of shit he's positively drowning in it, thought Joe.

'Are they here now?' one of the girls asked, glancing around the room.

The Metronome looked at her intently. 'Would you like to find out?' He reached into his pocket, placing two blue pills on top of the piano.

Joe frowned. Everything they'd learned about Spook so far pointed to the pills being pink. A new product, perhaps, from a rival gang?

'This is Spook?' one of the girls asked.

The Metronome nodded. 'It'll show you things you won't believe.' He handed over a bottle of water. 'Welcome to a brave new world.'

The girls exchanged a look, then a smile. One after the other they took the pills.

The Metronome smiled. 'It'll happen quickly. Be ready.'

It happened quickly all right.

Both the effect of the drugs on the women and the confirmation that the Metronome dealt in weapons-grade bullshit.

Their eyes became glassy, but that wasn't because they'd become portals to view the dead; it was because their pupils were drowned in Rohypnol.

That wasn't all, because as Joe had approached the group,

30

there hadn't been the slightest hint of recognition from any of them.

The Metronome couldn't see Joe.

Couldn't hear him, either.

He no more used Spook than employed the vaguest sense of decency. He was a miserable small-time sex offender.

That didn't mean he couldn't be haunted.

The girls slumped off their seats unconscious, the crack they made on the studio floor eliciting a snigger from the Metronome. He rolled the sleeves of his turtleneck up like he was getting ready for an honest day's labour.

'If you can't handle your drugs, you shouldn't take them,' he said, moving closer to them. 'Lot of bad men around, willing to take advantage. Luckily for you, you've got me to keep you safe.'

Joe's fists clenched. He knew what men like this did to keep girls 'safe'.

The more the techno music played in the background – the more he listened – the more he feared he'd been one of those men once. Not a rapist, but an abuser in other ways.

A manipulator. Someone who used others for his purposes and benefit.

He told himself he wasn't now.

He also knew that the rules governing the dead didn't apply any more. Lucia and Hans had drilled that into him. There were no punishments for interacting with the living. No punishments for beating the living piss out of them, either.

As the Metronome reached for one of the girls, Joe caught him by the wrist, jamming it sharply upwards and taking no little satisfaction from the scream of pain and the sound of snapping bone. The musician looked wildly around as Joe grabbed him by the throat, then dragged him back towards the piano.

'You can't see me,' said Joe, 'or hear me, because you're a

fucking fake. But I like to think that on some level you can understand me.'

He drove the younger man's face into the keys, the cartilage in his nose snapping, his mouth howling, blood streaming.

'Nah,' said Joe, 'I don't think you've got it yet.'

He forced the Metronome down onto the stool, grabbing his uninjured hand and forcing it onto the keys.

'Sweaty rapists,' he said, 'don't deserve nice things.'

He raised the lid, then slammed it down, the Metronome's fingers cracking under the pressure. Again and again Joe brought the lid down, the musician screaming as his fingers became mushed sausages. On the fifth slam, he passed out.

Joe stepped back, allowing the Metronome to collapse off the stool, unconscious.

It wouldn't have been most people's idea of justice.

Most people weren't him.

'You took your time.'

'I wasted my time,' said Joe, joining Hans as he leaned against the car. 'The guy's a fake. I doubt he can spell Spook. He's certainly never taken it.'

'How do you know?' said Hans.

'Because I was in the same room as him, and he didn't so much as blink at me. He's a dead end.'

Hans nodded at the passenger side. 'Just as well as I've got a lead for us, then. There's been another Spook overdose. At teenage girl, at SO36.'

'What's SO36?'

'A punk club. Now stop asking stupid questions and get your dead arse in the car.'

Joe cast a final glance at the recording studio. He'd lost himself in there. Or maybe he'd found himself.

Neither of those possibilities brought him much comfort.

Chapter 4

Nothingness had never seemed so intimidating.

Mabel stared resolutely ahead, her hand firmly on the airship's tiller, the eyes of forty children on her back, the one called Chestnut older than the others and staring twice as hard because of it.

To the uninformed, the scene through the cockpit screen was a void of blackness. Mabel, fortunately, wasn't uninformed; she had the navigational controls of the blimp to guide her, but she didn't need them. She knew where she was going by instinct. How could she not, when you considered who she was on her way to see?

'You ever been this far out before?' asked Chestnut, plunging her hand into the leather satchel that lay at her feet.

'No one's ever been this far out before,' said Mabel, her eyes fixed on the cockpit screen.

'How do you know where we're going, then?

'I just do. Trust in that, girl.'

Chestnut took out a roll of stickers from the satchel and held them up. Each one contained a fresh insult.

I BLOW GOATS
I SHAG DOGS
I DRINK PISS

'What's this?' she asked.

Mabel smirked. 'Daisy-May's idea of a joke. Dying Squad, when they go to the soil, they have name tags to remind them of who they are. Fella called Joe Lazarus, she'd always play tricks on him. Swap one of these insults for his name tag.'

Chestnut smiled as she came across one that said *GIRL BOSS*, ripping it off and sticking it onto her T-shirt, then dropping the roll of stickers back into the bag. She turned towards the main display screen, moving closer to it and tapping it with her finger. 'It's pound-shop space out there, man. Low-budget, like they couldn't afford the fucking stars.'

Mabel shook her head. 'Mouth on you. It's like you're doing a cover version of Daisy-May. You used to put flowers in her hair, you know that?'

'So everyone keeps saying. Amazing what being half poisoned in the Gloop can do for your temperament.'

They both looked behind them at the unconscious form of Daisy-May. It was impossible not to. Her presence in the cockpit was massive, despite the frailty of her frame.

The cockpit screen – and the blanket of blankness it showed – drew them back soon enough.

'Beyond the Pen wall. Crazy times,' said Chestnut.

'We're not beyond it yet,' said Mabel.

'But we went past it. Left it behind thirty minutes ago.'

'May have looked like that, but we didn't. When we're properly clear of it, you'll bloody know about it, believe me.'

'Why? How?'

'Check on Daisy-May, would you?' Mabel replied. 'Some nursemaid you are. She could be bleeding out her ears and you'd be too busy gabbing to notice.'

Chestnut harrumphed, jumped off the control console and kneeled down next to the dozing Warden of the Pen. 'She looks a bit paler than last time she passed out. She's breathing, though. Or whatever it is we do.'

Mabel nodded.

'How much longer? Till she becomes deader than she already is, I mean?'

'Same as I told you last time.'

'You said you didn't know.'

'There you go, then.'

'I'm going to get sick, aren't I?' said Chestnut.

Mabel stiffened. She'd been expecting such a question from the girl. Was a little surprised, in fact, that it had taken so long to come.

'You're fine now, so there's no reason to think that.'

'I was in the Gloop longer than Daisy-May was,' said Chestnut. 'Plenty of time passed before she pulled me out.'

'But she gave you her respirator. I gave you a drug infusion. Would have given Daisy-May one too, if she hadn't been trying to stop the Dispossessed. It's a miracle she's made it this far, to be honest with you.'

And Mabel was being honest: it *was* a miracle. The exposure to the irradiated Gloop meant Daisy-May should have been dead long ago, because when you died the first time, that soil wasn't the end. In the afterlife, there was always another level of dead you could hit.

Like the place we're headed right now. That's chock bleeding full of people who died a second time. This suicide mission's about making sure Daisy-May doesn't join them.

Daisy-May had to survive. The future of the Pen depended upon it. Without her, it would be left to the traitorous Remus, the Warden's supposed right-hand man. The woman who didn't glimmer, too, whoever that witch was.

Mabel shivered, looking down at her bare arm as it erupted with goose prickles.

'You felt that too?' said Chestnut.

'Best strap yourself in,' said Mabel, crunching deeper into her captain's seat. 'Things are about to get pretty bloody real.'

That realness began as a speck of light on the horizon.

It looked like a pinprick at first, a barely glowing dot in an ocean of darkness. Mabel knew better. That dot would soon grow exponentially until it became something else. Something far wilder than the Pen they'd left behind them. If she faltered, if she displayed anything less than total clarity of mind and conviction of heart, they'd be lost. Which made her sound like a hardened pro at what they were about to encounter when in fact she was a rank bloody amateur.

She grasped the blimp's helm and offered up a quick prayer. She didn't think it would do much good, but her hundreds of years of existence hadn't quite extinguished all her optimism yet.

'Holy fuck,' said Chestnut.

'Yep,' said Mabel. 'That about covers it.'

What they were looking at was difficult to process, but Mabel had to.

It was like looking at an X-ray of a deity's migraine.

There were shards of crackling blue light and malleable clay-like buildings forming then collapsing in front of them. A structure would coalesce, then melt before their eyes like it had waived its right to exist. There were figures, too, floating in this abominable nothingness, men, women and children made of formless clay. Just as some sort of definition was beginning to take hold, it was as if they were showered in acid; like the buildings, they gave up the ghost and melted away into sludge.

Place is like a tumour, thought Mabel. Rachel had some

stones, banishing the old cow here. Hell would have been kinder.

'What is this place?' asked Chestnut. 'And why the fuck have you brought us here?'

Good question, thought Mabel, as a shock wave hit the blimp, causing the children in the back to scream. Chestnut was tossed off her feet, Mabel's death grip on the helm just about keeping her upright. Lightning slashes tore into the darkness ahead of them, illuminating the mounds of mush that were trying to be humans.

'Most people think the Pen is purgatory, and they're right, but there's this place too,' said Mabel. 'It's called Oblivion, and it's more limbo than limbo. This is where souls who die in the afterlife come. It's where Daisy-May will come if we can't save her.'

Another wave of fuck-knows-what assaulted the craft, causing another collective scream.

'That's *what* this place is. But why are we here?' asked Chestnut. 'Shouldn't we be trying to keep Daisy-May away from here?'

Mabel gritted her teeth, fighting the buffeting. 'There's no swerving Oblivion if that's the way it goes for her. There's someone here who can save her, though. If she chooses to.'

'Who the hell lives in a place like this?' asked Chestnut. 'Who'd be insane enough?'

'Insanity. Well, the old dear we're going to see's got spoonfuls of that. Living here isn't a choice she made, though. She was banished here by the Duchess.'

'For what?'

'It's a long story,' said Mabel, 'and I'm too bloody short-tempered to tell it. Last place I wanted to bring any of you, this. Last place I wanted to come myself, but Remus's little insurrection back at the Pen hasn't left me much choice.'

37

Another whipcrack of lightning tore at the sky, illuminating the cockpit like a nightmare.

'That was close,' said Chestnut, her fists clenched in terror.

'There,' Mabel shouted, unable to keep the triumph out of her voice. 'That's where we need to head.'

She wrestled the helm to the left, the airship pitching in the same direction.

When you saw it, you questioned how you'd ever missed it in the first place.

That wasn't because the building was particularly remarkable; it was a four-storey tenement block, the sort that New York specialised in, intent on cramming as many refugee souls into it as possible, ladders running up its sides, boxy windows allowing as much light in as it saw fit. It was the solidity of the building that stood out, though; in a world of gravy-like sludge, the faded red brickwork shone like a lighthouse.

Who knew Rachel had such a good sense of humour? thought Mabel, a rare grin on her face. Never thought I'd see this place again.

She pointed at the building. 'Going to land us on the roof.'

A boom of sonic fury sounded.

'Sounds like Oblivion heard you,' said Chestnut.

'Oblivion can stick it up its arse,' said Mabel. 'We're landing this ship.'

The girl was right, though. It was like voicing that intention had angered Oblivion and the shapeless beings it contained. The lightning raged more fiercely, the wind whipping the blimp ever more aggressively, and if she didn't know better, it seemed to Mabel that the formless beings were a little less formless.

Wouldn't put it past the sainted Duchess. Always had a flare

38

for torture, even if she never liked to admit it. She didn't want anyone coming for the old girl.

'Are those birds?'

Chestnut's question snapped Mabel from her reverie. They were several hundred feet from the tenement building now, despite Oblivion's efforts to push them away. Mabel squinted, then reached down, bringing up a pair of gold-plated goggles and sliding them onto her face. The lenses whirred and whined, adjusting and magnifying.

'Those ain't birds,' she said, swallowing. 'What kind of shot are you, girl?'

'With a gun, you mean?' said Chestnut.

'I didn't mean with your gob.'

'Never held a gun in my life.'

Of course she hasn't. Not everyone had our upbringing. Our life.

'Going to need you to hold us steady, then,' said Mabel.

'You mean pilot the ship?'

'Piloting the ship would involve you piloting the ship. All I want you to do is plant those twig legs of yours, grab hold of the helm and hold us bloody steady. I'll do the rest.'

Chestnut gawped as what she'd thought were birds finally came clearly into view. 'I hope you've got a big gun.'

'I've always got a big gun,' said Mabel.

The gun turrets owed much to the old Lancaster bombers the Allies had used in the Second World War. They were contained in a plastic bubble that jutted out from the blimp's cockpit, a gunnery designed for the lithe and young, not the more generously sized older markswoman. Mabel swore and sweated her way into the bucket seat, squeezing her way into the unsqueezable, the goggles on her face refocusing to their new environment.

What they showed her wasn't particularly welcome.

39

Chestnut had thought they were birds, and the creatures certainly had wings, after a sort. Spanning at least a couple of feet, they were like bats' wings, veiny and fragile-looking. Embedded within them were rows of malformed teeth, jutting haphazardly from papery skin.

It was the creature's face that shocked the most, though. It was almost human enough to be recognisable as such – there were eyes, a mouth and the approximation of a regular-sized head – but it was a visage ripped from the worst excesses of a Lovecraftian nightmare. A beak had been badly stitched over its mouth, its body reminding Mabel of a diseased dinosaur. It was fully formed, but still retained the loose, clay-like texture of the beings they'd seen earlier. It was as if something was keeping it in an unnatural state of being, and causing it a tremendous amount of pain because of that fact.

Defences courtesy of the Duchess. She really doesn't want anyone visiting the old girl, does she?

Mabel considered her options and, more importantly, her armoury. She had a bag full of scorpion bombs kicking around somewhere, and those things had a *kick*; they'd blow a hole in heaven itself. They worked better on big, immovable objects, though, not these flying beasts. No, *they* called for something else.

She flung the goggles aside, instead relying on the glass in front of her, her two eyes, and the onrushing closeness of the creatures. She grasped the twin gun handles, her fingers finding the red plastic triggers.

'Right then, you buggers,' she said, a half-smile on her face, 'let's be having you.'

As she moved the fat slab of metal that was the gun, the plastic bubble enclosing her moved with it. She sighted one of the creatures and pressed down on the triggers, a whine responding, the heat from the gun directed onto her face.

The cannon kicked against her as hundreds of translucent

light discs were spat from its turrets, searing the blackness and thudding into the creatures. Their almost-human faces screamed as their wings began to dissolve under the onslaught, a yell sounding from Mabel as she moved the weapon from left to right, scoring the sky with light-disc death.

The Duchess had never thought anyone'd be mad enough to come out here, and she sure as shit hadn't thought they'd be armed with one of these cannons if they did. These things were target practice.

Just as she thought this, one of the creatures peeled off from the others. Mabel tried to track it as she finished off those still flying, the gun billowing heat and shoving the smell of burned petrol up her nostrils.

The skies now clear, she yanked the gun to the left, not stopping firing for a second, green bullets punching through nothingness, the remaining creature gone.

Shit, she thought, hunting for it.

Back and forth, back and forth she went, the gun cooling in her hands, steam rising from it, squinting, searching for a sign of the beast.

Maybe it got scared. An animal sees every one of its kin picked off, that animal bloody runs.

'You spot any more of them up there?' she called out to Chestnut.

'Nope,' the girl called back. 'You got 'em all.'

Except I didn't, but maybe that doesn't matter.

She did a final sweep.

It was time to land this thing and get Daisy-May inside.

Something slammed into the glass bubble, instantly causing a spider web of cracks to appear. Mabel looked on in horror as she saw the dinosaur-bird-man, its hand-foot digging into the flimsy enclosure and wrenching it clean off. The air – or whatever passed for it in Oblivion – stung Mabel's skin as she shoved herself back into the seat, trying to keep out of range of the thing's snapping beak, the plastic bubble tumbling into nothingness.

'You all right down there?' called out Chestnut.

'Just keep flying,' Mabel shouted back, the beak missing her by inches. 'Nothing I can't handle.'

She says, with a monster an inch away from her and literal fucking oblivion waiting for her the other side of it.

She reached back, grabbing a rung of the ladder that would lead her up to the cockpit.

And the kids. Chestnut too. No way can I let this monster get up there. Have to end it now.

Still, she couldn't stay in the seat. Not if she wanted to keep her intestines.

She ducked away from the snapping beak, her old bones protesting, her free hand reaching for the pendant around her neck. They both had them, the Duchess and her; Rachel had used hers to halt the progress of the Dispossessed, poisoning the Gloop in the process.

Mabel's was a little less nuclear, though no less deadly for it.

Ripping it free, she smashed it into the thing's beak, its human eyes wide open in surprise, its hold on the ship loosening a little.

What had been enclosed within the pendant wasn't visible to the naked eye. If Mabel had been able to see it, she would have glimpsed a minuscule scarab beetle burrowing itself into the creature's fur, multiplying exponentially as it did so, a colony growing and growing and growing.

She winced as the beast began to scream and dissolve in front of her eyes, its skin eaten away by something she couldn't see but knew was there just the same.

Within seconds, she could say the same thing about the beast. It was like it had never existed at all.

'You took your time.'

Mabel hauled herself from the stepladder to the cockpit proper, slamming the hatch shut with a full-stop relish. 'I was busy saving our arses.'

Chestnut tapped the ship's wheel proudly. 'You impressed with my flying?'

'All you did was hold her steady,' said Mabel. 'I did all the shooting.'

'Tough crowd,' Chestnut said, shrugging.

Mabel grunted, nudging the girl aside and taking control of the helm. 'Going to moor us directly over the building, then winch down with Daisy-May. Get the rope ready.'

'I'm coming too, right?' said Chestnut.

'Nope. I need you to stay here with the kids.'

Chestnut looked doubtfully at the collection of children. 'What am I supposed to do with them?'

'Guard them. Keep them safe. Play pat-a-cake, pat-a-cake with them for all I bleeding care.'

'What's pat-a-cake, pat-a-cake?'

Mabel looked at the ragtag collection of children. They'd spent God-knows-how-long enduring unspeakable tortures. All they knew was pain, abuse and broken trust.

'You'll work it out. Compared to what they're used to, it'll seem like heaven.'

Strange that the atmosphere wasn't poisonous, except for the mild sting. Or at least not as poisonous as the Gloop. Perhaps it was because it wasn't so different to the Pen; Oblivion was essentially an extension of it, one that had been knocked up by fly-by-night builders.

The rope lurched downwards, Daisy-May, strapped to Mabel's front, moaning slightly at the jarring motion. Mabel looked up at the blimp and scowled. 'Take it easy, girl,' she yelled. 'You'll have killed us by the time we reach the roof.'

Chestnut was just about visible on the ship above, her hand working the winch.

'Moan, moan, moan with you,' she shouted back.

Mabel looked down, the roof just twenty feet or so away. Would there be a final surprise when they reached it, one last line of defence? She didn't think so. It wasn't necessary.

And she won't be pleased to see me, you can take that as given. Not that I need her to be. I just need her to be intrigued enough to want to help.

Her feet thudded into the building's concrete roof and she quickly released them both from the winch, scanning left and right, hunting for threats. None presented themselves; it was still just the unformed nightmare of before, all electric-blue light and rootless, formless clay figures and buildings.

Hauling Daisy-May onto her shoulder like a pack of spuds, she made her way towards a rusted metal door.

Hang in there, girl. Help's almost here. Though it'll probably look like the biggest hindrance you've ever bloody seen.

The door opened with a slight push and led to a dingily lit corridor.

Nostalgia whipped at Mabel.

Never thought I'd see this place again. It's exactly as I remember it. That feeling of dozens of different lives squashed behind the doors, waiting to spill out. Like the building's got indigestion. Like it's bloated.

As she walked down the corridor, Daisy-May distressingly light on her shoulder, she felt those lives either side of her, all their frustrations, hopes and dreams unfulfilled. Such was the pressure in the corridor, it felt like her head had been placed in a vice.

Because that's what it was like here when we were girls. All of us wanted to get out, and all of us knew we never would. Not when we'd

44

been marked down as sisters of the Pen. No escaping that, either in the living world or the dead.

At the end of the corridor was a set of stairs, and she headed down them. As she reached the third-floor landing, a knot of nervous fear tightened in her stomach. She wasn't used to being afraid for herself – others, like Daisy-May, she had plenty of experience of – but then the person she was here to see was the original bogeywoman, a childhood figure that had loomed large in both life and death.

She arrived at Room 237 and took a deep breath of stale air.

Daisy-May groaned on her shoulder, almost as if she knew what was coming.

Mabel rapped sharply on the door.

A grunt from inside.

Feet on floorboards, getting closer.

The sound of a lock sliding back.

The door creaked open. A yellowed eye was just about visible through the crack.

A guttural chuckle, then the door swung fully open.

An ancient-looking woman stood there. Her grey hair streaked away from her scalp like it had somewhere more urgent to be. Her teeth were sporadic, a wisp of whiskers sprouting from the bottom of her chin. She looked half dead, like the Grim Reaper had taken one look at her then sent her back as damaged goods.

'Hello, Oma Jankie,' Mabel said to her grandmother.

Part 2

No Future

Chapter 5

Before Himmler took me to the laboratory, he took me to the chamber.

He had a sense of theatre, Heinrich. All the Nazi royalty did. There was something of the amateur dramatist about their fondness for the uniform and the flag. They loved the pomp and circumstance. Maybe it was what helped them do the deeds they did. The uniform insulated them from the inhumanity.

The chamber was impressive. Flaming torches had been placed a few feet apart from each other, throwing shadows onto the stone walls. Between these torches were shields containing coats of arms. A mighty round table sat in the centre of the room. I thought back to a story we'd been told in school about King Arthur and his knights.

Himmler gazed upon it all proudly; it was as if the chamber was a favoured son. 'You are one of the first to see this,' he told me. 'This will be our Camelot, where we rebuild the world.' He stroked the table lovingly. 'If you help us – if you do what I believe you're capable of doing – you could sit at this table one day. What do you think about that?'

'I don't understand what you want from me,' I replied.

49

But I did. At least I was beginning to.

Himmler pulled out a chair from underneath the mighty oak table and slid into it.

'One of the great gifts the Führer possesses is his vision. Herr Hitler and I believe the Aryan race are descended from Atlantean gods; that this is not something of myth, but of historical fact. As such, we have set out to prove it. Take a seat, Jacob.'

I did, although it was like the seat took me. As soon as I sat, a malignant circular lip began to lower the table, concrete grinding against gears. Himmler smirked at my reaction as I looked around, half in terror, half in wonder, as we began to descend into the depths.

'To obtain the proof of these theories, we send expeditions out into the world,' he continued. 'Tibet. Western Eurasia. Iceland. Vienna. Our teams have uncovered priceless artefacts that prove our theories.' He smiled at me. 'None, though, are quite as priceless as you.'

I gazed around as we continued to descend. We passed through rooms containing row after row of glass display cases, the expeditions having plundered hundreds of artefacts. Skulls and spears and parchments that proved Himmler's wild theories because he wanted to prove them, because men like him weren't swayed by logic, or facts, or science. Their dogma was so ingrained they'd see truth where they wanted to see it.

And I was part of that truth. He knew what I was, some-how, knew too that when you cast the net of insanity far and wide, eventually you landed something that sounded insane but wasn't.

The light below us shifted from musty brown to bleached white. The table lift began to slow.

'Good,' said Himmler. 'We're about to arrive.'

The chamber was what Himmler felt the past should be; the laboratory was what he demanded of the future.

It gleamed with Teutonic ambition, the stone of above replaced by stainless steel. Benches of microscopes lined up like sentries. Lab coats clung to technicians as they went about their work. If they were surprised at my presence, they didn't show it.

At the back of the room was a wall of glass that looked out onto another, smaller room. Wiligut lurked by the window, kneading impatient hands, hovering next to a long chrome control desk peppered with dials, knobs and a balding, bespectacled technician.

His nose wrinkled at the sight of me.

'Show some appreciation,' said Himmler, putting his arm around me. 'This boy, in his Youth finery, is going to help us conquer worlds.'

Wiligut looked away, his gaze sneaking back to the glass wall. 'A mission dependent on a Jew. Who would credit it?'

'The vessel isn't important,' Himmler replied. 'The destination is.'

I looked at the room behind the glass wall. A mattress was laid upon a metal gurney, straps dangling from it like sleeping snakes. A tangle of electronica cocooned the bed, leads of different colours and thicknesses sprouting from chunks of chrome and steel.

'What do you want from me?' I asked, unable to drag my eyes away.

Himmler kneeled down next to me. I supposed he thought it reassuring, dropping to my height. I never found stale sweat and cigarettes particularly reassuring.

'To the moment of truth, Jacob. You know why I've brought you here, don't you? Why I have taken you from your parents?'

I shook my head.

He nodded his.

'It's right that you guard such a secret. I would, too. I'm sure there are times when that secret – that destiny – weighs heavily upon you. I don't envy you the responsibility, but I am willing to help you shoulder it.'

I told him I didn't know what he was talking about.

I didn't see the backhand coming.

I felt it, though, as the rough skin of his hand crunched my face. Dots danced as I stumbled backwards. I cursed the sob of pain that came out.

'I didn't want to do that,' said Himmler, every fibre of his being showing the lie of those words.

He stood up, taking me by the arm and dragging me towards Wiligut and the wall of glass.

'You have been blessed. It baffles me that one of your tribe *could* be blessed in such a way, but my research confirms it beyond all reasonable doubt. You are destined for greatness in the afterlife. A god in everything but title.'

I said nothing.

'I believe – and Herr Hitler agrees – that you could be of great use to us, because quite frankly, when you're about to take on the world, it pays to have a god on your side.'

I was only half listening now. Instead, I was staring at the technician at the control desk. Different to the one I saw when I first came in. Young. Fresh faced. He was watching me closely. His face was a kabuki mask of neutrality, but his hands betrayed him; he passed a pen from one hand to the other, twirling it like a baton, unable to settle. He was excited, this man who looked barely old enough to shave. Excited by my presence. Excited by whatever he planned to do to me.

'Are you ready, Schmidt?'

He swallowed. I realised he wasn't excited, but nervous. At

best, both. He bowed his head, taking solace in the floor. 'Yes, Herr Himmler. But—'

'I dislike buts, Schmidt. They reek of weakness and muddiness of thought.'

Schmidt twisted his hands together. 'The procedure carries risk, Herr Himmler. It may not be possible for me to bring him back.'

Himmler took a step towards him. 'The risk will be greater to you if you don't.'

Schmidt licked his lips, then followed it with a vigorous nod.

I knew deep down that the room behind the wall of glass was meant for me. I couldn't have guessed what they intended to do to me in there, though.

A source of eternal shame (and there were so many sources, over the years) was how I didn't struggle. I would like to be able to say I fought the good fight, that it took three of them to bind me to the hospital bed, but it didn't. I allowed myself to be led like the meekest of lambs, resigned to whatever atrocities they had in mind for me.

When the last strap was fastened, I turned my face towards Himmler. He stood next to a slurp of steel that sat on a metal trolley. Cupcake dials protruding from machinery, two metal pads resting on top of it, coiled wire dangling from them.

'Ah,' he said, patting the machine proudly. 'You've noticed the defibrillator, as well you might; this machine will be your salvation, young Jacob. It will bring you back.'

'Back from where?' I asked, eyeing it warily. The dials reminded me of a spiteful face.

'The afterlife, of course,' said Himmler, smiling.

I felt a needle invade my skin and whipped my head round. The technician had injected me with something.

'You'll feel no pain,' said Himmler. 'Not at first, anyway.'

Something was wrong with the room.

One moment it was there, sterile, solid, firm; then it was as if someone had taken an eraser to it, carefully rubbing out the edges and sanding away the lines. I tried to move, but the bindings around me were still all too real. Finally, as the room became a mush of light, the bindings fell away and I *could* move. I leaped from the bed, darting a glance through the glass wall. Himmler and Schmidt were staring intently at the control desk, ignoring me altogether.

Behind them was a short, stumpy middle-aged woman so out of place it was incredible that I hadn't noticed her before. Stranger too when you considered how familiar she looked. Was it the ruddiness of her cheeks that sparked some remembrance in me? Her waddling walk?

She raised a hand in greeting. Before I could think about it, I raised one back.

'Stay right there, lad,' said the woman, glaring at Himmler and his assistant. 'I'll come to you.'

With that, she walked through the wall.

I'd heard tell of it before, of course. How could I not, when you consider what I'd been brought up to be? The teachings I'd been subjected to, as soon as I could crawl? I was a future leader of the Pen, the Warden-to-be of purgatory. Spirits weren't a thing of fantasy in my family. They were a stark, joyous reality.

Still, it was one thing to hear of them and quite another to see one in the room with me.

'You must be someone important, lad, to have me come fetch you,' the woman said, offering me her hand. 'Name's Mabel.'

I stared at it wonderingly, took it cautiously. 'Am I dead?'

Mabel nodded, looking back at Himmler and Schmidt, still

hunched over the control desk. 'Got the animals out there to thank for that. Seen some things in my time – on the soil, and in the what-comes-after – but these Nazis, they're the worst of them. Things'll only get worse, an' all. Least, till they get better.'

It's difficult to describe, the sensation of looking at your own dead body. It feels a little like someone's playing an elaborate practical joke on you, that at any moment someone will jump in and surprise you. Perhaps that's because you want it to happen; it's your brain's way of coping with the enormity of it all. The finality.

The door opened and Himmler, accompanied by yet another man in a lab coat, strode in. I found it interesting that he couldn't see Mabel, – or me, for that matter – but it was as if he could see *something*; he skirted around us, his eyes searching the room.

He stopped when he came to my corpse, leaning over it, feeling my pulse. 'Charge it,' he said to the technician. 'It's been two minutes since his heart stopped.'

Two minutes? It had felt like three seconds.

'What's all this then?' Mabel said, looking quizzically at the technician as he hovered over my cooling body, paddles in hands. Himmler ripped my shirt open as an electric whine filled the air.

'Give me your hands, lad,' she said, a frown appearing on her weather-beaten forehead.

I did as I was told, but half-heartedly; I was fascinated by the machine that sounded like electricity waking up, intrigued by the man and his paddles.

'It's charged,' said the man.

Himmler took a step back. 'Do it.'

The technician pressed the paddles down onto my chest. My physical body convulsed, and so too did the one I now

55

inhabited, jerking me away from Mabel, wrenching my hands from her. Her form began to blur, like someone had drizzled fog over her.

'Come back to me,' came her garbled voice. 'Come back to me, lad.'

The machine screamed a one-note refrain.

'Again,' said Himmler.

The man slammed the paddles down, my dead body buckarooing, pain present this time in my spirit form, a burning in my chest as well as a thumping in my head.

'Again,' said Himmler.

A whine of sound, a crackle of anticipation, a snap of electric whiplash, and I was dragged backwards into my body. It was like I was trapped inside that cooling husk. My eyeballs were someone else's, my vision blurred between the horizontal and the vertical.

'I have a pulse,' said the technician, a man I observed from my body on the gurney and the last vestiges of my spirit, which stood several feet away.

'I'm sorry,' said Mabel, her speech slurred, barely discernible.

My vision finally snapped into focus, and I saw Himmler's face inches from mine.

'He's awake.'

This was a truthful lie, because although my eyes were open, I felt like I was in a fugue state of death, like a bit of me had broken off when I'd crossed over, a splinter, perhaps, in the hands of the dowdy woman called Mabel.

I struggled up, my breath raging, seeking purchase.

'Herr Himmler.'

Schmidt, in the doorway, a child on Christmas morning. Himmler's head shapped up, hunger in his eyes. 'Did it work?'

'It's easier for me to show you.'

★

They wanted me to see.

I felt weak, half dead when I'd been wholly dead just moments ago, but they wanted me to see.

The technician took my weight, shuffling me along to the control desk, where Himmler and Schmidt stared, rapt, at a wireless with a screen encased within it. It was like nothing I'd ever seen before, a cinema screen shrunk in the wash, mated with a transistor radio.

Static ebbed and flowed on the screen, indistinct, ghostly.

There was something there, though, a figure captured, her profile frozen for posterity.

'Did you see her?' Himmler enquired, his magpie eyes hungry for the prize. I thought about lying, then decided against it.

I nodded. It was Mabel, the spirit I had spoken to when I was dead. They'd seen the whole thing.

'Do you know what this means, Jacob?' Himmler asked, smiling his cancer smile.

I shook my head, even though I was beginning to.

'It means we have proof of the afterlife's existence. And with the finest scientific minds in the country, the means to tame it and make it our own.'

I would have laughed at such deranged ambition if I didn't think he was right.

Chapter 6

Clayton was a gone-to-seed conurbation that had eaten its own young.

Three miles east of Manchester's city centre, the area contained row upon row of houses left to die, their skeletons desecrated by steel shutters bolted over their hollowed-out windows and doors. As it did with the dead that lingered too long on its soil, the earth was intent on reclaiming its own; vines grew out of the crumbling brickwork, the warren of streets an apocalypse of desolation.

Among it all, a Lowry-like light smudge sat on a canvas of darkness, one lone house stubbornly holding the line. It squatted on the end of the terraced row, light burning from its windows, tub-thumping sound groaning from its insides like drum-and-bass stomach ache, the street lights opposite it snuffed out along with everything else.

'Feels like the end of the world, doesn't it?' said Megan.

Bits shook his head. 'Shame. Used to be a good area.'

'You lived here?'

'Girlfriend did. I'd stay over sometimes, when her mum was doing the night shift.'

'So what's the plan?' Megan nodded at the house across the way.

'You go in the front, say Spooky Dave sent you. See what's what. Meantime, I'll go in the back, all unseen like, and snoop around, see what I can find.'

'That doesn't sound like much of a plan,' said Megan.

'This is how it is in the Dying Squad,' said Bits. 'You try shit, and often that shit leads to other shit. It's sort of like unwrapping an onion, except you're wearing goalie gloves when you're doing it. And a blindfold.'

Megan frowned.

'It works,' said Bits. 'We found you, didn't we?'

'It just seems that the level of risk is a lot higher for me then you.' She folded her arms and stared at the lit-up house. 'They can see me. Hurt me, too, if they choose too. You're already dead.'

Bits sneered. 'Yeah, I'm the lucky one in this deal.'

'You know what I mean.'

'I do, and we're all volunteers here. You want to sit this one out, I get it. No way of knowing what you'll be walking into.'

Megan shifted her weight from foot to foot. 'Need you to promise me something. It's something you've already promised me, but I need to hear you say it again.'

'What?'

'You'll help me find out about my past. It's not going to be something that just gets lost down the sofa in the hunt for Joe.'

'Course it won't,' said Bits. 'When we get him back, you're going to have two coppers working on it, too. One of them shit hot at the old detecting lark.'

Megan looked at him awkwardly. 'Seems to me there's something we haven't considered here.'

'What's that?' said Bits.

'What if Joe's back to his old self?'

Bits scowled at her. 'His old self's a stand-up fucking bloke.'

'The way you told it to me, that's his *new* self. What if that personality makeover didn't take? We don't know what happened to him after he chased the Generation Killer down, but if he's still on the soil – and if Dave's telling the truth, he is – then his memory will be shot to pieces. What if he's slipped into old ways?'

'He won't have,' said Bits. 'Joe's fucking *solid*, man. I know him. You don't.'

Megan held her hands up, placatory. 'You say it, I believe you. Might not kill us to keep an open mind, though.'

Bits considered for a moment, then gave her a grudging nod.

Megan turned back to the heavily fortified house and sighed. 'Fuck it. I've photographed worse places than this.'

Yeah, and it got you kidnapped by a serial killer, Bits thought but didn't say.

'You'll have been spotted a good ten minutes ago,' he did say, nodding towards the house. 'Gazelle amongst the lions, a girl like you in a place like this. If you're going to do this thing, you need to do it now.'

'Then stop talking,' said Megan, 'and start walking.'

It wasn't like she'd never bought drugs before.

Indeed, for as long as she could remember, people had seemed intent on forcing pills on her. Doctors, particularly. There were the before times, of course, which she couldn't remember, but everything from the age of thirteen was as sharp as a fucking tack. It was a by-product of seeing the dead: admitting it tended to gain the attention of the medical profession and make them insist on you taking antipsychotic drugs. And she did, for a time, and those drugs worked, walling her off from the spirits.

Then she began to miss them. They weren't so much old friends as the only family she'd ever really known. So out went the antipsychotics and in came the ghouls. Some party drugs even enhanced her ability to see them. That was the excuse she told herself, anyway.

She hadn't visited many crack houses, though, and that was what this place was. It might have not shared the boarded-up neglect of its brothers and sisters around it, but it was still built like a Mancunian Fort Knox. The front of the house contained metal slats for windows – to Megan's eye, they looked just wide enough to fit a gun barrel through – and the front door was a slavering chunk of steel.

It was madness to walk up to such a place, but then it was madness to have a ghost copper for a partner. At this point in her life, the most sensible thing seemed to be to embrace that madness.

Taking a deep breath, she prepared to knock on the front door.

Fuck, thought Bits. This takes me back.

Not the house itself – the back, like the front was so heavily fortified it bore virtually no relation to the home he remembered from his living, breathing youth – but the fact that he was attempting to sneak into a drugs den. He'd been good at it back in the day, his wiry, elastic body meaning he could squeeze into areas others couldn't, gathering intel or out-and-out trying to nick their drugs.

And now he didn't have to bother with the pesky problem of physics; he could just walk straight through the corrugated-steel shutter concealing the back door. There were advantages with this Dying Squad shit. That was what . . . someone had always tried to impress upon him.

Who?

Panic tugged at him. The brain fog had been threatening to settle in for a while now, and he'd been happily in denial about it.

He reached into his grubby jeans pocket, withdrawing a stick of gum. He should ration it really. Supplies were dwindling, and when it was gone, it was gone.

Which is why I've got to make this shit count when I can. I've got a lead, but that means nothing if I can't remember who it is I'm supposed to be chasing.

He tore off the silver wrapper and threw the pink gum into his mouth, chewing enthusiastically. Cool-breeze clarity descended upon him.

Joe.

Joe had told him to see the benefits of being dead, rather than just the downsides. And he'd been right. The ability to go anywhere and everywhere unobserved had allowed them to catch the Generation Killer. Save Megan, too. What Bits needed now was the ability to find his partner. He'd known on some gut level that Joe was still out there, but he hadn't expected him to be in Berlin, working with some bloke called Hans. Something strange was going on, and it was up to him – and Megan, if she was still game – to find out what that something was.

Because I'm Dying Squad, and so is Joe, no matter what doubts Megan has. If he's working with this Hans, it's for a reason. We just have to find out what that reason is.

It wasn't like there was a bell you could ring. There wasn't so much as a door knocker.

There was only, as far as Megan could see, a thin letter box halfway up the door. A CCTV camera too, several feet above the door itself and angled downwards. Bits was almost certainly right: she'd have been spotted a good while ago, and those inside were letting her come to them. No point rushing out only to find a rival gang or a waiting police raid.

The door was a thing of aggressive, you-shall-not-pass

intimidation. The only way you were getting through it was with a tank, and maybe not even then. She guessed you knocked on the door, the letter box opened, you told them your order, then they'd slip it out to you. A drive-through McDonald's for the narcotic generation.

She rapped sharply on the door. It had seemed to barely make a sound, but almost immediately, there was a scraping of steel as the letter box slot opened. Megan spied two piercing eyes peering out.

'Yes?' came a voice. 'How can I help you?'

Mancunian, she thought. But softly spoken with it.

'I'm here to speak to Julius.'

'And who are you?'

'A friend of Spooky Dave's. He sent me here. Said that he'd call ahead.'

The slot snapped shut.

Megan stood there squeezing her tense fists then releasing them again.

The sound of many locks sliding filled the air.

The door began to open.

As Bits stepped through the back door, he thought about Michelle. Truthfully, she was someone from his past he'd been glad to forget, and Spooky Dave's mention of her had stirred up a big pot of nothingness. There wasn't some pang for love lost or a life not lived; he hadn't given her a moment's thought since he'd passed over into the Pen. He didn't think this made him a bad person particularly; he suspected the feeling would be more than mutual. Him and Michelle had always been an on-again/off-again concern, a dirty, mutually convenient fuck. His death had probably caused no more than a ripple in her life.

Still, it was a shame she'd slid into the profession she clearly had. He wouldn't wish the life of a dealer on anyone, no matter how successful they'd become at it.

And she was clearly successful.

The crack houses he'd known were needle-strewn ruins where empty bottles fought for floor space with discarded fast-food cartons and mounds of faecal matter. The kitchen he'd just walked into was designer spotless: a table sat in the middle of the room, all chiselled Nordic cheekbones and sanded-off edges, a light suspended over it that looked so cheap it had to be expensive. Granite surfaces gleamed, a painfully angular fridge completing the picture. It was the sort of kitchen you'd find in a wanky coffee table book. The cooker looked like it was worth more than the bricks and mortar around it. Business must be booming.

Still, he'd known plenty of gangs where that had been the case and all it had meant was a bigger TV and a smarter pair of trainers. This wasn't a shithole with lashings of money; this was a home with lashings of style. That made him curious.

He passed through the kitchen door only to be faced with a narrow corridor. Pepperpot lights were recessed into the floor, casting the passageway in a warm, sympathetic hue. He knew little about interior design – it wasn't a big feature of the Pen – but he knew what he liked, and he liked this. If Spooky Dave hadn't been so specific, he'd have assumed he was in the wrong house.

And it even had *artwork*.

Proper photographs on the wall. Arty ones, some in black and white, and others in a sort of faded monochrome.

I've seen some of these before.

They were Megan's photos. The ones that looked like she took them with her eyes closed. It was only when Joe had sprayed his special shit on them that they saw the spirits she'd shot, too.

Bits tapped his finger against one taken outside the Lads

Club in Salford. That particular venue had been the scene of his most inglorious day on the Squad; he'd essentially executed another spirit there. That spirit had been a paedo piece of shit, but that hadn't excused the act.

He frowned at the last picture on the row. He might have an inexpert eye when it came to this sort of thing, but it was easy to tell it was different to the others.

This isn't one of Megan's, he thought. The era's different, for one thing. This is some punk-rock shit.

A two-piece band stood on stage, their mohawks proudly aloft, the frontman dressed in hand-me-down military attire, the drummer shirtless. The picture was black and white and immersed in grain, spidery writing at the bottom explaining that they were named the Ungrateful Dead and that the photo was taken in 1981.

What was special about this photo? The others were there presumably because of the hidden ghosts they contained, an Easter egg that few could see, and that included the dead. Was this picture the same?

He dug inside Joe's satchel – a piece of kit his partner had chased down the Generation Killer without – and retrieved the plastic bottle within. To all intents and purposes the thing looked fit for nothing but cleaning windows, but when it came to afterlife gadgets, looks could be deceiving. Bits pointed the nozzle at the picture and squeezed: a purple liquid instantly drenched the surface of the picture.

He took a step backwards; the last time he'd done this, the booby-trapped picture had burst into flames. This one didn't, but that didn't mean there wasn't a dramatic result, because it quickly became clear that there was someone else on stage with the band. A boy, leaping high, a look of pure joy on his face. He was dressed in shorts and a shirt, like he was ready for fascist finishing school.

Had the band known of the ghost boy's presence on stage? Was he a sort of spirit mascot? Intriguing, Bits thought, slipping the bottle back into his bag, but not what he was here for.

There was something else strange about this place: the drum-and-bass music he'd heard from outside had stopped. It was almost as if it had been a clichéd gangster ruse, what you'd expect to hear in a place like this. Now that he was in the house, there was another soundtrack being etched onto the airwaves: a classical one.

Gangsters playing classical music, thought Bits. It's all changed, man.

There was a closed door to his right, and he hovered next to it listening: classical music, muffled, maudlin, but undeniable. His skin prickled, a spider sense of danger he didn't really understand.

I'm dead, he thought, and fucking invisible. How much danger can there really be for someone like me?

He stepped through the oak door (again, he was very willing to believe this wasn't an original feature of the house) into what posh bastards would have called a dining room.

He quickly realised that he wasn't alone.

Megan didn't have a ton of experience with drug dens, but she was fairly sure this wasn't typical.

When the door had opened, a young guy had stood aside and beckoned her in. He'd been the exact opposite of what she'd expected – namely, a man with crack-ravaged teeth and a beaten-by-life face. Instead, this dude had to be roughly her own age – late twenties at the most – and dressed like a public-school model. Well-cut dark-blue chinos. A shirt and suit jacket so unassuming they had to be expensive, and clear-framed glasses that absolutely were. A pricey-as-fuck watch on his wrist, too. He looked like he should be boating at Oxford rather than slinging smack in Manchester.

There'd been something else. If Megan hadn't known better, it had looked like a flash of recognition in the man's eyes.

'Not what you expected?' he said, his voice clean and cool.

'To be honest, no,' Megan replied.

He held out a hand. 'I'm Julius.'

She took it. 'Megan.'

'Dave said you'd be coming.'

'*He's* a character.'

'People think he's insane,' said Julius, 'and they're right. Not because he says he can see the dead, though.'

Megan shifted uncomfortably on her feet.

'You know a little something about that yourself, do you not?' He looked at her closely. 'I've followed your work for quite some time.'

'Really?' said Megan, trying to disguise her surprise. She was more used to being followed by serial killers than art collectors.

'I can't see them, the spirits you take photographs of,' Julius said. 'It's enough for me to know they're there. To have a secret on the wall that only a few other people know about. I think your work is extraordinary.'

It was fair to say this wasn't going the way she'd expected it to. Not just Julius being a fan of her work, but Julius in general. There was an academic air to the drug dealer, one at odds with her clichés of cut-throat crime lords. A Mancunian accent but a soft one; there were no hard-edged Salford vowels on display here. It was like his words had been dipped in baby oil.

Which doesn't mean I should underestimate him, thought Megan. I bet people have been doing that his whole life. Most of them are probably dead.

★

The room Julius led to her kept up Megan's general level of disconcertion.

It was as beautiful as the outside of the house had been ugly. Furniture so lavish she was afraid to sit on it. A hi-fi system that looked more expensive than her old apartment, gracefully pumping out a concerto. Wooden parquet flooring. A svelte TV in the corner. Every last bit of it the opposite of what she'd expected.

Something's not right here, she thought. Feels like Spooky Dave's a flat-out wind-up merchant. That, or he's set us up somehow.

Or maybe I'm just being paranoid. Not *everyone's* out to kidnap me.

Julius pointed to a chair in the corner. 'Please.'

Megan smiled in thanks and took it.

There was a table sitting between them, an ornate pot of tea resting patiently on it. Julius reached for it, pouring it into two dainty china cups.

Nope, thought Megan. Not your average drug dealer, our Julius. That's if he *is* a drug dealer.

She raised the cup to her mouth, taking a sip. It was good.

'What can I do for you?' said Julius, nursing his own cup.

'We need your help.'

'We?'

Fuck.

She took another sip of her tea, steadying herself.

'Me.'

'What is it I can help you with exactly?' He tilted his head slightly. 'As I mentioned, I'm aware of your work. I think you're extraordinary.'

'You do?' said Megan.

'It's the reason you got through the front door. But you're not here to talk about your art.'

Megan leaned forward. 'Dave said there's a new drug on the market that you've had some dealings with. Spook.'

Julius smiled at her, then rose from his seat, walking towards the hi-fi rack. He reached down, twisting a chunky circular dial on the jet-black receiver. The classical music jumped several leagues in volume, the walls almost shaking with it.

He turned back towards her.

He was holding a gun.

Up, he mouthed.

Bits stared at the room, trying to take it in. To make sense of it.

There were six places laid at the dining room table. The chairs next to those places were occupied. If you squinted, you would have assumed the figures were children. They sat patiently, their arms out in front of them, their heads half turned towards each other as if in conversation. The plates in front of them were piled high with food at odds with their age; there were no fairy cakes here, no childish fancies. Instead, beef Wellington sat in pools of gravy, and full-to-the brim wine glasses waited impatiently to be drunk.

Bits saw, all too clearly, that the children weren't really children.

They were dolls. Incredibly lifelike ones. Their hair was shiny, their skin a close approximation of the genuine thing, their eyes dead and glassy.

The food in front of them was all too real, though. The flies that swarmed and swam in the oceans of gravy confirmed that.

A wailing filled the air. It sounded almost as mournful as the classical music in the dining room.

Glad of the excuse to leave such a creepy scene, Bits decided to follow it.

★

The volume of the wails increased as Bits ascended the stairs. Chances were, Megan was inside by now. He didn't like the idea of not being there to keep an eye on her, but he had to use this time to properly stake the place out; if things went south, she'd be able to see what was in front of her. He could keep an eye on what was coming for her from behind.

The wailing had been replaced by a whispered whimper, and he followed its trail, arriving on a landing just as tasteful as its downstairs cousin. In fact, it was almost too tasteful; the energy had been drained from it, transfused instead with good taste.

No fucking soul, man. No fucking life, either. The Pen might be shabby as fuck, but at least it's got chaos in its veins. I'd be afraid to fart in a place like this. The only room that didn't have airs and graces was the dolls' dining room.

The house hadn't been like this in his youth, he was sure of that. This was new.

But then everything was new when you'd been dead for the best part of thirty years.

The doors on the top landing were all shut – one even had a fat old padlock jutting out of it. The one he was interested in was just behind him. That was the one that had the whimpering noise leaking from it.

He walked clean through the door, unable to lose the gangster swagger he'd always employed when striding into the unknown.

The unknown was a children's room that contained an old adult.

There was a crib in the corner – untouched, from the look of it, by the presence of a baby – with a battalion of teddy bears guarding it. Toy cars were parked neatly by the window, Star Wars curtains shutting the world out, and the room had been painted a deep navy blue, lit by a mushroom-shaped lamp in the corner.

70

That was the kids' room bit. The adult bit was more jarring.

A woman sat in a chair, rocking forwards and backwards, staring into space. She held a baby-shaped object in her arms, swaddled in an eggshell-blue shawl. What Bits had taken for whimpering and wailing was the woman singing a lullaby.

At least he assumed it was a woman. She sat in profile to him, her lank hair straggling over the back of the rocking chair, flecks of silver streaked into it, her frame frail and slight.

Bits moved round to get a better look, and his undead breath caught.

Michelle.

Or rather, the old woman she'd become.

Her eyes were closed, the lids mottled and heavy, her face lined with decades of hard life. She was an addict, he would have bet anything on it.

Which ain't any sort of judgement. I was no better when I was living. Still need the gum to keep me going when I'm dead. Life's tough. You do what you need to get by.

He frowned, taking a step closer. The bundle in Michelle's arms wasn't a baby, but a doll. She was still singing to it, only stopping to place kisses on its head.

A chill ran down his spine. It was like the dolls downstairs. Incredibly lifelike, and all the more terrifying for it.

Michelle's eyes opened. She looked right at him.

'I knew you'd come back one day,' she said.

When a guy you didn't know pointed a gun at you and told you to get up, you got up.

Megan rose slowly to her feet, keeping her eyes on the gun's barrel. It wasn't the first time she'd had one pointed at her – the Generation Killer had popped that particular cherry – but it was an experience where familiarity definitely bred contempt.

Julius motioned upwards again, using his other hand to lift his shirt.

Ah. He thinks I'm wearing a wire. Or at least, he wants to confirm that I'm not.

She nodded, pulling up her chunky black woollen sweater, her heart pumping, her anxiety half convincing her that she was actually wired up and ready to narc.

Julius nodded, twirling his gun three hundred and sixty degrees.

Megan obliged.

When she was facing him again, she let the sweater drop.

He lowered the gun, then reached back, dipping the stereo volume down. 'You can't be too careful in my game. People either want to shoot you or betray you.'

'Neither of those things would do me much good,' said Megan, attempting a smile and landing on a grimace. 'All I want is information.'

Julius nodded, setting the gun aside, his movements prim and considered. 'On Spook.'

'More on someone who might be investigating it.'

He sat down and crossed his legs, smoothing down his trousers, then beckoned for her to sit too.

Megan did, taking another slug of tea as she settled, trying, and failing, to disguise her shaking hand.

'It's quite the trip, Spook, so I'm told,' said Julius.

'You haven't tried it?'

He smiled. 'It's enough for me to know that there's a life beyond this one; I don't want to glimpse it before it's my time. That's why I find your photographs such a delight – the wonders they contain are richer in my imagination.'

He sounds like a philosophy professor, thought Megan. One who'll shoot me if I give him a wrong answer. 'You're happy enough to sell it, though.'

'I'm happy enough to provide a service people need. If I don't, someone else will. But you're not here to talk to me about my life choices.' He leaned forward, adjusting his glasses slightly. 'Why *are* you here?'

'I'm trying to find someone. A ghost policeman, if you can believe it.'

'I can't, but that doesn't mean I'm not intrigued by it.'

'A friend of mine needs to track this policeman down, and I have reason to believe you may have met someone he's working with,' said Megan. 'A German national called Hans.'

Julius raised his eyebrows. 'Are you hoping to join this spectral police force?'

'All I'm hoping to do is help someone who helped me. He needs to find this spirit, who goes by the name of Joe Lazarus. Lazarus is looking for people who deal in Spook.'

'Why?'

'I don't know,' said Megan, 'but I'm guessing it has something to do with the guy he's with.'

Julius sat back, readjusting himself. 'Hans got in contact with me two weeks ago, in Berlin.'

'What did he want?'

'He wanted to know if I dealt in Spook.'

'What did you tell him?'

'What did I tell someone I didn't know, who arrived unannounced at my hotel and whose demeanour screamed ex-security services? What do you think I told him?' He removed his glasses, breathed on the lenses, then wiped them against his crisp white shirt. 'He was mildly impressive, I suppose: a man used to intimidating people. Certainly he intended to intimidate me.'

'Into doing what?' asked Megan.

'Dropping my supply of Spook. He was there to warn me off it, without specifically warning me off it.'

73

'Why was he doing that?'

Julius inspected his glasses, then, apparently satisfied, put them back on. 'There will be a price for all these questions. You understand that?'

Megan nodded.

'He said he was a concerned citizen, representing a committee of other concerned citizens. Nonsense, of course.'

Nonsense, thought Megan. Who uses a word like nonsense when they're under fifty? This lad's playing a part. Which doesn't make him any less dangerous.

'What did you say to him?' she asked.

'That I didn't have the first idea what he was talking about. That if that state of affairs changed at some point in the future, he'd be the first to know. He left me his number to that effect.'

Doesn't make any sense that Joe would be working with a guy like this. Not going on what Bits has told me about him. There's something at play here that I can't see.

Or maybe my theory's right. Maybe Joe forgot about the good guy he was trying to be and remembered the bad guy he actually was.

If that's the case, I get the impression we're all in a lot of trouble.

'You can see me?' said Bits, as his ex-girlfriend stared right at him.

Michelle looked from him to the doll in her hands, patting it tenderly on the back. 'Course I can.'

'How?'

'The medicine Julius gives me.'

Bits swallowed. 'Don't understand.'

'All sorts turn up here, you know. The dead, and those that are dead but don't know it. Wondered whether I'd see your grandad at some point.'

'I saw him, before the end.' Bits shook his head. 'Fucking *mad*, this.'

'You haven't changed,' said Michelle, looking him up and down. 'Even got the same tracksuit on.'

'Thing about being dead, isn't it? Your personal shopper loses all fucking interest.'

'Did it hurt? Dying?'

'Nah. One minute you're alive and the next you ain't. Both feel the same.'

'What's heaven like?' she asked, twirling a lank piece of hair around her fingers.

'I ever get there, I'll let you know.'

She turned her attention back to the doll.

'What you got there, love?' said Bits.

'This is Kai,' said Michelle, stroking the doll's head. 'Beautiful, isn't he?'

He nodded. 'Suppose he is.'

'He's my seventh bairn. Other six are downstairs, having their teas.'

Bits swallowed. 'Yeah, I've met them.'

'They never stick. Bairns all come out wrong with me.' Michelle held the doll away from her, gazing lovingly into its eyes. 'That's why Kai here is a present from God. My kids downstairs, too.'

Bits squeezed then unsqueezed his fists. He didn't know what to say.

'The first was yours.'

His stomach dropped. 'What?'

She looked at him without really looking at him and said nothing.

Bits swallowed, his mouth a desert. 'What do you mean?'

Michelle dragged her attention away from the doll and looked him dead in the eye. 'I was pregnant when you got yourself blown up in the Arndale.'

'I never knew,' he said, his legs jelly. 'You never told me.'

'Didn't know myself until a week after.' Tears began to swell in her eyes. 'Lost it soon after. Never knew whether it were a girl or a boy. Six more times I tried. Never happened. Something would always go wrong. Thought it might be you, cursing me.'

'It wasn't,' said Bits.

Michelle walked over to the crib, placing the doll carefully into it then tucking the blanket over it. 'Took whatever drugs I could find for years. Helped me forget. *You* know.'

'I do,' he said, looking at the desiccated human form of a woman he used to know.

'Then our Julius came to me with something new. That ghost drug, Spook. They'll come back to me one of these days, those babbies. When they do, I need to be able to see them. How will I be able to look after them otherwise?'

Bits opened his mouth, then realised there were no words to put in it.

Megan had to concede that it was a stroke of genius.

Julius had hollowed out the terrace, knocking through the walls until it was one long twenty-house millipede, then shoved the guts of a drug factory inside. Everyone in Manchester knew the street was deserted, that it had been abandoned, but nobody knew what was really going on there.

She had no frame of reference for such a thing, but it screamed state-of-the-art. Steel canisters stretched from floor to ceiling, reminding her of a thriving micro-brewery. White-coated technicians hovered over spotlessly clean benches, studiously going about their work.

It was like a science lab had double-dropped a party pill.

'The way the Spooky Daves of this world do business is over,' said Julius, his hands behind his back, a look of pride on his face. 'Too vulnerable to the vagaries of others, the windiness of supply chains. I'm going to do it differently.'

Megan began to feel hot. It was like someone had cranked up her internal thermometer by several degrees.

I don't know where this is going, she thought. But I'm guessing it's nowhere good.

'You're going to produce your own drugs,' she said, turning to him.

Julius smiled. 'I already am. And Spook's going to be my premium product.'

'How?'

'It's my belief that Spook has been produced by a private military contractor. For what purpose, I'm unsure, but you can be certain it isn't to give clubbers kicks. I'm going to reproduce it in this lab.'

'That can't be easy,' said Megan.

'Nothing worthwhile ever is.'

She took a breath. It was becoming increasingly difficult to concentrate.

'Where do I come in?'

Julius adjusted his glasses. 'The process is proving to be difficult. Our attempts at reverse-engineering the drug have so far been unsuccessful. I believe that Spook was designed with the assistance of someone like yourself: someone who can see the dead. I require a blood sample from you. To carry out a few simple tests, too.'

'And if I agree, you'll set up the meeting with Hans?'

He nodded. 'You have my word.'

Whatever the word of a drug dealer means, thought Megan, even one as well dressed as this. Still, we're getting somewhere. There's a clear link between Spook, and this Hans guy. We find Hans, we find Joe.

She began to feel dizzy, like someone was trying to whip away the floor from underneath her feet.

'I'm not feeling too great,' she said.

Julius stood watching her, a small smile on his lips.

He began to blur.

The tea, she thought. He put something . . .

She fell.

Chapter 7

The streets of Berlin were never quiet, but night-time was when they properly roared into life, a witching hour that encouraged the city's hedonistic denizens to come out and play. Still, Joe thought, it could have been worse. There was a trickle of old punks lining the streets, but the majority seemed to have departed the club. Ambulances and policemen tended to have that effect.

Although SO36's blue and red sign still glowed, the shutters across its entrance suggested it was closed, which was pretty much how you wanted a crime scene to be if you had intentions to skulk and suss without the distraction of the living.

Hans killed the car's engine. They sat in silence, the only noise the tinny techno coming from the vehicle's speakers.

'Why are we here?' Hans said finally.

Joe reached for his notebook.

'Try without that.'

He noticed the long cylindrical object Hans was holding. It whined and whispered.

'A girl OD'd here an hour ago. Our contact on the police force said she'd taken Spook.'

'Go on,' said Hans.

Joe swallowed. 'You're waiting to find out what hospital she's been taken to. Once you know, we'll go there and question her.'

Hans nodded. 'And?'

Joe looked down at the cattle prod in Hans's fist. 'I . . .'

A whine filled the air.

A crackle of sulphur garnished it.

'I don't want to do this, Lazarus,' said Hans. 'Please don't make me.'

'I . . .'

Hans drove the cattle prod into Joe's side. His jaw clenched as his body spasmed.

'I hate this a lot more than you do,' Hans said, jabbing the prod deeper.

'Doubt that . . . somehow,' Joe replied, his teeth gritted.

'It's the only way I can get you to remember things.'

'I know,' panted Joe.

'I want you to go into the club and poke around there,' said Hans. 'We can't have this shit on the street. It's killing kids. Every death is our responsibility. Got it?'

'Got . . . it,' Joe gasped.

Hans nodded, then flicked a switch on the metal rod. The sulphur whine dimmed.

The pain Joe experienced didn't.

'Hate that you made me do that,' said Hans.

'I . . . know.'

'Only way we have of keeping your memory sharp. When that memory comes back all the way, I won't need to do it any more, and you know what? Nothing will make me happier.'

Joe nodded, closing his eyes.

'Now go in there and see what you can find,' Hans said. 'Partner.'

As Joe passed formlessly through the artfully crumbling club entrance (noting in the distance the neon glow of a cross on the building opposite), the pain in his side raged. It wasn't the first time he'd been blasted by Hans; the pain stuck around for a good half-hour after the original jab. He didn't know about the science behind it, but he couldn't deny it was a motivator. Any time he felt memories slipping, he remembered the raging agony in his side. He couldn't quite shake the feeling that Hans enjoyed it a little too much, though.

The reception of the club – an altogether too grand a description for it – was a study in punk-rock nostalgia. The walls were plastered with old gig posters. Joe mouthed the names. The Sex Pistols. Bowie. Iggy. The Ramones. All of them artfully browned and curled at the edges, but Joe was willing to bet that was a design statement rather than a historical eventuality. These posters were years young, not decades old.

There was a large poster stuck above the doorway to what he assumed was the club's main room. The title *THE UNGRATE-FUL DEAD* headed it, then, underneath that, the exhortation to *BRING DOWN THE WALL*. A defiant-looking punk band, all cut-to-ribbons clothing and spiked hair, stood next to a graffitied Berlin Wall. *12 November 1989* was written at the bottom, along with *CELEBRATION CONCERT. FREE. WE ARE THE PEOPLE! WE ARE THE POWER!*

The band were called the Ungrateful Dead.

That name rang a bell. Why?

He went to his notebook, turning past the information about the investigation's objective. There were other scribblings after that, not always in the most rigid of structures.

There.

The Ungrateful Dead were the band who'd headlined here tonight. Judging by the aged poster above him, they were at the heritage end of rock and roll, rather than its cutting edge. Hardly surprising in a place like this, where the past wasn't so much celebrated as deified.

81

Walking through the door spat Joe into the guts of the club. Or its colon, judging by its dishevelled appearance.

It was deserted, lit only by emergency red lighting. The stage stood directly in front of him, full of drums, amps and guitars. It looked like the band hadn't been able to load out. OD'ing kids and the emergency services they brought would do that.

Behind him was the bar, with a row of cash registers. He didn't doubt that if he'd still been alive, his feet would have stuck to the floor. This place had booze soaked into its soul, not to mention its cheap vinyl flooring. He could almost smell the cigarette smoke.

The walls themselves were daubed in graffiti. *TOO MUCH FUTURE. DESTROY WHAT'S DESTROYING YOU.*
WE ARE THE PEOPLE! WE ARE THE POWER!

Manufactured nihilism, with a side order of hope and empowerment. He supposed there were worse mission statements.

Behind the stage itself was a wall of fraying plaster. A mural had been painted on it: a depiction of the singer from the Ungrateful Dead, and a red-haired punk on the drums.

'What are you drinking?'

As he turned, he realised he'd been wrong to assume the club was deserted: there was someone standing at the bar, or rather, behind it.

Flame-red hair teased into spikes so sharp they looked like they'd take your eye out. An eye that *had* been taken out, replaced by a vine. Vines that covered much of the man's face, which told Joe he had a potential witness, but one who couldn't be relied upon: decay like that meant he'd been dead for a long time. His memory would be Swiss cheese.

Still, he'd never been one to say no to a free drink.

He walked over to the bar and nodded at the barman. 'I'll take a Jack and Coke.'

He knew he wouldn't be able to actually drink it, but that was OK, because there was no way the barman could actually serve it. That didn't stop him trying. Joe watched as his form-less arms passed through the bottle of Jack Daniel's pinned to the wall in front of him.

He remembers what Jack Daniel's is, then. Which means he might not be such a useless witness after all.

'Were you here earlier tonight? The Ungrateful Dead were playing. A young girl OD'd.'

'What are you drinking?' the man replied.

Joe sighed.

'A teenage girl collapsed, just after the band came on. Do you remember her? Did you see anyone with her?'

The flame-haired man's one good eye pierced Joe's face.

'What are you drinking.'

The words may be the same, but the tone's different. It sounded like he was agreeing with me.

'You saw her?'

'What are you drinking!'

A definite yes tone, and the slightest of nods.

'Did you see who gave her the pill? Did you see anything suspicious at all?'

The barman didn't answer, instead walking clean through the bar and past Joe towards the stage. He looked up at the mural.

'What are you drinking.'

No questioning in the tone at all. More a statement of fact.

Joe looked from the mural to the man with one eye. There was no similarity between him and the lead singer. More so with the drummer – they shared the same hairstyle, at least – but it was difficult to tell, such was the blizzard of vines covering his face and body.

'What are you drinking,' the barman said again, nodding at the mural.

Some connection between the band and the OD'ing girl, maybe? It was difficult to tell when your witness had one stock-in-trade phrase. Not to mention one eye.

Something rumbled in the phantom detective's gut.

A million years ago, Joe would have called it a hunch.

Considering she was over three hundred years old, Berlin's Charité hospital still looked damn good. Germany's largest (and oldest) hospital, it had originally been conceived as an out-of-town plague house before reimagining itself as a place of healing and renewal. It was named after the French word for charity, and did its best to live up to it.

The glowing cross that sat astride the building next to it wasn't quite as ancient.

'What's with those neon crosses?' asked Joe. 'They're every-where.'

'You remember seeing them before?' Hans replied.

Joe shrugged. 'I guess so.'

'They belong to a rock-and-roll deacon. He's got churches all over the city. Glowing crosses, leather jackets instead of cassocks. Trying to get the youth, or some bullshit, and the way I hear it, he's succeeding. Those neon crosses have helped; they're his brand. He was a big noise in East Germany before the Wall fell, apparently.'

Joe tapped his fingers on the dashboard. 'If he's plugged into the youth, he could be worth checking out. He might have heard about Spook, at least.'

'Maybe,' said Hans.

'Club I was just at seemed to have links to the past, before the Wall came down. Think there's some sort of connection?'

'Everything in this city's linked to the past,' said Hans, 'whether it likes it or not. The girl in this place is our priority, not some crusty old punks. Stay focused.'

Joe and Hans sat opposite the hospital entrance, their dozing car coughing into the night's cool air.

'Not a reason in the world why I should be in that hospital,' Hans said, 'which is why you're here. Need you to go in and find out what the girl who OD'd knows.'

'How do you know she's in this hospital?' said Joe.

'Because that's what my source told me,' Hans replied, 'and he's never wrong.'

Joe kneaded his hands together.

'Remember what you were like when Lucia found you,' said Hans. 'You were a mess. A joke.'

'That's true,' said Joe. 'I owe Lucia a lot. The Dying Squad, too.'

'Now it's time to repay her. You have your kitbag?'

Joe nodded, reaching down into the footwell next to him, lifting up a leather backpack and trying to ignore the raging pain in his side.

'Then go to work.'

What struck Joe about the hospital was the number of spirits walking its wards.

There were several on each floor, all of them in varying degrees of decrepitude. They seemed to be crawling out of the walls. It was like there'd been an event for them, one that said it was OK to be seen in public.

He stepped aside as the double doors in front of him were thrown open, and two paramedics rushed through pushing a hospital gurney containing a man in a shirt sodden with blood. Joe noted the puncture wound. A knife attack, he'd guess; he'd seen enough of them when he'd been alive. That was a memory trinket he didn't have to dig deep for.

Taking out his notebook, he flipped through it until he arrived at the name of the girl he sought: Ella Wagner.

Hans had shown him a picture, too. Sixteen. Blonde. He'd even found which ward she'd been taken to. Money could buy you anything, apparently.

He scanned the directory and discovered that her ward was on the fifth floor.

Normally he wouldn't have had a chance in hell of communicating with a living witness, but Ella had taken Spook. That meant that for the next few hours, the drug would allow her to see the dead. He intended to take advantage of that.

Someone had sold her that Spook, and Joe needed to know who. It wasn't like a tab of Ecstasy that you bought off a random dealer; Spook was specialised, a drug dealt in trust.

He knew something was wrong even before he heard the alarm.

There was a feeling in the air of rupture and pain, of the unnatural forced into being. Orderlies ran clean through him, pounding towards a room at the end of the corridor. A doctor, too. Joe followed them, picking up his pace.

It's Ella. I don't know how I know that, I just do.

He rounded the corner, plunging through the door that had been thrown open by the hospital staff, hating the fact that he'd been right.

His fists squeezed together instinctively.

A teenage girl hung from the opposite doorway. A knotted sheet was wrapped tightly around her neck, her body limp. The orderlies were rushing to get her down, but Joe knew it was too late. The lifeless shape of her spoke to that.

What a waste, he thought. What a fucking waste.

The room was bathed in almost-darkness, lit only by a night light in the corner. It offered up just enough illumination to show a chart pinned to the end of what had been Ella's bed. Ignoring the orderlies, Joe kneeled in front of it, scanning the details. Name, date checked into hospital, date of birth, height, all things he didn't need to know. Initial diagnosis was more helpful, although the doctor's broken-wristed scrawl wasn't.

Patient admitted due to toxic reaction to undetermined narcotics. Bloods to be taken to ascertain the nature of toxicity. Full psychiatric evaluation to be conducted when the patient's condition had stabilised. Patient was in a state of extreme agitation when admitted. Stated she was hallucinating, and 'seeing the dead'. Restraint necessary. Observations to be taken every hour.

Joe got to his feet. Those restraints obviously hadn't done their job.

He looked at the bag on his shoulder.

He thought about what was in that bag.

It was worth a shot.

Lucia called it the Trifecta. Joe was never sure why exactly, but he was sure of the device's innate wrongness, just as he was sure it was the only chance he had of being able to question Ella.

She'd been placed on the bed by the orderlies, the doctor having confirmed her time of death. He had a few moments, he guessed, before she was taken down to the morgue. He didn't know whether that would be enough – didn't know whether this was going to work, even if it was – but at least it guaranteed him an empty room and a fighting chance.

He drew out the first piece of the Trifecta, and truly, it was difficult to imagine anything more functional. The device – and its two brothers – looked like a metal hockey puck. Joe placed all three on Ella's cooling midriff, a few inches apart from each other. Her face was already a little waxy, her lips blue. It might be too late. In a way, Joe hoped it was; what he was about to do was wrong, no matter how right the reasons.

He pushed the small black button on each of the metal dishes regardless.

There was a whine, then a crackle in the air.

A hum, too. One he had felt before.

A glimmer began to appear over Ella's body, like a double-exposure haze.

A soul-shredding scream punctured the air.

Ella jerked up. Or rather, the double exposure version of her did: she shimmered and glimmered, her face slightly indistinct, like a half-developed photograph yanked from the darkroom too early.

Would you look at that, thought Joe. It actually worked.

'Get the fuck away from me.'

Her eyes were open and staring right at him. Joe saw a mixture of anger and fear in them. Both those things were eminently understandable.

'It's OK, Ella. I'm here to help.'

'You glimmer,' she said. 'You're one of them. You're dead.'

Joe nodded. 'I am.'

Ella blinked. 'You talk.'

'With words and everything,' he said, smiling.

She closed her eyes. 'This is like a bad dream.'

It's much worse than that.

Ella tried to jump off the bed, but grunted in surprise. 'I can't move.'

'That's short-term. I just need to ask you a few questions.'

'Are you real? Are any of the things I see real?'

'All of it's real,' said Joe, 'including me. There's nothing to be afraid of.'

Ella scrunched her eyes shut again. 'I took a pill. It made me see things. Horrible things.'

'At the club?'

She nodded, keeping her eyes closed. 'The things I saw scared me. Then the ambulance crew brought me here, and it was worse.'

A sound began in the back of her throat, and she started to shake violently. Sobs burst from her chest, galloping against each other.

'I . . . just . . . wanted to see . . . my dad . . . again. He . . . said . . . it would let me, if I . . . took it.'

'Who said?' Joe asked, swaddling his words with care. 'Who sold you the drug, Ella?'

Ella looked down, seeing the waxy form of her flesh-and-blood body.

The sobbed chokes caught in her throat. 'What the fuck's . . . going on?'

Joe reached out a hand, placing it on the girl's arm. 'There's no easy way to say this. You're dead, Ella.'

She laughed. Not the reaction Joe expected particularly, but no one really has a frame of reference for being told they're dead.

He'd been in this situation once. When? Who was it that had delivered the fateful news? It didn't feel right that it was Hans and Lucia. Rang untrue somehow.

'That's bullshit,' said Ella. 'I'd know if I was dead.'

'It doesn't feel that different. You still feel like you.'

She rubbed her eyes and stuck her chin out defiantly. 'This is a hallucination. Just like the one I had in the club. Like I had when I got to this shithole.' Her face twitched at the memory. 'I saw people with vines all over their faces. They . . . they . . .'

'They weren't hallucinations,' said Joe. 'That was the Spook, letting you see what was really there.'

He was wasting time he didn't have. The Trifecta acted as a sort of holding cell for the dead person's spirit before they were taken to the Next Place, hell or the Pen – at least that was what Lucia had told him. It didn't stop them being dragged off to those places, but it bought you a little time with them. It had limited uses when you were trying to discover how a spirit had met its end, because they usually couldn't remember (Ella's blank memory concerning her hanging herself a case in point), but it gave you a fighting chance of finding out other details.

Like, who sold her the Spook.

'Everything's going to be OK,' said Joe. 'I give you my word.'

Ella laughed again. 'The word of a ghost. I don't know what's crazier: that you're there to give it, or that I believe it.'

'Who sold you the Spook, Ella?'

She shook her head. 'I just wanted to see my dad again. They were his favourite band. I thought he'd be there.'

Have to Sunday-drive my way to this, thought Joe, even though I only have the time to drink-drive. 'The Ungrateful Dead, right? What's their story?'

Ella shifted on the bed. She seemed to welcome the distraction. 'The Dead go way back. As in, East Germany before the Wall fell. They were one of the main bands in the punk scene there. True pioneers.' She smiled like she was remembering a bedtime story. 'There's a myth about them. One I always thought was bullshit until tonight.'

'Which is?'

She leaned forward. 'They say that in the band's early days, a ghost performed on stage with them. A boy. He'd dance to the music, sort of like a mascot.'

'Who's "they"?'

'A few people at the gigs,' said Ella, 'and a few was all it took. It became part of their legend.'

'But you thought it was bullshit.'

She nodded. 'Until tonight, when I saw a boy onstage with them. He wasn't dancing, though. It was more like he was glimmering. Like you are.' She squinted at Joe. 'Do you think he's real?'

'Am *I* real?'

'I don't know,' said Ella.' She looked away. 'All I know is, I

90

wanted to see my dad again. The day he died, we'd had a big argument. I said some shitty things. I never got to say sorry.'

'I'm sure he knew,' Joe said.

'People always say that,' Ella replied. 'And it's always bullshit.'

A crack of light started to appear in the doorway that she had hanged herself in.

Time's up.

'They wouldn't leave me alone her, the monsters,' she said. 'The hallucinations. It felt like my brain was exploding. I needed a way out.' She looked behind her at the doorway. 'I . . . I . . .'

'The dealer who sold you the Spook,' Joe said quickly. 'Do you know him?'

'He was a friend of my dad's,' said Ella, seemingly hypnotised by the growing crack of light. 'Name's Klaus. He works out of Berghain.'

'Berghain?'

'It's a club.'

She got to her feet, the Trifecta seemingly unable to hold her in place any more. 'You're lucky you're dead. You wouldn't make it through the door of that place otherwise.'

Joe turned away as the room burned white.

When he looked back, only Ella's cooling corpse and the three metal Trifecta dishes remained.

Hans was where Joe had left him. When you had a soil-addled memory, that was always something to be thankful for.

The black Mercedes dozed, coughing fumes discreetly from its exhaust, Hans visible in the illuminated driver's seat. Joe rapped on the window.

Hans lowered it like it was a chore. His square jaw was set defiantly out in front of him. Music drifted from the car's speakers through the open window. 'Well?'

'Got a lead. Berghain.'

'What's in that shithole?'

'Our lead.'

Hans glared at him.

'The guy who's been dealing Spook operates out of there,' Joe continued. 'Way I figure it, if he's not the Mr Big we're looking for, he can lead us to him.'

Hans nodded, either satisfied or satisfied enough to not be completely unsatisfied. He reached across, opening the passenger door and letting it swing wide.

Joe thought of Ella's young, wasted body. The way her lips had turned blue. A lifetime of opportunity snuffed out because of the poison someone had sold her.

He swayed on his feet, the world lurching.

His eyes swam.

He saw two images, superimposed over one another.

The first – the more vivid – was of the girl he'd just seen in the hospital, hanging dead from a beam.

The second was less clear, but that didn't mean he couldn't pick out details.

A girl of a similar age was slouched on the floor behind Ella. She had a mane of shocking-pink hair, and a black Ramones T-shirt.

Joe knew her. He just didn't know *how* he knew her.

He searched for the memory.

He couldn't find it.

She meant something to me. What?

The song playing on the car's stereo ended, to be replaced by the innane chatter of a DJ.

The image faded from his mind completely.

Chapter 8

Back at the old homestead. Mabel could hardly believe it.

Every detail was exactly as she remembered. The old carriage clock on the mantelpiece. The faded grey sofa, its stuffing
sporadically unspooling. The peeling paintwork. The smell
of undetermined meats stewing in watery sauces. A parade of
photographs depicting long-dead and never-met relations, all
of them good servants of the Pen.

And at the centre of it all, her feared and reviled grandmother.

'Little Mabel,' said Oma Jankie, running a tongue over her
whiskered lips. 'You've got awfully fat.'

'Banishment hasn't improved your manners none,' Mabel
replied. 'Can't say I'm surprised, judging by what we had to go
through to get here.'

'Oh, she's a frightful cunt, your Duchess,' said Oma Jankie,
grinning. 'She's made me proud in that respect. Even I wouldn't
have thrown anyone into Oblivion.'

'You would,' said Mabel. 'You did.'

'*You'd* hold my head under the water if I was dying,' said
Oma Jankie.

'I've not come here to squabble with you,' said Mabel, taking
a step towards her. 'Actually pleased to see you, if you can
believe that.'

'I can't,' said Oma Jankie.

'You'll always be my Oma,' said Mabel. 'Not much either of us can do about that.'

'But you'd like to have,' said the old woman, a grin wicked with mischief on her face. 'I was harsh on you because I knew what you'd face in the Pen. Knew it was the only way to prepare you for days like this.'

'The past don't interest me much,' said Mabel. 'It's things in the here and now I care about.'

Oma Jankie nodded towards the sofa. Daisy-May lay on it, unconscious.

'This pile of rag and bones? The one your idiot sister made Warden?'

Mabel frowned. 'You know about that?'

'I know everything you three girls think, let alone do. What do you imagine that voice in your head was?'

'The devil on my shoulder,' said Mabel. 'My conscience gone wrong. Never thought for a minute it was actually you.'

'Well, it was. Rachel might have banished my body here, but she doesn't get rid of my mind so easily. That can still go where it wants, when it wants.'

'Think I'd find that worse somehow,' said Mabel. 'Frustrating to see us girls mess up, and all you can do is hector us about it. Pretty much all you did when we were alive on the soil.'

'Thank you for explaining the nature of my punishment to me,' Oma Jankie said, ice in her smile. 'I haven't had a single second to consider it.'

'You must have mellowed,' said Mabel. 'You'd have come for me with a cane back in the old days.'

'She took my bloody cane,' Oma Jankie spat. 'Along with my purpose.'

'The purpose bit, I can help you with,' said Mabel, walking

94

to the sofa and sitting down next to the curled-up form of Daisy-May, ''cos the girl needs your help.'

Oma Jankie scowled. 'Why should I help that mongrel? She's no Warden of the Pen. Never was, no matter what that blasted sister of yours said. Not the way these things are done, giving the title away to any stray who wanders across her path. The succession line has been traced back centuries. Traced forward centuries more.'

'Except it wasn't,' said Mabel, ''cos I never got the nod to fetch that Jacob lad again. Who knows where the poor mite ended up after the Nazis had him? All Rachel knew was *her* time was up and she needed a successor.'

Oma Jankie pointed a gnarled finger at Daisy-May. 'And this is who she chose? A common gutter rat?'

Mabel got to her feet. 'That common gutter rat's got more courage than you and me combined. More than *every* bleeding relative of ours. She's good and pure in a way you can't imagine. She swam through the Gloop after Rachel had poisoned it, and despite the damage that did to her, she tore that Uriel bastard to shreds with her bare hands. She's more worthy of the Warden mantle than anyone you've ever met.'

Oma Jankie considered this. Silence lingered between them.

Finally she spoke. 'If she's so worthy, what's she doing here?'

'Swimming through the Gloop poisoned her. Don't know how much longer she'll last without your help. 'Cos we both know you can help her.'

Oma Jankie placed her hands on her hips. 'Why should I, if this is something Rachel would want? That *you* would want, for that matter?'

'Not stupid enough to waste my time appealing to your conscience,' said Mabel.

'Good.'

'But that girl there's your best chance of getting back to the Pen. We both know why.'

Oma Jankie sniffed. '*If* she completes the trials.'

'There are no guarantees in the afterlife. No one knows that better than you. But what do you have to lose?'

Oma Jankie laughed. 'Less than you, that's for sure. You must be desperate, offering me that. Coming all this way, too.'

Mabel swallowed. The old cow was right: she *was* desperate. Oma Jankie was a last throw of the dice, the sort of desperate move a degenerate gambler would use when he was down to his last dollar.

The sad truth was, she was that gambler, and she was down to her last quarter.

'Do it,' she said to the old woman. 'I know the cost.'

Preparing for the operation (although really Mabel saw it more as a ceremony) didn't take long. A space was cleared on the boxy living room floor, and a saucepan full of a foul-smelling, tar-black goop stood ready a foot or so away. Oma Jankie gave it a final stir, then got to her feet, assessing Daisy-May, who lay on the cold stone floor.

'You know that this cure is nothing of the sort, little Mabel? That any healing will come from the girl herself?'

'I know well enough, seeing as I went through the same thing. Rachel, too. Hardly likely to forget, are we?'

'It was the making of you.'

'It was almost the death of me,' said Mabel.

Oma Jankie laughed, walking back to the saucepan of toxic tar and lifting it up. 'Almost doesn't count. Now, hold her down.'

Mabel frowned, but nevertheless did as she was told. 'You really think I need to? Girl barely has the strength of a kitten.'

'You'll see."

She nodded, placing her chapped, weathered hands on Daisy-May's bony shoulders.

Come on, girl, she thought. I know you can get through this. You *have* to get through this.

Oma Jankie positioned the saucepan over Daisy-May's face, holding it there for a few seconds.

She's enjoying this, thought Mabel.

Then she locked her eyes with Mabel's and began to pour.

For a second, Mabel thought her grandmother had oversold the prospect of Daisy-May reacting. A few drops of the liquid hit the girl's face and she didn't so much as flinch. It was only when it began to fall in earnest that she started to move, her back arching as the toxic substance covered her eyes and mouth. Mabel winced as she pushed her back down, telling herself that this was her only chance, that it was this or eternal oblivion.

As more and more of the goop covered her face, Mabel saw that it was beginning to harden, crusting into a sort of obscene face mask.

'This is going to kill her,' she said as Daisy-May started to gag.

Oma Jankie wasn't listening, though, or rather, she had lost the ability to; her eyes had rolled back into her skull, leaving pupils of pure white. Her throat seemed similarly afflicted; she was making a choking sound very like Daisy-May's.

It had begun.

Daisy-May's eyes popped open, along with her gasping-for-air mouth. To begin with, she feared she'd gone blind, so complete was the darkness. Then her eyes began to adjust. She couldn't pick out objects or people – anything, in fact, that would allow her to place where she actually was – but she started to differentiate between the different shades of black.

Like I used to do at Grandma June's house. I wanted a night light,

97

but she taught me how not to be afraid of the dark. That was one in the cool granny ledger.

Then she begged me to kill her, which sort of chalked it off.

She got to her feet and tried to think of the last thing she could remember. There'd been kids in a laboratory, held against their will. Dispossessed ones, from the poorest part of the Pen. A woman who didn't glimmer who was behind it all somehow.

And Remus. Her right-hand man, who had betrayed her.

Plus, that freaky-as-fuck demon that wore human skin like a bad suit. Uriel. The one whose wings she'd ripped off. She could remember all that, which meant she wasn't on the soil. Didn't feel like the Pen either, though. Not really.

Wherever she was, she felt like herself. Her body was real. Solid.

She flexed her fists, jumped up on her toes. Where before there'd been sickness, now there was the sense of her body being in a truce with itself.

How long would that last?

'You must be wondering where you are.'

An old woman's voice sounded all around her. One flavoured with cackle sprinkled with bile.

'Guessing it's nowhere good,' said Daisy-May, looking for the woman who'd spoken. 'Not if everything's in darkness and there a booming voice of God bouncing around the place.'

The woman laughed. It was the sound of a bird dying.

'I've never been called a god before. I could get used to it.'

'Don't doubt it,' said Daisy-May. 'Never met a deity that didn't have a God complex.'

'I heard you were feisty.'

'Feisty. A dirty word for "having an opinion".'

'Do you know where you are, girl? What you're here to do?'

Daisy-May sighed. 'How would I? How many pitch-black netherworlds do you think I've woken up in?'

98

The reply was silence.

'To be fair, this isn't the first,' she said. 'Hell was hell, but at least being tortured gave me something to look at. This place is dull as fuck.'

'This "place" is a sacred link between two minds. It's as old as the Almighty himself, and just as hallowed.'

Daisy-May snorted. 'Peeps are always banging on about how sacred the afterlife is. Time to kill those cows, mate.'

'I've never heard such impertinence.'

'Give it five, I'm just getting my eye in.'

'Do you know why you're here, child? Do you know how close to death you are?'

She thought back. That did ring a bell, now the booming woman's voice came to mention it. It was since she'd taken that swim in the Gloop; she'd got sicker and sicker. Passed out after the big face-off with Uriel.

'I'm guessing I've not made it to the Next Place.'

The old woman laughed. 'That isn't for the likes of you.'

'What is then? What's more limbo than limbo?'

'Your soul is poisoned. To stand any chance of purifying it, you must undergo the trials.'

Daisy-May sighed. 'Sounds like hard work.'

'Saving one's soul usually is,' the woman replied.

'What do these trials involve?'

There was a shimmer directly in front of her, a ripple of light in a sea of darkness. An old woman stepped through it. She was withered, with a shock of electrocuted grey hair and hungry-looking eyes. There was something familiar about her.

'Seen worse entrances,' said Daisy-May. 'Have we met? You look familiar.'

'I've never had the displeasure,' the old woman said. 'My name, though, I'm sure you're familiar with. My granddaughters have delighted in dragging it through the mud over the years.'

Realisation dawned. 'Fucking hell, you're the demon grand-ma.' Daisy-May clicked her fingers. 'Oma Jankie. You're Oma shitting Jankie.'

Oma Jankie glowered. 'You'll speak to me with respect.'

Daisy-May held her hands up. 'Absolutely. Heard nothing but bad things about you.'

The old woman smirked. 'I don't think you appreciate just how serious your position is. These trials aren't games, girl: they are the only way you're going to prove yourself worthy of purification. I know of only two people who have ever passed them: my granddaughters.'

'House always wins, right?'

'I showed no favouritism. It was only by passing these trials that they proved themselves worthy of their positions. It is why you simply being handed the mantle of Warden was such a travesty. You did nothing to earn the title.'

'You don't know anything about my life,' said Daisy-May, 'and you don't have the first clue as to how I earned that title.'

'I know all.'

'You know jack shit, mate.' She clenched her fists. 'People like you are the reason the Dispossessed revolted, and why the Duchess picked me. I'm the future. You're barely the past.'

Oma Jankie licked her lips. 'You'll need that spirit if you're to pass the trials.'

'What are these trials? What do I have to do?'

'Pass them to survive,' said Oma Jankie. 'That's all you need to know for now.' She stepped aside.

The doorway of light shimmered like it was inviting Daisy-May in.

It's never easy, she thought. And that's fine, 'cos all I've ever known is hard.

Squeezing her hands into fists and her fears into deeds, she walked through the doorway.

Chapter 9

Wewelsburg Castle, 1941

You smell the laboratory before you see it. It's not like the first time I was taken there. A lot has happened since then. None of it's good. That isn't the way Schmidt and Himmler see it, but they're not the ones in the cage. They don't get killed and resurrected every day. Daily death and rebirth give you a certain worldview.

There's a mania about the place. Fevered conversations, although not on account of my arrival. That doesn't prompt a second look from the technicians. They should pay me more respect. I'm the main event. I'm why *he's* coming here.

Their Führer. Their Hitler.

Today's going to be different, but not in the way they think. They're on the brink of bridging the worlds of the living and the dead. I can't allow that to happen.

I must blow up the bridge, even if I'm on it.

Especially if I'm on it.

They don't call it the cage: the room in which they kill me every day is called the testing booth. It makes it sounds like the perfumery of a department store when it's more the slaughter room of an abattoir. I said this to Himmler once. I didn't say it twice.

Today, though, Himmler looks at me almost with deference. He knows how valuable I am. I'm a priceless Ming vase he can't afford to drop. If he does, it's Hitler he'll have to answer to.

'I don't like his heart rhythms,' says Schmidt, looking at the chart in front of him. 'I'd feel better if we could delay.'

Himmler sniggers. 'The Führer would love that.'

'The impact on the human body is enormous,' says Schmidt. 'The constant stopping then restarting of his heart has weakened it considerably. I don't know how many more times we can do it.'

Himmler smiles that smile. 'If today goes well, we won't need to do it many more times: only once. That will be something to celebrate, will it not?'

Schmidt nods, biting his bottom lip.

'Prep the boy,' says Himmler. 'The Führer will be here within the hour.'

I don't wait to be led. As I walk towards the cage, my hand goes to my pocket and the suicide pill that sits within it. It's the one that was gifted to me by my father.

Today's the day. I intend to turn the eve of their greatest triumph into the day of their greatest failure. And all it's going to take is my suicide.

When I was put under the first time, the room was stripped bare of everything but a hospital gurney and a defibrillator. Now it's as if electronics have bred within the four walls.

Two banks of machinery flank the bed. They don't bother with the straps any more. They know I'm broken, compliant. I'll do what they say when they say it, and not offer up a sniffle of complaint. I'm a good lab rat.

Situated in the four corners of the room are metal towers that reach almost to the ceiling, bending in on themselves. They installed them a week ago. It is difficult to imagine they're to improve my condition.

A buzz surges through the room.

He's here, someone says.

Be ready, someone says.

The Führer, someone says, awe stuck in his teeth.

Schmidt says nothing. He has too much at stake. Himmler too, though he is no doubt insulated against Hitler's rages. Schmidt isn't. I'm his ticket to Nazi immortality. If something goes wrong with me, something will go wrong with him. If he's lucky, it will only be his career.

I sit on a stool, swinging my legs, feeling like a child brought into a parent's place of work. Technicians crane their heads. Someone giggles nervously. What they are trying to achieve here is the stuff of madness and legend. It cannot possibly work.

I finger the pill in my pocket. It's been half whittled away over my time here by my nervy fingers. Destiny lurks within it.

The Nazis mean to bridge the world between the living and the dead. I know this, because they've told me. I have become an emaciated mascot to them. I'll never be one of them, but I've been around long enough for them to lower their guard. Or make them believe one is no longer necessary.

The time they leave before bringing me back from the dead has grown longer. It makes the pain even greater, but that's of little consequence to them. As long as I keep coming back, they learn more of the connection between the living and the dead. And they've learned a lot.

They've learned that a different spirit greets me each time my heart is stopped. I never saw the dumpy woman, Mabel, again. Perhaps I'm not important enough. Perhaps she was too important and thought me a time-waster. Or perhaps she knew something was amiss here. Certainly she knew of the evil of the Nazis. Theirs is an evil sufficient to scare even the dead.

They say very little, these spirits that come to me. It's like they know that Himmler and his lackeys are listening in. They're wise, if that's the reason for their silent watchfulness, because that's something Himmler and Schmidt have learned to do. They record on their machinery, technology that defies description. They play it back to me. The last two spirits spoke to me. Crackly words filtered through a mangle of distortion, but coherent, just. How excited my tormentors were.

How excited they knew Hitler would be.

Now, he's here. What wonders they plan to show him.

If I have anything to do with it, he won't see a damn thing.

I swallow the tablet.

Suddenly, he's there.

He's shorter than I expected. There's something manic about him. His eyes flit this way and that, like he's focusing on everything and nothing. In photographs he always seems pristine, composed. Sculptured, even. Here, all I see is a short man in a uniform that's too big for him, with lanky, sweaty hair and a sense of decay.

The men here see something different. They flank him, standing to attention, lab technicians and soldiers alike, their eyes hungrily searching for his. A flash of approval. A nod of respect. Something to take home to the wife. *I saw him. He nodded at me. There was understanding there. The Führer knows what I would do for him. What I would do for the Fatherland.*

They will go home disappointed. Hitler only has eyes for me.

He approaches, Himmler to the right of him, Schmidt to the left, and I feel unchanged. The pill hasn't worked. Perhaps my fingers have worried the poison out of it. Perhaps it was never really poison. Perhaps it hasn't taken effect yet. A thousand questions, all of them unanswered.

He stops a foot or so away from me. He licks his lips. Whether this is for effect or merely something he does unconsciously, who can say?

'This is him?'

His voice is high-pitched. There's no gravel to it. No bass.

'Yes, Herr Hitler,' Himmler replies, looking at me almost fondly.

'He looks thin.'

'A side effect of the programme. We give him drinks to build him back up. There are inevitable consequences to what we do here.'

Hitler nods, as if he himself has made similar sacrifices.

He takes the cane that's in his right hand and touches it to my face. He moves my head left then right with the steel tip.

'Will he survive what we will do here today?'

Himmler looks at Schmidt expectantly. The scientist smiles nervously. 'Yes, Mein Führer. You have my guarantee.'

'Your guarantee,' Hitler replies. 'Is that something worth having? It's been offered to me many times over the years. Sometimes it means something, sometimes it doesn't.'

'Schmidt is our most brilliant technician,' says Himmler, smiling. 'Everything you are about to see is down to his genius.'

Hitler snorts. 'If it's a success, I'm sure you will borrow some of that genius for yourself, Heinrich. Certainly I will allocate some of the blame if it's not.'

Himmler is caught between nervous admittance and confident denial.

'What do you make of this, boy?' Hitler looks at me as if observing a snake in a zoo.

'What do I make of what?' I reply, my mouth dry, my heart still stubbornly beating, despite the pill I have ingested.

'The ambition of the living to broach the world of the dead? The designs we have of conquering that world?'

'I think the idea is as insane as you.' The words are out of my mouth before my brain can process them, fuelled by bravery I didn't know I had.

Hitler stares at me.

Himmler goes to strike me.

I close my eyes, waiting for a sting that doesn't come. Hitler has raised his cane, stilling Himmler's hand.

'We will see if you're right,' he says, smiling in a way I don't understand.

I'm led into the testing room as usual. Strapped down as usual. Schmidt is the difference. Instead of hovering at the control desk outside, he's in the room with me, encased inside a suit. It's something a deep-sea diver might use when dropping to the depths of the ocean. Wires trail from the suit to the ceiling. His helmet fogs up.

He's nervous. I can smell it on him.

I'm nervous too, because he's in here with me, and because the pill I took hasn't worked. My father said it would kill me in seconds, yet here I lie, minutes later, alive. If you can call this living.

One of Schmidt's underlings hovers next to me. He has a needle in his hand. This is how it goes. They stick it in my arm. I die. I stand on the brink of the afterlife. They pull me back. It was supposed to be different this time. I took the suicide pill. I'm supposed to stay there. Wait there until it's my turn to take on the mantle of Warden of the Pen.

I look over at Schmidt in his ridiculous oversized diving suit and realise he means to stay there too.

The needle slides into a vein next to my big toe. My arms are such a criss-cross of slashes, they are no longer an option.

The familiar grind of slipping away settles on me. I know its stench by now. I'm sick of it. There is nothing left for me. No comfort. No relief.

First there is the drop, then the ascent. I clamber wearily from my skin-and-bone body, looking at it disdainfully. It can do nothing for me. It's useless, like a coat that doesn't fit any more.

The room loses its clarity. Hitler and his entourage are huddled around the control desk outside, smudgy line-drawings. The look on Hitler's face can be seen, though. He's like a child at Christmas, one who asked for a hobby horse and instead received a full-grown stallion.

I glance around the room to see what spirit they've sent me this time. It's a woman. She considers me. She doesn't speak yet. It would be wrong to say she's old. She is, but it would be wrong to say it, because it would suggest decrepitude. Instead, a sense of power radiates from her. It's like she's been chiselled from a block of ice. Sculpted cheekbones. Scraped-back hair.

'Hello, Jacob,' she says. 'I'm the Duchess.'

'They're listening,' I say.

'I know.' She nods behind me. 'They're watching, too.'

I look over my shoulder. Schmidt stands there in his suit. He should be indistinct, but he's as pin-sharp as if I was still living and breathing. He's here, with us.

'This is incredible,' he says, giddy.

The Duchess takes a step towards me. 'I'm sorry for what these animals have done to you. You shouldn't have had to go through it.'

I swallow. 'Can you take me now?'

'There's nothing I'd like more.'

From the corner of my eye, I see Schmidt move forward. He's like an over-eager suitor at a prom. His attention flicks between us and the jiggling Hitler in the room outside.

'It's your birthright,' says the Duchess. 'Never in the history of the Pen has an ordained Warden not taken up that mantle.'

Fear prickles, because *but* lurks behind her words.

She glances to her right, at the smeary men outside the room. 'I must break that cycle with you. For now, anyway.'

'What do you mean?' I ask.

'These devils, with their technology, cannot be allowed access to the Pen. I have come in person to tell you that we won't be back.'

She looks at Schmidt, then to Hitler outside. 'Do you hear me, Herr Hitler? While you monsters breathe, we won't be back. It doesn't matter how many times you kill this boy. This is the last time you'll see us. Your tinpot regime won't last for ever. Believe this: none of you will ever see the Pen.'

'You can't leave me here.'

The words are less of an order and more of a plea. I look imploringly at this Duchess who I'm supposed to replace.

'Strength, Jacob. Now is not the time for your ascension to the Pen. Know that when it is – when I am given the command from up high to come and get you – I'll be there, ready to take your hand.'

She tries to smile at me.

There's a blinding flash of white. Schmidt cries out, raising his arm.

I blink away the glare. She's gone.

'Bring him back,' Schmidt says, pointing to me, his voice distorted by the suit's helmet. The distortion can't hide the resignation. The resentment.

Two lackeys quickly enter, and I watch from the corner of the room as they huddle around my cooling cage of a body. They'll inject me. I'll be revived. It will hurt worse than death. I'll still be a prisoner here. It will never end.

My flesh-and-blood body bucks under the electric paddles they always shock me with. It's strange, because although the first shock never brings me back, I usually feel a tingle. This time there's nothing. I'm just watching a boy who looks like me getting electrocuted.

'Something's wrong,' says one of the men. He must be new. This is what always happens.

'Shock him again,' says Schmidt.

They do. My body jackknifes.

I slump to the floor in the corner. I've seen this play. It always ends the same way.

Perhaps it's not the end of the world that it seems to be, though. I need only to survive the Nazis' rule, and the Duchess will return. I must be strong, like she said. Must endure.

'His mouth.'

There's panic in Schmidt's voice, and I see why. My earthly body has begun frothing at the mouth.

The machine I am hooked up to wails.

They can't bring me back.

'Again,' Schmidt screams, trying to get out of the diving suit.

The pill I took. It must have worked after all. It took its time, but the rabid froth spilling from my mouth indicates it got there in the end.

Panic seizes me. I can't die for good, not now. Not while the Duchess will stay away. What will become of me? I'll be a bastard spirit, wandering this vile land alone. There is no telling how long the reign of the Nazis might last.

I could escape, though. How would they keep me here, with my earthly body cold and dead? I'd be a formless apparition. Their technology, their way of monitoring me, extends no further than this room. It wouldn't be the freedom I crave, but it would be freedom.

Schmidt looks outside. Himmler and Hitler stand there, their faces stone, unblinking.

'Again,' he says, his voice high and wobbly.

'Herr Schmidt,' begins one of his underlings, 'there is nothing more we can do.'

'Again,' Schmidt says, quieter this time.

The men nod and shock me once again.

Schmidt bows his head.

I walk towards the window while he's distracted. This is my chance. If I can just get out of the room and out of this damnable castle, then perhaps the Duchess will return. She can liberate me from this hell.

A humming fills the room. It tickles my teeth and dribbles from my eyeballs. Instinctively I look up at the four pylons in the corners. They haven't done a damn thing that I know of before today, yet now they seem to have sprung into life.

I reach the glass. By rights I should be able to pass clear through it. I've read the texts. My father said it would be so.

I reach out with my hand. It strikes the glass like it doesn't know I'm dead yet.

I hear laughing from the other side.

Himmler and Hitler sneer at me.

I strike the glass again. It repels me again.

'Silly boy,' says Schmidt from behind me.

My body spasms. This time I do feel the electricity.

I drop to the floor, gasping. Schmidt stands there with a long metal device in his hand. It looks like a cattle prod.

'Death isn't the release you think it is,' he says.

Wewelsburg Castle, 13 March 1945

I now know what it is to haunt a place.

Perhaps the spirits that are accused of such crimes are like me.

Imprisoned in a room by technology they don't understand. Bouncing off walls, trying to find a way out. They're nothing to be scared of. They're desperate. They just want to be free.

I almost miss the early weeks of being inside this cage. Then I was fawned over, admired. Hitler himself came back several times to look at me, an entourage of High Command with him. The Gestapo were particularly fascinated with me. I considered learning to juggle. You have to put on a show.

Then the stomach of the great war rumbled hungrily, and the visits became less and less. The scientists stayed for a time, running their experiments, trying to use me as a conduit to the afterlife. Schmidt claimed there were pockets of Nazi scientists behind enemy lines in places like Manchester and New York who were trying to channel spirits to work for them.

They failed. Their numbers diminished, pulled back for the war effort.

Now there is only Schmidt and me.

Explosions sound night and day, getting closer. It seems the Duchess was right. The time of the Nazis is drawing to a close. This should bring me joy, but doesn't. What will their fall mean for me? Will the Duchess return? Will I finally break free from the shackles I am kept in? All I can remember is this cell. The maddening, never-ending humming within it that somehow keeps me whole, and which makes escape impossible.

Another explosion, closer this time. The laboratory rattles its approval. Schmidt can't bear to leave me, or rather, he can't bear to leave the work. He says he's close. The means to bridge the worlds of the living and the dead is at hand. I have my doubts.

Here he is now. Scarecrow-thin. Lab coat hanging off him. Himmler and Hitler long gone. Schmidt's work has been forgotten, amnesia brought on by the Allies' bombs and bullets. He'll be an urban myth when defeat is finally declared. Something gaudy to be written about, along with the Nazis' search for Atlantis and their quest for gods and monsters. No one will ever know how close they came.

'They're here, Jacob.'

He looks behind him, almost as if he expects a tank to trundle through the wall at any moment.

'Who's here?'

He places his hands against the wall of my cage. 'The Americans. They're at the gates. It's over.'

I walk to the glass. 'Could you free me? What good am I now?'

He looks over at the control desk. 'Perhaps I should. They wouldn't understand my research. Would consider it godless, if they managed to grasp it at all.'

He walks over to the desk. I swallow, struggling to believe that freedom is finally at hand.

'I was so close,' he says, more to himself than to me. 'So close.'

His finger moves towards a button on the desk.

'And you could get closer still, Herr Schmidt.'

He whips round, his jungle of hair bouncing as he does so.

A platoon of soldiers lingers at the entrance to the laboratory. Guns sit in their arms, but there's no spite to them. It's like they know they won't be needed.

At the centre of the group is a man dressed in army fatigues. He's not like the soldiers who flank him. He's more of a society dandy. His skin is olive brown. A razor-edge moustache balances on his top lip. There's an aura about him.

Schmidt has got a gun from somewhere. His hands are shaking.

The soldiers bristle, their own guns raised as one. Schmidt doesn't look like much of a shot. These men do.

'Easy,' says the man with olive skin, motioning to the soldiers to lower their weapons. 'There's no need for shooting.'

'You're the enemy,' says Schmidt.

'In the wider context, you're probably right,' says the American, his words warm, sunny and jostling with each other. 'In this context, you're absolutely wrong.'

He looks over Schmidt's shoulder. It's like he's looking right at me, which is impossible, because the only way to see me is through the monitors on the machine. The soldiers either side of him see nothing.

'I'd prefer it if you put your gun down,' says the American, returning his attention to Schmidt. 'You have nothing to fear from us. There'll be no trial for you, Herr Schmidt. I want to work with you, not punish you.'

He smiles. He has the whitest teeth I've ever seen.

Schmidt lowers the gun. He may be devoted to the cause, but he's no idiot. Dead martyrs don't leave much of a scientific legacy. 'I don't understand.'

'The United States is in need of you, Doctor,' says the American, flashing his million-dollar smile again and striding towards Schmidt. 'You, and your research.'

Schmidt takes a step backwards, instinctively shielding me from sight. 'My research?'

The American looks around admiringly at the laboratory, then sticks out a hand. 'Isiah Matthews.'

Schmidt regards the hand like it's diseased, but takes it nonetheless.

Matthews pumps it fiercely. 'We know all about the work you've been doing here, the advances you've made. There are wars to come after this one has been won, and we'll need men like you to help fight them.' He stands next to Schmidt, placing an arm around his shoulders. He looks me dead in the eye. 'You and your friend here, of course.'

He winks at me.

'Hello, Jacob,' he says.

Chapter 10

He couldn't find her.

That hadn't been down to not looking. He'd searched every inch of the house for Megan, and hadn't seen hide nor hair of her. The only evidence of her presence had been the two china teacups he'd found in the living room, a pot of tea sitting between them.

Which he was guessing meant she'd got an audience with Julius. What she'd done with that audience was another matter.

There was one last door he hadn't checked, leading off from the kitchen. It was strange. Out of place. A metal barrier more at home in a freezer than a designer kitchen. He wouldn't have stood a chance in hell of getting through it if he'd been alive.

Luckily for him, he wasn't.

It didn't make any sense.

Bits had passed formlessly through the door into a dimly lit corridor. What was strange about the corridor was that it wasn't part of the house itself; it was like they'd punched through to the adjoining house. Basic LED lights stood on rickety-looking stands, casting the bare, sand-blasted walls in a harsh light.

No chance they'd have got planning permission for this caper, he thought. What the fuck's going on here?

There was another door at the end of the corridor, a similar thing of steel and might.

He quickened his pace towards it.

Bits had a lot of time for Megan. She had ice in her veins and a lion's heart in her chest.

Her habit of getting kidnapped, though, could get in the bin.

He'd walked into what could only be described as an operating theatre. The room was tiled, the floor and ceiling dazzling in their whiteness. A blood bag had been strapped to some sort of heart-rate machine, a thin tube stretching out from it to Megan's arm where she lay unmoving on a medical gurney.

It didn't seem likely she was taking a disco nap.

'Megan.'

Nothing.

Bits walked over to her. She looked *out*; if not for the slightest movement of her chest rising and falling, he would have worried it was permanent.

Still might be, unless I can get her awake and out of this psycho pit. Don't know why she's been drugged, but it isn't to let her catch up on her beauty sleep. Don't like the rate that bag's filling up with blood, neither. It was a mistake coming here. Doesn't matter whether Spooky Dave set us up, or whether he's just ignorant of what a fucking madhouse this place is. All that matters is getting Megan out of here.

He called her name again, still receiving no reply.

He heard the trundle of wheels in the distance. A trolley of some sort.

He leaned over Megan, reaching for her arm, wincing on her behalf at the cannula that was sticking out of it. Blood continued to flow from it, filling the bag just above her. No time for subtlety; if he had to wrench the cannula out, then so be it.

Except he couldn't touch her.

His hand passed straight through her arm.

Fuck.

He tried again, getting the same result.

He tended not to interact with the living world – old habits and older Xylophone Men died hard – but since the knowledge that such an act now brought no punishment, it was something he'd employed when he needed to. Or at least he tried to: the ability seemed to come and go, often deserting him when he most needed it. He most needed it now.

The door swung open. A young guy was standing there – Bits would have put him in his twenties – dressed in a pristine white lab coat. He was pushing a metal trolley; the surgical instruments that rested on top of it gleamed under the tungsten lights.

'Yeah, you need to wake up, Megan,' Bits said. 'Like now, 'cos there might not be a later if you don't.'

The man pushed the trolley forward, bringing it to a stop next to the gurney. He bent and lifted one of Megan's eyelids, nodding, apparently satisfied with what he saw.

Fucking horror show, this. One I walked us both into. Now it's up to me to walk us both out.

The man checked the blood bag, a small smile on his lips.

Have to take him down. Before it's too late.

Bits shoved his fists forwards. They merely passed through the lab-coated body of the young man.

It wasn't working. There was one option left open to him, one that had even less chance of success than his failed attempt to push the man away.

The man picked up a scalpel from the trolley, holding it up, seemingly hypnotised by the way the light reflected off the blade.

Fuck, thought Bits, shoving his hand into the kitbag on his shoulder. I hope this works.

Though there's a part of me that hopes it doesn't.

It had been the second day on the Squad when Joe had shown them the kitbag.

Bits had slouched and insolently endured the first day of training, resenting the lectures and the patronising *you're lucky to be here* tone. The field kit they'd take with them to the soil had tweaked his interest, though. There was the gun, of course, the UV wand, and the essential gum to keep their memories intact. It was the vial of powder in the thick plastic case that had grabbed his attention most, mainly because Joe had studiously avoided talking about it.

'What's this?' Bits had asked, holding up the vial and looking curiously at the rust-coloured contents.

'It's older than God, and twice as dangerous,' said Joe. 'You don't want to be messing around with it.'

'If I don't want to be messing around with it, what's it doing in the bag?'

Joe had stiffened. 'This is your second day. Let's get back to the basics.'

'If we're going to be partners, we need to trust each other, right?' said Bits. 'Tricky to do that if you hold out on me. Decide what I don't need to know rather than what I do.'

Joe had taken the vial from him. 'This is a last-resort tool, one that gets used so rarely it's barely worth mentioning.'

'It's still in the bag, though, yeah? Has to be a reason for that.'

He sighed, passing the vial from his left hand to his right. 'You ever been to a seance?'

Bits snorted. 'Don't believe in all that sweaty bollocks.'

'You're *literally* a ghost.'

'Doesn't mean I can speak to the living, does it? Or that I'd want to.'

'That's the thing,' said Joe, passing the vial back to him.

'With this stuff, you can. And people do, and have, through the ages. Clairvoyants, spiritualists, whatever you want to call them, they inhale this shit, they can speak to the dead. Or rather, the dead can speak, and act, through them.'

'Full of charlatans, that game, man.'

'There are plenty of bad pennies, sure,' said Joe. 'But there are also legit practitioners. Some people can see the dead without any stimulants, it's natural for them. Others inhale this powder. By doing that, they open themselves up not just to seeing the dead, but to being possessed by them, too.'

'Why the fuck would anyone want that?' Bits had asked.

'Maybe they want to know whether a loved one is all right. Maybe they want to be close to them again. That's what a real clairvoyant is: an intermediary between the living and the dead. This powder used to be the building blocks to make that happen.'

'Used to be? Like, not any more?'

Joe nodded. 'It was seen as too dangerous. The powder allows a soul to take residence in your body, sure, but once it's in there, it's sometimes tricky to get it back out again. Maybe it likes having an earthly body to stay in, or it can't get back out when it tries to: either way, the clairvoyant's in a lot of trouble. Apparently there's a way of doing it without the powder, but that involves breaking off a piece of your soul. Real black-magic stuff that only a few can do.'

'So what are exorcisms, then?' Bits asked.

'An exorcism is like using a sledgehammer to crack a nut,' said Joe. 'Sometimes it'll work, but there won't be much left of the nut.'

'If this shit's such bad news, why have it in the bag at all?'

'I asked Daisy-May – the Warden to you – that very same question. She said that if the situation arises where you need to use it in an investigation, and the living host accepts the possession of their own free will, then the transfer's allowed. Rare as rocking-horse shit, though, those circumstances, and if the host isn't willing, you're risking the Xylophone Man.'

Joe had tucked the vial away, deep in the bag. 'It's an inelegant weapon for a more savage age. No place for it in the Dying Squad.'

That was then. What would Joe make of that weapon, and the need to use it, now? Faced with Megan unconscious on an operating table and about to be carved apart?

Got to try, no matter what the risks, thought Bits. Might be dangerous as fuck, but it can't be any worse than a nutter with a scalpel.

He uncorked the vial and, allowing himself no time to change his mind, poured the contents over Megan's face.

If the psycho butcher in the lab coat could see this, he was showing no sign of it, though something gave him pause, his scalpel hovering inches over her pale skin.

All at once, Megan opened her mouth as if she were yawning, like the prospect of having her skin sliced to pieces was one that bored her. Bits began to gag, his mouth opening too of its own accord, his windpipe constricting. The sensation was one of being violently shoved down a dark tunnel.

That was when he experienced what he could only describe as an out-of-body experience. The sensation of rushing towards Megan's body continued, but as he looked back, he saw his own body standing a few feet away. Except standing wasn't quite right; it was like his body was dissolving, parts of it falling off, devoured by the air.

He got a final look at what was left of his face, then his head was wrenched forward and he slammed into Megan's supine figure. There were a few seconds of blackness, then he blinked.

He was looking up directly into the lab-coated man's eyes.

Fucking hell. It worked. It's like I'm squatting on her soul.

That's mad.

—You in here, Megan? he thought. —'Cos if you are, now'd be a great time to wake up.

A slurred mumble came back to him, one of fuzziness and sleep.

—Tell me to go and I'll go. Need your consent to possess you, 'cos this is a fucked-up thing I'm about to do.

Another mumble. Then: *Stay.*

Pain seared as the scalpel dug into his arm.

Except it's not my arm. It's Megan's.

He turned her head slightly and saw the mad scientist (*Julius* — the name popped into his head, narrated by Megan) draw back in surprise.

Stay, came Megan's voice, a little stronger this time.

Fine then, Bits thought.

He commanded Megan's left arm to move, and it did, grabbing Julius's wrist and pushing the scalpel clumsily away.

'That's impossible,' Julius said. 'I put you under.'

Ignoring the pain in his (her — *fuck, this is trippy*) right arm where the man had made a cut, Bits jolted Megan upwards, all the time feeling like both the puppet master and the marionette.

Have to use this element of surprise while I have it. Wonder if I can rotate her head round all the way, Exorcist style? That'd shit him up.

He settled for lashing out with Megan's right foot, though really it was more of a sluggish shove; his mind might have been sharp and racing, but Megan's body was still weary from whatever drug she'd been given. Still, it was enough to push Julius backwards, making him drop the scalpel in the process.

Gritting Megan's teeth, Bits ripped the cannula from her arm, blood spraying Julius and splattering on the white-tiled wall behind him.

'I'm going to kill you,' he said, and the tone and quality of

Megan's voice startled even him. It was guttural and bassy, like it had been scooped out of hell's slop bucket.

Julius backed away, a look of naked terror on his face.

Because I – we – sound fucking demonic. Maybe I'll tell him his mother sucks cocks in hell. Really *shit him up.*

He turned Megan's head. Her eyes alighted on the trolley with its various surgical instruments. Ones that would work just as well as torture instruments.

He reached out for a particularly gruesome-looking device, all flashing metal teeth and rib-breaking intentions. Just as he closed Megan's hand around it, Julius lurched for the scalpel on the floor. Bits commanded Megan's foot to kick out, and it did, with more authority this time, connecting with Julius's ribs, eliciting a jolt of pain from both of them and sending the man sprawling.

Grabbing the device from the trolley, ignoring the pain in her foot, Bits/Megan dived at Julius, pinning him to the ground with her legs, driving her weight onto his stomach and winding him.

She held the device against Julius's neck, using just enough pressure to draw blood.

'Why did you drug her?'

Megan's voice flipped this way and that in pitch, parts of some words deep, others high-pitched.

Julius winced. 'Her? Don't you mean you?'

Bits applied just a little more pressure, drawing a gasp from the man.

Careful, said Megan's voice.

'I know what I mean,' said Bits.

'You're a prize specimen,' Julius gasped. 'With your blood, your DNA, I could have created my own version of Spook.'

'Did Dave deliberately send us here? Does he know what you are? What you intended to do?'

'David's a businessman,' said Julius. 'He saw an opportunity and he took it.'

'What opportunity?'

'I'm the future of this city. By gifting you to me, he guaranteed himself a place in that future.'

Ask him about Hans. Ask him how we find Hans. Megan's voice. Stronger now. Useful, too.

—In a minute, Bits thought. —I need to ask him about Michelle first.

'Michelle your aunt then, is she?' He could see the resemblance if he squinted.

'Yes,' was Julius's slightly strangled reply.

'She needs professional help, not to be in this nut house,' said Bits, in his best demon voice. 'Those dolls are sick. Plain wrong.'

'They help her,' said Julius. 'You don't understand.'

'I understand you're taking advantage of a damaged woman, one who meant something to me once. You're going to do right by her. Get her the help she needs. Right?'

Julius swallowed. 'All right.'

And I believe he will, thought Bits, because I sound like the devil himself, and you don't fuck with the devil. He's got the best tunes, but he's got a million ways to hurt you, too. Probably invented most of them.

He pressed Megan's knees down tighter, drawing a groan from Julius.

'And you're going to give me this Hans's contact details.'

'He'll kill me if I do.'

Bits looked Julius dead in the eye.

'What do you think we'll do to you?'

Julius had been remarkably complicit when it came to handing over the details. Willing, too, to sew Megan's arm back up. But then he'd already got the blood from her; perhaps he realised it wasn't so important to have his pound of flesh, too.

He was scared, Megan said. *Who can blame him? It's not every day you come face to face with a possessed nutcase like me.*

—Like us, Bits silently replied. —And it worked, didn't it? I got you out of there.

He spotted the sanctuary of a bus shelter, throwing a glance backwards. There were no signs of pursuit, nor did he expect any; they'd properly rattled Julius.

They'd have properly rattled anyone. Would continue to do so, because Bits felt Megan tense then relax around him, and that had to be a problem on the outside as well as the inside. He could feel her body twitch, right on the verge of spasming. She was getting stronger, pushing him out, reclaiming her body as well as her soul.

It was time to end this thing.

How do you end it? Megan said. *How do you get out of me?*

—Saucy cow, said Bits.

That's not really an answer. Also: urgh. Sometimes I forget you're a nineties lad.

—To be honest, I'm not really sure. Whenever Joe talked about possession, it was more to say how we should never, ever do it.

What?

—Wasn't left with much of a choice, was I? If I hadn't done it, you'd have been burger patty by now.

Can't believe you just let Julius go, said Megan. *I'd have killed him.*

—It's the Dying Squad, said Bits, —not the death squad. We solve crimes, not commit them. I'm going to call in Julius's drugs factory to the feds, or rather, you are, just as soon as we get this separation done.

So do it.

—All right, I will. Open your mouth.

Why?

—Because that's how I entered you to begin with.

Again, urgh – but is it really that literal?

—Think I know what the fuck's going on? Think I've done this before?

All right, all right. Wait, though: could you just open my mouth without my say-so?

—Suppose so, said Bits. —I controlled you when you were passed out, but I'd rather not make a habit of it. Feels like taking a dump in someone else's toilet.

Lovely. I bet you bought Loaded, *didn't you? Had* FHM *posters on your wall?*

—Proper mags, those. None of this namby-pamby cancelling rubbish you get today.

Your words make me sad.

Bits felt Megan's mouth open.

He tried to think back to the original briefing with Joe. What had he said about separating from a living host after possession?

'It's a flip of a coin whether it's even possible.' That was it. 'It depends on the host, and the spirit. You visualise separation – picture yourself literally stepping out of the living host, out of their mouth – and if it's going to work, it will. But even if it does, chances are there'll be something of your soul left in the host.'

He'd just have to take the chance. Bits couldn't imagine Manchester was stuffed to the cassocks with exorcists.

He visualised them separating.

Nothing happened.

He tried again.

Less happened.

This is starting to hurt, Megan said.

—Hurt how? asked Bits.

Like I'm trying to take a massive shit but can't.

—Beautiful, that, said Bits. —You're a real princess.

He tried again.

He failed again.

It's not working, is it? You can't separate from me.

—No, Bits replied. —I can't. Not just now, anyway.

So when?

—I don't know. But I know a man who will. We've just got to get to Berlin to find him. Joe'll know what to do.

You still think there's a Joe to get back?

—Not this nonsense again.

It stinks, Bits. He's knee-deep involved with this Spook drug.

—Probably undercover, isn't he? Getting intel so he can bring the gang down.

Where does Hans fit into that? Megan wondered. *Way Julius and Dave told it, he sounded suss as anything. Why's Joe working with him? What's his angle?*

—Got Hans's number now. We get to Berlin, we set up a meet, and we get Joe back. He'll know how to separate us.

I hope, Bits thought.

I heard that, said Megan.

Chapter 11

Frankie Knuckles, accurately labelled the Godfather of House Music, once described the Warehouse – the club that is widely acknowledged to have birthed the house genre – as being a church for people who have fallen from grace. Lost to music in 2014, Frankie would have loved Berghain.

Stealing its name from the nearby neighbourhoods of Kreuzberg and Friedrichshain, Berghain was a massive concrete dollop that had kept much of its original architecture while gaining the title of Best Club in the World. The local concern had become an international phenomenon, clubbers and tourists alike converging on it, lured in by lurid rumours of sex, drugs and the finest minimal techno in the world, the venue's fascist-like desire for secrecy only adding to its walled-off mystique.

'Place is a piss trench for derelicts,' said Hans.

Not everyone was a fan.

Joe walked alongside his partner, skirting round a neat square of wasteland, observing the queue of people snaking back hundreds of feet, the club's pounding techno reverberating. Glowing in the distance was a thin, flashing spike attached to a bulbous glowing golf ball: the TV Tower of the old Germany looking out upon the new.

They reached the head of the line. 'So?' Joe asked. 'What's the plan?'

'This is a two-man job,' said Hans. 'We go in together. You ID the dealer, I'll sweep him up. He'll be the Spook supplier we're looking for, or he'll lead us to them. If the little dead girl wasn't lying to you, that is.'

'She had no reason to,' said Joe.

Hans adjusted his suit jacket and straightened his glasses. 'Let's get this thing done.'

Joe looked from his partner – all immaculate black suit and slave-to-the-industrial-military-machine haircut – to the queuing clubbers. Their clothes may have shared Hans's colour palette, but that was where the similarity ended: everyone seemed to be in a regulation outfit of black T-shirts or singlets, with spray-on black jeans, and black trainers to boot.

'You haven't really come dressed for it,' he said.

Hans adjusted his tie and straightened his sneer. 'Watch and learn.'

Facing them at the doorway to the club was a black-suited behemoth. The man's grey hair was swept back from his face, and two steel pins pierced his lips. Barbed-wire tattoos were tangled onto his face, a wild-abandon grey beard covering the lower part of it. A shimmering gold chain dangling around his neck completed the picture. The normal reaction at such a specimen, Joe thought, would be cowed awe.

Hans, it seemed, was going to go with arrogance and bribery instead. He held out a hand, the notes rolled in it all too visible. 'How you doing?'

The bouncer looked from Hans's outstretched hand to his gleaming shark-black eyes.

He shook his head. 'Not tonight.'

Hans smiled, nodded down to his still-outstretched hand. 'I don't think you appreciate how grateful I'll be.'

The doorman ran a hand through his mane of grey hair, then shook his head again dismissively.

Hans glowered, going into his pocket and drawing out more notes.

'Don't embarrass yourself,' said the doorman. 'It's not going to happen.'

Joe placed a hand on Hans's arm. 'Let me go in there and flush him out. It's the point of having me here, right? I can't be seen or heard.'

Hans pocketed the money and took a step backwards, turning away from the bouncer. 'Do your thing. I'll be in the car.'

Joe nodded, and began to walk towards the club's entrance.

'Oh, and Lazarus?'

He turned back to his partner.

'Never put a hand on me like that again. Understand?'

He didn't. Hans's animosity came from a place that was alien to him.

He still said, 'Yes, guv.'

This is what life looks like, thought Joe. This, God got right.

Berghain was humanity filtered through a prism of speaker stacks and bass-in-the-soul beats. Sixty-foot-high ceilings were supported by colourless concrete pillars, a cathedral of writhing, committed clubbers laid out in front of him, music piped in from techno-heaven.

It was like a religion. One that wouldn't judge you when you fucked up.

There was an air of sexualised spirituality to it all, one he would have loved to lose himself in and come stumbling out of several days later. It was tempting, that inner voice selling him the virtues of such a surrender. Tempting, but not quite tempting enough. Not when he had work to do.

The opportunity to do that work was, however, proving

to be problematic. The place was a maze: corridors leading to dead ends that were in fact nothing of the sort, packed, sweating bodies funnelling him this way and that, each lap throwing up a new gloomy rabbit hole of throw-care-to the-wind debauchery. A difficult assignment to find one man in all of this, even if the description of that man had been a vivid one; a middle-aged punk should be easy enough to spot amongst the sea of black uniforms.

That was if he was here at all.

Ordinarily, the music would have proved to be a screaming distraction, but the deeper Joe went into the club – and the closer he went to the speakers – the easier he found it to order his thoughts. It was something about the beat and the bass; it was like it was performing a spit and polish on his memories. Snatches were beginning to come back to him.

Images of a one-armed man. The vision he'd seen of the girl, outside the hospital, the one with the pink hair. A lanky whippet of a man, all round-shouldered arrogance and front, who'd been something to him once.

All these people meant something to him. What?

Focus, a voice said. *Keep to the task at hand.*

Good advice.

He did another sweep of the dance floor, tingles surging through him as he passed among the dancing clubbers. It might have been his imagination, but he was sure that he'd been the recipient of the occasional double-take. It was possible, he sup-posed, if any of the people dancing were on Spook.

Or maybe they were out of their minds on something else.

He stood on the upper gantry and closed his eyes, letting the rat-a-tat-tat beats soak into him, the minimal *tsk tsk tsk* helping his thoughts coalesce and solidify.

These people don't know how lucky they've got it. Mum always said life was wasted on the living.

He blinked. He hadn't thought about his mum since the accident. Couldn't even remember if he had one.

He did, though. And he had a feeling he'd seen her after he died. Was she dead too? That sounded right, somehow.

That was when he saw him.

Klaus, that was what Ella had said the dealer's name was. An old punk in a punch-drunk trench coat, the little hair he had gelled into reluctant spikes. Roughly seventy feet away, lurking in a corner, letting the punters come to him. Made sense. When you were a fixture at a place like this, you didn't need to make the dance-floor trawl; the dance floor trawled its way to you.

Klaus looked from left to right, then moved away from his pitch, heading towards a staircase.

Joe followed.

Holding back a little, unable to throw aside a lifetime's instinct of tailing someone despite his invisibility, he just about managed to keep Klaus in sight, weaving around a group of people coming the other way.

He allowed himself a smile. It had been a while since he'd been on the hunt like this.

At least, he thought it had.

The hunt led to the slightly more civilised Panorama Bar. Different DJs and a different vibe set high above the main dance floor, where avid clubbers could catch their breath, then decide whether to let it go again. Judging by the state of the people here, they'd been pondering that conundrum for days.

The music wasn't quieter here as such, just a little less pound-your-fillings loud. Certainly it seemed to be low enough to (just about) hold a conversation: Klaus was doing just that, sitting opposite a couple of women. Both wore all-black ensembles, the woman on the left's faded Guns N' Roses logo the only nod to a different colour.

A pitcher sat between them, three empty glasses waiting to be filled. The sofa backing onto their area was free, so Joe slipped into it, watching them intently, waiting to see what he could hear.

'This shit's the shit,' said Klaus, taking the pitcher and filling two of the glasses. 'In six months, it'll be bigger than Ecstasy when *that* first dropped. Like the summer of love, but this'll be the summer of death.'

'What is it?' yelled Guns N' Roses woman.

'Spook,' Klaus replied. 'One sip and you'll be able to see ghosts, baby.'

Shit, thought Joe. If he's legit, that means he'll be able to see me. Although maybe that won't be a bad thing. I play this right, I can work it to my favour.

The woman's friend shook her head. 'Heard about this. It's bullshit. Dangerous if it isn't.'

Klaus wagged a disapproving finger. 'It's actually a really beautiful experience. I take it all the time.'

The woman looked him up and down. 'I can believe it.'

'I'll try it,' said Guns N' Roses, picking up a glass.

Her friend looked at her disapprovingly.

'Live a little,' said the woman, winking at her.

'That's the spirit,' said Klaus. 'And I'm here to make sure it goes smooth.'

Lucky her, thought Joe.

Guns N' Roses tipped her glass back and emptied it in one go.

'Good girl,' said Klaus.

Her friend visibly shuddered.

'How long will it take to kick in?'

'Depends,' said Klaus. 'You're thin and sexy, so it should be pretty fast.'

'You're a creep.'

He simply grinned.

The woman who'd downed the drink began to blink. 'Wait. Wait.' She squinted. 'That seat was empty a moment ago, wasn't it? I think it's working,' she added. 'Are they supposed to glimmer like that?'

Klaus glanced behind him.

'Hello, Klaus,' said Joe.

The ageing punk jumped to his feet, a look of horror on his face.

'They speak?' said the woman. 'I didn't expect them to speak. How does it know your name?'

Klaus didn't wait to answer; taking a final look at Joe, he lurched towards the stairs.

Good, thought Joe. I could use the exercise.

He looked at the woman, who was still staring at him open-mouthed.

'That drug is dangerous, madam. If I were you, I'd reassess your life choices.'

She nodded dazedly.

Joe smiled. 'Have a good evening.'

It was never going to be much of a chase.

Joe could pass through people and objects at will, whereas Klaus, middle-aged spread and all, had to barge sweatily past them. And there were so many to barge past; the dance floor was packed tight with bodies heaving to the music. Joe stood on the balcony, watching as Klaus tried to squeeze his way through.

As the music reached a glitchy crescendo, he jumped, lasers exploding all around him. His timing couldn't have been more perfect; he landed on the dance floor just a foot or so away from the horror-stricken Klaus. It was a move that would have resulted in broken ankles if he'd still been a living, breathing copper, but as an undead one, there was only the muscle memory of what it should feel like.

And I've got better at controlling that, he thought. On my first case, walking through walls made me feel sick, now I can jump off balconies like Batman.

Another memory. A farmhouse in the countryside, the first time he'd walked through a wall. A run-down one.

It was the music. He didn't know how or why it was making him remember things, only that it was, and here, with these ear-splitting beats, it was like the effect was supercharged.

The aggrieved crowd were helping do his work for him too; they pushed the corpulent punk away from them and towards Joe.

No consequences any more for interacting with the living, he thought, reaching forward and grabbing Klaus by his collar. Long-term, can't help feeling that'll end badly. Short term, it'll do nicely.

He dragged the man away from the throng, a bizarre sight no doubt to those they were leaving behind. But then if even half the legends about what went on in Berghain were true, the sight of an old punk manhandling himself off the dance floor wouldn't warrant more than a glance.

Joe pinned him to the wall, ensconced a little way from the dance floor in a concealed crevice.

'How is this possible?' said Klaus, to himself as much as Joe.

'You've been getting high on your own supply,' said Joe. 'Know what a cliché that makes you?'

'How do you know who I am?' Klaus asked, staring at him in slack-jawed wonder. 'How can you touch me?'

'I'm asking the questions,' said Joe. 'You'll be the one answering them.'

A little of the cocky arrogance he had seen upstairs returned to Klaus's face. 'Or what? What are you going to do? Haunt it out of me?'

Joe's fist connected with Klaus's stomach, knocking the wind from him and deflating him like a dying balloon. He let the man gasp for air, then pinned him back against the wall.

'That clarify things for you?'

Klaus nodded quickly.

'Spook: who's your supplier?'

'Spook?' said Klaus. 'Never heard of it.'

Joe sighed and drove his knee into Klaus's groin. The punk cried out, buckling over in pain.

'I can do whatever I like to you and no one will ever know,' said Joe. 'There's no one to stop me.'

He lifted Klaus's head up so they were staring directly at each other. 'You killed a girl, do you know that? You might not have pulled the trigger, but you sold her Spook and now she's dead.'

A look of horror flashed in Klaus's eyes. 'Ella?'

Joe nodded, then leaned in, his face inches from the punk's. 'Talk.'

Klaus swallowed. 'Colonel. He's who you want.'

Joe frowned. 'Who's Colonel?'

Klaus shook his head. 'I can't believe I'm snitching to a ghost.'

'No one ever can. Who's Colonel?'

'He's a singer in a band. The Ungrateful Dead.'

The Ungrateful Dead.

The band at the club. The one that had been playing earlier tonight. The one Ella had gone to see. That was what the barman had been trying to tell him when he pointed out the poster.

'What's Colonel's connection to Spook?'

'He's the main supplier for it in Berlin,' said Klaus. 'You want Spook in this town, you go to him.'

134

'Where can I find him?' said Joe, relaxing his grip just a little.

'He lives at Hotel Control.'

'He lives in a hotel?'

'It's a rock-star themed hotel. He's a fucking cliché. What can I tell you?'

Joe pulled him closer. 'You warn him I'm coming, I'll find you. Do you doubt it?'

Klaus shook his head.

Joe released him, watching as the punk scuttled off. It was a risk letting him go, but it wasn't like he was overburdened with other options. Besides, the Klauses of this world had a yellow streak a mile wide; the last thing he'd do would be to run back towards danger.

There was a stack of speakers a few feet away, raised slightly on a small stage. Joe walked over to them, then hopped up onto the stage, the bass reverberating through him, the insistent electronica helping to settle and order his thoughts.

The pink-haired girl appeared in his mind again. Had she been his partner? That felt true and untrue. She'd been something to him.

She called me Joey, not Joe. She knew it wound me up.

The pink-haired vision smiled. He was getting somewhere.

Another one popped up. He was in a storm drain, running. No, chasing. He was chasing a one-armed man. The man was firing some sort of weapon at him.

The Generation Killer, that was what he'd been called. Hans had already told him that, but now Joe remembered it for himself.

A cheer went up from the crowd, and he was snapped out of his reverie. He looked up to see that an image of a girl with white hair had been projected onto the cavernous far wall. The clubbers were raising their hands to her like she was a golden god.

I know her, thought Joe, closing his eyes and placing his head next to the speaker stack, the bass and the melody coursing through his brain. Where from?

The graffiti at the recording studio

Somewhere else, too.

A sample had been drizzled into the harsh industrial beats.

'My name is Hanna Jankie,' it began, 'and I died a very long time ago.'

Another roar from the crowd.

Tsk tsk tsk went the beat.

'I'm no ghost, no wandering spirit striving for peace that's just out of reach. I'm a person, with hopes, and dreams, and ambitions, just like you.'

The clubbers celebrated these words with another roar.

'There is an afterlife. There is something afterwards.'

Her words were punchy, like a mission statement, the urgency of the rhythm beneath making them even more so.

'Take peace in that.'

Except you didn't, did you?

Joe's eyes snapped open.

He was beginning to remember. The full film this time, not just badly edited highlights.

The girl projected onto the wall – the one whose voice had been sampled – was called Hanna. She'd tried to take over the Pen. Daisy-May had told him about it. Shown him footage of her, too.

Daisy-May.

The trickle became a waterfall.

He began to remember.

He remembered what type of person he'd been when he was alive.

He remembered the type of person he'd been trying to be since he died. Since he'd been given a second chance.

He remembered the Dying Squad. The one in the Pen, not the one Lucia and Hans had told him about. They'd never so much as mentioned purgatory, and Joe's role there.

When he came to think of it, they'd barely told him anything at all.

They said that was because he had to come by the memories himself, that it was no good if they just fed them to him.

What if that was bollocks? What if they were using him, feeding him just enough half-truths to keep him in line. Keep him useful?

He had no evidence that that was the case, and his job was about evidence. Gathering it. Sorting it. Using it to get to the truth.

He intended to do just that. While he did it, he'd keep the partial reclamation of his memories to himself. Just to be safe.

He stared up to the image of Hanna. The looped, glitchy sample of her voice continued to ring around the club.

The Duchess. The Duchess had gone to Tokyo to stop her. She'd failed. Hans had told him that Hanna had blown up half the city.

Someone needed to hold her to account for that.

If what Joe remembered of the Dying Squad was accurate, someone would.

Chapter 12

When she'd walked through the doorway of light, Daisy-May had swapped one world of darkness for another.

There was more nuance to this new darkness, though. Whereas the last one had tied its mast to jet-black nothingness, this one was made up of different shades: a hint of grey here, a dash of black-brown there.

This was a place based in the real world, too, even if it wasn't *of* the real world. Water dripped somewhere close by. There was a cold, aggressive dampness. The ceiling was low – she was sure of that – and it had the feel of being underground.

She wasn't alone, either. She couldn't hear or see anyone, but she could feel their presence. They were close by. More than one person, too, if she had to guess.

'Is this the trials, then?' she called out. 'Just standing around waiting to catch my death?'

The filament of a bulb caught life, flooding the room with light. Daisy-May threw up a hand, her eyes protesting. She squinted and they settled, focusing in on what an ambitious estate agent would have described as a bijou room with potential but she would have labelled an underground sex dungeon.

Because it was a dungeon, or as close as you got without buying a castle. The ceiling was as low as she'd sensed, cold, damp tiles curving in the middle, just a couple of feet from her head. The walls were similarly tiled, with a film of green moss clinging to their clammy surface.

Three chains – fat, chunky things – dropped from the ceiling, finding a home around the necks of three women. They were unconscious, their chests rising and falling, their heads slumped forward in their metal harnesses. A thick oak table stood before them. On it, in front of each of the women, was a glass of water and two round pills.

Probably not for their hangovers, thought Daisy-May.

'What's this all about?' she called out, searching for Oma Jankie. 'I'm on the clock here, Grandma. There's a Pen that needs saving from a fascist uprising.'

Oma Jankie stepped out of the shadows.

'Got a flare for the dramatic, you Jankie girls,' said Daisy-May. 'Couldn't you just have given me the rule book to read or something?'

'This isn't a game, girl,' said Oma Jankie. 'The trials are a matter of life and death. Primarily yours.'

Daisy-May nodded towards the three women. 'What about their lives? Who are they?'

Oma Jankie licked her lips in anticipation and sat on the edge of the table just a few feet from one of the women. 'There was once a Russian called Leonid Yahontov. He was a good child of the revolution, working for the KGB in pursuit of the eventual triumph of socialism over capitalism. This loyalty wouldn't save him when it was discovered that he had kidnapped, murdered, then butchered over a hundred women.'

'Jesus,' said Daisy-May.

Oma Jankie waved a hand at the women in chains. 'These women were his fifteenth, sixteenth and seventeenth victims. Women who did little more than go about their business, until Leonid Yahontov was their business and ultimately their death.'

Daisy-May felt her fists ball. 'What's all this got to do with me? Especially if this has already happened?'

Oma Jankie smiled. 'Today, these women get a second chance. If you manage to save them, their souls will be plucked from the Pen and spirited to the Next Place. Eternal paradise awaits them.'

'What if I don't save them?'

'Then they'll descend to hell.'

'Looks like they're already in it,' said Daisy-May.

'They are,' said Oma Jankie, and Daisy-May felt revulsion at the smile that lingered on the old woman's lips. 'This is where they'll stay if you fail them. Each woman you allow to die will linger here to die again, and again, and again. You know a little about that sort of hell, do you not?'

Daisy-May did. The Xylophone Man had made her relive her own murder when he'd taken her to hell to punish her for interfering with the living, a double hit when you considered she'd learned of Joe Lazarus's part in it. It was vinegar-in-the-wound pain the likes of which she'd never known before, or since, one she wouldn't have wished on her worst enemy, let alone these poor souls.

'So,' she said, 'how do I help them?'

There was the sound of a key turning in a lock, and a door Daisy-May hadn't noticed began to scrape open. It was a sound sufficient to stir consciousness in the restrained women; they blinked awake, looking with a great deal of trepidation towards the now open doorway. A giant of a man was silhouetted against it. Daisy-May would have put him at six foot five, easily, and this was no gangling beanpole; he was linebacker-broad.

Who's been eating my porridge?

Leonid took a step forward, an action that did nothing to dispel the feeling that he'd emerged from some Brothers Grimm nightmare. He was almost completely bald, with just a shadow of hair on his head and face. He wore the outfit of a Russian soldier, but it barely fitted him; his body seemed at war with it, bulging in places it shouldn't.

As he advanced, his gaze swept the room, passing through Oma Jankie and Daisy-May without the merest hint of recognition.

'This maniac is about to present these women with a puzzle,' said Oma Jankie. 'Solve it, and you'll save their lives.'

'How?' said Daisy-May. 'Frankenstein over there can't see us, so stands to reason he can't hear us, either. Nor will these women be able to. How will they know what decision I make?'

'It will pop into their heads. They will naturally assume they have made the decision themselves.'

'What decision?' said Daisy-May.

'Stop prattling and listen.'

Leonid smiled at the women. Daisy-May noted the way in which they were dressed: simple sackcloth dresses that could have been made hundreds of years ago.

'Good evening, ladies,' he said, his Russian dialect somehow understandable to Daisy-May's ears. 'I am sorry to have kept you waiting. I had urgent matters to attend to. Kindly cast your eyes downward.'

The women obeyed.

'In front of each of you are two tablets. Do you see them?'

They said nothing.

The smile slipped from Leonid's face. 'Do you *see* them.'

The women, as one, confirmed that they did.

Leonid walked over to the woman on the far left-hand side. 'These tablets are the same, but different. To the naked eye – certainly to the uneducated one – they look identical. There are subtle differences, though, and when it comes to their chemical properties, these differences become starker.'

The gargantuan Russian smiled like a beatific grandfather.

'One of these pills is harmless, a placebo. The other is so laced with poison it will kill you within a minute of ingesting it.'

One of the women began to cry.

'If you pick the placebo, you have my word that you may go free,' he continued. 'If you pick the poison pill, you have my word that you will die quickly and painfully.'

'This guy's a fucking arsehole,' said Daisy-May.

'Yes,' said Oma Jankie. 'Whether he becomes a murdering arsehole is up to you.'

'So I've got to do what, pick the right pill? How am I supposed to do that?'

'Listen,' said Oma Jankie.

'I am not an unfair man,' said Leonid. 'Whichever pill you choose, I will swallow the other one. You have a 50/50 chance of survival, I have a 50/50 chance of death. There is symmetry in that, no?'

'This was a common KGB torture technique,' said Oma Jankie. Daisy-May noted the fondness in her tone. 'Leonid here elevated it to a different level during his reign of terror.'

'What happens if I can't figure out the right one?'

'Then these women will die, and their souls will be trapped in hell for ever.'

'No pressure, then,' said Daisy-May. 'What if I get the first one wrong and the second one right?'

'The pill takes a minute to kill,' said Oma Jankie, a sly look on her face. 'Choose quickly enough on the second, and you have a chance of saving the first.'

'Think I'll just get it right the first time.' Daisy-May turned to the old woman. 'How does this scrub the poison out of *my* system, exactly? These trials just sound like torture for everybody involved. Fucking sadism, man.'

'Ceremonies like this have been used to purify the soul for millennia,' said Oma Jankie. 'The manifest goal of such purification is to prepare the individual for communication with, and acceptance by, the supernatural. Think of it as a way of wiping the slate clean and allowing you to start again.'

She nodded towards the three chained women. 'Now, it is time for you to choose.'

Daisy-May walked towards the table. The tablets really did look identical; both of them white, the slightest dusting of powder on their outer shell, innocuous-looking, harmless.

How am I supposed to work this out? she asked herself. There's no skill to it, no deduction; it's a roulette wheel spin, nothing more.

There was only one slight difference between the two pills, so small that if you weren't looking for it, you'd have missed it. A tiny 'P' stamped in the centre of one of them.

'Choose,' Leonid said to the first woman.

If 'P' is for poison, that just makes me think it's a double bluff. That's the clean one – has to be.

'I choose the pill on the left,' said Daisy-May. 'The one with the subtle-as-fuck "P" on it.'

'Is that your final answer?' said Oma Jankie.

'Final as death.'

The first woman reached forward, picking up the 'P' pill with her left hand and the glass of water with her right. She placed the pill on her tongue and washed it down with the water.

Leonid mirrored the action, throwing the remaining pill down his throat and swallowing it in one gulp.

He grinned at the women.

He's looking pretty confident, thought Daisy-May. Which makes me feel pretty fucking nervous.

The first woman looked expectantly at Leonid, as if she were waiting for permission to die.

She soon got it.

Her hands went to her throat as she began to gag. Froth formed at her mouth, her eyes bulging.

'Wrong choice,' said Leonid, smiling. He moved to the second woman, who was looking at her neighbour in horror. 'Perhaps you will have more luck, my dear.'

The woman shook her head.

'You chose badly last time,' said Oma Jankie. 'Quickly now, or the first woman's soul will be lost for ever.'

Easy, thought Daisy-May. The placebo has to be the plain pill.

And try saying that after a couple of shots of sambuca.

'It has to be the one on the right,' she said. 'The plain pill. That's the one.'

'You're sure?' said Oma Jankie.

'I said so, didn't I?'

The second woman reached out for the pill, popping it into her mouth and quickly washing it down with the glass of water.

Leonid took the remaining pill, once again throwing it into his mouth and swallowing it clean down.

Come on. That has to be the right one, because if it's not, I don't know what is.

She wasn't surprised when the second woman started choking as well, though.

'This is a trick. The deck's loaded.'

'There is a way to save these women,' said Oma Jankie, a smug smirk on her face. 'It's just that you're not intelligent enough to work it out.'

'How can there be?' said Daisy-May. 'Two women, two different pills, the same result. The fix is fucking *in*, mate.'

'That first poor soul has twenty seconds of life left, if that,' said Oma Jankie, as the second woman began to foam at the mouth. 'Think, girl.'

Daisy-May swallowed, panic nipping at her heels, willing her to trip up. There was a way out of this, there had to be.

She took a breath. There had been something about the way the Russian psycho had swallowed the pills that had bothered her, something that had been off. Had he not swallowed them at all, perhaps?

Though even if he hadn't, so what? The women had taken one of each pill, so one of them should have been unaffected. It didn't make any sense.

I have to think this through. See it as a crime scene. This is the sort of shit I used to solve when I was Dying Squad.

She took a step closer to the table, trying to block out the gasping of the women, because if she couldn't concentrate and think this thing through, they were dead anyway. There was little to examine; just the two empty glasses.

A thought fired.

A smile flowered on her face.

The water. Both women had drunk from a glass of water.

Leonid hadn't. He'd dry-swallowed both tablets down. He hadn't touched the glass.

'He put the poison in the water,' said Daisy-May, no little triumph in her voice. 'It was never in the tablets at all. It doesn't matter which one of those they take, because they're harmless. The bad stuff's in the glass.'

'Are you sure?' said Oma Jankie.

'You bet I fucking am,' said Daisy-May. 'Final answer.'

The third woman picked up the first pill and swallowed it whole. She then took the second and dry-swallowed that down too, much to Leonid's horror.

With a smile, she pushed the untouched glass towards him. 'Would you like a drink of water?' she said. 'You look parched.'

'That's my girl,' said Daisy-May.

Oma Jankie growled. 'A lucky guess, but this was the simplest of the three trials. You may not fare as well on the next one.'

'Don't bet on it,' said Daisy-May, her back straight, eyes burning. 'We breed 'em tough in Nottingham, duck, and smart as fuck, too.' She took a step towards Oma Jankie. 'Free these women's souls and take me to the next trial. I've got a realm to save.'

Oma Jankie scowled, then waved her hand.

Just before a haze of white descended, Daisy-May saw the three women smile at her.

Saw Leonid rage, too, at the injustice of it all. It reminded her of the rantings and ravings of the Xylophone Man when he was similarly outwitted.

Wonder what ever happened to him? she thought, as the whiteness scrubbed out the rest of the room.

Part 3

We are the people!
We are the power!

Chapter 13

Project Phenomena government facility, America, 1953

It's the sunshine I can't get used to.

In Germany, it was harsh and bright. Unsubtle. Here, it's as if it's been filtered through a prism in heaven. Not everyone in the facility gets to see it, so I appreciate how lucky I am.

An hour a day, I get to go outside. It feels like an eternity. The facility is miles from anything – for all I know, hundreds of miles from anything – but I don't care. I don't need roads, or cars, or bustle and hustle. I just need these fields. The sounds of unseen birds. Sunshine that massages my muscle memory, reminds me what it's like to have my skin warmed. It's a paradise.

Paradise never lasts, though. Just ask Adam and Eve.

A cloud of dust appears on the horizon. In all the times I've been allowed out here, it's the first sign of life that I've seen. The birds don't like it. They cough and squawk nervously. I feel the weight of the building behind me. A concrete leviathan without windows that looks like it could withstand a nuclear blast. Matthews claims it's been built to.

There's a fence, hundreds of feet away. I'm not allowed near it, but that diktat doesn't extend to the soldiers who patrol it. They've seen the cloud. They seem to expect it – their guns stay on their shoulders, but their bodies snap to attention. It's someone important at the centre of this cloud. They'd have to be to be coming here, because *here* doesn't exist. That's what Director Matthews says.

'You've seen it, then?'

I turn to see Matthews himself behind me. He's wearing a suit and tie I haven't seen before. Smart, even by his standards. He always looks like he's dressed for an evening at the country club.

I nod. 'Someone's coming?'

He laughs. 'The President of the United States is coming.'

'You're making fun of me.'

'Not this time. Can you believe it? Ike himself, coming at the behest of an old carnie huckster like me. That's America for you, Jacob. Anyone can be anyone as long as they believe hard enough.'

I think he believes it. But that doesn't mean it's true.

Three black slugs park a few feet away from the entrance to the compound. They're more whale than car. Black-suited men with sunglasses get out, their heads twitching this way and that, looking for threats. Hoping for them. None of them see me. I can always tell. There's no telltale double-take.

Director Matthews twitches alongside me. I've never seen him nervous before. His mouth doesn't know what to do with itself; it fidgets, unable to settle. Even his gleaming teeth seem on edge.

One of the suited men walks to the car in the middle while the others stand to attention. He opens a door, and a man in a grey suit gets out.

'Is that him?' I ask. 'Is that the president?'

Matthews swallows. 'General Dwight D. Eisenhower. Supreme Allied Commander in Europe. War hero. Dogged.

Loved. A wartime president for peacetime. What will he make of our little operation, Jacob? What will he make of our ghosts?'

'Will he be able to see me?'

'Not without assistance. Technology has moved on since your Nazi lab. Let's hope it's moved on enough to impress the good general.'

The president strides towards us, his swivel-headed agents either side of him. A man in an army suit stands to the right of him. The sun bounces off his medals. If the president's a man who usually smiles when meeting people, he doesn't here. He runs his steely gaze over Director Matthews' fancy shoes and fancier teeth.

He reaches us and sticks out a hand.

'Matthews?'

'Yes, sir,' says the director, smiling widely, grasping the president's offered hand. 'So glad that you could find time to see us today.'

'I wouldn't be too glad,' says Eisenhower, 'because I'm of a mind to close you down. You have exactly one hour to persuade me otherwise.'

If the compound has an official name, I've never heard Matthews use it. Or anyone else, for that matter. It's either the compound, or the clink. For most, it's a prison. For the likes of me, spirits kept on a metaphorical and literal chain, but also for those who work there. The work is so secret the employees are rarely allowed to leave. They sleep on site. This is a calling, and once you've heard that call, you can't simply shut your ears to it.

To that end, the compound is essentially a barn pretending to be a city. A vacuum-packed carton of concrete housing hundreds of rooms. All of them with identical doors and unclear intentions. There are shops. A couple of bars. It's designed so you don't need to leave.

Not that Matthews shows the slightest inclination to. He's a zealot. The leader of a cult who demands complete faith and absolute devotion, and usually gets it. Judging by the look on the president's face, he won't be getting it from him.

We walk through the trunk of the compound, the roof hundreds of feet above us, a platoon of workers standing to attention on either side, the door that will lead us to the labs getting closer. My presence goes unnoticed by Eisenhower. I'm a lapdog that can't be seen or heard.

'Tell me about yourself, Matthews.'

The president barks the command. It's like he's irritated Matthews hasn't volunteered the information already.

Matthews smiles, trying to keep pace with the older man. He's unsettled, off balance.

'My origins are humble, Mr President. I come from poor stock, but I flatter myself the Matthews are a hard-working breed.'

Eisenhower laughs. It's like a seal barking.

'Hard-working, is it? Well, from what I've heard, that's true enough. A shyster may not punch a clock, but he has to put the hours in if he's to be successful.'

Matthews tugs at his tie. 'I'm not sure I understand.'

'Oh, I'm quite sure you do,' says the president, stopping and forcing Matthews to stop too. 'You have quite the family, Director Matthews. Travelling folk, were they not? They would have been called carnies in my day. Maybe they still are.'

Matthews smiles weakly. 'My family were evangelists, Mr President. They carried the Lord's word to the four corners of this great land.'

'They were common hucksters, sir, who were driven out of every state they practised in. You should know. You were the star attraction.'

Matthews swallows. 'I was blessed, Mr President.'

'Blessed? You are far too modest. Why, you were named the miracle child, were you not? Grieving widows would flock to you. Inconsolable fathers would seek you out. Mourning mothers would throw themselves at your sainted feet, because you could see and communicate with the dead. This gift, it seems, worked particularly well when the grieving party gave your parents money.'

'Gave the *church* money, sir,' says Matthews. I can sense the anger in his voice, as well as no little fear. 'We received not a penny. My parents were simple God-fearing folk and saw a way in which my gift could serve the Lord.'

'And fill their own coffers,' says Eisenhower. He waves expansively at the compound. 'Is that what this is to you, sir? A grift? A con?'

'No one believes in this programme more than me,' says Matthews, 'and with the greatest of respect, that was good enough for your predecessor.'

Eisenhower bristles. 'I am not my predecessor. President Truman was a great man, but he made several decisions that baffled me, none more so than financing this ghoul show. It's one thing to take our pick of the Nazis' best scientists and spirit them away, quite another to spirit away their ghosts. Ghosts only you can see, apparently.'

'You will be able to see them too,' says Matthews, 'and you won't need faith to do so. This is an operation of science, Mr President, not spiritual mumbo-jumbo. I intend to prove that to you today.'

Eisenhower stares at him coldly, like he's auditing his soul. 'How?'

I stand next to Matthews, both of us looking at a glass cube fifty feet away. Eisenhower and three of his servicemen sit inside it, visibly agitated. He's not used to being kept waiting, this president, and he's even less used to sitting inside a glass-walled cage with darkened windows. Whatever Matthews has planned, it had better be spectacular.

'I want you to go into that room,' Matthews says, as if reading my mind, 'and listen to everything they say. Then leave and report back to me.'

'That's it?' I say, confused.

'That's it,' he replies.

'But what's the point?'

'The point is if an unseen spirit can spy on the President of the United States of America, what's to stop him spying on the First Secretary of the Soviet Union?'

I ease through the darkened glass, utterly formless. Matthews trusts me enough to allow this now. I'm still solidified when I'm in my room, but we have built trust, the director and I. He needs me, and I need him. He knows I'll come back.

One of Eisenhower's suited protectors is waving a small steel device around the room. Seemingly satisfied, he pops it back into his jacket. 'Room's clean, Mr President.'

'You're sure?' says Eisenhower.

'I am, sir. There are no bugs in this room. You can speak safely.'

'What do you think?' The president turns to the man dressed like a general.

'About the director?'

He nods.

'I think his teeth cost more than my house.'

Eisenhower smiles. 'He's like a game-show host. I don't know what Truman was thinking, putting him in charge of the operation.'

'Doesn't seem a man of science.'

'He's not. That's Schmidt's department. Scientist we took

154

from Germany. Although from what I understand, he's more of an occultist.'

'Nazis went big on that shit, huh?' says the general. 'Depraved fucks.'

'Not just the Nazis. It's the reason we're sitting here today. The reason I haven't shut down this freak show already. It's the Russians, Ted. You've seen the latest?'

'The ESP shit? I wouldn't read too much into that, Mr President.'

'It's my job to read something into it. Your job too, as much as I'm loath to tell you how to do it. That Russian woman, Kulagina, she's got plenty of people spooked.'

'Some commie bitch moving objects with her brain? You could see the wires in that TV footage, Ike, or as good as.'

'I didn't see any wires. Plenty others didn't either. They saw a middle-aged woman moving things on a table with her damn mind. Every instinct in my body tells me to close this place down, then tear it apart brick by brick. But what if I'm wrong? The Russians are putting millions into this hocus-pocus. What if they know something we don't? How can I take that chance?'

'What are you hoping to see here, though?' says the general, looking at the modest room they're contained in. 'A spoon-bend?'

'I don't know,' Eisenhower says, 'but if I don't see it soon, I'll have Matthews' balls in a cup.'

I slip away, passing through the wall. It seems enough to be going on with.

Eisenhower isn't trying to hide his impatience any more.

Matthews has brought him from the holding room where I eavesdropped on him into the guts of the laboratory. Row after row of glass cubes face us. To Eisenhower and his general, they are empty. To Director Matthews and myself, they are not.

'What am I doing here, Matthews? This is another room with a surplus of *nothing*.'

Matthews turns on his million-dollar smile, then turns it off again. He seems to realise it won't work with this audience. 'What would you say, Mr President, if I told you that I know every last word you said in that holding room?'

'I would say you're a liar, sir, an accusation you must have heard before.'

Matthews nods. 'I understand your distrust of men like myself. I do. There are a lot of charlatans around, people like Nina Kulagina. You're right to be sceptical of her, Ted.'

The general's head snaps towards us.

Matthews turns to Eisenhower and smiles. 'I couldn't see the wires either, Mr President, but believe me, she wasn't moving anything with her damn mind. Telekinesis is a sham. A con.'

Eisenhower and the general exchange a look.

Matthews flashes his teeth. 'And don't worry, General, these didn't cost more than your house. Your car, perhaps, and certainly your suit. Not your house, though.'

Eisenhower glares at him. 'You had the room bugged.'

'One of your men swept the room for bugs, did he not?' Matthews replies.

'Lip-reading,' says the general. 'You lip-read us.'

'Through darkened glass?'

A high-pitched German accent bounces around the room. Eisenhower and the general turn. Schmidt is standing in the doorway. He obviously didn't get the message to dress up, and is as raggedy as ever. Hair trying to escape his head. Clothes trying to escape his body. A suitcase in his hand. Perhaps he's sensed how this is going. Perhaps he knows he may have to flee.

'You're the Kraut,' the general says, looking at him as if he were liquefied faeces.

'I flatter myself I'm rather more than that,' says Schmidt, smiling widely. His teeth are wizened and yellow, falling out with each other. 'I'm your best weapon against the Russians. Or rather, my team is.'

'Your team?' Eisenhower barks. 'Just what exactly are you people running here?'

Schmidt looks to Matthews, who nods his approval.

Schmidt places the suitcase on the gantry next to the president and his general, then flicks up the clasps.

'What would you say, gentlemen, if I told you we could provide you with a team who are invisible, undetectable and impossible to kill. Who will swear total and utter loyalty to these United States of America?'

'I would say such a promise is easy to make,' Eisenhower replies, 'and almost impossible to fulfil.'

Schmidt smugly flips the suitcase open. If he was expecting a gasp, he is disappointed.

Inside the case is a large metal object, the type of thing you would see at an optician's. Something to slip over your head to test your eyesight. A whirring comes from the apparatus. A battery sits inside the case, black and metallic.

'What the hell is this?' asks Eisenhower.

'The means with which you can truly see,' replies Schmidt. 'Another world awaits you when you put this headset on, Mr President.'

'There's not a chance in hell of you putting that on, sir,' says the general.

'I can assure you, it's quite safe,' says Matthews from the back of the room. 'You called me gifted earlier, President Eisenhower. By putting on that headset, you'll get an idea of what that gift actually entails.'

Eisenhower eyes it warily.

'I advise against this,' repeats the general.

'We've come a long way,' says Eisenhower. 'Let's see what this horse and pony show actually looks like.'

Schmidt smiles, lifting the headset out of the case. It is obviously heavy: he strains slightly as he heaves it out.

'You are the first civilian to see this machine in action,' he says, raising it with difficulty above the president's head.

'That's the goddam president of the United States you're addressing,' spits the general. 'He's no civilian.'

Eisenhower reaches up, taking the strain and lowering the apparatus towards his head. As I agreed with Matthews beforehand, I stand in the corner of the room, a few feet away from the general.

'What do you see, sir?' asks the general.

The machine grumbles slightly as Eisenhower turns his head towards the back of the room.

'I see Matthews. It's like there's a black-and-white television right in front of my eyes.'

Matthews waves good-naturedly.

Slowly the president pans around the room.

'I see the room. The picture's breaking up a bit as I turn.'

'We're working on that,' says Schmidt impatiently. 'Keep looking.'

The general growls, but Eisenhower raises a placatory hand.

'I see you, Ted, and—' He stops dead as he looks directly at me. 'My God.'

'Wave to the president, Jacob,' says Matthews.

I do as I'm told.

'What is this?' says Eisenhower.

'More like *who*,' says Schmidt. 'This is Jacob Block, who died over nine years ago.'

'Bullshit,' says the general.

Eisenhower, trembling ever so slightly, removes the helmet and passes it to the general. The president scans the room, but of course he can no longer see me without the apparatus.

The general jams it quickly onto his own head and turns to me instantly.

'Nothing but a carnie trick,' he says uncertainly. I lurch towards him, causing him to jerk back in his chair.

'No trick,' says Matthews. 'Just a loyal spirit ready to fight for this great country. And he's not alone.'

'What do you mean?' says Eisenhower. The zeal in his eyes is unmistakable, even to me.

'Take a look out of that window,' says Matthews.

Eisenhower does as he's told. He's greeted by the sight of dozens of clear glass cages, a refinement of my prison in Germany. 'They're empty,' he says.

'General, if you please?' says Schmidt.

The general hands Eisenhower the helmet, and this time there is no uncertain handover. The president quickly places it on his head. Schmidt takes the suitcase from the table and walks with him as he moves to the window.

Eisenhower lets out the slightest yelp.

'What do you see?' asks the general, his scepticism apparently ebbing away.

'There are dozens of them, Ted. All of them like the boy in this room. All of them in cages.'

'All of them for *you*, Mr President,' says Matthews, putting an arm around Eisenhower's shoulders. 'A spirit platoon, awaiting your orders.'

Eisenhower removes the helmet, then passes it back to the general, who puts it on and whistles through his teeth.

'What do you think, Ted?'

'I think, Mr President,' the general replies, 'that we just won the Cold War.'

Chapter 14

Lucia had always relied on the deference of strangers.

It had been that way ever since she'd been a child. It was difficult to say why, exactly. Her eyes were striking, she supposed; emerald green, shaped like a cat's. Anyone who looked into them would become submerged, realising too late that they were out of their depth, that they demanded servitude.

Perhaps it was because of the wonders those eyes could see. They were her window into a world concealed from the living. She could never really decide whether her ability to see the dead was a blessing, a curse or an unholy combination of the two.

It was an ability that was quickly becoming commonplace, thanks to Spook. A ridiculous name for a drug unsuited to the unwashed masses. Lucia had spent her entire life learning the discipline of seeing the unseen; you couldn't just throw a pill down your neck and expect there to be no consequences. It was why it was so important to locate the source of the drugs that had been stolen from her.

Locate them and cut off the supply, as well as the head of the person distributing them.

She walked over to the wall-sized window in her office, passing a hand over the glass, its frosted surface instantly becoming clear. A scene of endeavour greeted her: dozens of men and women hunched over control desks and computers, not so much in the pursuit of science as bringing that disobedient cur to heel. Behind them was a bridge that seemed only halfway built, stopping dead in mid-air, a road to nowhere.

Except, of course, it wasn't. It was a road to somewhere wonderful. A road travelled only by the dead.

The dead, and her.

The phone rang, and wasn't that right, because there was always something and someone demanding your attention.

She passed her hand across the window again. It frosted in response, shutting the inside world out. It would still be there when she got back. It always was.

'Answer.'

The phone stopped ringing, then connected. The sound of a city could be heard, all muffled voices and mangled music. 'Just checking in, boss. Thought you'd appreciate a progress report.'

Hans.

'Have you found the supplier yet? That's the only real progress I'm interested in.'

'We're getting closer,' Hans's tinny voice said. 'We have a lead.'

'We?'

Silence on the other end of the line.

'Lazarus has a lead. For what that's worth.'

'For your sake, it better be worth a great deal. I want the supplier caught by the end of the day.' She placed her hands on the table, leaning forward slightly. 'Can you talk freely?'

'Yes,' came the immediate reply.

'Do you still believe we can trust Lazarus? His memory hasn't become too addled?'

'When it comes to the investigation, he retains the facts well enough. His instincts are sharp. It's remembering names that he's shabby on. He'll catch this dealer, I'm sure of that.'

'We don't want him to become too sharp. You're confident he still remembers nothing of his past? That he believes the facts we've fed him?'

'I am,' said Hans. 'In terms of that, he's a space cadet. The question is, what happens to him when we crack the case? The whole partner act's wearing thin.'

'Then he will have outlived his usefulness,' said Lucia. 'When that time comes, you know what to do.'

'Yes,' said Hans, 'I do.'

She could almost hear him smile.

It seemed to Joe that a lot of his job involved sitting around in cars watching Hans talk on the phone outside while trying to remember shit.

He *could* remember shit, though – at least he was beginning to – and the electronica bleeding from the car's speakers was helping. He'd feared that when he left the club and its dementia-fighting beats, amnesia and confusion would consume him once again. They hadn't – although how long that would remain so, he couldn't say – and with the musical accompaniment in the car, he was able to keep a firm grasp on the memories he'd got back so far.

He took his notebook from the inside of his coat (giving the Dragnet insignia a regulation rub), withdrew a pen, then flipped the notebook open. He needed to record what he'd relearned so far. He didn't know how long it would hang around for.

He leafed past the previous entries, which had recorded Hans and Lucia's details, along with his current assignment to unmask the city's Spook dealer. Hans could check those at any time; anything Joe recorded at the back, he was less likely to.

Because Joe didn't trust Hans. Not all the way. He'd been

keeping details of his past from him, and out-and-out lying about other things. Maybe there was a good reason for that – maybe it was part of Joe's recovery, like Hans and Lucia had claimed. Maybe it wasn't. Until he knew either way, he needed to keep an open mind.

He looked through the window. Hans was distracted, talking animatedly on the phone. To Lucia, no doubt; his slightly defensive posture said so.

Joe needed to be quick.

Pen nib met paper, and he began to write.

I'm Joe Lazarus.

I'm a detective with the Dying Squad, a spectral police force that solves crimes the flesh-and-blood police can't.

It's headed up by Daisy-May. She's the

He searched for the word.

Warden. She was the Warden.

He noted it down. Recorded, too, how he'd come to meet Daisy-May, and how he'd been responsible for her death on the soil. Writing it down helped make the facts seem more real somehow. They looked true. They looked *right*.

Hans had told him about his hunt for the Generation Killer, and that felt and sounded right, too. Joe had journeyed to the soil with a partner.

Bits. His name was Bits.

There was just one problem: that was where the memories dried up. He didn't remember whether he had caught that killer, or what came after it. Hans and Lucia were his only constants, and if it had been down to them, he'd be none the wiser about Daisy-May and the rest of the Squad.

He pocketed the notebook. He'd keep this partial reclamation of his past to himself, for now. He didn't know why it felt like a good idea to play brain-addled for Hans; it just did. Besides, memories were fragile things; worry them too vigorously and they tended to crumble.

The case he was on was real. Spook was real. The dead girl back at the hospital, Ella, was real. Whatever the circumstances that had led him here – whatever part Hans and Lucia had played in those circumstances – that meant something, because the one thing he *did* know was that he was police, and he had the crimes of his past to atone for. He could do that just fine while he tried to work out Hans and Lucia's motivations.

There was a tap on the window.

Hans.

He gestured for Joe to get out the car.

Joe obeyed, for now.

Hotel Control was every lascivious rock-and-roll cliché wrapped as a present, tied in a bow, then presented back to the Berlin public. It was difficult to know where the knowing kitsch started and the accidental cheese ended, but the hipsters didn't seem to mind; they flocked to the place in their archly styled droves, gagging to stay in the themed rooms (Bowie, Iggy and Lou Reed featuring heavily) and enjoy the Achtung, Baby! Bar.

Joe was just glad to remember who those musical acts were. His regained memory felt eggshell-fragile, liable to fracture at any moment. The scuzzy band in the corner were helping a little; the Kraut-rock they were kicking out helped his memories hold a temporary truce with amnesia. Not as much as the electronic music did, though. That was more effective, for some reason. Maybe it was the repetitiveness of the beats, their uniformity.

And then, suddenly, another memory resurfaced: an abandoned club in Manchester and the dancing spirits within it.

Elias had discovered that music helped stranded spirits regain some sense of themselves, plucking out buried memories.

It is the music. As long as I can hear it, I should be able to retain the memories I have. Who knows, maybe I'll be able to drag out a few more. And this is fucking Berlin; here, they hit you with a techno shovel while you're taking a shit.

Joe had expected Hotel Control's bar to be dead if not outright closed due to the lateness of the hour, but once again, it appeared that he'd underestimated Berlin's lust for life. The place was rammed with partygoers just starting their night out, and others determined not to let it end.

'Does anyone in this town actually work?' he wondered, shaking his head at the packed throng.

'They're all artists,' Hans replied. 'Paintbrushes don't expect you to punch a clock.' He looked at Joe expectantly. 'Well? What hotel room are we heading to?'

'You're coming too?' said Joe.

'Yes, I think so,' said Hans, smiling ice. 'This is our final stop. I want to hear this Colonel's confession with my own ears. He may be the main Spook dealer in Berlin, but he's still getting that supply from somewhere.'

'Maybe not,' said Joe. 'Maybe it stops with him.'

'If that happens to be true, I'll buy you a drink,' said Hans. 'If it doesn't, you can buy me two.'

Colonel's penthouse suite commanded the top floor of the hotel. The premier room got the premier rock star, too; a lovingly hand-painted mural of the Thin White Duke spread its way around the bright pink doorway. Joe walked up to it, putting an ear against the door, listening for any sign of life. There was nothing, except the repetitive click of a record stylus caught in a vinyl groove.

'Go in, do a recce, then report back,' said Hans.

Joe nodded, his foot already halfway through the gaudy hotel room door.

Joe didn't need his years of experience to tell him something was wrong. A hotel porter would have clocked a similar vibe. It was something in the air, like death had tweaked its nose, then started laughing at the resulting nosebleed.

The penthouse was made up of several rooms. The one he was in, with its floor-to-ceiling windows looking out onto the shining lights of Berlin, displayed all the signs of a struggle, and not a confected rock-and-roll one. Chairs and sofas were upturned, a table along with them. Something had gone down here, and it had obviously gone down before the record had finished its journey round the turntable. *Station to Station* sat on the platter, the needle stuck in the groove.

Tsk.

Tsk.

Tsk.

No consequences for touching things any more, Joe thought, smiling.

He reached out, taking the stylus and returning it to the beginning of the record, sound flooding the room, the notes scraping away the film of scum on his brain.

He stood there for a moment, his eyes closed, soaking up the music.

It was music that was his crutch. It was music that would save him.

Feeling invigorated, he turned his back on the room and walked towards the door at the far side that stood half open.

Has to be the bedroom. And as I don't hear a peep from it, I'm guessing something's gone south here. The air's thick with it.

★

You never really got used to the sight of a body bleeding out.

And maybe that was a good thing, Joe thought, kneeling next to the bed. Easy to get arrogant when you were searching for answers and were sure you were going to get them. Humility in the face of mortality seemed important, because death was the one thing you could never really beat, even when you were dead. Especially when you were dead.

He would have assumed the body belonged to Colonel even if the bedroom wall hadn't been covered in press cuttings about the aged punk. Although ones from his later years were fewer in number, there were enough for Joe to ID him. His ego and vanity had clung to him until the end, it seemed. From Colonel's pallor – and the fact that blood was still weakly weeping from the wound around his neck – he'd been killed recently. If not minutes ago, then within the last half-hour. Which meant the killer could still be here in the hotel.

It looked frenzied, the kill. The cut on the neck was jagged. Messy. A crime of passion rather than precision.

There was something else, too. A slogan, written on the wall above the bed: *WE ARE THE PEOPLE! WE ARE THE POWER!*

That meant something. He'd seen it before.

He reached for his notebook, flicking through it.

There: that same slogan that had been written on the wall of the punk club.

Because it's one of the phrases associated with Colonel. Something from his East German punk days.

Was it his past that had got him killed? Or was it the drugs?

Joe felt the doubts and questions fade away. All there was was the case.

The case, and a dead body.

'Fuck's sake.'

Hans stared at Colonel without remorse or revulsion, just annoyance at the fact that he was dead.

'He was murdered recently,' said Joe, crouching down next to the body, pointing at the slash scoured into Colonel's neck. 'The bleeding's almost stopped, but not quite. Hasn't crusted, either, which means we're talking within the hour. Look at the raggedness of the cut, too. Whoever killed him, they did it in a rage. It was personal.'

'He's a drug dealer,' said Hans. 'They make enemies.'

'I don't think Colonel believed whoever killed him *was* an enemy,' said Joe. 'There was clearly a struggle in the other room, sure, but there's no sign of forced entry, and a hotel room's easy to protect yourself in. You look through the peephole, and you don't let the scary hitman through the door.'

'So it was someone he knew.'

'Not just knew, trusted. You don't murder someone this viciously in silence, though. Why did no one hear it?'

'How does knowing that help us?' asked Hans.

'It tells us who *not* to look for as much as it tells us who we should. Colonel may have been a Spook dealer, but I don't think he was killed for drugs.' He pointed at the phrase written on the wall. 'I think he was killed because of that.'

'Fucking East German rock star, this Colonel,' said Hans, shaking his head. '*We are the people! We are the power!* That was his catchphrase. Couldn't move without some German crusty chanting it. He tried to copyright it and everything.'

Joe took a step towards the writing. 'Klaus – the deadbeat dealer who sold Ella the drugs – he fingered Colonel as Berlin's only Spook supplier. How does this phrase tie in? Someone from the old days, maybe, pissed off at what Colonel's become?'

'Hear lots of questions but not many answers.'

'I have an idea on how to get some,' said Joe. 'This is an almost brand-new hotel: it must have CCTV cameras. Whoever came into this room and committed this murder will have been captured on at least one of them. I don't care how much of a pro he or she is – they must have left some visual presence behind.'

'Which helps us how?' said Hans. 'I can't bribe my way into getting the hotel to hand it over to us, and the police will confiscate it sooner rather than later.'

Joe smiled. 'Let's go for sooner, then. I'm here to get into the places you can't, remember?'

The security room wasn't difficult to find, because security rooms never were; they were always in the same place, shoved deep into the building's backside. Customers didn't want to spend the night in windowless rooms with the sound of over-worked boilers and clanking machinery, and as they were the ones who paid the bills, they got the upper rooms with floor-to-ceiling windows. Security were left with sub-basement rooms, all pale-yellow walls, flickering tungsten lighting and a stark lack of hope.

A radio played music, at least, which Joe was grateful for, some flavour of techno that pounded away tinnily. He reached over, turning it up a little.

There was a bank of monitors on the desk, all of them showing pin-sharp high-definition images of the hotel. He spotted the still-full bar, a couple of lift cams and an ever-changing view of each floor. His eyes scanned the screen, looking for the floor in question.

There: penthouse level. Easy, in the respect that there was just the one suite, and the camera gave a clear, uninterrupted view of the corridor. Whoever had murdered Colonel would be on this tape, there was no doubt about it.

No surprise the security guards had missed it, he thought, as he looked around the empty room. They were either having a fag break or on extended leave. Either was fine, because it let him work uninterrupted. There wasn't a ton they could do to stop him if they *were* here, but that didn't mean he wanted to court attention.

He reached into his pocket and withdrew a small plastic case. Then he placed a single headphone bud in his left ear. It wasn't music he was intending to listen, to, though.

He eased the plastic box open, and something began to stir.

Joe had to hand it to Lucia: she knew her shit.

Or at least the technicians under her command did. This little gadget, if it worked, was some real miracle stuff. A sliver of metal uncoiled itself from the plastic box and a memory suddenly popped into Joe's head. It was like one of those plastic fortune-telling fish you got in Christmas crackers, whose bending and wiggling was supposed to predict your future. As he watched the metal worm drop onto the control panel in front of him, though, then burrow its way under the chunky circular dial, it wasn't the future Joe wanted to predict, but the past.

The Ghost in the Machine was what Lucia had jokingly called it. It was a means of the dead interacting with the technology of the living: you let the metal worm do its work, infesting the piece of technology you wanted to use, then, via the earpiece, you issued it commands.

Think of it as a super-injunction against the Xylophone Man, she had said. *You're* not interacting with the real world, the device is. That means he can't touch you for it.

How many other pieces of her technology had been rendered obsolete by the old Infernal Serpent's death? he wondered.

He heard voices in the corridor outside. Far away, but getting closer.

It was time to get to work.

'Rewind one hundred and twenty minutes, penthouse level,' he said, and as if by magic, the image on the centre screen began unspooling. He smiled. Even after everything he'd seen, there was an element of witchcraft to the technology.

He peered at the empty corridor on the screen as the video ran backwards. Hans appeared almost immediately, but then it would have been strange if he hadn't; Joe had let him into the penthouse suite just fifteen minutes ago.

Best to erase that. It'd probably raise the eyebrows of the soil police.

The Ghost in the Machine obeyed Joe's command, scrubbing that particular piece of footage.

He ordered it to keep rewinding.

Back, back it went, Colonel visibly absent, which meant he'd been in the hotel room for a good chunk of time.

Wait.

'Pause.'

The screen obeyed, a shimmer going through its freeze-frame shell.

A figure dressed in black was on screen. Its head was bowed towards the camera, a hood covering it.

Still, there might be something here Joe could use, some form of identification the killer couldn't quite hide.

If nothing else, he felt he could rule out a woman as the murderer. The frame of this person was too big, the shoulders too squared away. He couldn't say with a hundred per cent certainty that it was a man, but he was willing to go to ninety-five.

'Play at quarter-speed,' he commanded.

The CCTV system obeyed, the figure in black juddering its way down the corridor in staccato slow motion.

Joe waited, looking for a sign of anything. The face was

completely concealed; that didn't change, and he wasn't expecting it to. He just needed some small telltale sign.

Which black in Berlin isn't. Christ, it's like a uniform here.

'Pause.'

The command rang out again, and this time there was a note of triumph in it. The figure had arrived at the penthouse door, and two things stood out.

One, whoever it was had a key card in their hand, which they were raising towards the card reader. That meant Colonel might not have known them after all.

Secondly, although the person hadn't lowered their hood, they'd raised their head. Joe couldn't see the man's face – and it was a man, he could tell that for sure now – but he could see a hint of a grey beard.

Something else, too.

'Magnify one hundred per cent.'

The software obeyed.

Joe took a step closer to the screen, squinting. When he'd first seen this and commanded the clip to pause, he'd assumed his eyes had been playing tricks on him.

Turned out they hadn't.

A thin sliver of red was wrapped around the man's neck, sitting starkly within the sea of black that constituted the rest of his outfit.

It was a dog collar.

What, exactly, was a priest doing visiting an ageing rock star?

And if this man was the killer, why had he committed such a foul act?

Chapter 15

Here we go, thought Daisy-May. The magical shit-stery tour continues.

There was a door of white, and then there was a sea of black. She couldn't say she was mad keen on either of them. As her eyes adjusted, she saw that at least it was a sea of black she knew.

The thin pencil sketch of endless wall in the distance.

The sky of red and black, its clouds endlessly churning.

The barren landscape, with its sandy pockets of ground fog.

'This is the Pen,' said Daisy-May.

She felt a presence alongside her, and turned to see Oma Jankie.

'What is this, an apocalypse bar crawl? Where's next, Hiroshima?'

The old woman nodded at the landscape in front of them. 'Have you missed it?'

Daisy-May turned back, surveying the landscape. 'Yeah, if you can believe that.' She waved at the barren nothingness in front of her. 'Most people when they see this, all they think is of the desolation. Me, I see a refuge for souls that had a brutal life and have the promise of a better afterlife. It's a shithole, but it's *our* shithole.'

She frowned. 'Where are the Dispossessed? Barely a corner of the Pen that doesn't have a few of them, but I can't see any. Which is weird by itself, but I can't *hear* any either, which is even weirder.'

Oma Jankie smiled meanly. 'It's time for you to see the legacy you've left for your precious Dispossessed.'

The scene in front of her shook like someone had taken a hammer to a snow globe. As it re-formed, Daisy-May let out a sob of shock.

'This isn't real,' she said, her voice watery, her eyes disbelieving. 'This is another one of your bullshit tricks.'

'It's not my anything, girl,' said Oma Jankie. 'I don't set the trials.'

'Who does, then?'

'Even I don't know that. I'm simply one of the custodians. What you see in front of you is very real, I assure you.'

What Daisy-May saw in front of her was this: a gargantuan factory made of blackened stone, four chimneys sprouting from it like malignant growths, belching grey smoke into the air. Its design was brutal, its edges harsh and uncompromising. There was a familiarity to the building. It bore many of the same design flourishes as the one she'd broken the children out from. Cruelty architecture realised.

That was fitting when you considered the wretched souls stretching out endlessly in front of it. Hundreds of the Dispossessed had been tied together, a desperate chain gang shuffling forward in pairs towards the factory, their feet and hands bound, their heads bowed.

And they weren't alone.

A squadron of winged creatures towered over them, gigantic tar-black devils driving cat-o'-nine-tail whips into the Dispossessed, their faces featureless save for the gaping red maws of their mouths and their jagged, carved-in-blood eyes.

They look like Uriel, the fucker whose wings I tore off, thought Daisy-May.

'What is this?' she demanded.

'This is the world you left behind when you fled,' Oma Jankie said. 'The vacuum has been filled. The fallen angels have returned to the Pen, and they've been busy.'

'Busy doing what?'

'Getting on with the business of genocide.'

The world blurred again, and Daisy-May's stomach lurched along with it. Once it settled, she saw they were inside the factory. There was none of the gleaming high-tech trickery of the one she'd sprung the children from. This place was a thing of smelt and iron. Geysers of steam leaked from vats of molten fire, and the sound of metal striking metal could be heard.

Then there were the screams.

There were hundreds of Dispossessed inside the factory. As before, they'd been grouped into pairs and chained together, shuffling slowly into the factory. The same captors from outside were present too, lashing the prisoners with their jagged whips. When you considered where they were being led to, Daisy-May could see why they needed such 'encouragement'.

There was a vat at the centre of the room. It reminded her of an old coal works on the outskirts of Nottingham; the size and scale of its bloated concrete chimneys had always made her feel like an ant on a piece of bread. This vat had the same impact. The Dispossessed trudged up an endless spiral staircase towards its lip; the peak was consumed with steam rising from its flaming guts.

Then the steam cleared a little, and Daisy-May saw two insect-sized members of the Dispossessed standing on the platform, illuminated by the fire beneath them. They hesitated for the slightest of seconds, then jumped. Their frail, twig-like bodies twisted in the air as they fell, the flames below reaching for them. A flicker as their bodies hit the molten lake, then nothing.

'What's the point of this?' said Daisy-May, defiance propping up her words. 'Are you showing me some fucked-up future in the hope that I'll break down and cry?'

Oma Jankie chuckled. 'This is no alternative future. This is what's happening right here, right now, in the Pen. Remus opened the gates, and these devils walked in.'

'Why? To do what?'

'Euthanise the Dispossessed,' said Oma Jankie. 'They believe there are too many of them, that they've grown too free under your wardenship. They intend to cull their numbers.'

'This isn't real,' said Daisy-May.

'I wish that were true.'

She flexed her fists. 'What am I supposed to do about it? What's the trial, exactly?'

'It is important for you to see what has become of the place you were put in charge of,' said Oma Jankie. 'A place that hasn't yet been totally consumed, a place that may yet be saved, if you complete the trials.'

'Doesn't sound like much of a trial, that,' said Daisy-May. 'Let's call it passed, and then liberate the Pen from those winged fucks.'

Oma Jankie smiled. 'If only it were that simple.'

Daisy-May threw up her hand protectively as the world burned white, the scrunch of her eyes doing nothing to dispel the retina burn, the vat of death still repeating on her eyelids.

The light began to fade a little, and she winced at the warmth she felt on her face. It was different from the singe-your-eyebrows heat of the death furnace; this was the temperature of a comforting late-summer day. The sounds of the place backed that up, too. A lawnmower worked somewhere in the distance.

Birds sang. Insects chirruped. The smell of freshly cut grass filled her nostrils.

This is familiar, thought Daisy-May.

She slowly opened her eyes.

She was in a large garden surrounded by a hedge. The garden was comfortably half an acre, and situated in the countryside. A field stretched out lazily behind it. This wasn't the concrete isles of Nottingham.

A farmhouse sat in front of her. It was almost a cliché, so picture-perfect was it. A thatched roof for a head. Four windows looking out like eyes. A door standing open like a surprised mouth. It was like something out of a fairy story.

And *they* can go both ways, thought Daisy-May. Especially for the innocent young girl. They usually get royally fucked over. Lucky for me that I'm far from innocent.

She looked around her, trying to spot Oma Jankie, but there was no sign of her elderly torturer.

She started walking, the sun on her back, a sense of peace descending upon her. It was difficult to imagine anywhere more different to the Pen than this. Clear blue skies, just a sprinkling of cloud dust in them. Air so fresh it nettled her lungs. Life teeming all around her. She'd always had a fondness for the Pen – missed it whenever she'd been on a Dying Squad mission to the soil – but it couldn't compare to this. This was the best things about childhood, about life, crystallised and made whole.

As she neared the open back door, the smell of baking tickled her nose. Cookies, if she wasn't very much mistaken. When was the last time she'd eaten cookies? Grandma June had always baked them for her on the first day of the holidays. A welcome gift after the train journey from Nottingham. 'Though they're for me as much as you,' June would always say. 'Not the sort of tripe you get in the supermarket, with all that artificial sugar. Nothing but the real deal when I make them.'

Because that's where Oma Jankie has brought me, the old cow. This is Grandma's house, or a movie-of-the-week version of it. This is the only place I was ever really happy.

She walked through the door and gasped.

Part of her had expected to see her grandma – knew that was who she was being led by the nose to – but that didn't draw the sting from the shock of it. She watched for a minute as June went about her business, opening the oven door and taking out a tray of freshly baked cookies. (*Biscuits, not cookies,* that was what Grandma would always say. *We're not in bleeding America.*)

'Don't just stand there,' she said now, looking up at Daisy-May. 'Clear a space on the table, unless you want these to end up on the floor.'

'You can see me?' said Daisy-May.

'Course I can. Be a damn sight happier if I could see you clearing that table.'

Daisy-May felt like she was moving through treacle as she did as she was told, shifting a pile of magazines from the centre of the table onto one of the wicker chairs beneath it. She stared at her grandmother as she placed the laden tray carefully into the empty space.

June's eyes were clear, gleaming with recognition.

'You know who I am, don't you?' said Daisy-May.

June looked at her, a rumour of a smile on her face. 'Yep. You're the daft apeth of a granddaughter that always asks nutty questions.'

There's no Alzheimer's there. This woman isn't going to have hundreds of Post-it notes everywhere so she can remember who or what things are. She's as sharp as a fucking tack.

'Don't just stand there gawking, girl,' said June. 'Get your arse in gear and fetch his lordship. He's putting some shelves up in my bedroom. Got his uses, that boy. They don't always when they're that pretty.'

'His lordship?' said Daisy-May.

'You've had too much sun,' said June. 'Or not enough. Either way, you look halfway simple.' She clapped her hands together. 'Chop chop, or these things will be stone cold.'

Daisy-May left the kitchen, walking to the stairs (and the sound of intermittent banging) in a semi-daze, the house the same as she remembered it, but different, too, like it had been given a deep-clean makeover.

Because this is the perfect version of this place, and that doesn't mean it's spotless or modern, it just means it's the best it ever was, in my memory.

It means it's heaven.

Daisy-May was forced to reassess that opinion when she reached her grandmother's bedroom.

A young man stood inside, a hammer in his hand, a frown of concentration on his face. A baseball cap had been slung backwards on his head, and he had one eye closed as he tried to line up a nail with the shelf.

'Ryan?'

The word was out of her mouth before she could stop it.

He turned to her and smiled, and Daisy-May cursed the fucking weakness in her, because her heart responded in kind. The man in front of her was scum. He'd got her hooked on heroin, then turned her into a drugs mule, an action that had led to her murder. He was worthless. Morally bankrupt.

And none of that makes a lick of difference when he looks at me like that, because Ryan's a splinter in my thumb. I forget about him, spend months without thinking about him, and then my thumb will give a twinge and I'll remember how I used to feel about him. The way he made life seem exciting and safe all at the same time. The feeling of pride that came with being next to him. The way he made me feel like I was the centre of the fucking universe.

People say love's blind, but that's not right. Love haunts you, 'cos you're never quite free of it. You can move on, love again, but that first great love of your life – shit, even those that weren't great loves but got stuck between your teeth somehow – it lingers on the edges, waiting till you're asleep to fuck with you in your dreams. Sometimes that's not even a bad thing, because it reminds you you're alive.

Ryan winked at her. 'Just about done here, DM. Not going to claim it's totally straight, but it's totally *up*. Might even stay that way with a spit and polish and a lot of prayers.'

'What are you doing here?' said Daisy-May.

'Other than putting shelves up,' Ryan replied, 'and staring at your sexy mug?'

When it's like this, the age difference doesn't seem to matter. Is that wrong?

'You two better not be fooling around up there.' June's voice boomed from below. 'Not when these biscuits are going cold.'

'Biscuits?' said Ryan, with a look of mischief on his face. 'Shit, why didn't you say? They're about the only thing I'd pass up the chance to mess around with you for, and spoiler alert, I wouldn't really.'

He put the hammer down and stuck out a hand. 'You coming?'

As Daisy-May allowed herself to be led down the stairs, she tried to work out what exactly she was supposed to be doing here.

The first trial had been straightforward enough, in that it was a recognisable challenge, one of intellect and speed of thought. This, though: what was she supposed to do? Drown in good vibes? This was everything she'd ever wanted out of life. Her grandmother's house. The old lady who came with it. Ryan, but as she'd imagined him rather than the poisonous toerag he'd actually been. What was Oma Jankie's play here? What was expected of her?

'Nothing's expected of you,' said Oma Jankie.

Daisy-May whipped around to see the old woman sitting at the head of the table, helping herself to a cookie.

'For the first time in your life, that's actually true. You've won, Daisy-May.'

Daisy-May sat down opposite her, Ryan and her grandmother joshing to the right of her, seemingly oblivious. 'Won what?'

'This,' said Oma Jankie, waving expansively at the room. 'Everything you've ever wanted. Everything you've ever deserved.'

'I don't get it.'

'And I heard you were bright.'

'I've got a real blind spot when it comes to fake paradise,' said Daisy-May. 'It's my Achilles heel.'

Oma Jankie leaned forward. 'There's nothing fake about this place, or this scene. It's as real as the Pen I just showed you.'

'So, what, you're showing it just to torture me?'

'I'm showing what could be yours.'

'Still not getting it.'

Oma Jankie placed her hands together on the table. 'Paradise could be yours if you choose it.' She looked around the kitchen, a sneer on her face. 'This, apparently, would be paradise to you. This is the Next Place.'

Daisy-May frowned. 'I thought the Next Place wasn't for the likes of me.'

'If it was up to me, it wouldn't be,' said Oma Jankie. 'I don't set the trials; a greater force than either of us does. To be presented with this choice, that greater force must feel you've earned your ticket to paradise. Who am I to disagree?'

'So I could just stay here?' said Daisy-May. 'Would I always be in this place?'

'Paradise is what you make of it,' said Oma Jankie. 'It would be whatever you desired.'

'What about the Pen? What about me being Warden?'

'That wouldn't be your concern any more, obviously. Why should it be? You've served your time, done far more than most that enter the Next Place. It's time to stand down, Daisy-May. It's time to rest.'

'What would happen to the Dispossessed, though? What would happen to those winged monsters?'

'Why do you care? You'd have your own slice of ready-baked heaven. You wouldn't have to struggle any more. There'd be no more pain. Do you know what I'd give for that chance? What every single member of the Dispossessed would give? It's a once-in-an-afterlife opportunity.'

Daisy-May looked over at her grandma, who was playfully chiding Ryan over something. 'So I've just got to say, and I get to stay here for ever?'

'You got there in the end,' said Oma Jankie.

Her grandma turned to her. 'Not like you to miss a snack, love. Grab one before this great lunk finishes them all.'

Ryan winked at her. 'She's not lying. These cookies' – he looked sheepishly at June – 'sorry, *biscuits*, are too good. Strike soon, or I'll demolish the lot of them.'

Daisy-May reached out and picked one up. It was tempting, all right, and fuck, the *smell*; it was overpowering. This could be her life. No more pain, or nuclear-winter sky. No more suffocating responsibility of a job she hadn't asked for, one that a procession of people would slit her throat for. Oma Jankie was right – she didn't owe anyone anything any more. She'd served her time. She deserved this. Let someone else take the pain.

Everything she ever wanted was right here.

She brought the cookie close to her mouth, inhaling deeply. Damn, it smelled good. Hard to see how one mouthful could hurt.

From out of the corner of her eye, she saw that Oma Jankie was leaning forward expectantly.

Except that's probably what Eve thought before chowing down on the apple. She copped a lot of shit for that, and women have been copping it ever since.

Daisy-May placed the cookie back on the table and noted Ryan's frown.

She turned to Oma Jankie. 'What if I say no?'

'Why would you say no? You're being offered paradise, girl.'

'What you're offering me is too good to be true, and I won't insult your intelligence on how that one usually goes. Paradise isn't something you can hand out.'

'There's nothing for you back in the Pen,' said Oma Jankie. 'There's everything for you here.'

Daisy-May rose from her seat. Her grandmother and Ryan were watching her intently, and it could just have been her imagination, but their eyes looked different, or at least the expression in them did. They didn't look happy and loving any more.

They looked like addicts.

She stared at Oma Jankie with cool, clear eyes. 'I choose the Pen.'

The old woman's face twitched. 'Nonsense.'

'It's my decision. Least, you said it was. I choose the Pen.'

'What on earth for?' Oma Jankie said, her teeth grinding.

'Because it's my responsibility. The place might stink like a derelict swimming pool, it might be mad and chaotic and the people in it might be crazed maniacs, but they're *my* maniacs, and it's my responsibility. Place is under threat, with Remus and those devils he's let in. That's my problem, no one else's.'

'Final chance,' said Oma Jankie.

'Come on love.'

Daisy-May turned to see June smiling and holding out a hand.

'You're home. All you've got to do is believe it.'

'Your grandma's right, DM,' said Ryan. 'We're here. We're your family.'

Daisy-May smiled. 'You're nothing, mate. You're an old hag's conjuring trick. The real Ryan was a closet paedo and an out-and-out arsehole.'

She turned back to Oma Jankie. 'The Pen. For life.'

Oma Jankie nodded. 'Very well.'

With those words, it was like the room began to scream, the kitchen's acid reflux dissolving the walls and everything within them. Daisy-May looked over towards Ryan and June, recoiling in horror; the flesh had been flayed from them to reveal their pale-yellow humanoid forms. They had no eyes, and their mouths, such as they were, were bloodied, becoming more so when they opened them to scream.

Fucking hell, thought Daisy-May, looking at the thing that used to be Ryan. I almost got off with that.

'If you want the Pen, you shall have it,' said Oma Jankie. 'That is, if you pass the final test.'

'No sweat,' said Daisy-May, as a whistling filled her ears. 'There's nothing you can throw at me that I can't take.'

Oma Jankie chuckled. 'We'll see.'

Chapter 16

You didn't have to be dead to live in Tokyo's prime ministerial residence, but it helped.

Few buildings were reputed to be more haunted than the Kantei, which had been built amidst the rubble of the great earthquake of 1928. Assassins had stormed the premises in 1932, executing prime minister Tsuyoshi Inukai, then tried to finish the job by whacking his successor in 1936. This time the prime minister survived but five other people didn't; their spirits were said to haunt the place, their presence so rambunctious, an exorcism was held in 2005. Apparently, it didn't take; no prime minister had occupied the residence for decades.

They were, in the opinion of Hanna Jankie, quitters.

She'd been taken by the place the moment she'd stepped through the front door. There were spirits aplenty there – the old legends were true enough on that score – but it was the architecture she'd been most enraptured by. There was a grandeur and gravitas to the place that you just didn't get with modern buildings.

It helped, she supposed, if you didn't blow those modern buildings up. Nuclear devastation never showed a place in the best light.

It had been worth it, though. The nuclear facility meltdown

she'd brought about had devastated Tokyo, pumping poisonous radiation into the air and making it a no-go area for the living. The dead, on the other hand, were not only welcome but encouraged to migrate here. The nuclear winter she'd created allowed them to live and breathe on the soil, to retain a sense of themselves. Scores of the dead streamed in every day, Hanna's impassioned video message bouncing across the globe, a sticky bomb that gathered thousands of new recruits every time it was played.

A city of the dead, founded on the soil. It was everything she'd ever dreamed of.

Why then did she feel so dissatisfied?

It wasn't the prime minister's residence itself. The dust sheets had been thrown aside, and a degree of regal comfort had settled over the place. She was the queen of all she surveyed, a duchess in everything but name. One who had discovered the neatest of tricks. The deluge of radiation had changed her, somehow, allowing her to channel electrical current. All she had to do was touch a lamp – any electrical source – and it would flare into life.

It was a trick the Duchess would have found amusing. Her sister's meddling may have been infuriating, but Hanna hadn't wanted the Duchess killed. She'd still fostered hopes of Rachel and herself ruling New Tokyo together. That she'd essentially been atomised when the reactor exploded meant a fanciful dream had become an impossible one.

Hanna herself bore the scars of the Duchess's death. Half her face had been destroyed in the showdown at the power plant. She picked at the leather mask that straddled that blank side of her face. It made her look terrifying, like a possessed porcelain doll.

So be it. Terror wasn't a bad thing for a leader to foster.

It wasn't her face that troubled her, though, not really. It was

186

the thousands of souls that had been drawn to New Tokyo.

To begin with, the utopia she'd planned had come to pass. The spirits that flocked there were renewed by the radiation in the air, their consciousness and memories supercharged. They were suitably subservient to her, the language of the dead – and its sing-song dah-dah-*duh* refrain – picked up and passed around like a religious chant. It was a community of spirits, all in her service and image, everything she'd ever hoped for.

The living stayed away. Partly because of the radiation, partly because of the fear of the unknown. It was a truce, of sorts.

Then things began to change.

Like in the Pen, morning, afternoon and evening didn't really exist in the nuclear winter of New Tokyo. Morning was the most distinct, though, especially when the sun decided to out-muscle the clogged arteries of the clouds. Its beams lit them, giving them a radiance their poison didn't deserve. The sky behind them was never visible, but the glowing clouds at least reminded Hanna it was still there.

She exited through one of the palace's rear entrances, taking in a scene of ragtag beauty. Spirits lounged around, purposeless and comfortable with it. Before the explosion, this had been an ornate garden hundreds of years old; now, the leaves and grass had long since died, leaving nothing but naked gnarled branches and barren spaces where a lawn used to be.

It looked haunted, and not in a good way.

She walked down the long, winding pebbled path, trying to draw the attention of the spirits wandering aimlessly on either side of it. Their glazed eyes avoided hers.

'You,' said Hanna, pointing at a teenage boy in front of her. 'Have you seen Gertie?'

The boy ignored her, his gaze cast to the floor, his shambling gait taking him away from her.

'I'm talking to you,' said Hanna.

That fact didn't seem to concern the boy.

They're not listening to me any more. They used to hang on my every word. Now it's a triumph if I can elicit so much as a sideways glance.

She'd first noticed it a month ago. A sort of vagueness had begun to creep into the spirits' general demeanour, their eyes becoming glassy, their attention spans short and shifty. Hanna had kidded herself that it was her imagination; then, such was their detachment, she was forced to face facts: the spirits in new Tokyo had changed, and not for the better.

She called out to the boy again, this time employing the language of the dead. This, finally, hit the mark; he stopped in his tracks, turning back to her.

It wasn't like before, though. Then, he'd have been virtually slavering at the prospect of doing her bidding. Now, he was sulking like a truculent teenager.

How long before the language of the dead stopped working altogether?

'Have you seen Gertie?' she asked again.

The boy apparently had. He pointed into the distance.

Growing up, the Jankie girls had wanted for everything.

It was difficult to miss what you'd never had, but what Hanna had desired over everything else – what she'd begged for – was a trip to the Bronx zoo. It was elephants that obsessed her the most; it seemed impossible to believe that such a creature could exist in the real world. When she'd been alive, she'd never confirmed that it actually did.

So when she'd returned to the soil in death, she'd set about righting that childhood wrong. Tokyo zoo had escaped the reactor blast unscathed, and with no one to care for the animals, Hanna and her followers had set about liberating them. It was the elephant she was really after, though; Gertie had been the zoo's jewel in the crown, and Hanna had been delighted to learn she was still alive. She'd brought the elegant creature back to the prime minister's lodgings, where it eyed the spirits shepherding it warily. It wasn't so much a pet as a symbol of her new reign.

Unfortunately, that symbol now lay at her feet, dying.

She crouched next to the elephant, placing a hand on its side as its thick, leathery hide slowly rose and fell, a mighty warrior brought low, sprawled helpless in the street.

It's the radiation. It's been silently killing her. She's bigger than the rest of the animals we saved, so it took the longest, but it's done the job now.

Hanna looked up. Swathes of her followers were silently watching her. For the first time, she felt uneasy.

'Go about your day,' she called out, in the language of the dead.

They stayed where they were for a moment, staring at her insolently, then began to slowly disperse.

You're losing them.

Hanna closed her eyes. *Not now, Oma Jankie.*

I come in peace. Better yet, with a proposition.

I'm not interested in your propositions, said Hanna. *The only person they serve is you.*

You tried to create a new world, and I applaud you for it. It's over, though. The dead there have stopped listening to you.

As ever, telling me what I already know. It's the language of the dead. It's stopped working.

The language of the dead works fine. It's the spirits that have flocked to New Tokyo that don't. The radiation has fried their brains.

How can you possibly know that?

Tell me I'm wrong.

Hanna didn't reply.

189

You have to leave, before you lose control of them altogether.

And go where? asked Hanna.

Oma Jankie laughed. *Back to the Pen, of course.*

I don't know whether you've been keeping up with events, but I'm not exactly welcome there.

Let me worry about that.

What good are you, stuck in Oblivion? said Hanna. *You're wasting my time.*

If things go to plan, I won't be in Oblivion for much longer. I'll be back in the Pen, and I'll have the Warden with me. A Warden who's very dead, and so as vulnerable to the language of the dead as any other.

Hanna cursed the small smile that formed on her face.

Get back to the Pen, however you can, said Oma Jankie. *I'll take care of the rest. Then it will be time for you to take your rightful place as Warden.*

The elephant breathed for a final time, then trembled to stillness. She was gone.

It was time for Hanna to be gone, too. To seek out new pastures.

And she knew just the person to help her find them.

Hanna had been to Akihabara before. Been to the shop she was now headed towards, too.

It belonged to a gentleman known as Arata, and she'd slipped in, unseen, to steal a priceless piece of his technology, a device called the Dog Catcher. This was essentially a catcher's mitt, an impenetrable line of defence that had prevented the Japanese authorities from shutting down the nuclear reactor when she'd brought it back on line. Arata was a man who liked his secrets, and liked to guard them even more; his workshop had been heavily fortified and several levels below the surface.

It should have survived. And if it had, it should have a working network connection.

190

Akihabara looked deserted, though. The last time she'd been here, the area had been a hive of robot dogs, garishly made-up teens and shrieking, wouldn't-be-silenced technology. Now, it was anything but. The buildings had been melted and mangled into a guard of honour, half collapsed and leaning on each other, creating a canopy of steel and glass.

Arata's store, at least, was right where she'd left it, and virtually untouched. Squat, resembling little more than a concrete bunker. There were no windows, no sign; all there was, in fact, was a small illuminated keypad on the concrete front door.

That's for the tourists, thought Hanna. I prefer the servants' entrance.

Hanna squinted, her eyes adjusting to the darkness. There wasn't so much as a slap-and-tickle of emergency lighting to help her out. The place looked like it had been abandoned long ago.

Finally she began to pick out details. There were rows of metal racks full of spools of electronics and hundreds of cans of food.

She didn't find that particularly surprising. Arata had seemed beyond paranoid; he'd probably been preparing for an apocalyptic event since the age of five. He'd probably prayed for one.

Beyond the racks was the faint outline of the staircase. If her memory served, that should lead to the underground workshop. She descended the stairs, aware of an ever-increasing glow emanating from beneath. Something was down here, even if it was just a long-since-abandoned computer.

She squinted into the gloom. She could just about make out a figure sitting upright, lit partially by the monitor in front of it.

'Who's there?' said a distorted robotic voice.

The figure rose from its seat, stepping into the blue-screen light.

Arata.

At least Hanna assumed it was. There wasn't much of his face visible; that was consumed by a clunky-looking set of night goggles and a mouthpiece respirator.

'It's you,' Arata said. 'Hanna.' His voice was metallic, robot-ic. An effect of the respirator, Hanna assumed. His body was puny. Daylight-deprived. Three radiation suits hung from the wall opposite.

Hanna tilted her head towards him.

'You can see me.'

Arata nodded. 'After the reactor melted down, it was my first order of business. Seemed sensible to be able to see the enemy, so that I could hide from the enemy. The goggles help with that.'

Hanna folded her arms. 'Why haven't you moved on? Why did you stay here?'

Arata took a couple of steps backwards, his wary gaze not leaving her face. 'Because this is my home. Why should I be driven out of it? All my equipment is here, my research. My workshop is designed to withstand an earthquake, so a reactor meltdown was small bones. I'm protected from the radiation as long as I'm down here, and have a suit for when I have to venture outside. I do that far less now. The spirits have become unpredictable.'

'So I've discovered,' said Hanna.

'Not what you had in mind?' said Arata. 'Considering this was all your doing?'

'Don't be so modest,' said Hanna. 'You helped.'

She could feel his glare, despite not being able to see it through the respirator.

'The prototype you stole from me,' said Arata.

'Quite. I couldn't have done it without you. You're talented, clearly.'

He stuck his shoulders out. 'I'm much more than that.'

Hanna pointed at the respirator and goggles. 'You've developed technology to be able to communicate with the dead.'

Arata nodded. 'Not so difficult when you know what to look for.'

'What do you mean?'

He didn't reply.

'I need your help,' said Hanna.

The inventor bristled. 'Why should I help you, after you stole from me? After what you did to the city?'

'Because you're right about the spirits here,' she replied. 'They're close to being uncontrollable. Do you really think you can hide from them down here? They'll find you, and when they do, they'll kill you.'

Arata said nothing. Hanna noticed he didn't correct her.

Finally he asked: 'What do you need?'

Arata watched her from the corner of the room, arms folded, the red lighting illuminating him. 'You want to send an email.'

'Yes,' said Hanna.

'An email. You've brought a city to its knees – remade it in your own image – and you need help sending an email.'

She scowled at him. 'Computers weren't invented when I was alive. There was a dearth of them in hell, too.'

'You've been to hell?'

'Is that really so surprising?'

'No, not really,' said Arata. 'I could believe you invented it.'

Hanna smirked at him.

'Who's this email to?'

She told him.

'You're joking, right?'

'We're not really a joking family.'

'No,' said Arata. 'I can believe that, too.'

She felt him considering her. 'This Lucia, who you want to send a message to. She's the CEO of a company called Wraith. Have you heard of it?'

Hanna shook her head. 'Should I have?'

He jumped to his feet and began pacing the room excitedly. 'No. *Nobody's* heard of them.'

'Except you.'

He began rubbing his hands together, clearly grateful for an audience. 'Do you think it's new? This ability to produce technology that allows the living to see the dead?'

'There was nothing like it when I last walked the soil,' said Hanna. 'Admittedly, that was the best part of two hundred years ago.'

'The research goes back *decades*,' said Arata.' The Nazis made huge progress in the field. If you believe the rumours, communing with the dead was pretty much government policy.'

'I'm aware of the Nazis,' said Hanna. 'They have something of a loyalty card in hell.'

'I bet,' said Arata. 'It's my belief that Wraith – headed by your Lucia – have stood on the shoulders of those Nazis, used their technology to develop their own.'

'Where does this belief come from exactly?' said Hanna.

'I have my sources.'

'That sounds vague.'

'Trust me. You can find out anything on the dark web. After the Second World War, the Americans spirited away the Nazis' best paranormal scientists. The Russians had their own thing going. Then everything went quiet. You'd get the odd rumour of experiments on kids in Russia, ones that let them see the dead, but when aren't there those sorts of rumours? They're, like, standard.'

'You and I have very different definitions of standard,' said Hanna.

'Then, a few years ago, this new, ultra-secretive tech company appears on the scene,' continued Arata. 'They call themselves Wraith. No one really knows they exist, let alone what they're about. I do, though; some of their research into communication tech overlaps with my own, and I'm intrigued, because anyone who tries that hard to be under the radar usually has something pretty juicy to hide.'

'Presumably they did,' said Hanna.

Arata nodded. 'There's a guy who works for Wraith – or claims to – who posts on one of the sites I frequent. He comes out with some next-level shit. Says their main field is paranormal research, and they have a battery of tech that allows communication with the dead. Pills you can take. That's what got me excited, because that's a genuine product out in the world. The real revelation from this informant, though, is that Wraith have developed a way for the living to travel to the afterlife.'

'That's what Lucia told me,' said Hanna.

'Did you believe her?'

'I believed that she believed it, and she could see me, which gave her some credibility. She was running some sort of smuggling operation from the Pen to the soil, ferrying souls we call the Dispossessed to the Yakuza. Used the dead for all sorts of debauched shit. Building a bridge from the soil to the Pen, though? That flies in the face of everything I know.'

'Says the ghost on the soil.'

'There are ways of travelling between the lands of the living and the dead, I don't deny it,' said Hanna, 'and Lucia is clearly aware of them. It isn't something technology can facilitate.'

'Well, my contact at Wraith begged to differ,' said Arata, 'but I get your scepticism. I shared it, until he sent me the schematics for these' – he tapped the goggles he was wearing – 'and I realised they did everything they claimed he did. If he was telling the truth about the goggles, why wouldn't he be about everything else?'

Hanna considered it. She hadn't expected her belief in Lucia (desperate, no-other-option belief, admittedly) to be vindicated in this way, but was heartened nonetheless.

'I want you to send a message to her,' she said.

Arata took a seat behind a long metal desk, pulling an illuminated laptop closer to him.

'What do you want it to say?'

'Tell her I want a way out of this place,' said Hanna. 'Tell her I'm ready to talk.'

Part 4

'You are crazy, my child. You
must go to Berlin.'

Franz von Suppé, Austrian composer, 1800

Chapter 17

One kilometre south of Checkpoint Charlie, Berlin, 5 November 1979

The night's so cold, even I can feel it.

Frost clings to windows possessively. Ice hunkers down on anything concrete.

Everything's concrete.

The fog has a spiteful venom to it. It's a night for ghosts.

It's a night for us.

I am in a team of five. Five spirits of different ages and temperaments. I don't know how these men and women died, or how they were selected by Director Matthews. They all have a marking on their hands, though. A series of lines. It reminds me of the markings they put on us Jews when forcing us into concentration camps. My mother and father would have been branded like that. Hennie, too. It seems a lifetime since I last saw them.

We are not encouraged to talk to each other, the team. When the others look at me, all they see is a child. When I look at them, all I see is a void. They know nothing of my experiences, and I know nothing of theirs. I'm never paired with the same spirit twice. I believe it's because the spirits don't last. They wither, like flowers dying without water. Browned in the sun.

I don't, for some reason. Perhaps it's because of the Warden's role I'm supposed to fulfil. Perhaps it isn't. Regardless, I look the same, despite my half-century on the soil. And I remember everything.

These sorts of missions – the sort we are about to embark on tonight – have run for years. Reconnaissance. Spying. Information gathered behind enemy lines. I have no idea how useful the intel we provide is. I hear rumours of when things go wrong, though. I sometimes think this is deliberate. They want us to know that we're expendable.

There's a beast that stalks any spirit who physically interferes with the living world. They found that out, Director Matthews and Schmidt, on one of the early missions. It devoured two of my compatriots when they attempted to remove some documents from a KGB officer's house. They are happy for us to know its name, and the consequences it brings. If the Xylophone Man appears, they fail.

How the Nazis would have loved that beast. It would have been a bedtime story for Himmler. An anecdotal delight for Hitler. Their occult fantasies made real.

Night runs its fingers through its hair, dislodging a flurry of snow. Instinctively we huddle together against cold we can't feel. No one says anything. We're outside a bar, the sort that West Germany keeps to itself, unwilling to share with the East. A golden haze seeps from its long rectangular window, the glass misted, the bodies inside it reduced to silhouettes.

'Good night for it.'

Director Matthews emerges from the alley by the bar. He wears a thick military-style coat. The cut is Soviet. Expensive-looking leather gloves. Hair cut aggressively short. Every inch a good son of the Fatherland, one who looks nothing like the man I knew in California. He has mastered the art of disguise, Matthews, his spycraft enabling him to slip on different personas with ease. I wonder what he thinks of this field agent role. I rather suspect it isn't what he envisaged. We may be the ones to go behind enemy lines, but there's still danger for him, no matter how chameleon-like his appearance. With every successful mission, more attention is drawn towards him. Normally, I imagine he would enjoy this. The spy game isn't normal, though. You need to be a filing clerk, not a game-show host. Attention kills.

He looks over our shoulders and beckons us into the alleyway. His breath lingers in front of him. I wonder if my colleagues are as jealous of this as I am. To live. To breathe.

There's something different about Matthews tonight that goes beyond his appearance. He looks conflicted, like he's wrestling with something. Whatever it is, it seems to be winning.

'Tonight you will conduct a spying mission,' he says, clapping his hands together and smiling at me. 'Erich Honecker is to meet with the East German high command. You will observe, and report back to me.'

I look around at the team. 'All of us are required for the task?'

'This is too important an assignment to be trusted to you alone, Jacob,' says Matthews. 'Strength in numbers.'

I frown. This is irregular. For the team to number this many makes no sense.

'You have your orders,' he adds.

His mouth twitches, like there's something else to say.

'Good luck,' is what finally comes out.

I wondered what I'd feel, being back in Berlin after all this time. The answer is, not very much at all.

Much has changed. The Nazi wounds have mostly healed, at least in the West. The buildings shattered by the Allies' tanks and bombs have been rebuilt. The air of prosperity has returned to the place.

The main change is the Wall. The Nazis may have become extinct, but their legacy remains. You can see it whenever you look at the gash that's been cut down the centre of the city's gut. Barbed wire sews up the wound, while lashings of concrete try to salve it. It's a hack job done by a vindictive surgeon. This was my city once, and they've disfigured it. It makes me angry, and I was beginning to think that was something I was no longer capable of. I suppose I should be grateful.

I look at the team with me. They say nothing. Two men and two women. A jumble sale of clothes and eras squats on their bodies. I have no idea where Matthews sourced them from, or when they died, but they're spirits like me, ghosts from undefined eras. They're something less, too. There's less life to them. I retain my faculties. My soul, for want of a less religious interpretation. These automatons, I suggest, do not. There's a deadness behind their eyes.

Dead ghosts. Who would have thought it?

I know what I know. They're not like me. It's like they're sacrificial cattle, interacting with the physical world, which they know will result in their demise. Perhaps they crave that demise. I'm not above being released. I know what awaits me on the other side. My destiny. My birthright. But the Xylophone Man wouldn't grant me that release if I fought back against the living. He'd take me somewhere different. Somewhere worse. So I endure. I do what Matthews asks of me, and I know that release will find me in the end. Then I will be ready for the Pen. Ready to finally take my rightful place as Warden.

The woman at the front of our group stops, holding her hand up. Her clothes are from a similar time to my own. I wonder how she died. There are so many ways death can take a person. It's endlessly inventive. It's like its power bores it, forcing it to come up with new ways to kill.

'Why have we stopped?' I ask.

The woman doesn't reply. Instead, she sweeps her head left and right, looking for something. I see nothing.

Or rather, I see what I'm expected to see: a twelve-foot-tall concrete wall. Barbed wire drizzled across it. Sentry towers butting against the clogged fog that stubbornly lingers. Machine-gun muzzles in those towers. The odd glow of a cigarette. Houses on the eastern side blindly try to look out to their western kin, an act rendered impossible; their windows have been boarded up with concrete, the whole thing a tumour festooned to the city's soul. The Nazis never lost, not really, because this is their legacy. Their poison is trapped behind this wall. Fortifies them, even if it's a different ideology. A city divided. A country split in two. It's the eastern part of that city and country that we go to tonight.

The woman tugs on her starched grey suit, then nods to herself, raising her hand, indicating that we should follow.

The others do. I hold back slightly. There is something different about this mission. The energy is peculiar. It's difficult to trust, but then I learned a long time ago that trust is a luxury allowed to those who can afford it.

I cannot deny that our early missions carried with them a certain thrill. Director Matthews – and by extension, the president – quickly realised we were a resource that could be employed all over the world. Cuba, after the Bay of Pigs debacle. Asia. Theatres of war and amphitheatres of intrigue beckoned to us, and we answered the call. We reported back our findings, keeping our invisible ears to the ground.

This lack of physical interaction meant the Xylophone Man had no truck with us. Strange, how constricted a view the beast took on things, how rigid his worldview. Fortunate for us, certainly.

I travelled the globe on these missions. I had a purpose. I was needed.

I always knew what I was walking in to, though. Today, I don't.

At least, not in a figurative sense. What I've wandered into in a literal sense is all too clear: a concrete moat. Although that makes it sound almost medievally quaint, and this death strip is anything but: it's several feet wide, peppered with vomits of concrete at random points to stop vehicles breaching it. Not only that, but there's a bed of nails stretching its entire nine-foot width. If anyone is foolish – or brave – enough to scale the Wall, and lucky enough to dodge the hail of machine-gun bullets, they'll drop down to death by nails. Perhaps I was right after all when I thought of it as medieval. It is barbarism befitting that time.

I don't think much of this Berlin. I'm ready to leave it.

Still, there is work to do first, and these booby traps have no effect on us. We walk through them unaffected, the bed of nails not so much grazing our feet, the twitching machine guns oblivious to us, a slight thrill coursing down my spine at the power of this. I care little for the mission, whatever it is, but the simple act of it makes me feel alive. On nights like this one, with its biting fog and gnawing frost, that is enough, somehow.

We walk quickly and, although we can't be heard, quietly.

The eastern side of the Wall is shabby in sharp contrast to the western. It doesn't have the West's manufactured sheen, and the streets are emptier. The atmosphere stands apart, too. There's fear in it. The few souls on the street walk with their heads down, afraid of life and the questions it may ask. Those on the western side held their heads high, ready to embrace life's answers.

★

The woman in grey leads us down badly lit street after badly lit street. Half the buildings stand naked, bleeding rubble like they were never rebuilt after the war. Finally, a narrowing side street brings us out onto a grand open piazza. A monolith of a building waits for us at the end of it. Light burns from its windows, and a procession of cars is parked outside. Idling black chunks of steel, steam rising from them. The word *Volvo* is fastened onto them. They look new. Expensive. They contrast sharply with the other cars on the street: identical blobs of steel, designed to pootle and break down. Director Matthews describes these 'Trabis' as spark plugs with a roof.

The Volvos suggest that important people are inside this building.

We walk quickly now. The building looms ahead. Its architecture is forbidding. It is a structure that is intended to intimidate, and it does that job well. The light that spills from its windows looks like a cattle brand. This is a place of power that is to be kept from the people. Everyone on the eastern side of the Wall is supposed to be equal, though I'd wager the men in this building are more alike than the ones outside it. Not that I care. They mean nothing to me. Nothing on this earth truly does any more.

There are three armed guards at the entrance to the building. They wear thick Soviet-style coats. Director Matthews would no doubt despair of the cut. My father certainly would have. It's brutal.

The guards have dogs by their sides. They begin to bark. It's unfortunate, animals' ability to see us, but of no great consequence. Still, I flinch a little as we walk close to the dogs and their flashing, snapping teeth. The guards attempt to silence them, all the time straining their eyes, looking for the cause of the commotion. Not finding it. How could they? The Matthewses of this world, with their ability to see the dead, are few and far between. That is why we are so important. We're untraceable. Uncatchable.

Just like that, we're through the front door, the dogs' yelps fading into the distance. A grand reception area greets us. A curved staircase is situated at the back of the room. A polished marble floor lies underneath our feet. A solitary desk sits in the left-hand corner of the room. Two soldiers are gathered around it. They appear startled by the barking of the dogs outside. If only they knew how close we were. I could walk up to them, lick their faces and they wouldn't know we were here.

My teammates are apparently oblivious to this sort of whimsy. They stalk ahead as one towards the staircase and the marble wall beyond it. If there is any humanity left in these souls, it's beyond me to find it. It's like they're brainwashed, the mission the sole thing that powers them.

I envy them this. It brings me nothing but pain, the total recall I 'enjoy'.

The woman in the grey suit obviously remembers what she needs to; she ignores floors one to four, finally hopping quickly off the steps and striding down a faintly lit corridor on the fifth. The carpet beneath our soundless feet is thick. Peach in colour. The walls are painted a sickly yellow. It's a blind man's interpretation of good taste. These communists have no idea of class. My mother could have taught them much, if she was still alive.

I asked Director Matthews to find out what had become of my family. It seemed the least he could do. He agreed. Why would he not? He found them, eventually. Or at least what had happened to them. They'd died in a godforsaken camp in some hell-mouth corner of Germany. That was all he could tell me. What else was there to tell? What else would I want to know?

Voices can be heard, muffled by a door. There's laughter. This is the group we are to spy on, no doubt.

It has been necessary for me to learn other languages in order to complete missions of this nature. Russian. English. Spanish. When you are a spirit trapped in a jar, you are afforded time for such endeavours. I have a natural propensity for languages, and the ability to retain them. Now I begin to pick out words. Phrases. It appears some sort of celebration is occurring. Toasts are made and throatily embraced. Two guards stand outside the room. They do not see us, of course. Perhaps they can feel something, as one tugs at his collar as we approach, his eyes searching the corridor.

Then, just like that, we are through the door.

Within seconds, I know something is wrong.

The room is empty.

Or at least as good as. There are no men and women here, no one to spy on. Instead, two speakers rest on a mighty wooden table in the middle of the room, connected to some sort of PA system. The sounds of a party in full swing continues to blast from them.

This is a trap. They knew we were coming.

'We need to get out of here,' I say. 'Now.'

The woman in grey nods, then moves towards the door she just walked through. She reaches out to it. Her hand strikes it. It doesn't go through it.

There is the sound of electricity crackling.

A hissing makes itself known.

Below the curtained window are corrugated wooden shelves. Green gas is leaking from them.

This is the last thing I remember.

So many years, so many cages.

When I eventually regain consciousness – and how strange it is to discover that unconsciousness is something still afforded to me – I find myself once again imprisoned. My hand strikes the glass surface of the cage. It's very like the one the Nazis used. Electricity fizzes around me. I'm in a laboratory of some kind. The equipment here appears to be less refined than that used by the Americans, but no less effective. I'm someone else's toy now.

There's no sign of the team of spirits I was with.

'Good. You're awake.'

Director Matthews steps out of the gloom. He smiles, but doesn't mean it.

'What's going on?' I demand, already beginning to suspect. I may still look like a child, but my years on the soil have taught me that betrayal and cruelty win out over goodness and decency every time.

'Do you remember what President Eisenhower said about me once?' he asks. 'He called me a carnie huckster.'

I nod.

'He was right,' says Matthews, 'because I've betrayed you, Jacob. Betrayed my country, too, though I don't much care about that, because they betrayed me first. Decades of service I've given to America, and what do I have to show for it? A two-bedroom apartment, debt, and a pension a rat couldn't live on. My programme has made the United States the pre-eminent power on the globe, and how has she repaid me?'

'Is that what East Germany has done?' I ask. 'Repaid you?'

'I'm not proud of it,' says Matthews, taking a step towards the cage, 'but I'm not ashamed of it, either. I'll live like a king here. They value my abilities. Admire my legacy. Don't I deserve that?'

He places a hand on the glass screen separating us.

'This is the last time we'll see each other. My work here will take me elsewhere. I just wanted to say goodbye. And thank you.'

'For what?'

'For showing me there's some decency left in the world.'

With that, Matthews smiles, turns and leaves.

It is the Stasi that use me the most.

I perform a similar task to that I did for the Americans, in that I am required to spy. The Stasi suspect many people of conspiring against the state, and I am allowed off the leash to eavesdrop on those people. They have their bugs, of course, and their informants, but those methods aren't as effective as a spirit that can go anywhere and everywhere, completely unseen. My dispatches are used to destabilise the lives of enemies of the state.

The work is joyless. Grey. Lacking in ambition, just like the city I'm kept in.

I wonder, sometimes, about the trust they show in me. There's nothing to stop me escaping on those missions, just as there was nothing to stop me escaping when I worked for the Americans. I suppose both parties are aware of this simple fact: escape where? Where can a spirit like me go, exactly? There is no haven to aim for, no homeless shelter for ghosts. There is only what comes next in the Pen, and I have no way of knowing how to get there.

On the bad days, I've considered suicide. For someone like me, that is quite different to dying. I could interfere with the living world, call the Xylophone Man. He'd take me to God-knows-where. When I'm at my lowest, I question how it could be any worse than here. It would simply be a different sort of hell.

Then I think of the Duchess, and what she said to me. My time will come. I just need to endure. For my parents. For my sister, Hennie.

★

'Hello?'

I blink slightly as light floods the room. I have come to love the dark over the years. If I can't actually see my cage, it makes it seem more invisible.

A girl stands in the laboratory.

Eleven years old. Blonde hair.

She looks right at me.

She doesn't need the monitor to see me, like the technicians here. There is no Matthews amongst the ranks of German scientists, with his ability to see the dead. They require clunky equipment ripped from the grasp of dead Nazis. This girl swerves such devices. She looks directly at me. There is no fear on her face, no shock. It's as if we've met at a school dance.

She tilts her head slightly. We look to be of a similar age. For a second, I wonder if she's dead too, but she's not. I can always tell. There's life in her. This isn't a tangible thing I can measure, it's just something I feel instinctively.

I raise my hand in greeting.

She takes a step closer to my cage. 'I knew you were real. The others said you were a fairy story, but a fairy story's only make-believe unless you're actually living in it.'

'You can see me, then?' I ask.

'Of course I can,' she says. 'The others could too, if they were here.'

She steps right up to the cage and puts her hand against the glass. I see the marks on her hand. The ones that look like the Nazi brand used on Jews.

'What's your name?' asks the girl.

I tell her.

'How long have you been here for?'

'A long time. I can't measure time like you can, not any more.'

She taps her fingers on the glass. 'Doesn't it make you unhappy? Being trapped like this?'

I shrug my shoulders. 'I'm let out, sometimes. Go up to the surface.'

The girl frowns. 'I've only heard about the outside world. It doesn't sound that great to me.'

'You've never seen it?'

She shakes her head. 'What's it like up there?'

I raise my eyebrows. 'I thought it didn't sound that great.'

'I want to see that for myself. Maybe you can convince me.'

'I don't understand,' I say. 'How can you have never been outside?'

'I was born down here,' she replies, her eyes shifting downwards. 'We all were.'

'All?'

'The other children and me.'

'So you're a lab rat, just like me.'

She smiles. 'I suppose so. Do you think we're the unluckiest creatures on earth?'

I pause. 'I've met unluckier.'

She takes a step back from the cage. 'Can I come and see you again?'

I nod at this strangely confident girl with her knowing half-smile.

She begins to walk away.

'What's your name?' I call out.

She stops and turns back to me.

'Lucia,' she replies.

The Ministry for State Security, East Berlin, 1981

Lucia's visits grow more frequent as the scientists' become less so. At its peak, the lab was never as bustling as when the Nazis

or the Americans owned me, but the workforce further dimin-
ishes by the day. The tests on me are perfunctory, and I spend
more and more time in the cage. No more spying missions
for me. That's the reason my heart leaps when Lucia comes
to see me. The other scientists don't seem to mind; in fact, it's
one of the few times they seem truly engaged with me. They
watch her watching me. Those conversations are more stilted.
Awkward, with an audience. But she comes at night, too, and
we talk for many hours about everything and nothing. She
wants to know all there is to know about the outside world,
and I want to tell her.

We talk of how we'll leave this place one day. How we'll
explore the world together. The claustrophobia of the lab
doesn't feel as pronounced when we're making our plans. Perhaps because it's pure mainlined fantasy. Neither of us will ever
leave here.

Lucia loves my stories of the Pen, and of the role of Warden
I will one day assume. I think she only half believes them, but
her eyes twinkle in a way that makes my heart soar. The texts
my father forced me to learn come into their own as I recount
them, and she stares, rapt.

'We'll go there together one day.' That's what she always
says. 'We're meant for great things, Jacob, you and I, and we
can achieve them in the Pen.'

The way she says it, I almost believe her.

Then one night, she comes to me. Her eyes are red and
puffy. Grief rolls off her.

'They're taking us away tomorrow.'

'Taking you where?'

'To another facility. In Russia. I don't know any more
than that.'

'Why?' I say, as if she'll know.

She doesn't.

'I'll never see you again.' I hate the desperation in my voice. Have nothing but contempt for it, but it's there like a thorn in the words.

'I'll find you,' she says, putting her hand up to the glass. 'No matter how long it takes, I'll find you.'

We both know it's a lie.

Lucia is the last person I see for several months. Or years. How am I to know? The time is interminable down here. Whatever caused her to be moved also means I am forgotten. There are no more scientists, no more Stasi officials with spying missions for me. Just the cage, and the darkness. Why not release me, if they no longer have a use for me? What is to be gained by keeping me locked away?

Perhaps it's because they don't want anyone else to have me.

I would like to say the time passes quickly in my enforced solitary confinement, but it doesn't. Each day feels like a year, and each minute like a day. I don't know how my reason doesn't unspool completely. It would be kinder, perhaps, if it did. Instead, I'm left to pore over every detail of my life and death so far. It has been a florid existence, at least.

Lucia consumes my thoughts. She made me feel things I didn't think were possible. Affection. Friendship. Even love. I can never decide whether this is a gift, or a curse.

Every day I hope that an emissary from the Pen will arrive to rescue me from the torture.

They don't. My salvation comes in an altogether more un-likely form.

Chapter 18

'The seat-belt sign is on, madam.'

Megan raised her head, taking in the air hostess with the fake smile.

She was right, it *was* on.

She reached across, fastening the clasps across her stomach. 'Sorry.'

'No problem,' said the air hostess, flinching only a little at the guttural tone of Megan's voice. 'We'll be landing in around forty minutes. Can I get you anything before then?'

—A beer, said Bits, his voice reverberating around her head.

I don't want a beer, said Megan. *I don't even like beer.*

—I do, and I haven't had one in over twenty-five years.

I thought you were a recovering addict.

—Not like it's going to kill me, is it?

I need to keep a clear head. Think through strategy.

—*You* might. *I* need a beer.

No beer.

Megan frowned as her arm began to rise against her will. She reached out, grabbing it with her other hand.

Stop it.

—Just want a beer, man.

You can't try and control me like this. It's out of order.

—So's enforced sobriety.

She noticed that the couple across the aisle from her were staring as she wrestled with her own arm, unable to stop it jabbing at the call button.

You're going to get us arrested. People get twitchy if you fuck around on planes.

—Wouldn't know. This is the first time I've been on one.

You've never been on a plane before?

—Like taxis, nowadays, aren't they? Not like when I was alive.

'Can I help you, madam?'

Megan let go of her hand and looked up at the air hostess. 'I think I'll take a beer, if it's not too much trouble.'

Just one. A treat for getting me out of that slaughterhouse.

—Cheers, said Bits.

The air hostess stared at Megan and her oversized sunglasses for just a second.

Megan lowered them. 'Please?'

The woman had the good grace only to flinch for a couple of seconds when she saw Megan's eyes.

'Of course.'

—Probably thinks you're disabled, said Bits.

You trying to be offensive? Or does it just come naturally?

—It's a gift.

Besides, I have got a disability. I've got a ghost squatting in my soul.

—That's not a disability, man, that's a privilege.

It really isn't.

The air hostess returned with a can of condensation-soaked Heineken, setting it down with an ice-cube-heavy plastic cup.

Megan/Bits tugged fervently at the metal ring-pull and peeled it backwards.

Slow down, said Megan. *I'll do it, all right?*

—Wanted it this year, not next century.

Rude, she said, tilting the can and pouring the lager into the plastic cup.

She felt Bits's thoughts, joined with him in appreciating the moment, then picked up the cup and put it to her lips, drawing deeply from it.

—Fucking hell, that's good, said Bits. —Thanks.

You're welcome, she said. *You're not wrong.*

She took another sip, then set the cup down.

When we land, we call this Hans guy, right?

—Right, said Bits. —'Cos we're following the say-so of a mad bastard called Julius who tried to carve you up as his own little science project.

Like you said, Dying Squad's about chasing down the leads and trying stuff. This is our lead. Hopefully it will end up with Joe.

—Yeah. Hopefully.

All the while, me finding out about my past gets pushed to the back of the queue again.

—That's why we need Joe, love. He can help you.

What are you going to say to him when we find him?

Bits was silent for once.

Because I think you have to accept the possibility that he's not the guy he was.

Finally, he spoke.

—What worries me is that he *is*. On the soil, Joe was a wrong'un. Not judging him for that – there were few wronger than me – but like you say, what if he's become that person again? Being dead's like trying to stay sober – a daily fucking battle to keep on the straight and narrow, not slip into bad habits. Maybe something's caused Joe to slip into those bad habits. If it has, if his memory's gone, he won't even see them as bad, he'll just see them as habits.

Megan raised the beer to her lips once again and drank deeply.

She didn't know who needed the hit more: her or Bits.

There was a sort of poetry in the way Hans was attempting to eat the hot dog. It was like an inelegant dance, one in which it was never clear who was actually leading: Hans or the hot dog.

'Do you have to watch me when I eat?'

Joe raised his hands.

'It must be a novelty to the likes of you, I suppose. Can you remember food?'

'I struggle to remember what happened five minutes ago,' said Joe, 'let alone what Bockwurst tastes like.'

Hans took another bite, smiling ingratiatingly. 'You're really missing out.'

It was only half a joke, that, Joe's haziness beyond the five-minute mark, because they were out on the street and there was no music. There'd been music in the car, but when they'd got out and sidled over to the hot dog stand, there was only silence. Joe didn't know whether it was panic at that fact that was clouding his thoughts, or genuine memory loss.

It was gum before. That was how he retained his memory on the soil. Gum, and injections. An old woman had given him them, one who thought he was an absolute arsehole. *You'll crash hard when you stop taking them*, that was what she'd said. How hard would he crash with no music?

He had to assume very.

'Where are we off to?' he asked, doing his best to keep the panic from his voice. 'Keen to keep on the scent.'

'I'm keen to keep you on it too,' said Hans through a mouthful of sausage.

They moved away from the food stand, a sidestep shuffle that revealed a grand, ornate cathedral.

'You look like you've seen a ghost,' said Hans.

'I'm not too good with churches,' said Joe. 'I can't remember why that is.'

'How are you with priests?'

'Worse.'

'Well, that's unfortunate, because a priest is who we're here to see.'

Joe thought back to the CCTV footage. He could still do that, at least. 'The deacon with the red dog collar.'

Hans nodded. 'He's something of a local celebrity.'

'What's the red dog collar about it? It's a bit demonic, isn't it?'

Hans smirked. 'Deacon Voigt heads up a splinter group of the church. He's a proper East German, a zealot of the old anti-Stasi regime, and he's carried that zealotry into his missionary work. The church moved too slowly for him, so he's gone it alone. Travels the city giving out care packages to the poor and needy. His whole movement, it's kind of cool. Neon crosses, rock-and-roll imagery, that kind of thing. If Iggy and Bowie had been churchgoers, they'd have gone to Voigt's churches.'

Joe thought back to the neon crosses he'd seen dotted around the city. Another sign his memory hadn't gone completely. 'How do you know all this?'

'Because it's my job to,' said Hans.

Except that knowledge is obviously limited, thought Joe, or we wouldn't be on this wild goose chase.

'If Voigt's as pious and good as you say, what was he doing visiting a dealer like Colonel?'

'That's what you're going to ask him,' said Hans

'I'm going to ask him?' said Joe. 'How? He won't be able to see me.'

'Ah, little ghost, that's just the thing,' said Hans. 'The good deacon is a freak. He can see the undead without the need for Spook, or retina implants like mine. All you need to do is go and say hello.'

Joe shook his head. 'Again: how do you know that?'

Hans's face darkened. 'You're asking a lot of questions.'

'And you're not answering any of them.'

'It's Lucia's job to know everything that goes on in Berlin,' said Hans, 'so it's my job, too. Yours, when your memory returns. Believe it or not, you knew about Voigt before your accident. This knowledge has to come back to you naturally. It's no good me feeding you endless facts: you have to earn them yourself.'

Which is just another non-answer, thought Joe.

'I used to think I was special, being unseen,' he said. 'Now, it's quicker to make a list of all the people who can't see me, rather than those who can.'

'That's why we need to cut off the supply of Spook,' said Hans. 'It's unnatural, the living being able to see the likes of you. Cuts down on your effectiveness, too.'

'And you think this Deacon Voigt has something to do with Spook?'

'It's a mighty big coincidence if he doesn't,' said Hans, 'considering that within an hour of him entering Colonel's hotel room, Berlin's premier Spook dealer ended up dead. Wouldn't you agree?'

As Joe crossed the road towards the church, he was forced to admit that he did agree. In his career as a living copper (and his post-career as a dead one), he'd never experienced a coincidence that wasn't bullshit. There was no such thing as a coincidence: there was just evidence you hadn't discovered yet.

And one way or another, there'd be evidence to collect here and put in his little Dragnet notebook. They were getting closer, he could feel it. Why would the deacon have been visiting Colonel? He could have been there to offer spiritual absolution, true, but it was a strange time of the night to be making house calls. A strange house to call upon, too.

Going on the evidence he'd unearthed so far, Colonel didn't strike him as the religious type.

There was something insidious at play. Something that meant innocent girls like Ella took poison, then killed themselves because of it. He had to put a stop to the Spook supply. It wouldn't bring Ella back – wouldn't wipe the slate clean for the crimes he himself had committed in the past – but it was all he could do.

But his chance to be able to do that was fading along with his memories. He could still remember things OK, and the notebook helped. His thoughts were beginning to judder, though, like a car did when it was almost out of petrol. He needed a music top-up to refuel. Straighten out. Maybe there'd be an organist in the church who could bash out some minimal techno.

Maybe not.

Grateful that he could still remember to joke about forgetting, Joe passed through the church's front entrance.

The interior was discombobulating. He'd been expecting a thing of wood and stone – certainly that was what the outside of the building had hinted at – but instead, the place was a nod to the city's clubbing past and future. A huge glowing cross stood behind the altar, and a pair of decks were visible in the pulpit. The pews were actually leather-seated booths, the lamps above them throwing out a little light, pencilling shadows onto the gloom.

It was a church for hipsters.

He looked left and right; it was like someone was watching him. If they were, they were light of foot and heavy on their powers of concealment.

He stepped forward.

No one in the booths.

Someone at the front of the church. A foot, just about visible under the glowing cross, unmoving.

That doesn't look good, thought Joe. That doesn't look good at all.

It looked even worse when he reached the altar.

The deacon – at least Joe assumed it was the deacon – lay spreadeagled, a pistol held tightly in his hand. The weapon looked old – from the seventies, he would have guessed. Certainly not as svelte and modern as the weapons he'd seen (and used) when he'd been alive.

It appeared the deacon had turned it on himself. There was an entry wound at the side of his head; the contents of that head had been splattered across the altar. The angle of the exit wound was consistent with suicide.

So, what? The deacon kills Colonel, then kills himself? Why? Guilt at the heinousness of his crime? Something else?

Joe frowned. There was something written on the wall to the left of him. He could just about make it out in the murk. He walked over to it, squinting.

TOO MUCH FUTURE

The handwriting was the same as in Colonel's hotel room. A suicide note from the deacon? The phrase was familiar.

He found it in his notebook: it had been written on the wall at the punk club, just as the other phrase had. There was something he couldn't see properly, something from the city's fractured East German past. This had become much more than a simple hunt for a drug dealer. It was now a full-on murder investigation.

He took out his notebook, scribbling his findings down, then returned the book to his coat pocket.

He should search the deacon's body. Normally it would be a contaminate-the-crime-scene no-no, but that was the good thing about being dead: the usual rules didn't apply. He had no fingerprints to leave, no hair or fibres to confuse the forensics bods with. That didn't mean he didn't flinch slightly as he reached into the deacon's black jacket, or wince as he rifled through his pockets. It was wrong in a moral sense, if not in a bad-copper one.

It also proved to be pointless. There was nothing there but specks of dust and the odd sliver of lint.

There must be something. Something that explains why this bloke killed a dealer, then himself.

A thin slab of light covered the floor thirty feet away from him. It was coming from a partially open door. Never one to look a gift light in the mouth, Joe walked towards it.

He'd seen a good few vestries in his time, thanks to his vicar dad. That was another memory that had bobbed up through the memory scum. It should have been a moment of triumph, but he'd remembered the type of man his dad had actually been.

This vestry, unlike the clubbing experience outside, was as unremarkable as any of them. Wood panels. Ancient furniture that looked like it would collapse if you sneezed on it. A sense of decades in everything, all of it unchanged and fossilised.

There were a few swerves from the norm, admittedly. A couple of old hand-made punk posters that he found difficult to believe were standard church fare. A computer, too: the monitor sat on a rickety-looking desk, its screen blank, its red light glowing defiantly. Joe crouched down to see a jet-black tower underneath the desk, its old-school CD-ROM slot eyeing him invitingly.

That'd do nicely.

Reaching into his pocket, he took out the plastic box and eased the earpiece into his left ear. It was time to let the Ghost in the Machine rattle its chains again.

He eased off the plastic covering, the slim sliver of steel bending and curling in response. Pinching it between finger and thumb, he carefully slipped it into the tower's disk drive. The monitor flared into life, the tower chuntering and whirring, irritated that it had been woken from its slumber. Joe knew that somehow; it was like there was a connection between him and the machine, one that strengthened every time he used the device. It was the strangest thing, but he could almost hear the computer as it clicked away, eavesdrop on its processor as it issued commands.

What commands did he want it to issue?

The home page was a blank wall of blue. Not much to go on there.

'Open emails,' Joe said, and the deacon's Outlook account appeared. He commanded the computer to open the messages sequentially, but quickly realised there was little to go on; it was a roll call of righteousness and good deeds, concerned with food drops and charity drives, outreach centres and godliness.

Thing is, my dad was the same, and he ended up dead in a ditch because that charity work was paid for by drug money. Could be the same thing's true here. There must be something. Some clue as to why he's been so brutally murdered.

'Open photos,' Joe said, and the computer dutifully obeyed. It wasn't a particularly onerous task; there were just three images contained on the machine's hard drive.

The first captured the unlikeliest of scenes. A gig, in the very church he was now standing in. A stage had been set up in front of the altar, and a two-piece punk band bestrode it. Colonel and a drummer. He'd seen this photograph before, at the punk club.

The second photograph was more interesting. The deacon – a much younger, alive version – in front of the stage, with his arms around Colonel and the drummer, beaming. Early eighties, by the look of the fashions, and the ages of all those involved. An unlikely meeting of minds, but then unlikely was all he'd found in this case so far. It was time to go with that fact rather than fight against it.

The third photograph was stranger still, not just because it was shot in a selfie-style. It contained the deacon again, crouching in front of the stage. He even maintained the same arm-around-the-shoulder stance.

He had his arm around nobody.

There was a blank space where a person should be, and that person should have been short, based on the way the deacon was crouching. There was something familiar about the picture. He'd seen its like somewhere before, on another case. He tried to think where, but the memory fog was too dense, and wasn't for hacking back.

Still, it was like there was someone in that picture with the deacon. Someone Joe couldn't see.

He told the computer to magnify the image, which it immediately did, the pixels becoming ever blockier but no more revealing.

What else can I do? Just because I can control the computer doesn't mean I can make it do things it's not capable of. I can't magic up the person who's supposed to be in this photograph.

Which was true, but that didn't mean he couldn't make it do other things.

Opening a web page and steering towards a search engine, Joe dictated that it search for Deacon Voigt. He was instantly rewarded with a number of hits. An article from a month ago detailing his work in the community. One from several years ago describing his breakaway from the church, and the setting-up of his own rock-and-roll ministry, with the inevitable cries of cult. Interesting enough, but nothing that suggested why the man had ended up murdered in his own church.

Because other than the deacon being a drug kingpin, nothing could really explain that. And Joe wasn't ready to make that leap yet.

He frowned as he continued to pick his way through the news articles. There was little here but eulogies about the deacon's goodness. Telling, in its own way, because it showed how if his dealings were nefarious, he'd been able to hide in plain sight. That had certainly been the case with Joe's father.

In that third photo, there'd been a child-sized space next to the deacon. Ella had mentioned a child – a boy, to be specific – who had been a ghost mascot for Colonel's band. Joe had dismissed it as a confected record-label urban myth. Perhaps he'd been wrong to do so, because according to Hans, the deacon had been able to see the dead.

None of which explained why that same deacon had been transformed into a murderer, who had then killed himself.

There had to be something else here.

'Open address book.'

A book icon appeared, followed by a list in alphabetical order, a string of names that meant nothing to Joe. Why would they? He knew little about the deacon, let alone his associates.

He tapped his fingers on the desk. If there was anything worth seeing here, the dead holy man wouldn't have left in plain sight.

He'd have hidden it.

'Display all encrypted files,' said Joe.

The computer thought about it, the hard drive spluttering and coughing up a single folder.

'Open,' said Joe.

A password screen popped up.

Let's see if this toy is anything more than a wiggly-worm operating system.

'Input correct password.'

225

He winced slightly as a grinding sound filled his ears. It reminded him of an old modem dialling up to find an internet connection. Which makes sense, he thought, because that's what this conversation must sound like: a ton of zeros chatting with a fuck-load of ones, mediated by a dead guy with an ear-piece. What a world.

The first letter appeared in the password box, quickly followed by the rest.

ISEEGHOSTS_2

Joe smiled. He loved a dead deacon with a sense of humour.

The folder opened. It contained two images.

The first was another photo. It was of the deacon, again as a young man. He was smiling, looking directly at the camera. He appeared to be in some sort of club. Next to him, sitting close, was a slightly older, rakish-looking man with a fake tan and matinee-star looks.

The second image was of a scrap of paper. It contained a name and address:

Isiah Matthews
Residenz WestPoint,
Lichterfelder Ring 300
14321 Berlin

A quick Google search showed a nursing home at that address.

Have to assume this Isiah Matthews is a resident there, thought Joe. No idea who he is, but the deacon went to a lot of effort to hide his existence. That must mean something. My gut tells me that, as does good old-fashioned common sense.

He blinked, his memories frosting.

Where was he? What was he doing?

Fuck.

'Play music,' he commanded the computer.

The buzz saw of a throttled electric guitar fired up, and an old punk song played.

The brain fog began to ease slightly, the music scorching it back.

He placed his head next to the tower's inadequate speaker and closed his eyes. The yelping of the singer helped a little. He needed this top-up, but he also needed to get going.

He reached down next to the disk drive, and the thin sliver of metal uncurled from it onto his hand. After he'd popped it back into its plastic case, he copied the address on the screen into his notebook.

Isiah Matthews. That was the lead they needed to chase.

He didn't know what type of lead it was — or if it was going to be anything more than a dead end — but it was the only one they had.

Chapter 19

So, this was what the apocalypse looked like.

Daisy-May stood on the top floor of an apartment block, the window in the penthouse she'd been transported to torn out, wind screaming all around her, the world beneath her radiation-drenched and desolate. Buildings were demolished and half mangled. The faint outlines of char-grilled corpses were scattered over the landscape.

Then there were the spirits.

It was like being back in purgatory, watching convoys of Dispossessed traverse the wastelands of the Pen. Except this was the living world, and she'd never seen this many spirits grouped together on the soil before. This was an army, and they were streaming into the city and its desolation rather than away from it.

'A magnificent sight, is it not?'

She turned. Oma Jankie stood there, her hands behind her back, looking to all intents and purposes like she was taking the morning air.

'It looks like the end of the world,' said Daisy-May.

'Strange that you describe it as the end of something,' said Oma Jankie, 'when it is in fact the beginning.'

'What happened here?' asked Daisy-May, turning back to the city below. 'What is this place?'

'This is New Tokyo,' said Oma Jankie, 'and it's what happens when you send an old woman to do a young girl's job.'

A chill rippled down Daisy-May's spine. 'What?'

'The Duchess failed to stop Hanna from creating a nuclear winter in Tokyo, somewhere spirits stranded on the soil can live and thrive. It was quite brilliant of her, really.'

'Quite brilliant?' said Daisy-May, shaking her head at the destruction below. 'Thousands of people must have died.'

'Hundreds of thousands,' said Oma Jankie, 'but who's counting?'

Daisy-May stared defiantly at the old woman. 'None of this is real.'

'Everything you see in the trials is real. On that you have my word.'

'For all that means. What's the trial here, exactly?'

Oma Jankie smiled. 'It is to be a test of strength.'

Daisy-May lifted up a skinny arm. 'Not exactly playing to *my* strengths, that.'

'Strength isn't just about muscles, girl, it's about strength of will. It's about being able to choose the hard path when the easy also presents itself.'

'This should be a piece of piss, then,' said Daisy-May, ''cos all I know is hard.'

'We'll see,' said Oma Jankie.

She stepped into the shadows, melting out of sight.

So what the fuck do I do now? thought Daisy-May. Where do I go?

She frowned as a sound made itself known on the breeze.

It sounded almost like singing, but that wasn't quite right. Instead, it was more of a harmonic chant that ebbed and flowed with the wind. It soothed her in a way she didn't really understand.

It spoke to her, too. Told her it was important that she

descend from the building and go to the ground below.

She looked behind her. There was a doorway.

She began to walk towards it.

The chanting, the humming, the singing – the whatever-the-fuck-it-was – was louder on the ground. Now that she was out in the open, she realised the noise was all around her. It was part of the city, somehow, a constant three-note refrain.

Dah-dah-*duh*.

Dah-dah-*duh*.

Dah-dah-*duh*.

It rippled in waves, coursing through her, calming and soothing her. Why that was, Daisy-May couldn't say, only that it did. It made her feel connected to the earth and her surroundings, made her feel like she was part of something. Until now, she'd always been on the outside looking in, and that was as true of when she'd been living as it was now that she was dead. Becoming the Warden had only made that disconnection worse, because being the boss put you in a tribe of one.

Here, though, despite the destruction all around her, it felt like she was part of something bigger.

Maybe Oma Jankie was right. Maybe Hanna had done something good here.

Dah-dah-*duh*.

Dah-dah-*duh*.

The noise came from behind her, rising in power.

Daisy-May turned to see a group of spirits approaching. Such was the vibrancy of their glimmer, it was almost difficult to make them out. That didn't seem to matter, somehow; there was comfort in the glow they gave off. And now that she looked properly, it wasn't a nuclear wasteland they were in at all, it was actually kind of a paradise. A hard-to-define paradise, admittedly; more a sense of that this was where she was supposed to be.

Dah–dah–*duh*.

Dah–dah–*duh*.

She found her lips forming the words and parroting the chant. They felt good in her mouth, and even better out of it.

She realised that she had joined the convoy of spirits, her legs moving almost of their own accord. That was OK. Better than OK. It was *right*.

'Welcome, sister.'

A woman walked alongside her. She was short in stature but big in presence. The glimmer she gave off was almost blinding.

'Where are we going?' asked Daisy-May.

'Where would you like to go?' the woman replied.

Daisy-May realised that it didn't really matter. It was enough just to be with these people. She didn't have to worry about leading them, because somehow they were all leading each other. There were no hierarchies here, no bosses. They were all equal.

Dah–dah–*duh*.

Dah–dah–*duh*.

She'd come here to do something, but was struggling to re-call what that was exactly. If it was important, she'd remember it. If it wasn't, what did it matter?

Dah–dah–*duh*.

Dah–dah–*duh*.

There was part of her that baulked at the words, that found them unpalatable. She hated that part; it was the part that had meant she'd ended up in purgatory in the first place. It came from a place of weakness and of doubt. As long as she had these people around her – as long as they had the chant – everything would be all right. There was strength in unity.

'Hold, sister,' the woman alongside her said. 'There are devils amongst us.'

Daisy-May did as she was asked, and saw that her new friend was right.

It had been difficult to make out where she'd been walking to, such was the fierceness of the glimmer all around her. Now, it was if a break in the clouds had appeared.

There was a large open area of nothing in front of her. Within that square of nothing were five figures. Each one wore a chunky white outfit (*radiation suit* popped into Daisy-May's mind), and they were making their way cautiously towards her.

Dah-dah-*duh*, she mouthed.

Dah-dah-*duh*.

'Living souls,' the woman next to her said. 'The mistress calls them death tourists. They pay for the right to come here and gawk at us. A man-made drug called Spook lets them do that. They're invaders; this is *our* land, created by the mistress.'

'The . . . mistress?' said Daisy-May.

'You'll meet her soon,' the woman said, a smile in her words. 'It will be the best day of your life.'

Dah-dah-*duh*.

Dah-dah-*duh*.

Daisy-May found it increasingly difficult to remember what she was here for, and indeed, who she was. She would normally have been concerned about that, but now she drew peace from it. There was a sense that it didn't matter, that there was someone out there to take care of that sort of thing for her. What had the woman called her?

The mistress. That was familiar, somehow.

She felt a hand on her arm. The woman next to her was smiling at her. 'There's a way to make the mistress happy. A way to show you truly belong.'

That sounded good to Daisy-May. Belonging was something she was desperate for.

'These living souls are a scourge on our land,' the woman continued. 'They would wipe us from the face of it. Does that sound right to you? Does that sound fair?'

It didn't. What right did they have to do such a thing?

'What can we do?' Daisy-May asked.

'Destroy them,' said the woman, her confidence unswerving. 'A message must be sent. New Tokyo is ours. The living have so much already: why should they be allowed to take this place from us too?'

'They shouldn't,' said Daisy-May. 'Of course they shouldn't.'

'Join us, then,' said the woman. 'Help us drive them out.'

Dah–dah-*duh*.

Dah–dah-*duh*.

The chant swelled in power, and Daisy-May's resolve matched it. Of course she needed to drive them out. That nagging voice at the back of her mind, that she was here to do something; this was that something. She had to defend their land.

It *was* their land, right?

She shook her head, trying to dislodge the doubts.

The figures in the radiation suits had sensed their presence. More than that, they could see them.

The chant echoed all around as Daisy-May joined the others in forming a circle around the living souls.

Dah–dah-*duh*.

Dah–dah-*duh*.

Kill them.

Wipe them out.

Drive them out.

She felt her fists flex.

Her lips curled.

Her teeth bared.

They were as one. A pack.

She blinked. Weren't they?

It felt true, and not. Right, and not.

The spirits around her began to attack.

The living began to scream.

This wasn't right.

The chant said it was. The woman next to her said it was. But something in Daisy-May's gut made her doubt it. She was supposed to protect innocents, wasn't she? Fight for justice.

The spirits swarmed onto the living souls, tearing at their radiation suits. She'd thought of them as a pack before, had felt part of that pack, but was that a good thing? Packs could be wild. Feral.

Dah-dah-*duh*.

Dah-dah-*duh*.

The more Daisy-May listened, the more the chant sounded like an order rather than a soothing call to arms.

In its way, that was reassuring. She was so tired of giving orders. Exhausted with the weight of expectations on her. It was nice to let someone else take the strain.

The pack of spirits halted their attack, then turned as one to stare at her. It was as if they sensed her doubt, her exercise of free will. From the looks on their faces, they didn't like it.

It was as though she was being pulled in two different directions. Towards the pack of rampaging spirits, and away from them by someone or something else. What was it. Duty? Loyalty?

Dah-dah-*duh*.

Dah-dah-*duh*.

She was done with duty. Done with expectation. The chant was like a warm bath, and she was desperate to get in.

She clenched her fists. A woman was stumbling towards her, her radiation suit clunky and clumsy. The dopey heaviness of her thoughts dissolved. It was as though she'd freed herself from a meat hook.

That woman is the enemy.

She closed her eyes.

Took a breath.

Then she launched herself forward, colliding with the woman and knocking her to the ground.

Her fingers clawed at the mask covering the woman's face.

Dah–dah-*duh*.

Dah–dah-*duh*.

She ripped the mask off, screaming in triumph.

It was a scream that was taken up by her fellow attackers.

Out of the corner of her eye, she saw Oma Jankie smile. The old woman began to clap.

'Very good,' she called out. '*Very* good.'

Daisy-May looked down at the terrified woman she'd pinned to the ground.

Noticed, for the first time, the blood on the tips of her broken nails.

'You'll thank me for this one day, you know,' said Oma Jankie.

The world bleached out.

It's begun.

Oma Jankie's voice popped into Hanna's head, and for once, it wasn't a cause of excruciating irritation.

Daisy-May passed the trial? Hanna replied.

On the contrary, she failed it. She couldn't resist the language of the dead. And if she couldn't resist it in the trials, she certainly won't be able to resist it in the Pen.

You're sure?

As sure as I've ever been about anything, said Oma Jankie.

How long do I have? Hanna asked.

Make your way to the Pen as soon as possible. Daisy-May will be waiting for you. I personally guarantee it.

Chapter 20

Lucia never wore an environmental suit to the Pen. It would have been purely for show, and who exactly would she have been showing off to? The Dispossessed? She might have been the woman who didn't glimmer, but the point was, she was still recognisably a woman; throw a for-show spacesuit on and she'd have stuck out even more. You didn't need oxygen in the Pen, you just needed to not outstay your welcome.

She made sure that she never did. Normally she spoke to Remus on the communications array that she'd had set up, but sometimes you needed to show your face. Besides, travelling to the afterlife hadn't quite lost its novelty yet.

The doorway shimmered and flickered in front of her, the black and red clouds of the Pen just about visible, the bridge firm under her feet. It may have looked only partly built, a half-bridge to nowhere, but that was because the other half ended in the depths of the Pen. It was a feat of technological, religion-thrashing wonder that confounded even her. She had much to thank the Nazis and their research for, but she thought of herself standing on the shoulders of pygmies rather than giants. She and her team were the ones who'd joined the final dots.

As she passed through to the other side, emerging into what

she'd come to think of as the birthing pool – the point at which a soul passed from the land of the living into the land of the dead – she saw the changes Remus and his fallen angels had enacted upon the place.

Whenever she'd stepped off the bridge and through the doorway of light before (mercifully free of the white gunk the Dispossessed were always drenched in when they passed through), she'd been greeted by the sight of thousands of souls stumbling up vast concentric circles towards the Pen proper. As she gazed outwards, the circles were still there, but the fallen angels were a new addition. The eight-foot-tall beasts stood next to the entrance, corralling the Dispossessed into regimented lines. They still walked upwards, but this time it was a journey accompanied by the whips the beasts wielded, bringing them crashing down onto the confused, newly birthed souls, drawing screams from them.

My God, Remus. Is this what you really wanted? I ventured here to advance mankind. You've wasted your time on genocide and cruelty.

'Lucia.'

She turned to see another fallen angel – or grounded devil, depending on your perspective – towering over her. He was different to the others.

He didn't have any wings, for a start; all that was left of them was two twitching stumps. His body and face were covered by a bulging, ill-fitting skin-suit. It gave him a monstrous, freakish appearance, like a Frankenstein's monster gone to seed. The skin was particularly stretched around his elongated eyeballs, his general demeanour that of an angel that hadn't so much as fallen from heaven as been vindictively pushed.

'Hello, Uriel,' she said. 'You're looking well.'

Uriel laughed. The sound always reminded Lucia of beetles being crushed underneath the heel of a shoe.

'I look like a freak,' he said.

Lucia glanced at the malformed stumps where his wings should have been. 'We all have our bad-hair days.'

'Thanks to that little bitch, I'm shunned by my own kind. Laughed at. I disgust them.'

'You can barely notice,' said Lucia, keeping the straightest of faces. 'I wouldn't have, if you hadn't mentioned it. The skin's another matter. I'm not sure you're ever going to convince anyone you're still human, darling.'

Daisy-May had done quite the number on Uriel, one so comprehensive, in fact, that Lucia began to suspect she might have backed the wrong horse. The stick-thin girl had ripped his wings clean off, a display of power that made Lucia wonder what other tricks she might have up her sleeve. All Uriel and Remus seemed fit for was organising massacres. They were small creatures with large vats of bitterness.

'The girl will pay for what she did to me,' said Uriel, his oversized red eye-slashes boring into Lucia.

'Oh, have you found her?' She laced her words with mock surprise.

Uriel bared his jagged white teeth. 'It's only a matter of time.'

'Of course,' said Lucia, smiling sweetly. 'Now, if you don't mind, I'd like to see Remus.'

'He prefers to be called the Warden,' Uriel replied.

I bet he does. He's like every other tinpot dictator in history; he's so insecure in the power he's seized, he has to keep reminding you that he's seized it.

As they reached the Pen proper, its red and black clouds tumbling in the sky above her, Lucia wasn't sure whether she was supposed to be impressed or appalled by the transformation that had taken place.

Much was the same. The endless wall traced its way around the horizon, a Great Wall of China for the afterlife generation.

The various settlements that had grown up since Daisy-May had taken power were still there, although that was where the first signs of change could be seen: lazy trails of smoke drifted up from them, as well as the occasional lick of flame.

The real change, though, was on the horizon.

Dozens of burned-black factories were dotted around, four fat chimneys sticking up from each one, coughing smoke into the charred sky. Next to each was a line of slowly moving ants, or at least that was what it looked like to Lucia; there were noticeably bigger stick figures next to each line.

She counted thirty buildings at least, and they were just the ones she could see. There must be plenty of others she couldn't.

'You disapprove.'

Uriel stood alongside her, his jagged mouth smiling.

'If Remus wants to wipe out the Dispossessed, it makes no difference to me,' said Lucia. 'They're dead anyway.' She threw him a half-smile. 'Isn't it a little gauche, though, mass genocide? Hardly befitting your talents for death and destruction. These poor wretches can't present much of a challenge.'

'They are a means to an end,' said Uriel. 'Destroying them allowed us to come home.'

Lucia snorted. 'As I understand it, this place was never really home. There was heaven, and then there was hell. This was no more than a halfway house.'

Uriel bared his teeth. 'Little humans shouldn't concern themselves with the business of big gods.'

Lucia winked at him. 'Careful, darling. Your stumps are showing.'

Dear God, Lucia thought. He's built himself a palace.

When she'd first contacted Remus, they hadn't met at the compound; her lack of glimmer would have aroused suspicion. Instead, they'd convened at a bar in the down-at-heel Downs,

Remus cloaked and amusingly conspicuous because of it. The compound, she knew, was underground, all the better to hide from the Dispossessed's slack-jawed gaze. Or at least it used to be: now, someone had stuck a huge great building on top of it.

The architecture wasn't as brutal as the death factories she'd seen earlier, but neither could it be classed as sympathetic. There were windows, and even a door, but also a phalanx of guards standing outside, armed to the teeth.

At least they're human, thought Lucia. Or as human as the dead get.

Most striking of all was the colossal statue Remus had erected on the roof. It depicted himself – though a far more athletic and virile version – holding, of all things, a spear, every inch the powerful, all-conquering hero.

It was perhaps the most tragic thing she'd ever seen in her life.

The guards opened the door with the slightest of nods to her (had she imagined the faint look of revulsion when they'd looked at Uriel? She didn't think so), and she followed one of them along endless winding corridors until at last they reached a large briefing room full of television screens. For a moment, she assumed they were all static-filled, but once she'd stared at them for longer, it was apparent that she was wrong; they'd coalesced like one of those irritating magic eye pictures, each one containing a different crime scene.

'You can see them, then.'

'Hello, Remus,' said Lucia, turning to the older man as he hovered at her shoulder. 'This is where you get your famous Dying Squad cases, is it not?'

'It's where we *got* them,' Remus replied. 'I've disbanded the Squad.'

'Why?' asked Lucia.

'We have problems enough in the Pen without worrying

240

about those on the soil,' Remus replied. 'I always thought it one of the Duchess's more farcical vanity projects.'

'Thought it, but didn't say it,' smiled Lucia. 'What's it like being king, Remus? All you're missing is a crown. You have your heroic statue outside, I see.'

He glowered at her. 'I assume there's a reason why you're here, Lucia. One that couldn't be taken care of via communicator.'

'I was curious to see what you'd done with the place. You've been busy. Certainly the Dispossessed would say so.'

Remus laughed. 'Please don't tell me you're concerned about them all of a sudden. You've been using them as lab rats for months – their children, especially.'

Lucia held her hands up. 'What you do in the Pen is your business. You're the Warden, after all.'

Remus bared his teeth. 'That's just the problem: I'm not. Not officially. That vile girl didn't abdicate, so I'm seen by my people as nothing but a common dictator.'

Lucia inspected a nail. 'Whatever would give them that idea?'

He slammed his hand down on the desk. 'I won't be disrespected in my own realm.'

'You'd prefer I waited until you got to the soil?'

He leaned forward. 'Why do you think you're better than me? I'm genuinely curious.'

She matched his pose. 'Because the pain I've doled out to those pathetic creatures has always been in the name of science. The things we've learned can be adapted into technology to help the living. I'm no different to Louis Pasteur or Albert Einstein.'

Remus smiled. 'Josef Mengele would be a better comparison.'

Lucia smiled back. 'He'd certainly appreciate *your* flare for

241

genocide. I saw the factories, Remus. Your culling of the herd seems to be more of a wholesale slaughter.'

'What do you care?'

'I don't, particularly. In fact, I was more than happy to let our arrangement come to an end, but you did insist on setting up your own little colony on the soil. Seeing such widespread slaughter gives me pause.'

'I've lived in the Pen for so many years it defies belief,' said Remus. 'Living on the soil is my retirement. Thanks to your technology, it's one I'll be able to enjoy in peace, and in the best of memory.'

'Peace is still what you want, then?' said Lucia. 'Because your abattoirs suggest otherwise.'

'I'm merely course-correcting the Pen. Those Dispossessed that have developed "intelligence" are a cancer that needs to be blasted away. My methods are crude, I concede, but highly effective.'

'And the fallen angels you have doing your dirty work? What happens to them when that cancer has been blasted away? I can't see them being too keen on going back to hell.'

'Why are you here, Lucia?' said Remus. 'Why have you come?'

Lucia couldn't resist a final, triumphant smile. 'Because I'm about to lay my hands on the best Warden the Pen never had,' she said. 'And I was rather wondering whether you'd like her back.'

Hanna had to admit it: she could get used to modern technology.

The things that were possible now seemed like witchcraft to her, and she was someone who had rebooted, then blown up, a nuclear reactor.

Certainly it was technology that would help her get out of

New Tokyo. Or more pointedly, Arata's marshalling of that technology.

They looked up at a series of large video screens, each one containing a different map of the city.

'I don't see the problem,' said Hanna. 'According to Lucia's message, there's a plane waiting for us.'

'The problem is, the plane's not in central Tokyo,' said Arata. 'It's on a private landing strip four miles out.'

'Frustrating she couldn't find anything closer.'

'Apparently someone blew up a nuclear reactor and incinerated the inner-city airport.'

Hanna scowled. 'We go to the private landing strip, then.'

'It's not that simple,' said Arata. 'There are tens of thousands of spirits between us and the plane. Can you guarantee us safe passage?'

Hanna knew she couldn't. Her hold on them had slackened almost to nothingness. There'd been reports of spirits attacking the death tourists who ventured to New Tokyo. She'd forbidden this because it drew attention where she'd have preferred to avoid it. They'd done it anyway.

I'm not like them. That seems to matter somehow. They moved as one when they attacked the living. What will they do when they see that I don't move with them? How will I command them now that the language of the dead doesn't work any more?

I need to get out now, especially if what Oma Jankie says is true.

If her plan works, the afterlife will soon look very, very different.

It will look like mine.

'I'm assuming you have some sort of solution to this,' she said, 'considering the smug grin on your face and the fact that your life depends on you getting us there.'

'I have,' said Arata.

He tapped the monitor just above his head.

Seconds before, it had displayed a top-down view of the

city; when he touched the screen, a schematic overlaid it. The monitor next to it flared into life, showing a photograph of a cavernous room with dozens of massive stone pillars stretching from the floor to the sky.

'What am I looking at?' asked Hanna.

'It goes by several names,' said Arata, gazing at the monitor. 'The government calls it the Underground Temple, but I always preferred the Concrete Cathedral.'

Hanna stepped closer to the monitor. It was like looking at an optical illusion: the rows of giant-dwarfing concrete pillars appeared to be locked inside some sort of infinite loop, stretching on for ever.

'It reminds me of the Pen,' she said.

'What's the Pen?' said Arata.

'Somewhere you'd be unfortunate to end up. Continue.'

He nodded. 'Five silos, connected by four miles of underground tunnels. It's the largest storm-drainage system in the world. Tokyo sits on the Kanto flood plain: overflow from its rivers pour into these silos, reducing the risk of flooding. If you'd *really* wanted to fuck Tokyo up, you'd have destroyed the silos; you'd have been able to wash the whole place down the drain.'

'I never wanted to fuck Tokyo up,' said Hanna, staring at the screen. 'I just wanted to make it habitable to my kind.'

Still, she wished she'd known about the silos earlier.

'Why are you showing me this?'

'Because if we follow these tunnels, they'll bring us to half a kilometre away from the airstrip your friend Lucia told you about.'

'She's not my friend.'

'No, she's a means to an end, as am I,' Arata replied. 'I'll guide you through these tunnels if you guarantee me safe passage on the plane.'

'You can do that?' said Hanna.

'With access to the technology I have,' said Arata, 'I could guide us to hell if I needed to.'

'If that's true, I'd make sure you lost the map,' said Hanna.

The Concrete Cathedral was vast, designed, seemingly, to make you feel like a cosmic grub burrowing into the folds of the universe. The pillars facing them were unending, stretching upwards like they were auditioning for the temple of the gods. Hanna walked forward, the service hatch that had deposited them in the silo left open behind them.

'When I opened my shop, I wasn't looking for footfall,' Arata had said as he'd hauled on his radiation suit back at the shop. 'I was looking for close proximity to these storm drains. The great flood of '91 inundated thirty thousand homes and businesses; I couldn't afford for mine to be one of them.'

He laughed, his voice tinny through his respirator. 'Of course, I never expected a terrorist ghost to blow up a nuclear reactor.'

'Fail to prepare, prepare to fail,' Hanna had replied.

Now, as they trooped down the interminable tunnels, Arata's footsteps echoing, his laptop bag swinging from his shoulder, she knew she should have followed her own advice. It was pure luck that Lucia had fallen into her lap, and it was unlikely that her offer of escape would be consequence-free. People like that always wanted something in return, and Lucia's past conduct with spirits had been troubling.

Which was fine. Hanna just needed her plane. She wasn't looking for an adopted mother.

What to do about Arata once he'd led her to that plane? There were some benefits to keeping him around; he was savvy with technology in a way she never would be. It was unlikely, though, that there would be a seat for him. She needed him now. Later? Not so much.

'I'm a little surprised,' he said.

'About what?' said Hanna, picking up her pace a little.

'That we haven't encountered any spirits down here.'

'Why would we? I can't imagine the existence of these tunnels was widely known before the explosion.'

'It wasn't,' he admitted, 'but that doesn't mean some people didn't know about them. The homeless community, for instance. If you knew how to access the tunnels – and the information was passed around like Chinese whispers – they were a guaranteed roof over your head for the night. For a time, anyway.'

'What do you mean, for a time?'

'This place in a dry summer? It might be spooky as hell, but it's safe as houses. Safer than the streets if you're homeless, anyway. When it rains? Not so much. Rumour is, flash storms have caught out several groups here, but it was a couple of years ago, when the tsunami hit, that the tragedy really unfolded. A small town's-worth of people were fished out of here. Storm drove them underground, which was the last place they should be. The silo tanks filled up fast: with water, and the homeless.'

'And they say I'm a monster,' said Hanna. 'I was trying to create a society where all were equal, not driven underground in desperation.'

If Arata disagreed with this apparent contradiction, he held his tongue.

'I thought we'd have seen a few stragglers down here,' he said. 'I'm not complaining that we haven't, though.'

'Word about New Tokyo would have reached them,' said Hanna. 'I created a safe haven in death that they would not have enjoyed in life. They must have gone to the surface.'

'So safe, you're skulking around underground,' Arata said. 'Quite a haven, that.'

Hanna didn't reply. He had a point.

They could have been walking for ten minutes or ten hours, so unchanging were the pillar-filled tunnels, when Arata finally cried out in triumph.

'Is that a car?' said Hanna.

'It's an MSV. I was hoping we'd find one down here. I'm a little surprised it's taken us this long.'

'What the devil is an MSV?'

'A multi-service vehicle. They're used on building sites and facilities like this to transport heavy materials. Not the fastest thing around, but one thing's for sure: they're a lot faster than our feet. Particularly mine, wearing this damn radiation suit.'

'Will it still work?' said Hanna.

'It seems to be the one thing in this city you haven't blown up,' said Arata, 'so I'm keeping my fingers crossed.'

The good news was, the MSV was in one piece. In fact it looked virtually untouched. It even had a set of keys hanging from the ignition.

The bad news was, it wouldn't start.

'I thought you were supposed to be some sort of technological genius,' said Hanna.

'I am,' Arata replied.

'A genius that can't start a car.'

'It's not like starting a Kia. This is an industrial-grade vehicle, and we have no idea how long it's been down here.'

The MSV continued to cough and splutter, its engine irritated at the attempts to choke it back to life.

Hanna frowned, jumping off the back of it and squinting into the distance.

'What is it?' said Arata, his attention fixed on the vehicle.

Hanna didn't reply, taking several steps away from the MSV.

It wasn't that she'd heard something. She hadn't seen anything, either. It was more a feeling, a displacement of the air.

The MSV continued grumbling, a smoker coughing up his first nicotine breath of the morning.

Hanna squinted.

No.

'Arata.'

'What?' said Arata, his hand turning right then left, the engine stubbornly failing to turn over.

'We need to leave. Now.'

'What do you think I'm trying to do?' he fired back. 'I can't get the damn thing to start.'

'How much further is the airstrip?' said Hanna, backing towards the MSV.

'Another mile or so.' Arata cursed, then slammed his left hand onto the bonnet in frustration.

Too far, thought Hanna. We'll never make it.

'What is that?' said Arata, his vowels stretched by his respirator. He placed his hand over his mask as if shielding his eyes from the midday sun.

'Trouble,' said Hanna. 'You need to get that truck started.'

'It's not a truck,' said Arata, 'it's an—'

'I don't care what it's called. Just get it started.'

'Oh my God,' said Arata, finally seeing what Hanna had felt.

'He won't be much help, I'm afraid. We don't get on.'

There was no mistaking it now. The displacement in the air Hanna had felt had become a visual stampede. At least fifty spirits, heading straight for them. The homeless people who had drowned here, perhaps. Souls from the surface that had found their way down. She supposed it didn't much matter.

'Can you stop them?' said Arata. 'Will they listen to you?'

'I don't know. But I know we can't rely on them doing so.'

Arata reached for the ignition again.

'Come on,' he said, turning the key, the same starched cough coming from the engine.

Hanna kept her eyes on the onrushing mob. She'd been wrong when she'd said there were fifty. It was more like a hundred. There was an almost eerie beauty to the scene, so utterly silent were the spirits.

What living generals would give for such a force. An army that couldn't be seen by an opposing force, let alone hurt or killed. You'd be unbeatable. Unstoppable.

And she'd had that army. Before the radiation had rotted their minds, she could marshal the spirits here. She could have taken city after city in Japan, then branched out into world domination.

She'd almost succeeded in taking control of the Pen, before. Without the poisonous radiation on the soil, the language of the dead would still work there. She had unfinished business in purgatory. It was time to claim her birthright.

Which meant escaping this unhinged mob first.

Arata continued to swear at the vehicle as it still failed to start.

Hanna strode over to him.

'What's the problem with it?'

'Flat battery, if I had to guess. We need something to give it a nudge.'

'We have something,' she said.

'What?' asked Arata, his attention wandering back to the onrushing spirit mob.

'Me.'

She plunged her hand into the MSV's white bonnet; it passed through effortlessly, her fingers grasping for the engine.

'What are you doing?' said Arata.

'Shut up, and keep turning that ignition key.'

He did as he was told.

Hanna didn't pretend to understand the science behind it; she only knew the practical reality: that her spirit form carried some sort of electrical charge. Whether that had been enhanced by the radiation in the city, she wasn't sure, but the end result was that she was capable of pumping out electrical current. It varied in wattage, but she didn't need a lot; she just needed enough to spark this piece of junk into life.

She closed her eyes as her hand closed around the battery.

'Wait,' she said to Arata.

He stopped turning the key in the ignition.

Hanna visualised energy flowing through her fingertips. She didn't know if it was necessary, but it was necessary to her.

'Try it again,' she said.

Arata did as he was told.

The engine protested, but there was more guts to it. It was less a wet whine, more a throaty cough.

'Again,' said Hanna, her hand invisible in the bonnet.

This time, finally, it sparked into life.

She opened her eyes and looked towards the silent mob. They were a hundred feet away and closing at speed.

'How fast can this thing go?'

'We're about to find out,' said Arata. 'Jump on.'

The mob were close now, their hands grasping, and one look at them told Hanna that her language of the dead would be foreign to them. There was a blankness in their eyes that went far beyond the usual effect the soil's air had on the dead. It spoke of brain rot, of emptiness of thought, of reacting to instincts primal and visceral.

Their faces hinted at decay. Jaws were locked in a sort of rictus snarl; bodies were deformed, heads, legs and arms swollen.

Hanna gave the order for them to stop.

They ignored it.

Quite the legacy, Oma Jankie said. *You've created a city full of freaks. Disobedient ones, at that.*

Just as the spirits were on them, the MSV jerked forward, almost flipping Hanna off. She grasped the side, willing her hand solid, the vehicle picking up speed, wind beginning to whistle in her ears, the pillars blurring, the mob of spirits behind them reducing in size.

'We're going to make it,' shouted Arata, his gloved hands gripping the steering wheel in triumph.

I am, thought Hanna.

I don't know about you.

The MSV wasn't going to set any land-speed records, but it didn't need to; the access hatch they were after was actually less than a mile away. The vehicle began to scream in protest when it was pushed above thirty miles per hour, but it got them there quickly enough.

Arata brought it to a stop. The tunnel stretched on in front of them, but as far as Hanna was concerned, it could go on to the ends of the earth. It was the access hatch she was concerned with. It stood alone, thirty feet above their heads, a metal ladder leading up to it.

'That's it?'

'That's it,' said Arata. 'We get it open, it'll spit us out about half a kilometre from the airstrip.'

'Almost seems too easy,' said Hanna.

'I'd hate to see what hard looks like,' Arata replied.

Arata went up the ladder first.

It wasn't easy; the radiation suit he was wearing was hardly designed for climbing ladders, and the respirator and face mask reduced his visibility to almost nothing.

'Shit.'

Hanna looked upwards. Arata was grasping the handle of the metal hatch, desperately trying to force it open.

'It won't move,' he said.

A glance down.

The spirit mob had caught up with them. They were advancing as one.

Another curse from Arata. No matter how vigorously he yanked on the handle, it steadfastly refused to give.

The mob were closer now, moving in that deathly silent way of theirs. They'd be on them soon.

Why were they chasing them? Was it the living, breathing Arata they wanted? The smell of him? Or was it Hanna, their former leader? Why had the language of the dead stopped working?

It's like you say: they've had too much radiation, Oma Jankie's voice called out. *What you did was unnatural, against the order of things. This is the result. It's why you need to get out of there.*

'Let me try,' said Hanna.

Ignoring her grandmother's voice, she grasped the base of the ladder and quickly pulled herself up. She felt Arata shudder as her body passed through his; to the spirits below, they would have looked like a badly exposed negative, her teenage form inexpertly spliced over Arata's radiation-suited one.

'This will go better if you give me a little room to work in.'

Arata grumbled but obeyed, his wincing face just about visible as he made space for her.

'Hurry,' he said. 'They're almost here.'

Hanna allowed herself a final look at the spirits as they reached the base of the ladder. They had been her loyal subjects, souls that were supposed to welcome her new movement on the soil. Now they were nothing but a pack of slack-jawed slavering zombies. Still, they deserved something from her before she went. A final offering, for old times' sake.

She kicked out, the heel of her left foot connecting with Arata's masked head. He screamed in surprise as he plummeted down, his body hitting the concrete, the spirits quickly over-whelming him, tearing at the radiation suit.

He'd served his purpose, but there was no place for living souls in the future she intended to build.

She pushed her way formlessly through the hatch, the night sky greeting her, and got to her feet, kidding herself she could feel the difference in the air. She couldn't imagine that planes were usually allowed to land in the area – it was too close to the radiation epicentre – but it seemed Lucia had the power to circumnavigate that. An airport sat in the distance, its lights softly twinkling.

After a final look at the hatch – and taking a few seconds to listen to Arata's screams below – she started running to-wards them.

Chapter 21

East Berlin, 1984

Voices. Distant, but getting closer. Excited whispers and muted yelps. Two men.

It's so long since I've heard human beings. So long since I've seen any. Will they be able to see me? Possibly, if the equipment still works. The scientists here used the TV monitor and microphone to communicate with me. Lucia, of course, needed neither, but I couldn't get that lucky again. Whoever is making their way up these stairs will not have the ability to see the likes of me. Still. For me to see them will be enough. That will nourish me.

'This place is fucking *crazy*.'

'Sci-fi, man. Pure sci-fi.'

'You hear that crackle? Sounds like electricity or something.'

'You think it's safe?'

'Fucking East German, man, sure not to be. Nothing works here.'

Two men. German. The ease of their exchange I find heart-warming.

The lights flicker into life. They still work, then, which makes sense; they had to leave the power on to keep me imprisoned.

Two young men stand in the centre of the room, struck dumb. Their appearance is startling.

The one on the left wears a tatty trench coat. It's festooned with safety pins and, it appears, bottle tops. He wears fat leather boots, black in colour. His hair, I assume, must be some sort of accident. It's shaved at the sides but long and spiky in the middle, like a pink shark's fin. His companion is even more garishly attired; his hair is a tumbledown thicket of red spikes, and he wears a white T-shirt emblazoned with the words *FUCK WHITE POWER*.

I don't know what this means.

'Colonel,' says the man with the pink shark fin, 'what the fuck have we found here?'

'Flames,' Colonel replies, 'I don't fucking know.'

They come closer to my glass cage.

'Hello.' My voice crackles over the speakers.

The two men cry out in surprise.

'Who's there?' asks Colonel.

I step forward, pressing my face against the glass. Of course they can't see me.

'The monitor,' I say, my voice a hissy crackle. 'Look in the monitor.'

'Fuck,' says Flames, running his fingers through his red hair. 'Look at the *monitor*, man.'

Colonel does, then takes a step backwards. 'What the fuck?'

'This some sort of Stasi joke?' says Flames.

'It's coming from this room,' Colonel says. 'It's the cage in front of us.'

Flames looks from the monitor to the cage. 'There's nothing there.'

'There is,' I say, waving at the screen. 'There's me.'

The two garishly dressed men exchange a look.

'This is creepy, man,' Colonel says.

'Yeah,' says Flames. 'Cool, though. What is it? Like, a projection?'

'I'm not a projection,' I say. 'I'm a spirit. A ghost, if you prefer.'

'Yeah, right,' says Flames.

'You're arguing with a projection,' smirks Colonel, his face more confident than his tone.

'No,' I reply. 'He's not.'

Flames steps forward and taps on the glass.

Colonel watches, transfixed, as I tap back.

'What are you?' he asks. 'What's with the fucking Nazi Youth uniform?'

So I tell him.

Eventually they believe my story. Or at least they move beyond disbelieving it. There's only so long you can converse with a projection until you begin to accept the unacceptable. No one knows that better than I.

They tell me they're something called punks. They believe in everything and nothing. They want to bring down the corrupt socialist system they are governed by, but they want to headbutt the life out of life first.

It's not immediately obvious how they plan to do this.

'We're looking for somewhere to practise,' says Colonel.

'Practise what?' I ask.

'We're in a band,' Flames says, his chest puffing up.

'A brass band, you mean?'

The two punks exchange a look and a sneer.

'Punk rock, man,' says Colonel.

'We'll show you,' Flames adds.

And they do.

Their instrumentation is crude, the sound they make cruder. Colonel plays a guitar, the amplified noise it makes like a dying cat. He also sings, though it appears to me to be more like screaming. Flames sits behind a drum kit, savaging it with unrelenting fury. It is, by any qualification, a truly appalling sound.

It's also one of the most thrilling things I have ever seen.

There's a primal abandon to it that speaks to me, shakes me by my Hitler Youth lapels like a call to action, demands I take a stand. When they finally work out how to release me from my cage, I take to jerking to the racket, the music they generate gathering me up and spinning me around the room. All the rage and frustration that has festered within me bursting to come out, the songs they play allowing it to.

Colonel and Flames end up moving into the abandoned laboratory. I'm glad of it. After so long alone, I crave their company and conversation. They are as fascinated by me, as I am by them. I tell them about the experiments the Nazis carried out on me. How I was taken by the Americans and co-opted to spy for them. How I was sold to the East German security forces by Director Matthews and then abandoned here.

I don't tell them about the Pen. There's only so much the human mind can take on.

The two punks sit drinking one night. I am cross-legged in my cage, my form visible on the monitor.

Colonel waves a smouldering roll-up cigarette at me. 'You see, Jacob, you're just like us. You've been used by the state. They're all the same, West Germans, East Germans, Americans, whatever. They don't care about the common man. Only about what they can take from him.'

'That's true,' I say. 'People have been taking things from me all my life. My death, too.'

'Don't worry, brother,' Flames tells me, dragging deeply on his cigarette, 'because change is coming.'

'What do you mean?'

'There's lots of people like us,' Colonel replies. 'Angry at the way life is laid out for us by the state. Prepared to do something about it.'

'Laid out?'

Flames gets to his feet, seemingly energised by the question. 'The state decides what job we must do. Arrests us if we refuse to do it. Do you know it's illegal not to have a job? It's sick, man.'

'Too much future, that's what we call it,' Colonel says, grinding his cigarette into the concrete floor. 'Every last minute of our shitty lives mapped out. We say: fuck that. We say: we'll create our own future.'

'That's why our band's called the Ungrateful Dead,' Flames adds. 'East Germany's a zombie state. People here trudge along doing what they're told till they die. We're going to go on the road, show them there's another way. Carry the word. There are other punks in other cities. We're a fucking rallying cry for them. *We* are the people! *We* are the power!'

'Fucking right,' says Colonel, putting an arm around his bandmate.

'You're leaving, then?' I ask, inadequately keeping the disappointment from my voice.

Colonel looks at the monitor. 'You should come with us, Jacob. You're part of the band now.'

'Great idea, man,' Flames says. 'Pogo the fuck out of it on stage.'

'If I leave here, you won't be able to see. Hear me, either. I'll be invisible to you.'

'But we'll know you're there, man,' Colonel says enthusiastically. 'Be a fucking kick to know that, when none of the crowd does. Get you in our band photos, too. It'll be a secret, just between the three of us.'

This idea thrills and terrifies me in equal measure. To escape this room, to have a purpose again . . . it's almost too much to take in. But then it's so long since I've been anywhere else but here. This place has become a sort of sick comfort. And they wouldn't be able to talk to me any more. I'd be with them, but apart from them at the same time.

You might find Lucia.

The thought pops into my head uninvited. It's nonsense, of course. What are the chances of finding one person in a country as vast as East Germany? That's if she's returned from Russia. Still, logic can't quite choke down hope. And what's the alternative? Festering down here, hoping someone else comes along in a few years' time to befriend me?

'All right,' I say. 'I'll come.'

So follow the best years of my death.

Colonel has bought a van to transport the equipment on their impromptu tour of the country. There is a tension to every moment on the road, because what the men do is illegal, and punishable by prison, or worse. Their songs are inflammatory and defaming of the state. The performances they give are clandestine and all the more thrilling for it. The band have no licence to perform, essential in this tightly regulated country, but they don't care, and neither do their audience. They gather, these punks, in ever-increasing numbers as the Ungrateful Dead traverse the country. There are no signs or posters advertising these concerts, more an underground pulse that courses under East Germany's skin.

We are the people! We are the power!

The crowds get bigger. The concerts get better. And all the time I'm there, in the centre of it all, unseen, onstage with the band, allowing my body to be buffeted by the brutal chords and splintered melodies. Colonel and Flames look for me at each gig. They can't see me, of course, but I flatter myself that they can feel me somehow. Flatter myself that sometimes members of the audience can, too.

It's a strange existence. I am surrounded by life that is largely oblivious to me. It's both thrilling and miserable.

I don't find Lucia. I know I'll never see her again, but that doesn't stop me looking. Hoping. Praying.

A couple of months into the tour, Colonel and Flames play their biggest gig yet. It's in, of all places, a church.

The clergy, it transpires, are unlikely allies of the punks. The church is tolerated by the authorities, if not liked, and operates independently of many of the country's more draconian laws.

'Deacon Voigt is sympathetic to the cause, as are many in the church,' Colonel explains to a girl in a bar. 'They know we punks are persecuted, and so they give us a haven to come to. This concert will be important. Five punk bands, all political, all anti-authority. It's a call to arms. After tonight, everything changes.'

It transpires he's right, but not in the way he imagines.

The band sound-check at the front of the church. I've never seen them do this before – they feel it cuts into their time for drinking alcohol – so there can be little doubt that they are nervous, and that this concert is as important as they say. I sit in the front pew. I wish I could talk to them, let them know I'm there somehow. Instead, I'm back to being a wandering spirit. I observe life. I don't take part in it.

The pew behind me creaks. I turn to see a clergyman. He's staring at the band, a small smile on his lips, nodding his head ever so slightly in time to the music. He looks like no man of religion I've ever seen before. He has thick black hair that flows down past his shoulders, and a luxuriant black beard. His skin

260

is tanned. Leathered. He could be anything from twenty years old to fifty. His eyes are bewitching: one of them is green, one of them grey. They turn on me.

'Hello,' he says.

I look over my shoulder, assuming he's addressing the band. It's soon obvious that he isn't; that he's talking directly to me.

He smiles. 'Don't be alarmed. You're welcome here.'

'You can see me?'

He nods. 'A gift I've always enjoyed. And it is a gift, though many don't view it that way.' He leans forward, the pew groaning as he does so. 'My name is Ralf Voigt; I'm a deacon here. What's your name?'

'Jacob,' I reply, absurdly grateful that someone can see and hear me.

'A fine name. How long ago was it that you died, Jacob?'

'What year is it now?'

'Nineteen eighty-seven,' the deacon replies.

'Decades ago. In the forties.'

The deacon frowns. 'I suspected as much, by the uniform you wear.'

I look down at my Nazi Youth garb. I'm ashamed of it, yet I have no way of removing it.

'It's strange,' he continues. 'I've met spirits of your age before, and their faculties are always eroded. It's tragic. You're sharp as a tack, though.'

'I'm different.'

'Different how?'

'You wouldn't understand.'

He laughs. 'There's much I don't understand about life and death. You could teach me a lot, Jacob.'

The band's clatter fades to nothingness.

'What brings you here?' asks the deacon.

'Those men found me when I was at my lowest,' I reply.

'Three years ago, now. I believe in their mission. I follow them as they tour the country.'

'They can see you?'

'They could when they found me. Not any more.'

The deacon nods, seemingly satisfied with this. 'My door is always open if you ever want to come here to talk. I like to think I provide solace to both the living and the dead.'

I thank him, but think little of it. I assume I'll never see Deacon Voigt again after tonight.

I'm wrong.

Chapter 22

Music on the stereo. His partner sipping a turgid coffee. A border of condensation framing the windscreen. A darkened building opposite, hiding its light and secrets. Joe's memory might have been sketchy, but it felt like every stakeout he'd ever been on.

'Time's wasting, Lazarus,' said Hans. 'Whatever you're going to do, do it now.'

'When I hacked the deacon's computer, this address was one that was buried good and deep,' said Joe. 'Isiah Matthews, whoever he is, should be in this nursing home.'

'Why do we care?' asked Hans.

'There isn't a single trace of him online. I mean, not a single entry. That means he's gone to a great deal of effort to scrub out his digital footprint.'

'Well, go in and find that footprint,' said Hans, 'and if it gets us closer to the Spook dealer, so much the better.'

Joe still had his memories, and with each passing hour, he was adding to his collection.

He'd made sure to write them down in the back of his notebook, and was confident that Hans hadn't cottoned on to the fact. That still seemed to be the right call. It wasn't anything

Hans had done, more a gut feeling. Joe was sure he'd never heard about a Dying Squad division permanently sequestered on the soil before. It wouldn't make sense – should be impossible, in fact, as the living world's air would erode both memories and mission from Squad members' consciousness. He couldn't be certain – until a few hours ago, he'd struggled to remember his own name – but some instinct told him that was so.

If that instinct was correct, it meant Hans and Lucia had lied to him. That they had their own agenda. So he'd carry on playing memory-addled until their true intentions became clear. Not too memory-addled, though, because whatever their game was, he had a case to crack. There was someone at the end of this trail of breadcrumbs, a Mr or Mrs Big who was producing and funnelling out Spook – someone who was prepared to kill for it – and if it took a house call to a pensioner to find out who that someone was, then so be it.

A scan of the reception area didn't reveal any names or room numbers, but it did reveal a laptop computer. After doing the biz with the Ghost in the Machine, Joe was able to bring up a list of the home residents.

He scrolled down them, his eyes hunting for the prize.

There.

Isiah Matthews. Room 108.

Not dead, then.

Not that that meant much in his game.

The reception might have been deserted, but there were signs of life elsewhere: a couple of night-shift orderlies chatting on one floor, a half-arsed cleaner pushing a mop around on another. The floor he wanted, though, the first, was mercifully deserted.

He came to Room 108 and tried to look in. A blind had

been drawn over the window. He didn't know exactly what he was going to do when he got inside the room, just that he needed to do something. It'd work itself out. It always seemed to when time was short and the chips were down.

He eased through the door.

Given the lateness of the hour and the age of the resident, he'd assumed Isiah Matthews would be tucked up in bed. Instead, he was sitting bolt upright in a chair, legs crossed, facing the door. A cigarette rested between his fingers, glowing faintly. This was the man Joe had seen in the photo back at the church, he was sure of it. Older, of course, but those matinee-idol looks hadn't totally faded.

The room wasn't what he had expected. The nursing-home bedrooms he'd known were things of bleach and order; this one exuded bohemian clutter. Vinyl spun on a turntable, jazz seeping from it (Joe's mind settling gratefully on the groove), and a green lamp in the corner cast everything in a warm, comforting glow, highlighting the classic film posters that adorned the walls. The furniture, too, looked tastefully old. Certainly it wasn't nursing-home issue.

If Matthews (assuming this *was* Matthews) was afraid of being caught smoking indoors, he didn't show it. He exuded self-assurance, with his well-groomed pencil-thin moustache, his monogrammed slippers and his expensive-looking smoking jacket.

He was also staring directly at Joe.

'Hello,' he said quietly. 'Who are you?'

Joe blinked. 'You can see me?'

Matthews tapped his cigarette into the waiting ashtray, then took in a lungful of smoke. 'My eyesight's not what it was, but I don't think I'll ever lose that particular gift.'

American, thought Joe. 'Are you Isiah Matthews?'

Matthews gave him a sad smile. 'I suppose so. For a long

time, I pretended to be someone else. That's one of the few benefits of getting old: your need to pretend fades.' He nodded at Joe. 'And who might you be?'

Joe told him.

'And what are you doing here, Joe Lazarus? I've only ever met one spirit with your clarity of thought before.'

'Who was that?'

Matthews smiled. 'You haven't answered my question yet.'

Joe straightened up, switching into cop mode. 'I'm investigating a drug kingpin. A murder, too. That last part is what led me to you.'

Matthews waved his cigarette. 'I've heard about your sort. You're one of those spectral police officers. The Dying Squad, isn't it?'

Curiouser and curiouser, thought Joe. How does he know about the Squad?

'I am,' he admitted, 'though as much as anything, I'm a concerned citizen, one that doesn't want Berlin drowning in drugs.'

'You're referring to Spook, I assume,' said Matthews, grinding out his cigarette in the ashtray. 'The drug that lets regular people see the dead, like I can.'

Joe nodded.

'A wicked invention,' said Matthews. 'Living with a curse like mine requires years of discipline. You can't just pop a pill and expect there to be no consequences.'

He motioned to a chair opposite him. 'You're not the first visitor I've had tonight. It's a bad place to be when you can see the dead, a retirement home. Your room becomes a revolving door of confused spirits who've been unable to pass through to the other side. I can do little but listen to them and offer them solace.'

'I knew someone like that once,' said Joe. 'He turned out to be a cold-blooded killer.'

Matthews laughed. 'I'm no killer, though plenty would consider me a swindler and a betrayer. The President of the United States, for example.'

'And are you?' asked Joe.

The smile fell from Matthews' face. 'I'm a weak man who made mistakes during his life. That's why I've spent the last few decades hiding in Germany rather than living in America. Why are *you* here, Joe?'

Joe shuddered.

'Is something the matter?' said Matthews.

'It's been a long time since anyone actually used my first name. I forgot what it sounded like.'

'Strange how small kindnesses are often the biggest,' said Matthews, straightening his smoking jacket.

Joe finally slipped into the chair, noting its placement.

'As I said, you're not the first spirit I've had in here tonight,' said Matthews, noting Joe noting. 'Although when you get to my age, there's always the chance you'll be the last.'

'I'm here about Deacon Voigt,' said Joe. 'I believe you knew him.'

Matthews winced slightly. Reaching into his jacket, he took out a packet of cigarettes, liberating another cancer stick from the packet and lighting it. 'I always knew someone would come.'

'Why?'

He drew deeply on his cigarette. 'The deacon shares my gift for seeing the dead.'

'So I gather,' said Joe.

'There aren't many of us who can do it naturally. That marks us down as persons of interest.'

'How did you meet him?'

Matthews smiled ruefully, taking another drag. 'At a gay club, of all places.'

'Were you in a relationship with him?'

'A relationship sounds so formal. It was the great love affair of my life. Whether the same could be said for Ralf, well, you'd have to ask him.'

Joe shifted in his chair. 'That's going to be difficult. Ralf's dead.'

Matthews stared at him. 'That can't be true.'

'I assure you it is. I found his body an hour ago.'

The old man shook his head, as if trying to repel the truth. 'How?'

'Suicide,' said Joe. 'At least, that's what it looked like. Unless you know different. Is there anyone who would have wanted him dead?'

Matthews slumped back in his chair, the cigarette almost slipping through his fingers, a trail of ash falling from it. 'Ralf made a lot of enemies over the years. He was something of a firebrand under the old East German regime. Something of a figurehead, too. Anyone alternative in those days got grouped together; the queers, the punks, the hippies, they were united by people like Ralf. The church was seen as an enemy of the state, if a tolerated one.'

'The Wall fell a long time ago,' said Joe.

Matthews nodded, tossing the cigarette into the ashtray. 'No one worked harder for that than Ralf.'

'When was the last time you saw him?'

'Long enough for me to be no use to you. If that's what you're hoping.'

'Why did your relationship end?'

'What does it matter?'

'I need all the information I can find,' said Joe. 'It can help me get justice for Ralf, for one thing. I found a picture of the two of you, from your younger days. You still meant something to him, clearly.'

Matthews gave a wry smile. 'Aren't there living policemen around to do all this digging?'

'Things get missed that people like me can spot,' said Joe. 'Being dead has its advantages, believe it or not.'

'I do,' said Matthews. 'I was part of a government initiative that celebrated it.'

Joe leaned in. Now they were getting somewhere.

'What initiative?'

'I was part of a programme that used the dead in espionage work,' said Matthews. 'I collected them, then put them to work spying.'

Joe shook his head. 'You're joking.'

'Am I? I so rarely find anything funny nowadays, it's difficult to tell. I'm quite serious, Lazarus. It's hard to catch something you can't see. Even harder to know when they're spying on you.'

'Did the deacon know about this initiative?'

'He knew some of it,' Matthews said, 'but by the time he came into my life, I was done with it. Unfortunately, I went the way of many other poorly paid government officials: I sold out my country.'

Joe shifted in his seat. 'How?'

'How does anyone sell out? Another faction gives you money in exchange for your loyalty and principles. In this case, the East German government. They learned of a mission I was leading in Berlin and paid me handsomely to defect.' Matthews laughed. 'Thirty years ago, I'd have dressed that decision up. Now, what's the point? I took the money and ran. Or rather, stayed here.'

'What happened to the spirits under your care?'

He twitched slightly. 'That, I regret.'

He reached for the packet of cigarettes again, then thought better of it, resettling himself in his seat. 'There were five in the party. Most of the spirits we used were only good for one mission. It was their memories, you see; the longer they were in the living world, the less they could retain them.'

'You're preaching to the dead here,' said Joe.

'You seem to retain memories very well.'

'My memory's sketchy as hell.' He continued to soak up the jazz playing in the background, giving thanks for it.

'Regardless, you have *clarity*. The spirits I worked with didn't. They were trained for months to remember very specific details; to memorise documents or conversations, and this training was only ever good for a single mission. After that, they were useless and discarded as such.'

'Charming,' said Joe.

'I always rationalised it by seeing it as a kindness,' said Matthews, 'much as you would euthanise a terminally ill patient. The boy, though, was different.'

Joe frowned. 'The boy?'

'I first discovered Jacob in Germany. He was one of Himmler's occult projects, but truly, the Nazis never realised what they had with him. Unlike the others, Jacob never lost his memory. He was perfectly lucid, and fiercely intelligent. You can see what use such a child might be when it came to spying on your enemies.'

A boy. One who was dead. That meant something.

Joe retrieved his notebook, flicking through the pages. Ella, the overdosing punk fan, had mentioned a spirit child who was supposed to hang out with Colonel's band. Same city, but that didn't mean much.

Matthews nodded at it. 'You even have a notebook. You're adorable.'

'You were telling me about the boy,' said Joe.

'It was Jacob the East Germans paid me for,' said Matthews,

'and it was Jacob I felt the most guilt over. I'd developed a bond with him. It was almost like he was a real person.'

'Imagine,' said Joe.

'I had no idea what happened to him after I left him in the hands of the Stasi. I told Ralf about him, though, because Ralf knew *everyone*, including many of the stranded souls in the city. A spirit child who never lost his memory should have stood out.'

'And did Ralf – did Deacon Voigt – find him?' Joe asked.

'He did. Jacob turned up in his church one day. With a punk band, of all things.'

He turned up with a punk band. It is the same lad, then.

'How do you get from there to Voigt killing himself in his own church?' said Joe. 'I don't see the connection.'

Matthews sighed. 'As time went on, Ralf became more militant, more fixated on bringing the East German government down, and he didn't care who he used to further that cause. All of this brought unwanted attention in my direction, which was the opposite of what I wanted. It put me in a difficult position, and so I ended our relationship.'

Joe leaned forward. 'What would you say if I told you that I believe Ralf was one of the biggest drug dealers in the city?'

Matthews, who appeared to have aged by ten years, dipped his head. 'I would say that Ralf crossed so many lines in pursuit of what he thought was right, he wouldn't notice when he crossed ones he knew to be wrong.'

Joe considered this. 'Did you ever see Jacob again?'

'Ralf was my last contact with the boy. When our relationship ended, so did my connection to him.' The old man smiled. 'Jacob told me quite a tale once. Said he was destined to be a future leader of purgatory. Perhaps he's there now.'

'Perhaps he is,' said Joe.

But I'm willing to bet he isn't.

271

Joe walked, head down, towards the nursing home's reception area. There was a lot to unpack from what Matthews had told him; the trick was to pluck out the relevant bits. Certainly, the information on the deacon had value. Not his sexuality so much as his militancy. Old spies had long memories, and perhaps Voigt's disruptiveness in the past had caught up with him. Someone had murdered him, then made it look like suicide, perhaps. Why now, though? If he was the Spook dealer and someone was moving in on his territory, they wouldn't waste time mocking up a suicide; they'd just shoot the fucker in the face.

Sometimes suicide was just that. Maybe there was no conspiracy here, just tragedy.

Maybe the deacon simply couldn't cope with what he'd become.

Joe knew something about that.

Hans paced in front of his Mercedes, casting resentful looks towards the nursing home. He noticed Joe walking over and stiffened.

'You took your time.'

'Isiah Matthews was as chatty as he was surprising,' said Joe.

Hans opened the car door. 'Bore me with the details on the way. We need to go.'

'Go where?'

'I've got a lead on our Spook dealer. This is how real police work's done, Lazarus.'

Joe frowned. 'What lead?'

'Someone called. Said she has information.'

'And what does she want in return?'

'What does anyone want? Money.'

Hans slid into the driver's seat, a smug expression on his face.

Joe took his place in the passenger side. 'In this sort of investigation, if something comes easily to you, there's usually a reason.'

'The reason doesn't matter,' said Hans, 'only the result.'

'Which is what?'

'Our mystery informant giving us the name of the Spook supplier, and after that, us serving out cold, hard justice to them.'

Megan didn't notice that she'd dropped the phone on the ground.

She didn't notice the tourists who watched her with concern, momentarily ignoring the last remaining traces of the Berlin Wall. She didn't even notice the fact that she'd sunk to the concrete pavement, her knees kissing ice-cold puddles.

Her attention was centred on the fact that she was being suffocated from the inside.

It was like her whole body was in a vice, one that grew tighter by the second, making it impossible to breathe, let alone think.

—'Cept you *can* think, a voice said from somewhere. —A minute ago, you made a telephone call to a bloke called Hans. Set up a meeting. Remember?

Megan shut her eyes, hoping it would shut out the voice.

—It won't. It's me, Megs, Bits. I'm inside you. The pain of it's making it too much for you to cope with, but I can help you, if you let me.

Bits. She knew Bits. She *was* Bits, wasn't she?

—Fortunately for you, no, you're not. You're a great lass called Megan, who just happened to get possessed by the grubby likes of me. Remember?

She did, sort of. The pain made it hard to remember anything, but that made a weird sort of sense.

—We've got to get me out of you. When we find Joe, he's going to help with that. Until then, you just need to calm the fuck down. Me inside you this long, it's like being stuck in a tight-as-fuck tunnel. I'm going to break out. Understand?

Megan nodded, instantly regretting it as it unleashed a new tremor of pain.

—Need you to breathe. That's all. Easy as fuck. Take a breath in, hold it five seconds, then let it out. You ready?

She was.

—Breathe in.

She did.

—Hold it for five, four, three, two, one. Now: breathe out.

She did. It helped.

She repeated the process.

It helped a little more.

After several minutes, she felt the pressure ease.

She held a hand up to the collection of worried tourists who had gathered around. 'Panic attack,' she said, smiling weakly.

Those who understood her (and plenty who didn't) nodded, wandering away down the East Side Gallery.

Megan stuck out a hand to a wall depicting two men kissing, raising herself up.

Thanks. Not sure how many more of those I can take.

—We get Joe, you won't have to take any more. Just hold on a bit longer, love.

Megan leaned against the wall, looking out at the TV Tower in the distance.

Just a bit longer.

Chapter 23

When the blinding glare of white light faded (and it did so quickly this time) a sense of suffocating panic threatened to overwhelm Daisy-May. It was like she'd been buried alive, and for the first time in a long time, she remembered what it was to breathe, or to try to, her lungs screaming as she clawed desperately at the rubber mould covering her face.

Then she felt hands on her, strong, powerful, dependable things that promised salvation as she was hauled upwards, and felt those same hands on her face, helping her scrape free the death mask covering it.

A blurred vision of a room appeared, her mouth goldfish-bowling whatever passed for air into her lungs. Mabel stood over her, a look of concern on her face. 'You still with us, girl?'

Daisy-May convulsed with coughing, fighting to get her breath, the effort bending her double.

'She's not right,' she heard Mabel say.

'Give her a minute,' said Oma Jankie. 'It's always like this when they come up.'

As quickly as the coughing fit came, it went. Daisy-May got to her feet, Mabel steadying her. They seemed to be in an ancient apartment. The furniture was dated, too old to be antique, the style older than that.

'Where the fuck are we?'

'Oblivion,' said Mabel.

'Where the fuck's Oblivion?'

'Quite the mouth your Warden has,' said Oma Jankie, a sneer on her face. 'Doesn't even know about Oblivion. What have you been teaching her, Mabel?'

'Did it work?' said Mabel. 'Did she complete the trials?'

Daisy-May dusted herself off, pulling more air into her lungs. As she did so, she remembered what had happened in the last trial.

She hadn't been able to resist the language of the dead. She'd joined in with the slaughter of the living souls.

She'd enjoyed it, too.

She looked down at her hands. Her nails were broken, a crust of dried blood tattooed onto her fingertips.

'I—'

'She passed,' said Oma Jankie, interrupting her. 'I didn't think the girl had it in her.'

Daisy-May blinked. 'What?'

Mabel ran an appraising eye over her. 'That right?'

'I thought the trial was about strength,' said Daisy-May. 'I couldn't resist the language of the dead. I failed.'

'That wasn't the trial,' said Oma Jankie. 'The trial was about having the strength to work as part of a team when your natural inclination was to do the opposite. You're a loner, girl, yet you had the strength to be part of something bigger than yourself.'

'I helped slaughter innocents,' said Daisy-May.

'That wasn't real,' said Oma Jankie. 'Nothing in the trials is.'

Daisy-May held her fingers up. 'It felt fucking real.'

'What are you playing at, Oma?' Mabel was scowling.

'I thought you'd be happy,' Oma Jankie said. 'You wanted the girl restored, and here she is.'

Mabel looked suspiciously at the old woman, then reached

over to poke and prod Daisy-May. 'How do you feel?'

'Good. Better than good, to be honest. Pumped and ready to kick Remus's arse.'

'Not so fast,' said Oma Jankie. 'There's one final trial you must undergo.'

Daisy-May sighed. 'What have I got to do for the finale? Tap-dance with a bear?'

'The last trial is about sacrifice,' said Oma Jankie, 'because that's what the role of Warden is about. Sacrifice. Service.'

'Feel I proved myself on that score,' said Daisy-May.

Mabel nodded. 'More than once. What you planning, old woman?'

'It's nothing to do with what *I'm* planning,' Oma Jankie said primly. 'It's what the trials plan.'

'You've got an open bloody brief on that score,' said Mabel. 'You can't kid a kidder.'

Oma Jankie laughed. 'You always thought you knew better than me, little Mabel, even when you *were* little. When Rachel sent me here, she banished me, but she made me a custodian, too, one who could never leave.'

Daisy-May watched Mabel's face drop. 'What? What is it?'

'You must have known I'd ask it,' said Oma Jankie.

'Ask it or demand it?' said Mabel.

'They're the same thing.'

'Ask or demand *what*?' said Daisy-May. 'What are you two clowns on about?'

Oma Jankie turned to her. 'The sickness in you will be expunged if you pass one final trial.'

'Ex-what?'

'Obliterated, you illiterate. If you pass one final trial, you will be cured.'

'I feel fine,' said Daisy-May. 'Reckon that Gloop cancer's all the way gone.'

'It's not,' said Mabel. 'Not until you complete this last trial.'
She took her by the shoulders. 'There's only one answer you
can give to what she's about to ask you. Understand?'

'Nah, not really.'

'The role of Warden is one of sacrifice,' said Oma Jankie,
'and so you need to prove you're worthy of it by making one.'

Daisy-May thrust her hands into her pockets. 'What am I
supposed to do? Give up swearing? Abstain from piss-taking?'

Oma Jankie took a step closer to her. 'You need to choose
who is going to replace me here in Oblivion. Mabel – or you.'

Daisy-May frowned. 'What?'

'You're a wily old bitch,' said Mabel, shaking her head
in disgust.

'And you're a naïve one to think I'd have wanted anything
less,' said Oma Jankie.

'What do you mean, replace you?' said Daisy-May.

'I'm a custodian here,' said Oma Jankie. 'Responsible for
putting the chosen few through the trials. I can never return
to the Pen. Never go anywhere except this blasted apartment
room, unless I get someone to take my place.'

'And you want that to be me or Mabel,' said Daisy-May.
'Generous offer, love, but I think we'll probably pass.'

'One of us has to.'

She turned to Mabel. 'Why?'

Mabel cast a weary hand around the room. 'You can ask that
till you're blue in the face, girl, it's just the way of things. It's
written. Someone needs to be here to conduct the trials. The
Duchess honoured our grandmother by sending her here, but
it was a banishment in everything but name.'

She gathered herself. 'Obviously I'm the one who'll be
staying.'

'Will you fuck,' said Daisy-May.

'You think I've traipsed all this way to get you patched up, just to leave you here? The Pen needs you.'

Daisy-May thought back to the vision she'd had of the death camps, and the slaughtered Dispossessed within them.

'There has to be a way we can all leave this shithole,' she said. 'I'm the bleeding Warden, for Christ's sake. What's the point of being in charge if you can't demolish the odd law?'

'There isn't, and you can't,' said Oma Jankie.

'Being Warden's all about making hard decisions,' said Mabel. 'You're lucky, though, 'cos this one's a piece of piss. You choose me, then you get back to the Pen.'

She turned to her ancient grandmother. 'She's chosen. Let's get this show on the road.'

'It has to come from her,' said Oma Jankie. 'She has to say the words.'

'This is straight wrong,' said Daisy-May. 'I never signed up for anything like this.'

'No, the Duchess signed you up for worse,' said Mabel. 'Big part of me'll never forgive her for that, but what's done is done. You'll have worse choices in the years to come.'

Daisy-May kicked a toe into the dirt. 'What will you do here?'

'Going to be like a bleeding holiday,' said Mabel. 'No one mithering me for equipment. No Dispossessed pissing and wailing. An eternity of solitude sounds lovely. You'll be doing me a favour.'

'We both know that's bollocks.'

'It's time to choose,' said Oma Jankie.

'Bog off,' said Daisy-May. She considered the old woman. 'What happens to you if Mabel takes your place?'

Oma Jankie grinned, revealing missing teeth and a film of saliva. 'Isn't that obvious? I accompany you back to the Pen. There's much work to be done there.'

'The toilets *have* been playing up lately,' said Daisy-May. 'Best bring a plunger, you're gonna be busy.'

She turned to Mabel. 'I'll come back for you when I can.'

Mabel placed a rough hand on the girl's face. 'You won't. You'll live the afterlife that's due to you, and God willing, that'll take you to the Next Place. You won't give a single solitary thought to me, and you'll sure as hell shed me no tears.'

'Won't make a promise I can't keep there,' said Daisy-May.

'Remember who you are,' said Mabel. 'There'll be tests — voices — that'll make you doubt yourself. Block 'em out. You're Daisy-May, the bad-ass council-estate girl who became ruler of a realm. Remember that.'

Daisy-May nodded. 'Thanks for everything you've done for me.'

'When it comes to you, Daisy-May,' Mabel said, 'everything always felt like nothing at all.'

'What do you think of Berlin?'

Hanna watched as the city blurred by, the early-morning sunshine bathing it in a golden light it didn't seem to deserve. A cross glowed in the distance, straddling the top of a run-down building. Crumbling edifices rubbed shoulders with gleaming skyscrapers. The place, it seemed to her, was a collection of badly matched house guests, all trying to make it work.

'It's a city like any other,' she said eventually. 'The good and bad of that, I leave for you to decide.'

Lucia smiled, adjusting herself in the limo's back seat. 'Berlin's somewhere I've always drifted back to. The place seems to have a hold on me.'

'I envy you that,' Hanna replied. 'I've never felt that sort of connection to a place.'

'What about Tokyo? The Tokyo you crafted, I mean?'

Hanna tapped a finger against the window, seemingly bored. 'That turned out to be a disappointment.'

'Every visionary in history contended with a few failures,' said Lucia. 'I certainly did. It's what genius is powered by.'

Hanna smirked at her. 'That's what you'd count yourself as, is it?'

'It will do until a better word comes along.'

Hanna tilted her head, her leather mask creaking as she did so. 'And you can see me.'

Lucia nodded. 'I have your old paymasters to thank for that. The Pen had many fingers in many pies on the soil.'

'And you were one of those pies.'

'The programme I was co-opted into was, yes. Children genetically manipulated at birth to see the dead. A death sentence eventually, because to enable that state, to shock the body into it, your sister and her ilk engineered inoperable tumours to slowly grow within us. Mine haven't manifested themselves yet, but it's only a matter of time.'

'So this is about revenge, then,' said Hanna.

Lucia snorted. 'Revenge is for losers. I've brought you here because you're a winner, one who isn't afraid to make difficult decisions. Tokyo was a difficult decision, one many would have baulked at, yet you followed through. That's a rare quality.'

'A quality you need, apparently,' said Hanna, 'otherwise I wouldn't be here. I doubt you're in the habit of airlifting stranded spirits out of ruined cities.'

Lucia reached out and took a bottle of water from the door panel next to her. 'I made you an offer once, when we first met in Tokyo. It remains open. I want us to rule the Pen together.'

Hanna looked out of the window. 'I can't fault your ambition, even if I doubt your sanity.'

'It's that imagination that makes the impossible possible,' said Lucia. 'It means I can produce a drug that allows the living to see the dead. It allows me to co-opt amnesia-riddled ghost policemen to run missions for me. And it means I can build a bridge that links the land of the living with the land of the dead.'

The atmosphere in the car changed.

'You said that before,' said Hanna, 'and it was nonsense then. Man-made technology could never concoct such a thing.'

'Impossible is a concept I find rather passé,' said Lucia. 'I wave to it when it's in the rear-view mirror.'

'You're telling me you have a way of travelling to the Pen,' said Hanna, the excitement in her voice unmistakable.

Here we are, Oma Jankie's voice said. *I told you an opportunity would present itself.*

'I am,' Lucia said. 'I've travelled there myself, many times.'

Hanna shook her head. 'How?'

'I had a little help,' said Lucia, dragging a finger through the condensation on the bottle in her hand. 'Vision only takes you so far.'

'Help from whom?'

'That's not important. We finished what the Nazis started and built a bridge to the Pen. Now we just need someone to lead us over it.'

This is an opportunity, Hanna thought. New Tokyo was a worthwhile pursuit, but it was always a consolation prize, an attempt to re-create the Pen on the soil. If I could return to the real thing to rule . . .

Isn't this what I promised? said Oma Jankie. *Getting back there is only half the job, though. Remember that.*

I remember you promised to deliver Daisy-May on a platter for me.

Oma Jankie laughed. *And I will. Everything's going to plan.*

Hanna turned to Lucia.

'The current Warden you want me to usurp: what exactly is your plan concerning her?'

Lucia smiled. 'All in good time. Simply know that I have one.'

Daisy-May adjusted herself in the captain's seat, wanting it to consume her whole. Oma Jankie sat next to her, a wide grin on her face. Chestnut perched on the blimp's control desk, openly staring at the two of them.

'Going to get old fast, that gawping,' said Daisy-May.

'You're alive, though,' said Chestnut.

'Technically, I'm dead.'

'You know what I mean.'

'With you, I never really do,' said Daisy-May. 'It's one of your better qualities.'

Chestnut nodded towards Oma Jankie and spoke in a stage whisper. 'What happened to Mabel?'

'That's not Mabel, you tool.'

'Who is it, then?'

Oma Jankie grinned at Chestnut, enraptured. 'It talks. How does it talk?'

'I open my mouth and words come out,' said Chestnut.

'But you're Dispossessed,' said Oma Jankie.

'Plenty of shit's changed since you were abusing your grand-daughters on the soil,' said Daisy-May. 'It's a whole new world.'

Oma Jankie looked behind her. 'And there are more Dispossessed in the back. Children. It's almost like they're real people.'

'If you're going to come back to the Pen, you need to update your thinking,' said Daisy-May. 'Dispossessed are the same as you and me.'

'They're mongrels,' said Oma Jankie, 'and need to be treated as such. Remus has *that* right, at least.'

'That vision you showed me of the Pen: it's true, then?'

'Every last bit of it,' said Oma Jankie, a small smile on her lips.

Daisy-May shook her head. 'Fuck.'

'What are your intentions when you return to the Pen?' said Oma Jankie. 'Remus isn't the adversary you imagine. His methods are agricultural, but his heart's in the right place.'

'His heart's coal-fucking-black, which is probably why you two get on so well. He tried to force me to abdicate. Helped round up the kids in the back to be experimented on, too. He's going to get his, trust me.'

'I could be of great assistance to you there, you know,' said Oma Jankie, leaning forward conspiratorially. 'My whole purpose was to prepare my grandchildren for the Pen. My knowledge of it is encyclopedic. I know where all the bodies are buried, so to speak.'

I bet you do, thought Daisy-May. You probably dug half the graves.

'How about you guide us back to the Pen? Let's start with that, then see how we go from there.'

'Of course,' said Oma Jankie, bowing her head.

'You think you can pilot this thing?' Daisy-May said to Chestnut.

'Piece of piss,' Chestnut replied. 'And Mabel said we sail it, not pilot it.' She frowned. 'Where *is* Mabel?'

Daisy-May squeezed her fists together, trying to push down the anger, glaring at Oma Jankie. 'You just doomed your granddaughter to an eternity of isolation.'

'Actually, *you* did that.'

'Because you gave me no choice. You didn't even say goodbye.'

'It's not like that in our family,' said Oma Jankie. 'Your up-bringing was almost certainly more conventional.'

'My mum had a new boyfriend every week,' said Daisy-May. 'Lots of them used me as an ashtray. I know fuck-all about convention. And that doesn't explain why you couldn't have given Mabel a hug.'

Oma Jankie waved a hand dismissively. 'We're wasting time. What's your plan when we get back to the Pen?'

My plan? My plan's to watch you like a fucking hawk. I don't trust you. I don't like you. Going to proceed on the basis that you're a wolf amongst sheep and you'll eat the lot of us if given the chance.

Daisy-May shuddered. Her experience in the trials – particularly the last one – stuck to her. She'd lost control. Whatever Oma Jankie said, she'd failed that last trial. She hadn't been strong enough to resist the language of the dead. Which begged the question: why had the old crone passed her? What did she stand to gain from it?

Freedom, she supposed. She was patched up, and Mabel had been willing to take Oma Jankie's place just to get Daisy-May back in the game.

There was something else, though. Something she couldn't see yet.

'Well?' said Oma Jankie. 'What's next?'

Daisy-May stiffened. She looked out of the cockpit window, the aged apartment block receding in the distance. 'I need to round up an army. To stand any chance of doing that, I'm going to need a little legal advice.'

Clouds that looked like they'd been irrigated from someone's colon. Huge swathes of fuck-all. The pencil sketch of an unending wall in the distance. A blasted-free-of-colour landscape. Chlorine so strong it was like it was sweating from your pores.

God damn, it was good to see the Pen.

After they'd limped through Oblivion, they'd set the airship down in an area a few kilometres from the Downs. Daisy-May had half expected a battalion of Uriel-like demons to descend upon them, but their arrival had gone mercifully unnoticed, or so she hoped.

Not that everyone was happy about it.

'I'm not a fucking babysitter,' said Chestnut.

'You can say that again,' said Daisy-May. 'I'd be docking your potty mouth its wages if you were.'

'Why can't *she* do it,' said Chestnut, sticking a thumb in Oma Jankie's direction. 'She's an adult.'

'I'm not letting her within a hundred feet of those kids without me being there,' said Daisy-May quietly. 'You neither. She's got a lack of boundaries when it comes to the Dispossessed. Doesn't consider them real people. Not sure what Ofsted would say about putting someone like that in charge of a bunch of traumatised kids.'

'Why don't we let the kids go?' said Chestnut.

'Not until I know what we're letting them go *to*,' said Daisy-May. 'If half the shit's true that I saw in the trials, I want to keep them with us.'

Chestnut nodded towards Oma Jankie.

'So she's going with you?'

Daisy-May sighed. 'Yeah, she's going with me. Means I can keep an eye on the mad old cow.'

Chestnut shifted on her feet. 'You walking to the Downs?'

'Nah. Mabel's left me a present to speed things up a bit.'

Daisy-May had never ridden a motorbike before – let alone one with a sidecar attached – which she supposed was lucky, because the thing she was currently perched on barely passed as one.

It had the chassis of a motorbike, sure. Two wheels, and handlebars that looked like souped-up coat hangers. It was there that the similarities ended, though, because instead of metal, the bike's shell seemed to be more organic. When she touched it, it was like touching skin, though it seemed to be fragile, almost like tissue paper. This translated into the bike's weight, or lack of it; it had been laughably easy for her to drag it from the blimp's cargo bay.

Oma Jankie looked up at her from the sidecar, which, Daisy-May had noted, was made from the same material as the bike proper. With any luck, her bony arse would drop out of the bottom.

'What are we waiting for?' she said.

Good question.

There wasn't an ignition, which was fortunate, as Daisy-May didn't have a key. Instead, when she reached out and took hold of the handlebars, an engine she couldn't see roared into life.

'Cool,' she said, remembering how to grin. 'Sit tight, Janko. Got a feeling this might be a bumpy ride.'

She twisted the throttle and the bike jackknifed forwards, fortunately not tipping her over the handlebars but instead staying rigid between her legs, the sidecar to her left loose but not too loose, moving when she moved, dipping when she dipped, the wind yanking her short pink hair this way and that, an undeniable sense of elation filling her. She was still here. She was still breathing, or whatever it was that the dead did. She was still fighting.

Going to keep it that way, she thought, 'cos those smacked-arse demons aren't going to take themselves down.

That enthusiasm didn't last long: what Daisy-May saw as they reached the peak of the hill was enough for her to kill the bike's engine.

'What I saw in the trials. It was reality, rather than a glimpse of what might be.'

'I did warn you,' said Oma Jankie.

'Warning someone, then that someone seeing it with their own peepers are two different things.'

287

And they were, because it had been like watching TV foot-age compared to what she was seeing now.

On the horizon, now as much of a fixture as the Pen wall, were dozens of defiant black squares. All of them had pencil-sketch chimneys jutting from their roofs, wisps of sick smoke leaking from them. They looked like they'd been there for ever, as unmovable a part of the Pen as the smell of bleach and the teeming Dispossessed, who were lined up like ants outside the factories, their number so vast it was as if they weren't really moving at all.

This was what she'd seen in the trials.

What she hadn't seen was the damage to the Downs itself. The rabbit warren of Dispossessed shacks and buildings had been razed to the ground. Burned smoke drifted lazily, most of the settlements concertinaed flat. Whereas before the streets had hummed and buzzed with life, now there was nothing save for smouldering piles of rubble. There was just one building that was still intact, and it was that one building that gave Daisy-May hope.

The courthouse, where she'd met the Judge for the first time and sought his counsel. Where he'd given that counsel on the woman who didn't glimmer and the missing children. The fact that it was still standing meant there was still a chance the Judge was, too. During the short period of time she'd spent with him, he'd struck her as the sort to fight with the last drop of his undead breath. Certainly that was what she was counting on.

'There's nothing left here, girl. You're wasting time,' said Oma Jankie.

'There's nothing left here, *ma'am*,' said Daisy-May, not look-ing at the old woman. 'And you're wrong, 'cos there is.'

She guided the bike down the hill towards the Downs, the silence that greeted them eerie and unsettling. Normally this was a place of screams and curses, of clicks and whistles, not the euthanised ghost town that lay before her. Daisy-May's skin prickled unpleasantly as they drove down the winding street to the courthouse. Bodies had been piled on the sides of the road, some of them still smoking.

Because those ballsy fuckers fought to the end. They weren't content to be led to their death in the factories. They made a last stand and died where they fell.

'It's too quiet,' said Oma Jankie. 'I don't like it.'

'In rare agreement with you there,' said Daisy-May, letting the motorbike coast. 'Keep those old peepers of yours open.'

'What are you hoping to achieve here?'

'Enlightenment. Inner peace.'

'You're not making any sense, girl.'

'Not trying to. An old mucker of mine used to run this town. Hoping he's still in a fit state to do so again.'

'Look around you. Everyone and everything here has been destroyed.'

Daisy-May brought the bike to a halt and looked up at the courthouse. 'Not everything.'

As she crept towards the courthouse – Oma Jankie just behind her, mercifully quiet and surprisingly light-footed – Daisy-May mentally poked and prodded her body for weaknesses, signs that there was still sickness infecting her bones. She didn't find any. She felt like she had before her swim in the Gloop. Better, even. Which was useful, considering what was to come. Before slipping into a coma, she'd managed to rip Uriel wing from wing. She'd have to call upon that power again if she was to take on the fallen angels that currently ruled over the Pen.

Silently they passed through the courthouse's main entrance.

Daisy-May was dismayed to see that the place was in ruins. The chairs were scattered and splayed, the Judge's seating area overturned and smouldering. The bar that had been attached to the side of the courtroom was also in a bad way; hundreds of broken bottles and glasses littered the floor, and several of the booths had been ripped clean out.

'This is your grand plan?' Oma Jankie muttered. 'This is to be the birthplace of the revolution?'

Daisy-May held a hand up for quiet.

There were voices in the distance, both raised and unseen.

Beckoning for the old woman to follow, Daisy-May began to creep towards them.

There was a doorway at the back of the courtroom, just behind the Judge's bench (or what was left of it), and that was where the voices were coming from. The Judge's tone was recognisable instantly, that good-old-boy Deep South evangelical twang soaring and dipping deliciously. There were two other sets of voices: guttural, filthy things that sounded like they'd been tarred and feathered.

The door was open just a crack, and Daisy-May sidled up to it, already confident of what she was going to see, nevertheless disturbed when she saw it.

The good news was that the Judge was still alive. In fine fettle, too, judging by the volume of his voice. The bad news was that he was in a room with two of the fallen angels, and they, due to their height, were more difficult to see; she could just about make out their crouched, stooped legs, and the tar-black wings that covered them.

She had to cover up a yelp of surprise as a hand took her arm. Oma Jankie shook her head, then pointed back the way they'd come.

Daisy-May gave a head-shake of her own, then placed a finger to her lips. She needed the Judge. They weren't leaving without him.

Need to test my power, too, she thought. Need to know it's still there. Need to know there's more of it if I need it.

First, though, she'd listen, and see just what these devils wanted.

'I don't know how many different ways you want me to say it,' said the Judge.

(*Say-ah-it. Bloke's lost none of his accent.*)

'There are no more Dispossessed here,' he went on. 'You've slaughtered them all.'

'We know you're lying,' one of the fallen angels said. 'We know you're hiding them somewhere.'

'The streets are paved with the lie of those words, sir,' the Judge replied. 'Bodies immolated by your own hand smoulder outside. Surely you could not have forgotten that so soon?'

'We got but a tiny fraction of those that foul these lands,' the other devil replied. 'We know there are more. It won't end well for you if you don't give them up, Judge.'

Daisy-May saw the Judge bristle. 'You will address me as "your honour" when you are in my courtroom, sir.'

'I'll address you as I see fit. I'll snap you over my knee if I choose to.'

'That was not our agreement,' said the Judge. 'You should be standing in front of my bench for breach of—'

He began to gargle as one of the fallen angels reached out and grabbed him by the throat, yanking him up and suspending him several feet off the ground.

'You have misunderstood our arrangement. You give us the location of hidden Dispossessed camps, and we let you live. If you won't keep your side of the bargain, why should we?'

Daisy-May frowned. She didn't like the sound of the Judge shopping the Dispossessed, but maybe the tar-black creature in front of her was full of shit. She needed to hear it from the Judge himself, not the devil that had his tongue.

She stepped back and closed her eyes.

'What are you doing?' hissed Oma Jankie.

Making an entrance, thought Daisy-May.

When she'd used the power before, it had been necessary for her to conjure up a distinct emotion. Anger, sadness, grief, it didn't really seem to matter, it just needed to be raw and unfiltered. She dug deep now for such an emotion, thinking of the burned-to-a-crisp bodies she'd seen outside, the callous way they'd just been flung onto the ground.

Yeah. That'd do it.

She'd just meant to punch a hole in the wall in front of her, maybe rip out the doorway, but instead the whole wall collapsed, pushed by some unseen force onto the angels in an explosion of masonry and wood. It was the strangest thing; although her eyes were closed, she could see it in pin-sharp clarity, the chunks of wall knocking the fallen angels off their feet as the Judge dived for cover under the desk, dust swirling.

'What now?' said Oma Jankie, a hint of desperation in her voice.

'That was just the sound check,' said Daisy-May, a small smile on her face.

The devils got to their feet, swiping claws at the clouds of dust, trying to see who'd had the nerve to assault them in such a way.

One of them laughed. 'It's just a girl.'

'It's not just a girl,' said the other. 'It's the Warden.'

'This guy knows what's what,' said Daisy-May.

'You've climbed out from under your rock, then?' said the angel on the left. 'We've been searching for you, girl. The reward for finding you will be considerable.'

Daisy-May bared her teeth at the same time as she clenched

her fists. 'Would it kill you fuckers, just for once, to call me ma'am?'

The angel swung a clawed fist towards her, frowning as it froze inches from her face. He moved his other hand to it, trying to free it from the mid-air quicksand.

'No force on earth could shift that arm now,' Daisy-May said, closing her eyes once again. 'Fortunately for you, we're not on earth.'

She whipped her hand to the left, wrenching a scream of pain from the fallen angel and its arm clean out of its socket.

A jet of clotted black blood sprayed out, drenching her.

She barely felt it.

The second demon roared, its wings unfurling, ripping chunks out of the wall as they did so, a display of theatre ignored by Daisy-May. Instead, she stuck her right arm out, and the demon began to choke, clawing at its throat, its pitchfork-red eyes engorged.

'Learned this from a film,' she said, a look of sly glee on her face. 'Bloke that did it was kind of an arsehole, but the old bucket head got shit *done.*'

The demon's eyes bulged, its talons slashing at its neck, disgorging strips of black flesh as it tried to lessen the pressure on its throat.

Its colleague got shakily to its feet, its arm lying on the floor, blood gushing from the exit wound.

'Need you to hang around for a sec, Chuckles,' said Daisy-May, her left hand shoving the demon backwards and pinning it against the wall.

Its colleague gagged for a final time, then fell face first to the floor, its black cottage-cheese blood trickling from its self-inflicted throat wound.

Daisy-May rolled her neck, then turned her attention towards the creature trapped against the wall. She walked up to it as it desperately strained against its mental bindings.

'Half a mind to cut you loose. Let you take a message back to all your little demon mates that the sheriff's back in town and she's pissed off. Need some answers from you first, though.'

'I'll tell you nothing, mongrel.'

Daisy-May considered the creature. 'You know what? I believe you.'

She flicked her finger to the left, and the demon's head crunched sickeningly in the same direction, then flopped lifelessly forward.

Daisy-May put her hands in her pockets as the beast fell to the floor.

She felt eyes on the back of her neck, and turned to Oma Jankie. The old woman looked shell-shocked.

'What's up with you?' said Daisy-May.

'I did not expect such a display of power. Such a lack of mercy.'

'You think these fuckers know anything about mercy? They'd kill you where you stand, just for being different. They're monsters. We're not.'

She caught sight of herself in the window behind the judge's desk. Her clothes, hair and face were covered in matted black blood.

We're not.

'You can come out now, your honour. The fighting's over.'

The Judge poked his head out from underneath his miraculously intact desk. 'I owe you a debt of honour, Warden.'

'There's going to be ways to repay it, believe me,' said Daisy-May, watching as he struggled to his feet and dusted down his robes. 'Was what those fuckers said true? Have you been shopping the Dispossessed to them?'

The Judge stuck out his chin. 'Yes and no.'

Daisy-May took a step towards him. 'Was looking for an indignant-as-fuck "no" there.'

He matched her stance. 'Child, I have saved more Dispossessed in the last month than you can possibly imagine. I am the reason there aren't mountains of bodies outside.'

'There's plenty of big hills,' said Daisy-May. 'I saw them on the way here.'

'I have been working with the Dispossessed. Feeding those devils carefully selected pieces of disinformation, and putting myself at considerable risk while doing so.'

'Talk's cheap,' said Daisy-May. 'All I see's a pile of bodies outside.'

'Then it is time you opened your eyes, ma'am.'

The Judge scowled as he placed his hands underneath the lip of the desk, his face turning puce as he strained against it, roaring as he finally managed to upend it, flipping it over, the mighty oak monument creaking and cracking as it hit the floor. He rubbed a gowned arm against his perspiring face, then nodded at the floor.

There was a hatch, a metal ring at its centre, like it had been ripped from the nose of a bull and transplanted there.

'See for yourself,' he said, nodding at it.

'You first,' said Daisy-May, eyeing it warily.

'As you wish.'

The Judge leaned down, yanking at the hatch. Finally, with a reluctant creak, it gave way. He beckoned her towards it.

'Trusting there isn't some foul monster down here,' said Daisy-May, walking towards the opening. ''Cos if there is, I'm going to be mighty pissed.'

Blackness bled from the hole. She swallowed, then carefully levered herself down. The drop wasn't a long one, and her feet, when they connected with the floor, found reassuring solidity.

That wasn't all she found.

The light wasn't bright, but it was enough to illuminate the room she'd landed in.

Really, it was more of a cellar stuffed with people.

Dozens upon dozens of Dispossessed eyes looked out at her.

A grunt sounded. The Judge dropped down. He got to his feet, panting heavily. 'Do you see now, Warden?'

'How many are there?'

'Five hundred and three souls, though their number grows larger by the day. Dispossessed that would have ended up in the killing fields if it was not for my intervention.'

Daisy-May nodded. 'Five hundred and three, you say?'

'I did,' replied the Judge.

'We need more,' Daisy-May replied.

Chapter 24

Auferstehungskirche, East Berlin, 1987

This concert is different to the others.

They were modest in size, small tribes of like-minded people congregating for a common cause. Here, the church already heaves, the vestry swollen with men and women of every type. There are the punks, of course, shark-finned, drawing-pinned revolutionaries. There are the hippies, too, men with longer hair than the women, gathered under a banner of peace but also of wanting the rule they are subjected to dragged to the ground and smashed to pieces.

Then there are the skinheads. There are fewer of them, but they make up for that with sheer gristle. Their hunting eyes charge the atmosphere. They look as though they'd like nothing better than to throw punches at the beatniks and punks around them, but for now, they settle for stares and glares.

The atmosphere crackles. It is easy to believe the slightest spark could cause it to burst into flame, and the band haven't even taken to the stage yet.

I slip through into the vestry, where an impromptu green room has been set up. Bands drink and talk nervous nonsense. None of them are used to playing to crowds of this size. Music seems altogether incidental to the cause: these people want to be apart from society, or they want to demolish that society so that they can create something better. All fear the Stasi. My previous employers, the ones who bored of me, will want nothing more than to stop this night from happening. I'm a little surprised they haven't tried to stop it already.

This is apparent in the mood. There's a skittishness to it all. A feeling that this could be the last night of freedom, so best make it count. The only person who doesn't seem nervous is the person who has the most cause to. Deacon Voigt moves effortlessly through both the crowd and the bands backstage, shaking hands, pumping fists, settling nerves. If he fears the Stasi – and he should – he doesn't show it. Perhaps he thinks God will protect him. Perhaps he believes the Almighty to be an honorary punk.

Perhaps he is.

At last Flames and Colonel make their way to the stage. I follow them. They won't know I'm there, but perhaps they will believe it just the same.

The church overflows. Everyone stands, the pews buckling under their weight. Steam rises from bodies. The air bites. The deacon watches from the side of the stage, smiling at me as I go past. This gives me comfort. At least one person will be able to see me.

Of course I scan the crowd for Lucia. Of course she isn't there. Why would she be?

Colonel shakes as he picks up his guitar then clumsily stuffs its lead into the amplifier. Waves of feedback spill from the stage. Flames takes his place behind the drum kit. I kid myself that they both look at me. We have come a long way from rehearsing in the abandoned laboratory.

We. Because I am part of this. For the first time since I was with my family, I am part of something. I believe in something. I am needed.

Colonel walks to the microphone, his amp still spitting feed-back. He raises a hand in the air.

'*We* are the people!' he yells. '*We* are the power!'

The clarion call is quickly picked up by the crowd. A two-sentence chant that gets passed around and added to, bile, anger and hope drenching the words in spittle.

He strikes the first chord, and the room explodes. It's a glorious thrashing of limbs and lungs. The lyrics are screamed back at him as he orally assaults the microphone, his hand a blur on his battered home-made guitar, a look of pure deranged glee on Flames's face as his drumsticks pound the cymbals. I stand a couple of feet to the right of Colonel, jerking my body like I'm having a fit. I have no control over it. The music has taken hold of me. Finally, I have purpose. Finally, I understand why I have been kept back here. Why I haven't yet made the journey to the Pen.

Then, carnage.

Stained-glass windows shatter and men begin to climb through them. All have shaved heads. Their scalped kin in the crowd respond to this signal and start throwing punches at the people next to them. Women scream. Men too. Colonel stops playing. Flames isn't far behind him.

A man – though in truth he's little older than a boy – stands in the shattered frame of one of the windows.

'Heil Hitler!' he screams, thrusting his arm out in the salute.

I look at the blood and the carnage, and see that the other skinheads have the brand of the Nazi on them. Swastika stamps around their arms. Tattooed onto knuckles. Many of them are little older than children. How can this be happening? Don't these fools know what it was like under the jackboot of those devils? This was supposed to represent something else. Lessons were supposed to have been learned.

Colonel leaps into the crowd below, swinging his guitar like a jackhammer, cracking it into the neo-Nazi hordes. They scatter like skittles, Colonel screaming like an avenging banshee, Flames right behind him, fists like windmills against the shaven-headed swarm. Inspired by their example, others fight back, and before long, the invading Nazis are pinned at the back of the church.

'Fuck fascism!' Flames screams. 'Fuck you.'

A whistle pierces the air.

Wood breaks.

The front door of the church swings open.

Policemen pile in.

They ignore the skinheads, going straight for the punks. Batons thudding against desperate arms, they go about their work with zeal. They are indiscriminate: the merest sight of brightly coloured hair or ragamuffin clothes is enough for them to swing wildly. The punks are defenceless seals under such an onslaught. The skinheads use this distraction to escape, streaming like rats out of the front door.

Flames finds himself surrounded by four policemen. Colonel is dragged away by another three officers, screaming, 'We are the people! We are the power!' Flames looks around. He realises he's outnumbered. He realises his fellow punks have been routed.

He raises his hands and says, 'I surrender.'

The policemen look at each other and smile.

That's when Flames realises they have no intention of arresting him.

He crouches down, putting his hands over his head as the batons rain down.

The foetal position can't protect him. Not for long. The batons are already bathed in blood and want more.

I step forward. 'Stop it.'

They can't hear me.

I take another step forward, standing in front of Flames. I could stop this. Block the blows. But then I'd doom myself to hell, and these men would continue to strike him anyway.

Bone cracks under batons.

I'm powerless. I've always been powerless. The punks' cause gave me hope and purpose, made me believe that perhaps I didn't need to wander the soil alone, that I could be needed again. Be part of something.

That was madness.

Madness, too, to think humanity could change. There is no escaping the jackboot of oppression. It will always win out.

Flames stops moving.

That doesn't mean the policemen stop hitting him.

It takes a couple of hours for them to fully clear the church.

The ambulances take away the injured. There are plenty. Some aren't so lucky. There are plenty of them, as well.

Flames doesn't make it. A selfish part of me wants his spirit to remain behind, so that I have some company. It doesn't. He's led a good, fruitful life. It's the Next Place for him, or at worst, the Pen. Perhaps I'll see him there one day. The thought gives me some comfort, no matter how unlikely it is.

The deacon moves amongst it all, tending those less badly injured. He bears his own wounds from the struggle. A black eye. A cut on his forehead. There will be repercussions for that too, I wouldn't wonder. You don't strike a deacon, even in this corrupt cesspit of a country.

'Deacon Voigt.'

He looks up. 'I'm sorry you had to see that, Jacob.'

'I can't be hurt,' I reply. 'Others had it far worse.'

He gets to his feet. 'Pain isn't always physical. Bones heal. Better than hearts, anyway.'

301

'They killed Flames.'

The deacon nods grimly. 'Others too. They fear them, the Stasi, because they represent something dangerous to them. Free thinking. Freedom from the oppression of the state. You share those beliefs, I think.'

'I did. What good are they when faced with such violence?'

Fire burns within him, his green and grey eyes flashing. 'You can't think like that, Jacob. If you do, Flames's death is for nothing. You dishonour it.'

I lower my head.

'I wonder if you might do me a favour.'

I look up again. 'Anything.'

'Colonel was arrested. He will have been taken to the central Ministry for State Security. Can you go there? Find him, see if he's all right?' He smiles at me. 'I would do it myself, but my ability to slip through walls unseen isn't what it was.'

'Can you draw me a map?' I reply, trying to return the smile.

Stasi headquarters is as grey and soulless as the rest of this blasted city.

A long, thin concrete slab of nothingness with dozens of peephole windows sewn into it, it has a battalion of armoured guards in front of it. The Stasi may have put me to work in the past, but they never showed me their home. As I stand a few feet from the main entrance, I think back to that time, many years ago, when my team was ambushed and trapped in Berlin. There always seem to be men with the best of intentions sending me into buildings that contain men with the worst.

This is different, though. The deacon is a man of God. He is not so very different from the man I must be in the Pen. And Colonel is my friend. It will be good to know he's well.

I ease through the front entrance. The deacon has explained that the holding cells will be in the basement. He knows this because he himself has been arrested and detained there. I pass through faceless corridors of faded grey paint as I make my way to the stairwell. It's like the colour and life have been drained from them. Perhaps it's so the prisoners who are led down these corridors lose hope. I'm sure it works, if so.

When I finally reach the basement, I hear the prisoners before I see them.

Their bellows and chants carry along the corridor towards me. Being incarcerated obviously hasn't robbed them of their revolutionary vigour.

'We are the people! We are the power!'

The chant sparked by Colonel in the church rings out and leads me by the nose towards it. These men have been beaten, but not broken; their spirit and belief remain unbowed. If they can say that, with the hardships they have endured, then so must I. The belief is still there. It's up to me to carry that flame.

I arrive at a thick steel door with three mighty bars cut into the top of it, just as several baton-wielding officers approach. They scream for quiet but don't seem to actually want it; they look like they want nothing more than to yank the cell door open and beat the men into silence.

Ten men are crammed into the cell. All have injuries. None seem to care.

My heart leaps when I realise that Colonel is amongst them. He leads the chant, screaming it from the summit of his lungs.

'We are the people! We are the power!'

The cell door opens and the guards pile in. They set about their work gleefully. The punks attempt to fight back, but they're still reeling from the beatings at the church. Two guards quickly separate Colonel from the rest of the pack, and drag him kicking and chanting from the cell.

'We are the people! We are the power!' he yells, again and again.

They haul him along the corridor, the tips of his feet barely touching the floor.

'Fucking pigs,' he spits, when he surely knows it will bring him pain. 'Fucking scum.'

The corridor bends to the right. The guards stop when they get to a brown door. One of them opens it, while the other shoves Colonel through. He falls head-first onto the grimy concrete floor. The two guards follow him in, shutting the door behind them.

Fear fills me as I pass through it. I can't lose both of my friends on the same night.

'Fuck,' says Colonel, as the two guards help him to his feet. 'Did you have to be so rough?'

I don't understand.

One of the men dusts him down. 'It has to look convincing. What would all your little punk friends think if they knew their spiritual leader was a Stasi informant?'

Colonel scowls. 'I'm no informant.'

The guard perches on the rickety-looking wooden desk behind him. 'You give us information about your friends for money, Herr Colonel. What do you think that makes you?'

This is difficult to believe. If I wasn't seeing it with my own eyes, I wouldn't.

Colonel is steadfast. True of mind and spirit. There is nothing more important to him than the cause.

'I'm no whore,' he says, flexing his arms. 'I gave you that information for my freedom.'

'And you'll get that freedom,' replies the guard. 'This time tomorrow, your worthless arse will be on the other side of the Wall. We don't need your sort here.'

Colonel doesn't reply.

It's true, then. He's betrayed his friends. Betrayed me.

'It's just a shame your little friend didn't decide to take us up on our offer,' says the other guard.

Colonel stares at him. 'What do you mean?'

'Your information about the concert was useful, don't get me wrong. It allowed us to recruit those skinhead thugs to do much of our work for us. We decided to keep your friend Flames for ourselves, though. There'll be no defection for him.'

The colour drains from Colonel's face. 'What did you do to him?'

'He did it to himself. Anyone who seeks to bring the government down does.'

The guards go to the door and open it. The taller of the two smiles. 'Perhaps you could write one of your punk songs to play at Flames's funeral. It would be a fitting epitaph, no?'

They laugh. They leave.

So do I.

After the discovery of Colonel's betrayal, I return to espionage.

The deacon doesn't ask me to do this. He wouldn't take advantage of me like that. The truth is, I want to do it. The deacon's a good man, doing God's work, and I feel it my duty to assist him. I cannot say how much it comforts me, being seen. I can have conversations, and not just in soulless laboratories. So it's a small price to pay to slip into government buildings and find out what the authorities plan to do with Deacon Voigt and his punk followers.

He's become quite the celebrity with the Stasi, the deacon, although the church has stripped him of that title. They feel he no longer represents them in the best light. He laughs at this. 'God doesn't care about titles. All he cares about is what's right and what's wrong. I believe I'm on the side of right. What else matters?'

He organises marches. Heads up a newspaper that celebrates anti-government ideals and beliefs. Many punks work with him. The movement is stronger than ever. Flames's death was a lightning rod, as was the defection of Colonel. Here on the eastern side, he is reviled, but in his new western home he is celebrated, or so the deacon tells me. He has a new band, which sings of a time when the Wall will be pulled down and we will all be as one again.

I cannot forget his betrayal, nor forgive it.

The sea of humanity around me is overwhelming.

There must be close to half a million people gathered in Alexanderplatz. They have gathered – and now march – on the strength of a rumour. Who can blame them when that rumour, if true, will in fact be a miracle?

The gates of the Berlin Wall are to be opened. The government have announced it – or more importantly, they have not denounced it. I stand side by side with the deacon. Chants and songs of hope ring all around us. Decades of protest and pain are about to be justified.

'We are the people! We are the power!'

The chant has taken on a life of its own. It isn't Colonel's any more. He doesn't deserve it. It's the people's now. They have taken it and made it something purer.

With the excitement comes a sense of trepidation. What comes after the Wall falls for me? Surely then it will be time for me to journey to the Pen?

When the surge of people from the East to the West happens, it does so with a whisper rather than a rebel yell.

There is no running battle with the guards. They simply

stand aside, open the gates and let people through. The deacon seems almost disappointed.

'It's too easy, don't you think?' he says. 'It's hard to fully trust it.'

We're just a few short feet of the Wall. Even though I've been free to come and go as I please through it for years, there is a certain charge to seeing the gates open. What future will I be walking through to?

Guitar notes can be heard. I see the thin outline of a stage in the distance.

We are the people! We are the power! is sung, over and over again.

We pass together through the gates, the deacon and I.

We are in West Germany.

A band plays on a stage fifty feet away.

Colonel fronts them. The important few know what he did to get on that stage, and won't forget it.

I certainly won't.

The scenes are apocalyptic, in the best possible way.

Hundreds of people sit on top of the Wall. Graffiti is enthusiastically daubed onto it. Many others take whatever is to hand and strike it, some to smash it down, some, perhaps, to keep part of it for posterity. The deacon dances with a group of punks, screaming nonsense lyrics like he's speaking in tongues.

I stand apart. There is no way for me to take part in these celebrations. No guttural punk scream for me to dance to. I am, as ever, completely alone.

'Jacob.'

A tremor runs down my spine. The voice is familiar.

I turn.

There's a young woman standing there. She's looking straight at me.

Blonde hair. Cool blue eyes.

Older than the last time I saw her, but still unmistakably the girl who means more to me than anything.

'I knew it was you,' she says, smiling.

Lucia.

She's found me.

Chapter 25

The Berliner Fernsehturm had been built as a five-hundred-foot fuck-you to the West, a TV tower that showed in all its muscular glory the technological might of both East Germany and the communist state. Spitting out television and radio signals to the masses, it also operated as a bar with a three-hundred-and-sixty-degree observation platform, all the better to gaze at the good socialist children of the revolution below.

That was in the old, before-the-Wall-fell Berlin, anyway. In the new, proudly inclusive city, the tower had come to represent reunification, an establishing shot for the many films made there, as recognisable as the Brandenburg Gate or the Reichstag building.

And, if you were Megan, a piece of piss to stake out.

She sat outside the Espresso House café sipping a coffee, her eyes peeled at the tram stop opposite, the TV Tower's entrance behind her, just fifty feet away. It had the virtue of being the only way into the tower and the only way out, which was why it had been chosen.

—Hans will know that too, said Bits, wriggling inside her. —Doubt he's stupid.

Wouldn't suggest that he is, said Megan. *It's his curiosity we're playing on, not his intelligence. He thinks we've got the info on the main Spook dealer; that's all he's going to be interested in.*

—What happens when he realises we don't know anything about any Spook dealers?

We know just enough to sound credible. Julius, the psycho who wanted to carve me up, will work nicely as a foot in the door.

—Sounds weak, man.

Only if something has happened to Joe that means he's not Joe any more. If that's the case, this isn't a rescue operation we're on. It's a sting.

—What you chatting about a sting?

You have to accept the possibility that Joe's not the man you remember. If that's true, you might have to arrest him, not rescue him.

Bits's silence was deafening.

Besides, this is your plan, pointed out Megan. *It's a bit late for second thoughts.*

—It's never too late for second thoughts. That's why they're called second thoughts.

It's a good plan, in that it's our only plan. Keep the faith.

—Faith? said Bits. —We're fucked if that's our crutch.

Megan winced as a spasm of pain passed through her, causing her to spill the coffee in her hand and set it shakily down. She'd been getting these cramps ever since they'd touched down in Berlin. This was one of the lighter ones – the pain wasn't anything like it had been at the East Side Gallery – but it was an early-warning signal from her body that something was wrong.

—Something *is* wrong, said Bits. —You've got another soul in you. Never much for biology, but that isn't how it's supposed to work.

Not sure biology's got much to do with it. Always had a distinct lack of soul chat in the lessons I went to.

—Fuck, said Bits. —That's him.

Megan raised her cup, taking a sip of jet-black coffee as she

310

squinted slightly. Bits was right: that *was* Joe, walking towards the TV Tower's entrance. He wore the same trench coat — the exact same outfit — as when he'd rescued her from the Generation Killer. The man alongside him, tall, dressed all in black, with a blonde bristle-top crew cut, looked like he meant business.

—Has to be Hans, said Bits. —Looks like a squaddie going to a funeral.

Let's just hope it's not mine, said Megan.

Joe followed Hans's lead, scanning the main square as they walked towards the TV Tower.

'Anything?' said Hans.

Was there? The girl sitting sipping coffee looked familiar, somehow. He couldn't place where he knew her from. God, what he'd give for a sub-stack of speakers and some pounding techno beats: they'd be able to massage a name to go along with the face. Something told him she'd been part of a previous case, but he'd be damned if he knew which one.

'We're clear,' said Joe. 'Whoever this is, they're not watching us.'

Because if that woman *was* the someone, Joe didn't want Hans to know. Not before he'd figured out who she was. The dumb routine was working nicely, for now.

Hans nodded, giving the square a once-over himself, then, apparently satisfied, headed towards the tower's entrance.

Joe looked up, raising a hand as the sun peeked out from the tower's bulbous steel head. 'You sure this place is going to be open?'

'This is Berlin,' said Hans. 'It never closes.'

They walked in silence to the lift, Hans nodding at the attendant as she smiled, tapping the call button.

As they stepped in, Joe was grateful for the techno muzak

that played tinnily; it firmed his mind up, giving him a chance to assess the case and stress-test it for weaknesses.

See if *there* was a case any more.

Ella, the girl at the club, had OD'd on Spook then killed herself, unable to cope with the hellish visions of the dead she'd unleashed.

Klaus had sold her the Spook. Joe had tracked him down to Berghain, where he'd given up Colonel as his supplier. Joe had then found Colonel, an ageing punk turned drug kingpin, murdered in his hotel room.

The CCTV footage he'd examined had shown Deacon Voigt visiting that hotel room. Voigt originated from East Germany just like Colonel, and was apparently something of a revolutionary in his day. Joe had found Voigt dead in his own church. It had looked like suicide, but a clumsy niggle in Joe's gut told him it was something else.

He'd searched the deacon's computer. Found a series of strange photos and a name – Isiah Matthews.

He'd visited Matthews in his nursing home. The American had been in a relationship with Voigt, and, like him, had been able to see the dead. He'd defected, selling the East German authorities a spirit called Jacob. That same boy had cropped up from the start of the investigation: he was linked to Colonel's band, too. A future Warden of the Pen no less, according to Matthews.

Was the deacon the dealer, or was the Colonel the ultimate kingpin? With both men dead, did that mean the Spook supply was dead, too? Joe hoped so, but it felt unsatisfactory. He didn't feel like he'd got any sort of justice for Ella.

Maybe that didn't matter. Maybe that was more about him than any sort of actual justice.

Then there was the woman he'd recognised outside.

Was she their informant?

Whoever she was, Joe hoped she knew what she was doing.

I wish I knew what I was doing, said Megan.

—You do. Getting Joe back.

You make it sound like the easiest thing in the world.

—It is, as long as his memory's not fucked. And he's not returned to his wicked ways.

Megan walked towards the TV Tower. Joe and Hans had already slipped through the entrance and out of sight.

Feels weird, having you possess me. It's like I'm carrying an obese baby. Then it lightens, and I get a burst of energy. Reckon I'll need it for this Hans.

—You'll need your wits more, said Bits. —That's what's going to help us get Joe out.

That's what you're here for. You're supposed to be a copper, after all.

—A ghost copper. Dying Squad are more Hellboy than Sherlock Holmes.

I don't know what that means.

The lift attendant smiled uncertainly at her. 'Can I help you?'

'I've got a meeting upstairs,' Megan said. 'I should be on the list.'

The attendant only flinched a little at the sound of her voice. She looked down at the tablet in her hand. 'What was the name?'

Megan told her, wincing at her tone. It was like someone had pickled her vocal cords.

—They have, said Bits. —'Cept I don't mean to, it's just how it's coming out. Like there's not enough space for me, and the shit-scary thing is, that space keeps getting less and less.

For me too, agreed Megan. *That's why we need to extract Joe and get him to separate us before we both suffocate to death.*

313

—I'm already dead.

Don't get cocky, said Megan. *In the afterlife there always seems to be a next level of dead you can reach.*

The lift attendant found the name she was looking for, smiled and tapped the button.

Megan took a deep breath, then walked into the open lift.

Joe had been expecting a classy, minimalist dining experience. Instead, it was like they'd chanced upon an annex of Berghain.

Early-morning light flooded through the windows, giving the sprawling legions of frazzled-comedown clubbers an almost angelic look. A DJ had set up in front of one of the curved floor-to-ceiling windows, the beats easing down the energy of the room, the city far below them, its stragglers nothing but ants.

The crowd, Joe noticed, was different from at Berghain; they were preppier, more jeans, shoes and upturned collars than understated black cool.

Because these are the sort of people who get turned away at the door. They're paying for the Berlin clubbing experience, and not suffering in line to get access to it.

He scanned the room, looking for the woman he'd seen downstairs. Not that he knew what he'd do if he found her.

'You're my eyes and ears,' said Hans. 'Whoever we're meeting isn't going to be able to see you. That's an advantage we can use.'

He walked towards the bar, taking a beer from the bartender and giving back a curt nod. There was an empty seat by one of the windows and he headed for it, Joe a couple of paces back, sweeping the room. It was a collection of wasted good-looking people loudly talking about how unwasted they were and proudly declaring themselves masters of the universe, conversations he was sure were on a ten-minute loop.

Hans took his seat.

Joe stood to the left of him, waiting.

There they are, said Megan.

—I can see that. Joe's looking right at us.

Doesn't exactly look pleased to see me, does he? His eyes are cold as fuck.

—He might not recognise you. Soil air might have addled his brain.

'Might' is doing a lot of heavy lifting there, Bits.

—But it *is* doing the lifting. Not a reason in the world to think Joe's lost to us. If he is, it's my responsibility to bring him back.

Well then, let's do that.

Megan began walking towards him.

Joe had finally worked out where he knew the girl from, and it was all thanks to the ambient beats in the background. Music had once again worked its magic; it was like a shammy on the muck on his mind.

This was the kidnapped girl he'd rescued from the clutches of the Generation Killer.

Megan. Her name was Megan.

Except it wasn't just Joe who had rescued her. It was his partner, Bits, as well.

Why had he suddenly remembered that?

It was something about Megan's face. Actually, not just her face; it was the way she moved, too. It was like she was in someone else's body, her slight frame ungainly somehow, awkward and unwilling.

Hans should recognise her, thought Joe. He was involved in the Generation Killer investigation, or so he says. If I rescued her, as he claims, he has to know her.

'You recognise her?' he said.

'Never seen her before in my life.'

Joe would have known he was lying even if he hadn't known he was lying. It was the slightest flicker in those dead black eyes that had betrayed him.

Joe stood to one side as Megan approached, seeking out her gaze but getting nothing in return.

We've met, he thought. I helped rescue her. Why is she pretending not to know me? Why is she here at all?

And where's Bits?

—No one's home with Joe, said Bits. —You mean fuck all to him.

Story of my life, said Megan. *That doesn't answer the question of whether he's turned bad again.*

—No one *turns* bad. It's fucking drip-feed.

Maybe he got a gallon of evil when his memory went, then. Maybe he's just reverted to type. Either way, we have to hope something sparks in him, or all this has been for nothing.

—Nothing's ever for nothing.

Thanks, Nietzsche.

—Met *him* in the Pen an' all.

Of course you did.

—Just make sure it's not obvious you can see Joe. No reason a lass like you should be able to see a ghost. You need to be subtle, like, otherwise it's a fuck-off big red flag.

Agreed.

Megan stuck out a hand as Hans turned and rose from his seat.

'Hans, I presume?'

He nodded, frowning curiously at her, then taking her hand. 'And who am I speaking to?'

'Someone who can help you.'

316

'I like people who can help me,' he said. 'So we're off to a good start.'

He sat down, gesturing to the seat next to him.

Megan took it.

Hans nodded towards the bar. 'Drink?'

'I'm here for business, not beer,' said Megan.

She looked out of the corner of her eye at Joe. She didn't want Hans to cotton on to her ability to see the dead, but she also needed some sign from Joe.

None was forthcoming. He stared blankly back at her.

'Straight to it. I respect that.' Hans studied her curiously. 'That's quite a cold you've got there.'

'I'm sorry?'

'Your voice. Sounds like you've got a frog in your throat.'

'Shall we crack on?' Megan said.

'Of course. What do you have for me?'

'Money first. When I see that, you get the info.'

'I'm hardly likely to have it here, am I? Not the amount you asked for.'

Megan shifted in her seat, trying to keep the spasms under control. 'Where *do* you have it, then?'

'Downstairs.'

She frowned. 'Where downstairs?'

Hans smiled, gesturing at the sky lounge they sat in. 'This, here? It's for tourists. The real bar is thirty feet underneath the base of this monstrosity. That's where your money is.'

'I wanted you to bring it here,' said Megan.

'I want lots of things,' said Hans. 'Not many of them ever happen.' He got to his feet. 'Shall we?'

—What's our play here? said Bits.

We need to go along with him. See why Joe's working with this guy. Figure out what his *play is.*

—That's a lot of playing. How are we going to do that?

317

By improvising, said Megan.

—Fuck's sake. This is the worst rescue in history.

We don't know it is a rescue yet. That's the problem. For all we know, it's about to turn into an arrest. Best you remember that.

They walked past the lift they'd come up in, instead working their way around to another, twenty feet or so past it. It was more industrial in design, a service lift in everything but name. A burly bouncer – Joe would have put his height at six foot five, easily – stood next to it. He nodded at Hans as he approached, hitting the call button.

The steel doors opened.

Hans didn't discuss any of this with me, thought Joe. Which goes to show he trusts me about as much as I trust him.

'This is the VIP lift, believe it or not,' said Hans. 'Back in the day, the Stasi royalty would wine and dine their comrades in the lounge in the clouds, then take them down for a nightcap.'

'Down where?' said Megan, eyeing the lift warily.

—Losing control, here, said Bits. This is a bad idea.

What choice do we have? Joe's still looking at me like I'm nothing. We leave now, we lose our shot at finding out what's going on with him.

The bouncer held out an arm, stopping the lift door from closing.

Hans entered, beckoning for Megan to follow him.

She flicked her eyes over to Joe, then back to Hans.

Fuck.

After a second's hesitation, she stepped in.

Joe followed closely behind Megan, noting again the odd way in which she moved. It was like she wasn't comfortable in her own skin. The way she was walking, it was hard to believe she'd be comfortable in anyone else's, either.

318

Still, there was something familiar about it. At times it was almost a strut, one he'd seen somewhere before.

Hans tapped the only button on the lift wall, and the doors closed behind them.

What's she doing here? wondered Joe, staring at Megan. How can she possibly be connected to Spook? What's her play if she's not?

Is she here for me?

Why did that possibility fill him with relief?

The lift juddered, then started to descend.

'You asked where we're going down to,' said Hans.

Megan nodded, looking around as if there were an escape route she hadn't found yet.

'Like I said, the Stasi used to take their Russian superiors for a little R and R deep underground. This was a special sort of service, one best not advertised to the unwashed proles on the surface.'

She frowned. 'Different times, I suppose.'

Hans continued. 'It was technically a brothel, but I doubt the Stasi referred to it as such. The highest-quality call girls East Germany had to offer, paid a monthly wage their contemporaries could only dream of. The downside was, they could never leave. They were kept down here for years at a time, separated from their families.'

The lift lurched to a stop.

'We thought it a shame,' he said, 'for that heritage to be forgotten.'

The doors began to open.

Joe took in the scene, and finally, beyond all reasonable doubt, he knew.

Hans wasn't Dying Squad. He wasn't any sort of law enforcement.

They were greeted by a corridor shrouded in red, like there

was an emergency Joe wasn't aware of yet. On either side were dozens of rooms. Some had their steel doors closed, some had them open. Hard-core techno played at almost Berghain-beating levels.

It didn't quite drown out the noises that were coming from within the rooms.

Hans exited the lift, beckoning for Megan to follow.

She stayed where she was. 'What is this place?'

'The corridor you walk down before you become rich,' said Hans. 'If you have the information I'm after, that is.'

'I have it.'

'Then follow me.'

Megan's eyes met Joe's for a second.

He recognises me.

—Wishful thinking, that, said Bits.

I'm telling you, he does.

—Who knows him better, me or you?

I saw recognition in his eyes.

—Which means what? What's the plan here? Can't just dawdle in this fucking lift.

This place looks bad news.

—Been a long time since we had any good. This was the plan. Come here, get Joe. We just need to work out which Joe it is we're getting: wrong'un, or right'un.

OK, said Megan. *OK*.

She stepped out of the lift.

She began to follow Hans.

The only good thing about the place was the music.

The driving beats seemed to work even better than Berghain, somehow; Joe felt sharper than he had in hours.

Sharp enough to know this was all wrong.

Hans wasn't Dying Squad. Neither was Lucia.

They were something else.

Something worse.

What did that make him? What crimes had he been responsible for, working alongside Hans?

And what did the answer to that question mean now that Megan was here?

The music played. Joe walked. Most of the doors in the corridor were closed. Some weren't. Joe looked into those ones.

Living souls lurked. Men. Old ones, who hadn't yet slipped into infirmity.

They wore military uniforms. The uniforms were old too, by the look of them.

Some of those uniforms were on the floor, the men who had been wearing them naked.

The men weren't alone. There were women in there with them. Though truthfully, some were barely older than girls.

They weren't alive. They were dead, like him. The glimmering spoke to that.

Joe didn't think it was possible for the dead to look haunted. He'd been wrong.

The spirits in the rooms looked desperate, their eyes dead and black.

A hum emanated from each room. It was familiar. Why?

The music helped him answer his own question.

Elias. He'd used similar technology in the sewers. It helped make spirits solid, somehow.

Helped to trap them, too.

Where?

In Megan's flat. They'd been unable to pass through the window when they'd realised they'd walked into a trap.

The music plunged into a break beat.

Joe remembered falling down the storm drain with Elias.

He remembered regaining consciousness.

He remembered what came afterwards.

What Hans was. What Lucia was.

He looked up at Megan, who walked a few feet away with Hans.

He barely noticed how tightly his fists were clenched.

—I've seen some fucked-up shit in this job, said Bits. —Think this tops it all, though.

Megan was forced to agree. It had been impossible not to peek into the rooms as she'd followed Hans down the corridor. The droopy, wrinkled folds of flesh she'd seen had belonged to the living. The wasted, glimmering skeletons had belonged to the dead. Women. Girls. All of them servicing the men.

How is it possible? Why would anyone want it to be so?

—You asking how it's possible for men to abuse women? said Bits. —'Cos you already know the answer to that. We've been doing it since the dawn of time. We'll be doing it beyond it, too.

Do you think these were the original women who worked down here? asked Megan as they reached the end of the corridor. *They've trapped their spirits down here somehow?*

—Yeah, I do. Seen this sort of tech before, when me and Joe were trying to find you. Makes me think that Hans here – and whoever he's working with – was behind that.

Which makes me think I'm closer to finding out about my past, too.

—Let's worry about your present, said Bits. —Namely, getting Joe, then getting the fuck out of this hellhole.

If Joe wants to be got, said Megan. *What if he's involved in all this? Responsible for it on some level?*

—He's not. Know it in my gut. Faith, love. Have a little.

I thought we were fucked if we had to rely on faith?

—Never said I was consistent, did I? Any good that's ever come out of this world comes from faith.

They'd reached the end of the corridor, coming out into a cavernous bar that reminded Joe of a set from a Kubrick film. The thick carpet was a vivid orange, the walls a faded white, like they'd hungrily soaked up decades' worth of cigarette smoke. Groups sat round white plastic tables, chatting, smoking, flirting, businessmen lolling by smoke-choked casino tables, losing money but being consoled by shimmering female spirits.

Soldiers, too, though like the men in the rooms they'd just walked past, these were dressed in the old uniform of the East German army. Depraved pensioners, clinging to a past that didn't exist any more, no matter how many busts of Lenin and Stalin the room contained.

The men here can see the spirits, thought Joe. Which means they must be on Spook. Hans and Lucia were never concerned with keeping it off the streets from a public safety point of view: they were concerned they'd lost control of the market, that whoever was trying to cut in on it – whether it was the deacon or Colonel – was eating into their profits, and drawing unwanted attention by doing so.

And I helped them. I was investigating rival drug dealers, helping them to remove the competition. Nothing more. They never gave a shit about girls like Ella. They just cared that her death was bad for business. They tried to keep the truth from me because they needed me. Now that they've got Megan – and they think she's the final piece of the puzzle, who'll lead them to their competitor – they don't need to pretend any more. They don't care about me seeing what kind of operation they're actually running.

That's bad news for Megan. Once they've got what they need from her, she's toast.

They won't need me any more, either.
Unfortunately for them, I remember everything.
I remember who I am. Who I was, and who I'm trying to be.
That Joe? The new one?
He's going to make these fuckers pay.

Chapter 26

Daisy-May stood on the blimp's observation deck, looking out upon a landscape infected with black factories. They'd been busy, Remus and his fallen angels. So busy it was like the death factories and the lines of Dispossessed leading to them had always been there.

She'd been in two minds on what to do with the children she'd rescued, eventually deciding that it was better to drop them off on a patch of wasteland. They ran the risk of falling foul of Remus's lackeys, that was true, but if they'd stayed, she would have been taking them right into the heart of danger.

Rather than the fucking artery I dumped them in. Best clean up this town, and make sure it doesn't matter.

'How can you trust this Judge?' said Oma Jankie. 'Men like that are only ever interested in one thing: their own best interests.'

'He didn't have to hide the Dispossessed away,' said Daisy-May. 'Didn't have to go to the Downs in the first place to deal out law and order. He's one of the good guys.'

Oma Jankie laughed. 'This isn't cops and robbers, girl.'

'That's what morally bankrupt fuckers like you always say. There's right, and there's wrong. The Judge'll be ready to do right when the time comes.'

'When will that time be, exactly?' Chestnut slouched over the blimp's controls, an insolent expression on her face. 'Since Old Mother Hubbard here showed up, you don't tell me anything. We're going to hit the compound, right? The Dying Squad digs. That's where Remus is hiding out.'

'Not yet,' said Daisy-May.

'Feels like a no-time-like-the-present situ to me, like.'

'The Dispossessed speaks inanely, if accurately,' said Oma Jankie. 'You won't be able to keep your return secret for long.'

'I'm not trying to keep it secret,' said Daisy-May. 'In fact, I'm going to scream it from the fucking rafters.'

Oma Jankie scowled at her. 'What do you mean?'

'We need to send a message to the rest of the Dispossessed,' said Daisy-May. 'We take down one factory – free the Dispossessed from there, with the help of the Judge and his people – and that sets off a ripple. It's how your girl Hanna almost fucked everything up in the Pen. The Dispossessed are looking for someone to believe in, 'cos before me and Hanna came along, they never had that. They get it, things'll catch fire quickly.'

'Trouble with fires is, sometimes they rage out of control,' said Chestnut. 'Sometimes you can't put them out.'

'Fuck, have you got philosophical,' said Daisy-May. 'You used to put . . .'

'. . . flowers in your hair, yeah, I know. Not much chance of ever being allowed to forget, is there?'

Oma Jankie took Daisy-May's arm and leaned in conspiratorially. 'A word with you, Warden.'

'Not really looking for any counsel at the moment, Janko,' Daisy-May replied. 'When I am, you'll be the last to know.'

'Your power is considerable,' the old woman said, ploughing on regardless. 'Greater, perhaps, than even Rachel's. She did well when she chose you.'

'Sure she'd be delighted to have your approval.'

'It's anger that fuels that power, is it not? You think of all the wrongs that have befallen you, and you use the pain of it to drive you.'

Daisy-May said nothing.

'I'll take your silence for a yes,' said Oma Jankie, 'and certainly, I don't judge you for it. Know this, though: anger is a fuel you should use sparingly. It rarely burns clean. It will consume you if you let it.'

'I'd best not let it, then,' said Daisy-May, placing a hand on the old woman's shoulder. 'I'm not Hanna. I'm not Rachel. I'm not even Mabel, I'm just me, for better and for worse. OK?'

Oma Jankie smiled toothily. 'Of course. *Ma'am.*'

'How we going to do this, then?' said Chestnut.

'How else?' said Daisy-May. 'We're going to blow shit up.'

The plan went like this: Daisy-May would blow a hole in the death factory's wall and the Judge, with his Dispossessed posse, would move in on the place. She'd then keep the fallen angels at bay while they liberated the in-chains Dispossessed.

Simple.

Anger rarely burns clean, that was what Oma Jankie had said to her, and although Daisy-May was inclined to disbelieve every word that came out of her mouth, on that one, she thought the old cow had a point. She'd never seen the Duchess so much as raise her voice when she'd been Warden of the Pen, but there'd never been any question of how much bad-ass power she wielded. It was hard to believe that power came from naked rage.

There was something else about the anger that filled her. It felt good. It had felt good to rip the wings from Uriel's back, and it had felt good when she'd killed the fallen angels back at the courthouse.

She needed to be careful, though, because nothing that felt that good usually was.

If there was something Mabel had excelled in, it was blowing shit up. Sometimes that had been with bazookas, sometimes it had been with explosive scarab beetles, and sometimes it had been with cannon-wielding diving suits.

This time, they were going to use a scorpion bomb.

A weapon that had been around since the second century, scorpion bombs were beautiful in their simplicity. The inhabitants of the fortress city of Hatra had once held off the attacking Romans by hurling pots full of poisonous scorpions onto the legionnaires below. Mabel had taken this principle and run with it. The stings of the scorpions she'd collected weren't filled with venom, though. She'd engorged them with nitroglycerine.

'Sort of like bees,' she'd said. 'Bees don't use their stinger unless they're desperate, 'cos they know that once they do, that's them done for. Same with my scorpions. Bundle them together, then make them feel threatened, they'll blow a hole in the Pen itself.'

Daisy-May was no expert on scorpion behaviour, but she had to figure that chucking them hundreds of feet through the air would make them feel pretty fucking threatened.

She dangled in the remains of the blimp's gunner cage, her left arm hooked around the stepladder that led back up to the cockpit, a canvas bag on her right shoulder, the contents squirming.

She removed the canvas bag from her shoulder with her free hand.

She pulled back her arm.

She threw the bag.

It wasn't much of a throw – it wouldn't have got within a

hundred feet of the factory, and they were at least four hundred feet away – but with her powers, it didn't need be. She mind-twanged the satchel, slingshotting it like it was a speeding, wriggling, constipated bullet.

It hit the side of the building in an explosion of light, sound and fury, carving open an abscess in its side.

That got the attention of whoever was inside. Now it was time for the Judge and his people to keep it.

Demolishing the factory wall had just the result Daisy-May intended: it allowed the Judge and his pack of baying Dispossessed helpers access to the factory.

It also drew the fallen angels out.

Two of them, anyway; they powered towards her now, their wings unfurled, their faces painted with malice. That was fine with Daisy-May – better they go for her then the Dispossessed down below.

She clung to the stepladder, the ground hundreds of feet below her, the willowy crack of the angels' blackened wings sounding as they flew towards her. She should have felt ex-posed up there, fragile and vulnerable, but she found she almost welcomed the isolation and vulnerability, such was the power coursing through her veins.

One of the devil angels pointed at her, and the other nodded.

Daisy-May risked a look away from them, down at the fac-tory. The Judge had made it to the hole she'd blown in the wall, the Dispossessed just a few feet behind him. He was an unlikely-looking general, but he had the loyalty of his troops. What else mattered? It wasn't like she screamed afterlife deity herself. She barely whimpered it.

The fallen angels drew nearer.

There'd been a time, a lifetime ago, when she'd dangled high in the air like this, letting go and trusting that the Dispossessed below would catch her. Now she was to put her trust in the impossible again. This time it wasn't a leap of faith that relied on others: instead, she had to trust herself, or rather, the powers she'd been granted as Warden.

She let go of the stepladder.

Wind screamed in her ears as she fell, the air prodding and pulling her, the angels peeling off from the airship and dive-bombing towards her.

Probably not too interested in catching me. They just want to make sure I go splat.

The air buffeted her as she held out her left arm.

The angel closest to her screamed in pain as she brought it under her control, her mind fighting against the efforts of the creature and of gravity itself.

Except gravity doesn't stand a chance against me, so what chance does one of those freaks have?

The angel screamed again as she dragged it towards her, both of them tumbling through the air. As it came within range, she hooked an arm around its throat, then hauled herself onto its bucking-bronco back, the ground rushing desperately towards them, uncaring about the impact it would make upon their bodies.

As the angel pulled up, slowing its descent by extending its wings even further, Daisy-May squeezed a fist, visualising the creature's insides compacting. It began to gag, black liquid spilling from its red maw of a mouth. With the ground almost upon them, she jumped, visualising the air around her acting as a sort of parachute, cushioning and slowing her descent.

It worked.

She touched down gently as the angel crashed into the floor with a crack and a crunch, its throat and insides already sand-blasted by her mind.

One down, one to go.

The second angel screamed in frustration, but didn't attack.

Because it's confused. I should be a mess of skin ribbons by now, except I'm fine and his mate's roadkill.

The angel flew in a small circle, dipping this way and that, seemingly unsure of what to do. Then it stopped dead, a look of resolution on its almost featureless face.

Come on, you fucker. I'm right here. Just a slip of a girl. You can take me. I'm nothing to you.

The angel, it seemed, agreed.

Its wings seemed to fold in on themselves as it dived, a missile heat-seeking her fragile form.

Daisy-May clenched her fists.

She stuck her chin out.

She pictured stripping apart the fallen angel, layer by layer, its tar-black skin flaying from its body, leaving nothing but a withered pink inner shell, its face crushed like an overripe grape, its arms broken at the elbows, jutting out like bent coat hangers, its insides on the outside, buffeted by the wind as it fell, its . . .

'Warden!'

. . . its ribcage ground into dust, its heart ripped out and in her hand . . .

'Daisy-May.'

The name was like a slap to her face. She turned to see Chestnut staring at her, terror dancing in her eyes.

'I think you got it,' she said.

Daisy-May looked down at her feet. The flayed remains of the fallen angel lay at them, its limbs wrenched out and scattered, its head a mush of tissue and flesh.

'I did that?'

'Well, it wasn't me,' said Chestnut, 'and magic-fascist Grandma's hiding back in the blimp.'

Daisy-May nodded to herself. 'All right.'

'*Are* you all right?' said Chestnut. 'Eyes went super-sketchy there.'

Daisy-May turned away from the remains of her vanquished foe. 'I'm fine. Come on, let's see how the Judge is getting on.'

When they entered the death factory, Daisy-May saw just how much work she still had to do to win the Dispossessed's hearts and minds.

The Judge had made it inside – most of his followers had, too – but they'd been backed into a corner by the remaining fallen angel. The enslaved Dispossessed hadn't moved a muscle. They were just as she'd seen them in the vision during the trials: cowed, beaten and seemingly accepting of their fate.

And that's not how revolutions start, she thought. *That's how genocides finish. I need fire in their eyes. I need them to be like they were when Hanna was here. She tricked them with her language-of-the-dead shit, but it was more than that; there was hundreds of years of mistreatment to fuel it all. They need to call upon it again. I could rip that fucker limb from limb, but what would that prove? They need to see that they have the power in their own hands.*

The fallen angel scooped up one of the Dispossessed, snapping its neck like a rag doll, then tossing it aside. The Judge roared in response, swinging at the beast with a gavel, a rash of nails sticking out from its wooden end.

Least he's got some stones.

Daisy-May closed her eyes, visualising the beast stumbling, watching in her mind as it came to pass. Killing it herself would send the wrong message, but there was no harm in giving the Judge a helping hand.

She looked upwards at the vast vat of death, an engorged water tower that stretched to the ceiling. Dots of Dispossessed were at the top, waiting to jump to their second death. She ran her tongue round her mouth, an idea forming.

The fallen angel unfurled its wings, rising into the sky. It hovered there, its talons clenched, its red scar eyes full of malevolent intent.

I need it to see they're not afraid, then for it to take that message out into the world. That's how revolutions start. One small spark that becomes a fire that burns the whole fucking forest down. Starting with this factory.

She stuck out a hand, freezing the angel in place.

Never tried to do two things at once with this power before. Maybe I won't need to. Maybe they'll help me get it done on their own.

Daisy-May caught the Judge's eye, then pointed to the vat in the centre of the room.

'We need to push that thing to the ground,' she called out. 'All of us. We work together, we can destroy this place and free every last soul in here.'

The Judge looked up at the leviathan death tower, then back down to Daisy-May. 'Its size is considerable, ma'am.'

The fallen angel screamed in frustration, its leathery wings beating against the air, pinned in place by Daisy-May's will.

'*We're* considerable,' said Daisy-May. 'There's nothing we can't do together. Who's with me?'

Murmurs from the Dispossessed, but without weight or power.

There were a few hundred gathered behind her. Many more on the steps leading up to the top of the water tower.

It just takes one spark.

She turned away from the group, striding to the base of the tower, setting herself and beginning to push, straining with all her might.

'Help the Warden.'

The Judge's voice rang out, loud and true. He marched to

Daisy-May's side, grunting as he began pushing against the tower leg.

Daisy-May's mind flinched as the angel continued to struggle. She turned to the Dispossessed behind her. 'We can do this,' she called out. 'All of us, together.'

They began to trickle over, just a few to begin with, but then more and more, all of them straining and heaving at the base of the tower.

It needs more, thought Daisy-May. It needs all of them.

She looked upwards – ignoring the angel's cursing – and took in the sight of the hundreds of Dispossessed that lined the stairway to the top of the death tower. Finally they'd been stirred into action; they were making their way down, the spell of doom that had lingered over them seemingly broken. Dozens jumped from the bottom steps, fighting for a space at the base of the tower to help bring it crashing down.

It began to sigh and grumble. They wouldn't have the strength to topple it by themselves, though. She was going to need to give it a helping hand.

'We're better together,' she called out. 'Together, there's *nothing* we can't do.'

The last of the Dispossessed jumped from the bottom of the stairs and began to push.

Here we go.

She visualised the vat being ripped from its base, the wood creaking and snapping, inadequate, ruptured and ruined, the poison within it sloshing out onto the factory floor, scorching the ground it fell upon, the paralysed angel witnessing every last second of it.

The tower began to groan.

The angel began to scream.

'Push!' yelled Daisy-May.

'Push!' cried the Judge. 'Push!'

The cry was taken up by a couple of the Dispossessed, then echoed by dozens more. It spread fast, a cry that quickly became a mass-effect command.

Daisy-May felt a pressure in her head as she visualised the tower toppling. This was a lot different from stripping one of the fallen angels down for parts; the vat and the deadly liquid within it had to weigh thousands of pounds.

Fuck the weight.

Fuck the impossibility of it all.

Those words weren't for show.

I meant them.

We're better together. Always.

At last the tower began to tip, the legs supporting it bending and splintering like matchsticks, the poison within it sloshing out, the fallen angel screaming as some of the liquid landed on its feet.

With a final anguished roar, the tower toppled, falling away from them, Daisy-May's body demanding she sag at the sheer effort of it all but her mind demanding she do the exact opposite; this was supposed to be the efforts of the Dispossessed, not one of her hyper-charged parlour tricks.

And it was, no matter how much of a helping hand I may have given it. That together thing isn't bullshit. It's the only way we're going to take back the Pen.

She blinked, releasing the angel. It tore away from them, shrieking in terror and regret, taking in the scene of destruction below it. Then it turned and flew through the open roof.

'It escapes,' said the Judge.

'Yep,' said Daisy-May.

'It will tell its brethren,' the Judge said. 'They will come looking for you.'

'Your honour,' Daisy-May replied, 'I'm absolutely fucking *counting* on it.'

Chapter 27

Wraith Headquarters, Berlin, 2022

'Really, Jacob, I think you're overreacting.'

'You always say that.'

'Only when you overreact.'

I sigh theatrically. I find that if you are to sigh, that is the best way to do it.

'You want to put me in a cage, Lucia. Whichever way you spin it, that's the truth.'

'I want to protect you,' Lucia replies. 'I've wanted that for the last thirty years.'

'You know what's best for me, is that right?'

'I know what's necessary to keep you safe. I know, too, that you're your own worst enemy when it comes to that safety.'

We've been squabbling like this for half an hour.

The technicians and their half-built bridge are oblivious to it, though I don't judge them for that. In terms of ambition, what they aim for makes the moon landing seem like a drive to the local shops. Even I'm excited by it. Which makes the fact that I have to hide in a cage all the more galling.

'The sacrifices we've both made, all these years. What was the point of them if I can't be there at the moment of triumph?'

'We don't know it's going to be the moment of triumph yet,' Lucia says. 'That's *my* point. We don't know what's going to happen when we turn on that machine. You've waited half a lifetime for this moment, Jacob. Can't you wait a few hours more?'

She smiles at me. There are more lines on her face, but her eyes burn just as bright as ever. She'll always be the little girl who kept me company when I was caged. The little girl I looked for all those years but who found *me*.

I say yes, because it's Lucia, and I always say yes to Lucia.

The night Lucia found me again in Berlin passed in a blur. Amongst the revelry of the Wall falling, we held our own celebration party.

She didn't wish to dwell on the time we'd spent apart. She furnished me with some details, though: about how she and the other children had been taken to Russia, and how she had eventually managed to escape her captors. She never revealed what happened to the others. It's hard to imagine it was anything good. She still bears the mark of that time on her hand, in the form of the barcode brand. She picks at it distractedly. She thinks I don't notice, but I do.

She made a promise to me on the night the Wall fell.

'I'm going to get you home to the Pen, Jacob. It's not going to be easy, but I've got backing now. Clever people with deep pockets. It might take decades, but I promise you this: before I die, you will see the Pen.'

I didn't believe her, but that was all right. I was just glad to be with her. It was something I'd dreamed about for the longest time, all those days and night spent alone, locked in my Stasi cell. Never for a moment did I think it would actually happen. So I was happy to sit back and listen to her claims of building a bridge, one that would allow the living to cross into the world of the dead. One that would take me home.

It didn't take me long to realise that she was serious. Both about her intentions to cross that divide, and about how she had the backing to do it. There were plentiful places to base ourselves for such an endeavour. Swathes of East Germany were left unoccupied as its residents streamed over to the West. Lucia took advantage of that. She picked clean the laboratory she'd first found me in, then wasted no time in moving on to bigger and better things.

It took some persuading for me to go back into my cage.

'It's for your safety,' Lucia explained patiently. 'I'm not the only one who knows of your existence. There are other parties who would snatch you away from me. Use you as a lab rat. The technology that comes from studying someone like you is priceless. Since the fall of the Wall, Germany's like the Wild West; without sufficient protection, you'll fall victim to that.'

So I trusted her. I knew she only wanted the best for me. Why else would she have spent so long looking for me? She is the one true love of my life, the only one I can rely on, save perhaps for Deacon Voigt.

I asked Lucia to find him. It would have been good to see him again, and I was curious to learn what had become of him in this brave new Germany. She was unable to, though. I question how hard she tried. I'm not stupid. I realise that what we are trying to achieve here would be misunderstood by many, particularly a man of God. There are others who no doubt crave the techno-logical leaps we have made, and aim to steal them.

So once again, I am confined. At night-time, anyway. It's a cage that isn't. A small house, just for myself, in the heart of an enormous warehouse. A bedroom. A living room. A kitchen. Home comforts that are practically useless, but that I appreciate nonetheless.

A shield is thrown around it at night to keep me safe. 'Like a mobile home in the middle of an exhibition hall' is how I

338

heard it described by one of the technicians. I don't know what that means, but it sounds right.

In the day, I am free to move around the facility. That is, when I'm not undergoing the battery of tests that Lucia insists are necessary. 'I know it's unpleasant,' she tells me at least once a day, 'but if we're going to get you home, we have to understand what makes you *you*. It won't be for ever, Jacob. It will be worth it, trust me.'

And I do.

Some of the technology that came from these tests has benefited me. Lucia and her team were able to manufacture a drug that when ingested allows the living to see the dead. The effect doesn't last long – an hour at the most – but it means I can be seen by the scientists I work with. They no longer need a screen and a microphone.

Judging by the way the organisation has grown, Lucia has been able to fashion many more gadgets. If she has, I have been kept in the dark about them. It matters little. All that does matter is the promise of getting me to the Pen.

Which brings us to the moment of truth, and a building the size of three football pitches.

This building is bleached white. It is vacuum-sealed, so no speck of dirt from the living world can infect it. The scientists traverse several deep-clean rooms before they are allowed access. Other than my mobile home, there is little else of note here.

Apart from the bridge, of course.

The bridge is made from what appears to be white moulded plastic and is only half built; it stops dead in the sky, with nothing to meet it in the middle. At this halfway point is a doorway, its metal skeleton slathered in gold foil. It reminds me of a video Lucia showed me once, of a craft that landed on the moon. It has that same fragile quality, which the room's tungsten light gleefully bounces off.

Lucia is nervous. She is never nervous.

The argument she had with me is magnified tenfold when it comes to her squabble with the scientists. She is insisting that she should be the first one to cross the bridge. It is madness, clearly, but she won't be dissuaded. They say we should test it with an animal first.

What are you expecting an animal to tell us? was her reply. *You can't debrief a goat.*

Someone expendable, then, I offer up. Someone like me.

'You're not expendable,' Lucia tells me. 'You're the most valuable person here. Without you, there is no programme.'

'But isn't the point of the programme to get me to the Pen?' I reply. 'If not now, when?'

'When I know it won't tear every one of your undead atoms to shreds,' she replies.

'What about your living atoms?'

She smiles at me. 'They're less important. And they're pretty tough.'

Lucia won't be dissuaded.

She stands at the bridge's tip, a hundred feet up in the air. She wears no protective suit. 'If I need anything like that, it will already be too late,' she told me earlier. 'I should be like a ghost there, as you are here. I will be perfectly safe.'

'How can you know that?'

'Never you mind,' she replied, winking at me. 'Trust me, Jacob. This is going to work.'

I wonder if she still feels confident now, standing on the edge of a lump of curved plastic, hundreds of feet in the air, opposite a tin-foil doorway. The thought that it will lead to the afterlife is comical. Or it would be if the dangers weren't so great, because Lucia will be offered little protection up there if something goes wrong.

Or if it goes right.

Technicians are gathered around desks. Thick veins of wires run away from them, feeding up to the bridge. It all looks woefully inadequate when you consider what they're trying to achieve.

'Turn it on,' calls Lucia, adjusting the miniature camera that has been fixed to her head, tightening the black leather band clinging to her scalp.

Someone does.

A whine can be heard. Faintly at first, but then gaining in volume and power. Whine becomes whistle and then a thousand whistles on top of that; it's as if the souls of the dead are being stretched on a torture rack. I cover my ears from the relative safety of my cage, as do the technicians gathered like trolls under the bridge. It's the sound of something unnatural. Something angry at being woken.

The air crackles, and the doorway in front of Lucia shimmers.

'My God,' she says. 'Can you see this?'

One of the technicians shouts a reply, but it's snatched away by the whistling screams.

Lucia steps through the doorway, and then she's gone.

The maiden voyage is a success.

Lucia becomes known in the Pen as 'the woman who doesn't glimmer'. She doesn't tell me this. That's left to one of the technicians. I don't see much of Lucia any more. I think she's ignoring me. She spends much of her time in the Pen. Her sojourns there grow longer with each visit. I don't know what she's doing there, but I hear rumours. Morsels I manage to extract from friendly scientists. Words I greedily steal when hiding behind walls. She oversees experiments on children. There are children there! That information astounds me. It was something I never imagined, but then why shouldn't it be so?

Are they children who are simply children, or creatures like me? Ones who look young but have ancient souls?

My soul certainly feels ancient. Hearing stories of the Pen only makes it more so.

Finally Lucia comes to me. It's late at night, so I sit quietly in my cell like a good little ghost.

She pulls up a chair in my fake living room, then sits opposite me. She's sad, even though her face argues that she's happy.

'I have something to tell you, Jacob.'

'This is it, isn't it?' I reply. 'I'm to return to the Pen.'

She looks down, troubled.

'I'll miss you too,' I say, smiling at her, 'but it's time. I don't belong here. I never did.'

'The Pen isn't what you imagine it to be.'

'What do you mean?'

She looks up, considering me. 'It's a wasteland, Jacob. There's nothing there.'

'That's not true.'

Because it isn't. I know the texts by heart. Know what I was told by my parents. I know of the wall. The Dispossessed. The spectral police force that keeps order there. I know, too, of what technicians sympathetic to me have told me.

'The Pen exists,' I say defiantly.

'I don't dispute that. Once, I'm sure it was glorious. Now, it's simply a wall and a desert. There's not a soul there. There's nothing to rule.'

'That isn't true.' A tremor infects my voice that I find impossible to control.

'I'm sorry,' Lucia replies. 'Truly I am. But you can stay here with me: will that really be so bad?'

When I don't reply, she gets to her feet. 'I'll leave you alone.'

'Let me see it for myself,' I call out as she gets to the door. 'I'm owed that, at least.'

'I wouldn't do it to you,' she replies. 'Besides, it could be catastrophic. The tests we've done, the readings, they all point to it being too dangerous for you. It explains why it's deserted, does it not? That would have been worse, almost, don't you think? To find it's a paradise you were supposed to rule, but then not be able to journey there?'

'I want to see it,' I say defiantly.

Lucia smiles at me, though there's no warmth in it, just sadness. 'My Jacob. I'm so sorry.'

I sit there for a good hour after she's gone, not moving. Where is there to go? What is there to see? It feels like I've died for a second time.

Three days after Lucia told me her truth, I resolve to go out and find my own.

I have no reason to disbelieve her tales of a desiccated Pen, and yet I can't bring myself to. Not fully. Why would she lie to me? She has always been a source of comfort and support in a life and death shorn of them. And yet. And yet. Her words do not ring true. To not even allow me to venture there: surely that is my choice to make? If it is such an irradiated wasteland, why does she keep going back?

No, I must see it for myself. Only then will I have a degree of closure. To do this, I must employ cunning.

I don't leave my apartment cage for a week. This is to lull the scientists into a false sense of security, but in truth, they have bathed in that state for a while now. Just as with the Stasi, I have become a forgotten plaything. There are more alluring trinkets in the lifeless Pen, apparently. I don't mind. In fact, it works in my favour, because they've become careless.

They've stopped locking me in.

I don't know whether this is because they forget to, or because they feel they no longer need to. It was only when Lucia went to the Pen that I was locked down before. There is no sulphur crackle of electricity when those two events happen now. I'm last Christmas's toy, and just as loved. I tested my new-found freedom last night. No one stopped me. No one saw me. They don't bother with the drugs any more.

Lucia is to enter the Pen again tonight.

And so am I.

The excitement generated by Lucia's forays into the Pen has waned.

Human beings are curious creatures. Present them with the extraordinary enough times and it becomes ordinary, even when it involves venturing to the afterlife. Although the crew has shrunk in number, there are still people required for the act. I see them filing past my cage. They talk amongst themselves, not giving me the slightest glance. Tonight, it doesn't bother me.

I always found it cruel, the placement of my mobile home. I am afforded a view of the bridge that takes Lucia to the afterlife, but no glimpse of what's beyond it. Tonight, though, I'm grateful for it. It allows me to visually place the location of the technicians.

It's now or never.

I've tried never. It's time to sample now.

I ease through the back door of my mobile home. This would be impossible if the shield was in place. So far, so good.

As I peer round the corner, I see that the bridge is visible, the tin-foil doorway at its tip empty, save for a rectangle of light that seeps through. There's no sign of Lucia. She must have already gone through. This is it. This is my chance.

I move forward quickly, that damnable scream-whistle filling the air. It seems strange that the air could be angry, but it unmistakably is. What goes on here is unnatural. I was blinded by my affection for Lucia and the chance of getting home, but it's no better than what the Nazis attempted. They're trying to open a path to the afterlife with a sledgehammer.

They don't see me as I make my way up the bridge. The steps are like cut lips, moulded into the white plastic. The higher I get, the greater the resistance. The doorway pulses with a faint pink light. It's like the sky is ill. A feeling of wrongness grows in me. Am I cheating, returning to the Pen in this way? The Duchess always said I would be brought there when the time was right. I've waited so long.

I grit my teeth against the buffeting wind. I will make it through. God can always spit me out if he chooses.

I stand at the doorway. What looks like a transparent pink tunnel faces me.

The wind screams louder.

I scream back as I step through.

A minute's walk through a wind tunnel, and I get to the other side.

My mind struggles to hear what my eyes are telling it.

I emerge into a cathedral of flesh. There are thousands of souls here. Perhaps tens of thousands. They push past me, blinking like foals cast from their mother's womb. The arena they're spat out into is vast; endless concentric steps flow up and down it. They too are drenched in souls. A sky of tumbling black and red clouds is just about visible above me.

Lucia told me this was a wasteland. She told me there was nothing here.

There's everything here. This place is saturated with life.

I see Lucia. She's just a few feet away, talking with one of the souls. A man.

There's a knife in her hand.

She reaches for the man, scoring the knife against his throat.

He tumbles to the floor.

She turns.

She sees me.

I don't know how long I've been here.

I don't know where here is, either. It's pitch black, so dark my eyes can't adjust to it. It's like being back in the Stasi prison.

I've been restrained, somehow. I can't move my arms or my legs. I'm sitting cross-legged on the floor.

I try and remember how I got here.

I was in the tunnel.

No, I'd got through the tunnel. I was in the Pen. I saw Lucia kill a man. A spirit. I didn't know such a thing was possible.

She saw me. Then, nothing.

I try to move, but pain racks my body. Am I in the Pen now?

Footsteps outside. Wherever outside is.

The sound of a door being opened.

Light floods the dark, drowning it.

My eyes adjust. I look around. I'm in a van of some sort. Steel is all around me. It's like I'm in a refrigerator. I believe it would be possible to see my breath, if I had any. There are shelves opposite me. Brown cardboard boxes are stacked and secured on either side of them.

'Jacob.'

Lucia walks into view. I barely recognise her. There's a sort of twisted anger buried beneath her skin. The light frames her like a halo. I try to talk, but can't.

'You betrayed my trust, Jacob. I told you the Pen wasn't safe, but you went there anyway. That's so disappointing. Our relationship works on trust. Without it, we don't have a relationship, it really is that simple.' She gives me a sad smile. 'I think this has gone as far as it can. It's time for us to move on.'

She's going to release me, at least.

She nods at someone I can't see.

The van's engine fires into life.

The door swings shut.

Blackness descends.

The people driving the van don't think I can hear them. Perhaps they don't know I'm here. Perhaps they do, and they simply don't care. I probably mean as much to them as the cardboard boxes stacked all around me, dry goods to be transported from point A to point B.

'It's fucked up, that's all I'm saying.' A young man's voice.

'You think too much.' A woman. Older.

'You say that like it's a bad thing.'

'It's a good thing if you're a scientist. If you're paid specifically not to think – not to ask questions, like we are – it's a bad thing.'

'You're telling me you think it's right, the things that go on in that place?'

'I think I'm being paid not to think,' the woman replies. 'I think conversations like this could get us killed.'

There's silence. I listen for sounds, trying to place where we are. Wherever it is, the air is built up. The noise of traffic surrounds us. How can Lucia have forsaken me like this? All I wanted was to see the Pen. Was that so wrong? So profound a breaking of trust that I should be banished?

'It's not natural, is what I'm saying,' the man continues. 'The things they do in there.'

'Natural is getting paid,' said the woman. 'Natural's shutting the fuck up when someone big and scary tells you to. Shit, *pays* you to.'

'You know what I hear about that bitch Lucia?'

'Do you *ever* shut up?' asks the woman. 'Ever take the hint that you should?'

'I hear that she was some sort of child assassin in Russia. Ended up killing her handlers or something.'

Before, I would have dismissed the story as nonsense. Now, who knows whether it is true or not? I'm beginning to suspect that I never really knew Lucia at all.

The woman audibly sighs. I'm beginning to like her.

'You watch too many films. You think that sounds realistic?'

'You're talking to me about realistic, after seeing what goes on—'

The man doesn't get a chance to finish his sentence, because something hits us.

The side of the van opposite me crunches inwards, the vehicle flipping like a top, my body held in place somehow as it turns and rolls. Metal splinters, human bones break, the boxes all around me fly, whatever is holding me in place finally snaps, choking out the gravity that held me firm and pitching me forward.

We finally come to a stop. There's no sound from the front.

Footsteps outside.

A grunt, as someone wrestles with the back door.

Finally, it's wrenched open. Night light from the street streams in.

I squint as a man's silhouette comes into view.

He has a greying beard and a face matted with piercings. Long, straggling hair down to his shoulders. One grey eye, one green.

I know this man. Or I did, when he was younger.

'Deacon Voigt?'

He smiles. 'Hello, Jacob.'

★

348

He's the deacon I knew back in East Berlin, but different.

There's his physical appearance, of course. There are no religious robes any more, just a well-cut black suit. A black shirt underneath that suit, with a thin red dog collar around his tattooed neck. He looks a little like a waiter, though it would be a bold person who told him so. There was always a steeliness to him, but it seems this has grown flintier. Fire still burns in his one grey eye and his one green one, but it's a cold fire.

It didn't escape my notice that his followers removed the boxes from the back of the van I was being transported in, loading them into one of their own. That vehicle went in one direction as we slipped into an unmarked black tank of a car and went in another.

'It's good to see you,' the deacon says, smiling at me, and for a second, the man I knew in East Germany returns.

'How did you know I'd be there?'

'I have my sources,' he replies, winking at me.

'You always did.'

He shrugs. 'Some things never change. Unlike Berlin.'

'I suppose. What became of you after the Wall fell?'

The deacon sits back in his seat. The city blurs past us, its pulse racing, unable to sleep. 'After the party, the headache. It took me a long time to adjust to our new world, the one we'd fought for. That's the problem with achieving your dreams, Jacob. You sometimes find out they were nightmares in disguise.' He considers me carefully. 'I think you know a little something about that, with Lucia.'

'What do you know about Lucia?' I spit the question, dousing it in venom.

The deacon smiles indulgently. 'Our little Jacob has developed some bite. Good for you.'

'Why are you here?' I ask. 'Where have you been?'

He closes his eyes and sits back in his seat. 'All in good time.

You're safe if you're with me, Jacob. That's all you need to know for now.'

After thirty minutes or so, we arrive in Kreuzberg. I seem bound to this area, unable to escape its gravitational pull.

The deacon has set himself up in one of the abandoned East German churches. Racks of temporary lighting glow, including a neon cross slung above the altar. The place looks like a foreclosed building site. Despite the lack of home comforts, many people reside here. They are tattooed, pierced. They laugh in corners and smirk in huddles. A couple of them can even see me. How can that be possible?

'There aren't many places like this left,' the deacon says, fondly running a hand over the crumbling brickwork behind him. 'Isn't it wonderful?'

'It reminds me of the old days in East Berlin.'

'It should. This is the church where we first met, Jacob, all those years ago. There's not much of East Berlin left. Buildings like this have been turned into apartment blocks, or knocked down altogether. Berlin's a shadow of the city it could have become.'

I look around at these people. That they're souls that need saving seems beyond doubt.

'What do you do now, Deacon? Are you still with the church?'

He laughs. 'I don't need stone buildings to carry out the Lord's work, nor do I need rotten, failing institutions. My ministry is on the streets. There are many souls that need my help, Jacob.'

I point to the ragged group dozing in the corner. 'Is that why these people are here?'

The deacon smiles. 'In a manner of speaking.'

Something seems wrong here, but I can't quite put my finger on why that is. 'How did you know I'd be in that van?' I ask again.

'I'd heard word that you were being kept captive,' says the deacon, looking away. 'You deserve better.' He turns back to me, fire in his eyes. 'I wonder if you still search for purpose, in the way that I do?'

'Of course. Whenever I think I've found it, though, it turns out to be something I didn't want. Something that ends up betraying me. Will that be true of you too, Deacon?'

He smiles. 'All I want to do is help people. Will you let me help you?'

'Help me how? By letting me spy for you?'

A laugh. 'I think we can do a little better than that. I'm guessing you don't know about the miracle that's taken place?'

'I don't believe in miracles. Not any more.'

The deacon winks at me. 'You'll believe in this one.'

With a whipcrack blur, he hurls a bottle at me. Decades of death haven't scraped away my self-preservation instincts: I thrust my arms forward in defence.

The bottle bounces harmlessly off them.

It doesn't pass through me.

It should have passed through me.

I look enquiringly at the deacon.

'I first noticed it a fortnight ago. I witnessed a distressed spirit knocking a man off his bar stool. The man assumed he'd slipped, of course, but I knew better. I waited for the spirit's demise. That's something I've seen before: when a spirit interferes with the living world, they're snatched away by a monster so hideous he defies description.'

'I know of it. Everyone does. A grim reaper for the dead.'

'It didn't come,' the deacon says. 'No punishment came down.'

'What does that mean?'

'It means that God's dead, Jacob. It means that you're free.'

★

For a time, that freedom tastes like a different flavour of servitude.

Still, it's in a good cause. The best of causes, because the deacon puts me to work helping the poor. What he has done in a newly healed Berlin is quite remarkable: he has a support network stretching all the way across the city, serving the needy.

'It's like a delivery service,' he explains. 'We take food and medical supplies to those who need it most.'

'How do you find such people?' I ask.

He smiles fondly. 'They find me. Those in need always have done. What's wonderful is that now you can help me to help them.'

'How?'

'There's a volunteer who works with me, a man called Klaus. His job is to deliver care packages all over the city. It's God's work, which means the devil loves nothing more than to disrupt it.'

'Disrupt it how?'

'Others would steal the packages. The police, for instance.'

'I thought the police were there to help people.'

'Some do,' says the deacon. 'There are many corrupt officers on the force, though, ones who would spirit away the care packages to resell. I'm in need of a lookout, someone unseen who can warn Klaus if danger looms.'

I say yes. I trust the deacon because I believe in my heart that he's a good man, and because after Lucia's betrayal, he's all I have left. My only connection with the past. The only one to have shown me kindness without agenda.

I find solace in the work. My partner, Klaus, is an old punk. He wears a green trench coat, a balding crown and reluctant hair spikes. He can also see me. The deacon explains that Klaus has the same gift he himself enjoys. I am grateful for this. It feels good to be seen. Klaus is reasonable company, though I don't care for the way he stares at me. It makes me feel like a sideshow freak.

If Lucia searches for me, I see no sign of it. I'm soiled rubbish to her, clearly.

The work sates my bitterness. I was put on this earth to help those in the Pen. Perhaps what I am doing here will be enough to get me there, finally.

One evening, Klaus tells me we have a different assignment to carry out.

'We're making a stop at Hotel Control,' he says.

'There are poor people who need supplies there?' It barely seems credible.

'Poor in spirit, perhaps,' he says with a smirk. 'I have no need of a lookout on this occasion. You wait in the car.'

I don't.

I don't know what it is that makes me disobey. Perhaps it's a lifetime of obeying.

I slip out of the car a few moments after Klaus does, keeping to the shadows, following him into the hotel's glitteringly opulent lobby. A grand sweeping staircase greets me and I'm taken back to my return to Berlin, working for the Americans. This building reminds me of the one we were captured in, with the addition of gaudy rock-and-roll accoutrements.

Klaus seems at home here. Perhaps the guests feel he's some sort of plant, paid to walk around like an old punk in their glitzy hotel. If he does, he does so unselfconsciously, winking at a smartly dressed couple as he waits for the lift, laughing as they scuttle off in fright. I wait for him to get into it, then look upwards at the digital readout. He's heading for the fifth floor. The penthouse is up there.

Taking the fire exit, I bound up the stairs, arriving at the fifth floor just as the lift does. Quietly now, not wanting to be seen by Klaus, I sneak down the corridor, pausing as he knocks on a door. It's just like old times. Spying. Except this time it's for me.

There's a mural of a dead rock star painted on the wall.

The door opens. Klaus enters.

There are raised voices inside. I hear them before I even get to the door.

If I keep out of Klaus's line of sight, they'll never know I was there.

The room looks like a high-class squat.

The furnishings scream luxury, the belongings anything but. A weathered duffel bag lies on the floor, clothes erupting from it. An old acoustic guitar stands alone in the corner. There must be thirty empty beer bottles scattered around. A couple of parched champagne bottles. Whoever's room this is, they're in the bathroom. This doesn't seem to stop Klaus communicating with them – he leans against the bathroom door, his back to it, while I crouch behind the unmade bed.

'The deacon's pissed, man.'

There's no reply.

'Knows the count's down. Knows it's you that's responsible.'

No reply.

'You think you're going to pin this all on me, you're in for a shock.'

No reply.

'I'll kill you if you've OD'ed in there.'

A toilet flushes.

The door opens.

A ghost stands there. Just not a dead one.

'You worry too much,' says Colonel, smirking. 'Now, what have you got for me?'

★

The rebel fire may have dimmed in his eyes, but Colonel is still recognisably Colonel. There is more of him and less of his hair, but his attire remains the same. It seems artfully dishevelled, though, like he's paid someone a great deal of money to make him look poor. In the old days, he got that poverty for free.

Klaus throws a brown paper package onto the bed. White surgical tape is wrapped around it. It's identical to the packages we've been taking to the city's poor. Their medical and food supplies.

Colonel takes out a knife and slits the bag open. There are dozens of tin-foil rolls inside.

I've seen them before. At Lucia's lab. In the van the deacon rescued me from.

They're the drugs that allow the living to see the dead.

Colonel picks up one of the rolls. 'This all you could get?'

'You're lucky to get that much,' Klaus says.

'Deacon figured out how to make more Spook yet?'

Klaus shakes his head. 'Got a team of mad scientists on it. A guy called Julius, in Manchester, who's trying to crack it. No joy yet, though. This'll be the last batch I can steal.'

Colonel frowns. 'The money, though, man. You know I've pre-sold these?'

'Deacon's going to take it global. Already got samples into Japan. The Yakuza there, they run tours into Tokyo. Promise you'll see spirits. You believe that shit?'

'He ever mention me?' Colonel asks, ignoring Klaus's rant. 'The deacon?'

Klaus snorts. 'He fucking hates you. Thinks you sold him out all those years ago.'

'Rich coming from a drug dealer who pretends to be a man of God.'

'He's still a man of God,' Klaus replies. 'He just thinks God's dead.'

Colonel laughs. 'He's only just figured that out?'

I return to the car, struggling to take in what I've heard.

The deacon is a good man. I've seen it with my own eyes. He may look different to when I knew him in East Berlin, but his heart remains the same. Surely he cannot have used me as a drugs mule? Surely I'm worth more than that?

Surely I'm is?

Or maybe I'm just lying to myself. The deacon was all I had left. Perhaps that fact blinded me to his true nature.

Colonel and Klaus approach. I slip into the back seat.

The central-locking system clunks.

Klaus opens the door and glances over at me.

'What you looking at?' asks Colonel.

'You want some Spook?' Klaus replies. 'You'll see an old friend if you do.'

'I don't have any old friends,' Colonel replies, sliding into his seat. 'And I don't take that shit.'

'Suit yourself,' Klaus says, smirking.

He pops a tablet into his mouth.

He has no 'gift'. The only reason he can see me is because of the drugs the deacon gives him.

The deacon lied to me. About that, and many other things.

They drive to an establishment called So36.

From its decrepit appearance, I assume the building to be condemned. Apparently not: a large line of people wait outside, keen on gaining entry. Klaus and Colonel ignore them, walking around the back. They're instantly waved through by the burly security guard.

It quickly becomes obvious that Colonel is to perform here.

356

He's greeted warmly by the various members of staff, then led to a room at the back of the club. I hung around enough green rooms with him in East Berlin to recognise one here. He greets the other band members cursorily. There is no camaraderie. They appear to be professionals, here to do a job. Or perhaps this is how bands behave nowadays. Another way in which the world changed when I was in captivity.

Klaus says his hellos, then peels off from the group. I follow him.

I don't know what I'm doing here. I just know I need to understand. There has to be more to this. The deacon has to be more than just a simple peddler of narcotics. He stands for something.

But then so did Colonel.

Klaus moves into the main belly of the club. My experience with these sorts of places is of battered squats and crumbling hovels. Here, much as it was with Colonel's clothes, that look appears to have been achieved at a cost. The clientele is old. As old as Colonel, and often older. Men and women looking to reclaim a little of their youth.

I jump onto the stage, surveying the room. It seems Klaus knows everyone here. Or at least knows who he needs to know. He moves through the room like a shark through water, a quick nod here, a sleight of hand there. The people he slips drugs to aren't needy. They aren't poor. They're simply hedonists looking for a cheap thrill. He speaks to a young girl. She's out of place here, by her age alone. That doesn't stop him selling to her.

I'm about to jump down from the stage when the lights dip and an expectant roar goes up from the crowd. The band troop on stage. Colonel struts to the front, soaking up the adulation. Sated, he takes the guitar that is handed to him from off stage.

It's interesting, watching him perform. In the old punk days, it was like he had no other choice; now, he makes it look like he'd rather be doing anything else. The outrage is confected, the anger and venom contrived. He no longer believes what he's singing. He no longer knows what he stands for.

I know how he feels.

The band are deep into their third song when I realise people can see me.

Not everyone, but those in the crowd who have taken Klaus's pills. They begin to point, pushing forward as if drawn to see whether I'm real or not. There was a time when I'd have craved such recognition. Not now. Not under these conditions.

I jump off the stage. I need to get out of here.

There is a commotion several rows back. The young girl I saw earlier has collapsed.

I want no part of any of this.

I walk. There is no design to the path I take. I need to put as much distance between the club and myself as possible.

I'm not ready to confront the deacon yet. I need to think things over. No matter how many times I churn my thoughts, one fact comes up: the deacon has lost his faith. He's no better than a common criminal, and he's made a common criminal of me by association. How could I have been so naïve? I might look like a child, but I have the soul of an adult. Not that you'd know it: my desire to see the best in people has been used and abused by all those I've met. Lucia. Director Matthews. Colonel. The deacon.

I look up. I wasn't taking notice of where I was walking.

I'm faced with the sight of thousands of concrete blocks, all of them illuminated by thin rectangular slabs of blue light. They look to be of a similar length and width, but the heights are different. Some are barely tall enough to reach my knees. Others dwarf me completely.

Each one looks like an upturned concrete coffin.

What is this place?

I walk deeper into the sea of grey. It would be easy to get lost. Perhaps that's what the architect intended. There is a serenity here that contrasts sharply with Berlin's usual mania. I stop, placing a hand against the cold grey stone of one of the blocks. That's when I realise that there are names stencilled into it. My eyes scan them, the blue backlight giving them an eerie, slightly morbid tinge. These are Jewish names.

I move to the next stone along. This too bears Jewish inscriptions.

Quickly I go from concrete block to concrete block. There's a pattern.

The names are in alphabetical order.

This is a memorial. To what?

So many names. So many men, women and children.

I move further into the concrete mass and see a plaque set into the floor.

Undead breath catches in my throat.

This is a memorial to the Jewish people murdered during the war.

My people.

My family.

They might be on one of these stones.

I hope they're not. I hope they survived the camps. I hope they lived good, happy lives.

I work my way backwards.

L.

K.

So many names. So much inhumanity.

J.

I.

Untold lives wiped out at the behest of a maniac, aided by thousands of enablers.

Finally, I find B. There are many Blocks, but I'm just looking for three.

Or preferably, none.

I sigh with relief when I realise my parents' names aren't on it.

That relief quickly curdles in my stomach.

Hennie. My sister's name is here. Her middle name, Mia, confirms it.

I drop to my knees. She's decades dead, but it feels like it happened seconds ago. I cannot imagine the horrors she endured.

Eventually I get to my feet. There's nothing I can do for Hennie now. Nothing, really, that I can do for myself.

I can do something about the deacon, though.

About Colonel, too.

I place my hand against Hennie's name. My blameless sister wasn't permitted to live. Why should those two men be? Men who have abused their position, and others?

They must be made to pay.

That will be my new purpose: revenge. An eye for an eye, and a tooth for a tooth.

I turn away from the memorial in case the memory of my sister is stained by such murderous thoughts.

Colonel and the deacon don't deserve to live. They must pay, in blood, by my hand.

That is my purpose now. *That* is why I have been kept on the soil.

I start running towards the hotel.

Chapter 28

Whichever way you looked at it, they were in a casino full of ghosts.

It was like East Germany still functioned here, its pulse faint but present. Perhaps, Joe thought, that was part of the appeal. Was this place any different to the punk club he'd visited a few hours ago? Both places stood as an antidote to modern life, intent on preserving a period of lapsed history.

This wasn't a re-enactment of days gone by like the punk club, though. The old men abusing the female spirits here were a different sort of animal entirely.

One that needed putting down.

Hans led Megan through the casino and up a flight of stairs into a large, empty room. Its floor-to-ceiling window looked down on the casino below.

He gestured to her. 'I want to show you something.'

Megan took her place next to him at the window.

'What do you see when you look out there?' said Hans.

She took a step closer to the window.

She could sense Joe's presence behind her. It felt malevolent. Dangerous. She told herself not to let her imagination run wild. Bits told her the same thing.

She looked out into the casino and saw a room full of ghosts. The spectral kind, as well as the living kind. The living souls were worse, somehow, in that they haunted their own lives, rather than actually living in them.

Hans didn't need to know about her ability to see the dead, though.

'I see a room full of people losing money,' she said. 'I'm here to make some.'

Hans laughed. 'You don't take Spook, then. You just sell it.'

'I don't sell that shit,' said Megan, with what she hoped was the right amount of indignation. 'But I know who does.'

'Right.'

Hans tapped on the window. 'I bring it up because it's quite a sight. There are all sorts of spooks and spectres down there. If you ask me, it's unnatural, but no one ever does. One of the spirits down there, he's naked, if you can believe that.'

Megan could, because she could see him. A spirit that looked to have been about sixty when he died, in a surgical gown, with a long cut down his centre that looked to have been badly stitched back up.

—Fucked up, that, said Bits. —Imagine having to walk around half naked for the rest of eternity.

'There's a story about this particular spirit,' said Hans, continuing, 'one that's relevant to the situation we find ourselves in. Would you like to hear it?'

'Not especially,' said Megan.

—Play nice, said Bits. —Least till we need to play nasty.

Hans smirked at her. 'You've got some front, I'll give you that.'

'Only some?'

He turned back to the window. 'Ugly naked ghost down there, he used to be a punter at this casino. Name of Spier. Real high roller, by all accounts; West German businessman who funnelled black-market goods into the East. One day, he loses big on the tables. As in, everything-he-owns big. He can't cope. Goes to the toilets. Kills himself.'

'Loving the story so far,' said Megan. 'Really feel-good.'

'Now, what many people don't know about casinos,' Hans continued, 'is that people killing themselves in the toilets is actually pretty common.'

He pointed to the wall to the left of them. A portable defibrillator sat in a glass box. 'That's why every casino has at least two defibrillators on site. I'd like to say it's for humanitarian reasons, but in reality, a dead gambler can't pay their debts. The house doesn't win if the gamblers cash out with their lives. These suicide attempts are so common – and successful – that most casinos have a secret passage built into the toilets. That way, when they're moving the body, they don't have to wheel it out in front of the punters. It's not an optic that's good for business.'

'No,' said Megan, 'I don't imagine it is.'

'So, when Spiers kills himself, the pit boss orders that he be wheeled to a morgue in the back of the casino. Calls the coroner and waits for the pickup. Here's the thing, though: it's all a con. Not Spier having money problems – he owes half of Germany, East *and* West – but the fact that he's dead. He's just taken a drug that makes it looks like he is. Slows his pulse and heart rate to nothing, and puts him into a semi-coma. The pit boss is Spier's man on the inside; he's sick of seeing the house always win. Their plan is this: Spier puts himself under, the pit boss goes to the morgue, then, with the help of this junkie ex-doctor, slices him open. Not to do a post-mortem, but to stash money they've lifted from the safe. Then they sew him back up and he's taken away by the ambulance service. The perfect heist.'

'This sounds like an old ghost's tale,' said Megan. 'A moronic one at that.'

'For Spier, it was,' said Hans, 'because the problem with junkie doctors is they're still junkies: the doc's high as a kite, and instead of avoiding the major organs, the fuck-up cuts through them, killing Spier. Not that the pit boss cares. He didn't need Spier alive: he just needed his body to transport the money out in.'

He tapped on the window again. 'Spier's ghost has haunted the place ever since. Can't leave, and asks everyone if they've seen his money. He flew close to the sun. Let greed blind him.' He turned to Megan. 'I hope that isn't what's happening here, Megan. I hope you can give me the information you say you can.'

'I've got the information,' said Megan, 'if you've got the money.'

Hans nodded, pointing towards a table in the centre of the room. Two chairs stood either side of a circular oak table, a leather holdall sitting at its centre.

Hans took one chair, Megan the other.

Hans leaned forward. 'Who's the Spook dealer?'

'Where's the money?' Megan shot back.

'Right next to you.'

Megan looked at the leather bag.

She unzipped it.

It was empty.

—We've been fucking played, said Bits. —There's not a penny in there.

Not really, said Megan, *because we never had the info in the first place. We just needed to find Joe.*

—Well now we have, and we've got ourselves locked in a room in an underground sex dungeon. This was a tapped plan from the start.

It was your plan. What do I know about gangsters?

—You know plenty about getting kidnapped.

364

How are we going to get out of this?

—He doesn't know you're two for the price of one, in terms of souls. Gives us the element of surprise, that.

Surprise, said Megan. *The shittest of all elements.*

Not when you've got a bad-ass ghost for a partner, thought Bits.

So now we come to it, thought Joe. A bag full of empty money. I don't pretend to know what Megan's doing here, or what her plan is, but I guess I'm about to find out.

'There's no money,' Megan said to Hans.

'There never was.'

She looked him dead in the eyes. 'You going to feed me some bullshit about letting me go if I tell you what I know?'

Hans shook his head. 'Nah. You're going to die tonight. You tell me what you know, I'll make it quick and painless. If you don't, I won't.'

'Hell of an offer.'

'Only one you've got.' He frowned. 'What's up with you? Your voice. Your eyes.'

'I'm possessed by a ghost copper.'

Hans laughed. 'Of course you are.'

He rose from his seat, leaning over the table towards Megan. 'Don't know how you got involved in Spook. Don't much care. All I need to know is the info on the supplier, then we'll get this over with.'

Megan took a breath like she was trying to inhale a conscience. 'You already met him.'

'What?'

'The Mancunian. Julius.'

Hans shook his head. 'Do better. That guy's small-time.'

'He's got designs on being big. He's moving into production, as well as supply. I should know. I've seen the lab.'

365

'I still say it's bullshit. What do you think, Lazarus?'

What do I think?

I think I've let this charade go on long enough.

Joe swung his right fist, rabbit-punching Hans in the kidneys, ripping a scream of pain from him, quickly following up with a punch to the back of his neck that sent him sprawling over the table and onto the floor.

The South African looked up at him dazedly. 'What the fuck are you doing?'

'What I should have done hours ago,' said Joe. 'Bringing your sorry arse to justice.'

'You work for me,' said Hans, scrabbling to his feet.

'Not any more,' said Joe.

Just as Hans was getting to his feet, Megan was getting to hers.

She shuffled backwards, aiming for the closed door, trying to make herself as small as possible as the two men faced each other.

—Knew he was in there, somewhere, said Bits. —Joe, back in the fucking *game*.

You think he knew this whole time? He was undercover, playing possum?

—Once he kicks this chump's arse, we can ask him.

Hans stood a couple of feet away, his fists raised, his black eyes glimmering.

Joe matched his stance, a small smile on his face.

The two men began to circle each other, the casino below them oblivious to it all. It was a showdown, whichever way you looked at it.

'What are you doing, Lazarus?'

'Stopping you.'

'You work for me. For the Squad.'

'You're not Dying Squad,' Joe replied. 'You're a budget gangster with flashy toys and a deep-pockets backer.'

Hans's face clouded with doubt. 'You're a dementia victim.'

'I was. Now I've remembered that I stop men like you, not work for them.'

They continued to circle.

'Sort of a relief, to tell you the truth,' said Hans. 'It's not right, your kind mixing with the living. Lucia said we could use you, though, and she was right. We did.'

He reached into his belt, his suit jacket rearing up as he did so, and withdrew a long, thin cylindrical pipe.

The cattle prod.

This time, he wouldn't have to pretend he didn't want to use it.

'I told Lucia we couldn't trust you,' said Hans, 'that eventually you'd remember.'

'That's the problem with being the hired help,' said Joe. 'Your opinions mean fuck-all.'

Hans flicked a switch, sparking the cattle prod into life. 'I'm going to enjoy this.'

—Mad, this, said Bits.

Megan inched backwards to the doorway, watching as the men continued to circle each other.

Hans looks bad-ass.

—Joe's a ghost, man. Hard to hurt a ghost, let alone kill one.

What do we do, then?

—Keep out of the way, and hope that I'm right.

Fights, in Joe's experience, weren't balletic wars waged by heroic, noble competitors. They were unskilled roars of violence that were over before they'd really begun.

The ones you won were, anyway.

That made Hans a dangerous opponent. He wasn't bothered about trading quips or one-liners; his only goal was Joe's destruction. A normal civilian would have struggled with such a task, Joe being dead and all, but Hans wasn't normal. With his cattle prod and his optical implants, he had the upper hand.

It was time, then, to even things up.

Joe took a step forward.

Hans glowered, the cattle prod crackling in his hand.

All this bloke wants is to wipe me out of existence.

I'll win by letting him.

Joe lurched forward, swinging a left hook he knew Hans would avoid, the mercenary going in for the kill, jabbing the cattle prod into his chest. Joe didn't want the pain the action brought, but he wanted the position it put him in: roaring through that pain, he reached out, digging his thumbs into Hans's eyes and pushing forwards. The South African screamed and the two men danced, Hans pushing the cattle prod further into Joe's chest, Joe digging his thumbs deeper into Hans's eyes, howls of pain from both men filling the air.

Biting hard on his cheek to stem the pain, Joe dropped his hands, drew back his head and brought it crashing into Hans's skull, cartilage dissolving, the cattle prod slipping from the South African's hand. Then he drove a fist into Hans's stomach, spasms coursing up his arm as it connected, doubling up his opponent.

He stood panting, pain flaring where the cattle prod had been jabbed.

He took a breath, then lashed out, pounding his fist into Hans's face.

The mercenary crumpled into unconsciousness.

Joe dropped to one knee.

'Joe?' said Megan, looking down at him. 'Are you OK?'

'Define . . . OK,' he panted, his head bowed, his eyes closed.

'What the fuck's going on?'

'It's a long story,' said Joe, his voice parched. 'Where's Bits?'

'That's a longer one,' said Megan.

Joe paced up and down on the office's orange carpet, his hands in his pockets, Megan leaning against the doorway watching him.

He's pissed off, she said.

—No shit, said Bits.

He's acting like it's our fault.

—He's acting like it's *my* fault, and it is. I made the call. I carried out the possession, with no way of knowing whether I could undo it.

You saved my life.

—There're some things that are worse than dying. Thinking this may be one of them, 'cos I'm not sure he knows how to separate us.

What makes you think that?

—The fact that he's stropping around with a face like thunder. Worry, too.

Joe stopped pacing, his head dropping like he was wrestling with some moral quandary.

He walked back to Megan and Bits, folding his arms.

—He's folding his arms, said Bits.

I can see that.

—Must be proper serious if he's folding his arms. Only does that when there's bad news.

'I've got good news and bad news,' said Joe. 'Which do you want first?'

'Always the good news,' said Megan.

'I know how to separate the two of you.'

'Great,' said Megan. 'What's the bad?'

Joe frowned. 'I need to kill you to do it.'

369

Chapter 29

The facility at Wraith was, Hanna had to admit, impressive.

Lucia's hype had been justified. The technology she'd created – the way she'd meshed the living and the dead together – was beyond anything Hanna could have imagined. And now here they were, looking at a strange half-built bridge that ended seemingly in mid-air. It almost made her believe that crossing back to the Pen was possible.

Almost.

Destiny awaits you over that bridge, said Oma Jankie. *All you need do is walk across it.*

It's too easy, Hanna replied, *and I don't trust easy. Neither should you.*

'I understand what your proposal would mean for me,' she said, addressing Lucia. 'What I don't understand is what's in it for you.'

'I would have thought that was obvious,' said Lucia.

'What can a living soul possibly want with the Pen? What favours would you need from me, as the price for installing me as Warden?'

'Power,' said Lucia. 'What else? All my life I've been under the control of others. Even now, I'm at the beck and call of shareholders. They're always men. They always think they know better, even when they know nothing at all. There's a glass ceiling on the soil, Hanna. One that was enforced on me at birth, But in the Pen, well, that's a different matter. There, *we* will rule. There'll be no one to abuse us. No one to keep us down.'

Hanna shook her head. 'Anyone can take power. It's a commodity to be bought and sold, just like any other.'

She stared at Lucia, realisation dawning. 'You need the language of the dead. Or rather, my ability to speak it.'

Lucia shrugged. 'It's a useful by-product of your presence, certainly.'

'It stopped working in New Tokyo. They were deaf to it, in the end.'

'That's because they were radiation-addled zombies. It will be different in the Pen.'

Hanna looked at her, curiosity on her face. 'How do you know?'

'Because I'm a scientist,' Lucia replied, 'and the workings of the dead are my science.'

Hanna considered her, a small smile forming on her lips. 'You're desperate.'

'What do you mean?' said Lucia.

'When you die, it's not purgatory you'll be headed to, I wager. You want power, but you want protection more. From the Pit, and the beast that resides in it. You intend to barricade yourself in purgatory with me so the devil can't take you to hell.'

Lucia's face became pinched. 'What does it matter *why* I want to help you? All that matters is I do.'

Hanna looked up at the half-built bridge. 'And you're going to help me with *that*?'

'You need proof?'

'Who wouldn't?'

'Then you'll have it. We'll venture to the Pen together.'

'What about Daisy-May? I can't imagine she'll relinquish her position easily.'

'That situation is in hand,' said Lucia.

Yes, Oma Jankie's voice said, *it is.*

Hanna kept her eyes on the bridge. 'Daisy-May has the ear of the Dispossessed. She didn't need the language of the dead to keep it, either. She's dangerous.'

'She fled,' said Lucia. 'Never to return. There's nothing to stand in our way, except an old man who's as deluded as he is powerless. When you slay Remus, the Pen will be ours.'

Remus knew that what he was seeing on the screens was real, but his brain refused to countenance it. Each screen told a story that was the same, but different.

Whereas before the displays had showed scores of Dispossessed being led into black factories, now they depicted scenes of revolution and chaos. Many of the death camps were on fire. Some showed all-out war, dozens of Dispossessed being mown down by the army of fallen angels, a hundred waiting to replace them and tear down their winged foes.

It's all falling apart, he thought. This whole thing rested on ruling by fear until I could cull the Dispossessed. There are still too many of them, and they're not afraid any more.

It's that blasted mongrel girl. I should have killed her when I had the chance.

He hadn't seen Daisy-May yet on any of the screens, but her presence could be felt on all of them. She'd made the Dispossessed believe in their own power, encouraged them to work together as one. They were supposed to be a rabble, yet to look at these screens, you'd think they were a tightly moulded fighting force.

'Sir?'

Remus closed his eyes. He'd forgotten the name of this underling. There had been so many, over the centuries.

'What is it?'

'Word has come down that the bridge is being activated.'

He gritted his teeth. 'A visit from Lucia so soon after the last one. What a blessing. You'd best prepare for her arrival, then.'

He felt the underling's presence linger.

'Was there something else?'

A gulp, loud enough to hear.

'There are reports from the Downs. Thousands of Dispossessed have been gathering there. More join them by the hour.'

'The Downs has been razed to the ground,' said Remus. 'What possible reason would they have to go there?'

'The Warden,' said the underling. 'They gather at her behest.'

'I'm the Warden,' snarled Remus.

The last time Daisy-May had been here, the Downs was little more than a collection of burned-out buildings and broken spirits. Now, it housed an army.

Or a garrison, at the least. Thousands of Dispossessed, many liberated from the death camps, many that had come out of hiding at the news of the uprising, all of them here because of her. They waited and they watched, their eyes heavy upon her as she stood on the carcass of a half-demolished building. She didn't like being so high, didn't like the impression of looking down upon them, but needs must.

Words were difficult at a time like this. They never carried as much weight as action did.

They need to hear what's next, though, thought Daisy-May. They need to hear what the end game is.

She took a breath.

She addressed her people.

'The guy who ordered your slaughter is called Remus. He's hiding in the compound. Until we bring him to justice, this isn't over. For him, it'll never be over, not until every last one of you is dead.'

She took another breath, trying to find as many pairs of eyes as she could.

'The compound's going to be guarded by the fallen angels. It's not going to be easy. A lot of you are going to die today, and it'll be a death you won't come back from. An oblivion death. Anyone who wants to stay behind, there'll be no judgement from me.'

She shifted on her feet, squeezing, and unsqueezing her fists.

'But for those who decide to stay and fight, I'll say this: we'll win. We'll kill the monsters. We'll rebuild the Pen, better than it was before. This will be worth it. The future will be worth it.

'Who's with me?'

Silence, for three of the longest seconds of Daisy-May's life.

I got this wrong, she thought. They're too scared.

Then an ear-blasting, soul-lifting roar sounded, a baton that was taken up and passed on, again and again. The Dispossessed punched their fists in the air, an army ready to do her bidding.

Daisy-May allowed herself a smile.

Lucia and Hanna stood underneath the bridge, an army of technicians scurrying this way and that.

'How long before it's ready?'

Another ten minutes was the answer. There was always something to double-check. Triple-check, if you were going to be truly thorough. Usually Lucia didn't have the patience for such rigour, but today she went with it. She needed it to go well with Hanna, needed the girl to be impressed.

Needed her full stop; Hanna's ability to speak the language

of the dead meant Lucia's position in the Pen would be unassailable. Let her have the throne, and Lucia could be the real power behind it.

That was how you truly ruled.

'Run that by me again.'

Joe stood opposite Megan, his arms folded, his ears hungry for the memory-enhancing music that played. 'Happy to. Story ends the same way, though.'

'You can separate Bits and me, but you need to kill me first.'

'That's about the size of it,' said Joe, looking down at the casino floor below. 'I was taught by Daisy-May that the art of possession means a dead soul bonding with a living one. If that soul isn't alive any more, the bond breaks.'

'That's good for Bits,' said Megan, 'but it's not great for me, is it? On account of me being dead.'

'I'm going to bring you back,' said Joe, 'and if we don't try it, you're going to die anyway.'

—Ask him how he's going to bring you back, said Bits.

'How are you going to bring me back?' said Megan.

Joe pointed at the defibrillator on the wall. 'With that.'

—What does he know about defibrillators? said Bits.

Megan relayed the question.

'More than I should,' replied Joe. 'A gangster of my . . . acquaintance had one. Used it when he wanted to indulge in the odd bit of torture. What people don't realise about defibrillators is, you use one on someone healthy, it'll stop their heart dead.'

'A gangster of your acquaintance,' said Megan. 'Do you mean you?'

Joe smiled. 'I turn it on, I apply the pads to your chest. That'll stop your heart. Two minutes later, I repeat it and restart it. Easy.'

Megan laughed drily. 'Easy. Right.'

'You'll only be dead for a very short period of time before I bring you back.'

'Is there no other way?'

'No,' said Joe. 'There isn't. I'm surprised Bits didn't tell you that before he possessed you.'

—Is he taking the piss?

'He really didn't have much of a choice,' said Megan. 'It was a life-and-death situation.'

Joe winced at the sound of her voice. 'As it is now. We leave this much longer, I won't need to stop your heart, Bits'll do it for you.'

—Arsehole.

Megan lay on the table in the centre of the office, her leg vibrating with sheer terror. Joe had removed the defibrillator from its plastic home on the wall and stood fiddling with it.

It was like the room was nervous, as if it knew what was about to happen.

—Not sure about this, said Bits. —Joe would struggle to put a plaster on your leg, let alone perform CPR.

We don't need a brain surgeon, said Megan. *We just need someone who can take those pads and shock the shit out of my body.*

—You make it sound simple.

He says he knows how to do it.

—He's said he'd *seen* how to do it. Big difference, that. Plus, his memories not exactly cast-iron, is it?

Joe glanced up at her, a small smile on his face. 'You look worried.'

'Yeah, it's the whole *you killing me* thing,' said Megan. 'It's the ultimate trust exercise.'

Joe picked up the pads, then flicked a button on the machine. It began to whine needily.

'You shock me once, it stops my heart, right?' said Megan.

'Not all the way,' said Joe. 'If it stops completely, it's already too late. The second electric shock I give you reminds your heart of its responsibilities, lets it find its rhythm again.'

'How long will I be under for before you start up with the pads?'

'Two minutes,' said Joe. 'Though the biggest tell is whether I see Bits or not. The second I do, and he's free from you, I jab you again and bring you back.'

'What if you haven't seen him at the two-minute mark?'

'I will,' said Joe.

—We've got no other choice, said Bits. —You're falling apart at the seams.

He was right. Her body was constantly trembling now, twitching of its own accord. Her eyeballs felt like they were on the brink of exploding, such was the pressure behind them.

She took in a breath of air. 'All right then. Do it.'

Here she was, lying down, aware that for the second time in the last twenty-four hours, a man was about to perform an impromptu operation on her. It was her past that meant she kept ending up in places like this. If she made it out of this room alive, she aimed to work out why that was exactly. Her past was still a murky, shifty thing, always ducking out of sight when she looked for it. It was time to pin it down, once and for all.

She'd kept her side of the bargain. She'd found Joe, and reunited him with Bits. If this worked, it was up to Bits to return the favour.

—It'll work, love, he said. —Then, no worries: we're going to do a deep dive on your fucked-up past.

Joe leaned over her with the pads, holding them inches from her exposed flesh.

She looked up at the clock in the centre of the room.

'See you in two minutes,' said Joe.

The pads touched her skin. Electricity soaked in pain ravaged its way through her body.

Blackness started to seep in from the edges of her vision.

Her eyelids became droopy.

They closed.

Megan found herself in a room.

It wasn't dark as such – there was light, even if it was a little murky – but the walls, floor and ceiling were painted in dark-of-night hues. In the centre of the room was a mirror, Gothic in style, and free-floating several feet above the floor. There was a simplicity to the room that Megan approved of.

Then she looked in the mirror, and approval was the very last thing on her mind.

Bits was wrapped around her like a tree.

It was like the Mancunian was growing out of her body. His toes jutted out of her knees. The tips of his fingers – and the nails attached to them – poked out of her cheeks. One of his elbows had erupted from her left side. His face was grafted onto her midriff.

He was screaming.

There was no volume to this scream. No more of Bits's thoughts in her head. Just his broken, deformed body spliced onto hers.

What do I do? she thought. What the fuck do I do?

Joe stood ready, defibrillator pads in his hands, the machine whining, ready to do its worst, the clock showing that thirty seconds had passed since he'd first shocked Megan.

He tightened his hands around the pads. Risked a look back at the clock.

Fifty seconds down.

Seventy seconds left before he had to bring Megan back.

Come on, Bits. Where are you?

Megan knew she should be grateful that something had started to happen, but the revulsion made it difficult.

More of Bits had appeared on her body, and unlike before, these body parts were moving. An eye on her cheek, the pupil within it pinging left and right. Three of his fingers on her right leg, flexing pathetically. A whole foot jutting out from her left hip, curling then uncurling. She tried to scream but couldn't; it was like there was a tongue lodged deep within her throat.

Because there is. It's happening. I can feel Bits being dislodged. It's like he's a pebble in my shoe that's working itself loose. I just don't want to watch as he's doing it.

It was impossible not to, though. She could feel two thumbs behind her eyelids, pressing down hard, jamming them open.

Her body writhed in the mirror.

Pain threatened to overwhelm her senses.

This had to be hell. Because if it wasn't, how could anything possibly be any worse?

Twenty seconds left.

Joe swallowed, his throat dry, the pads heavy in his hands, the whine from the defibrillator insistent. If this was going to work, he should have seen Bits by now. His partner should be clambering out of the unmoving body of Megan, ready with a Mancunian barb and a whip-smart insult. Instead, there was nothing.

Ten seconds left.

Come on, Bits. Let's be having you.

★

379

It was like every one of Bits's limbs had broken. The good thing was (if anything about this situation could be classed as good), Megan could see those limbs clearly now. Bits's splintered, rag-doll body was forcing its way out of hers, and although this was causing almost indescribable levels of pain, it meant it was working. There were two distinct people in that mirror.

She was almost certain that one of those people was still her.

Time's up.

Two minutes since he'd put her under.

Joe squeezed the pads. They were just inches from Megan's chest. If he waited much longer, he wouldn't be able to bring her back at all.

Then he saw it.

An elbow, appearing from Megan's chest. One that glimmered.

An arm.

Feet appearing from her stomach.

A leg.

Finally, a face, contorted in pain.

Bits.

Joe looked at the clock. Two minutes twenty seconds since he'd first shocked her.

'Hurry the fuck up,' he shouted.

Megan's body twitched.

He was almost completely free of her now. It was like a negative of Bits had been superimposed on top of her. That didn't mean that Megan felt any less pain, or that the sound of bones breaking, then resetting, was any less sickening.

She continued to stare into the mirror. She didn't know

why, only that it was important, somehow. It was an instinctive thing, deep and primeval. A wind whipped itself up from somewhere, chill and chilling, tugging at her hair.

Blackness once again seeped in from the sides.

She heard a whine, distant and unforgiving.

It's too late, she thought.

'Do it,' gasped Bits as his flickering, glimmering form wrenched itself free from Megan's spasming body. Joe didn't need to be asked twice; he jammed the pads onto her chest, her body jerking in response, the defibrillator flatlining.

Bits stumbled, then fell, and although Joe's attention was on Megan, he couldn't help noticing the flickering, indistinct form of his partner. It was like he was both there and somewhere else, a radio signal drifting in and out.

He waited, tapping his foot, impatient for the machine to recharge.

Ready.

He jammed the pads down again, and Megan's body bucked in response.

'Come on,' he yelled. 'Wake up.'

Megan examined herself in the mirror.

Bits was gone. The pain remained.

It was strange. Being possessed by him had been a violation of both her body and her spirit. Now that he was gone, though, she felt almost incomplete. She'd got used to his steadily constricting presence on her soul, his ever-present Mancunian tone in her ear.

A sense of peace descended upon her. The world seemed a heavy place all of a sudden. Perhaps she should close her eyes for a couple of minutes. She'd earned a rest.

★

'You're fucking losing her, man.'

Joe ignored Bits's bald statement of fact, instead shifting his gaze between the lifeless form of Megan and the shrieking defibrillator. The pads sat heavily in his hands. A few more seconds and he'd be able to shock her again.

Three minutes and counting, that was how long she'd been under. He had one more shot at bringing her back. If it didn't work this time, there wouldn't be another.

'She's gone, man,' said Bits.

'Is she fuck.'

He brought the pads down again.

It was like she'd been dunked in an ice bath.

The sense of comfort-blanket peace that had draped itself around Megan was whipped away, replaced by a shawl of pain and fury. She screamed, and this time she could hear it all too well. See it, too, although her reflection in the mirror was fading, replaced by another image: the treatment room Joe had shocked her in.

There he was now, pads in his hand, a look of concern on his face.

Bits was standing alongside him.

Cracks began to crawl across the mirror.

The room she was in started to collapse.

She reached forward.

Megan screamed, jerking upright, causing Joe and Bits to stumble backwards.

Her chest heaved, her head snapping left and right, her hair dank with sweat.

'Did it work?'

Bits stepped forward, half a smile on his face. 'If it didn't, we're both in hell.'

Megan was alive, and free of Bits. Joe wasn't going to say anything crazy like she was as good as new – he had no way of telling the damage he'd done to her heart by stopping then restarting it – but she was breathing, walking and talking. They had to chalk that up as a win.

Though they'd won nothing until they got out of the casino. The longer they stayed, the greater the danger that something would happen to Megan. Megan, who for some reason had come to save him, returning a favour Joe had only just remembered he was owed.

He had one more task before they left. One his conscience demanded he complete, because he was all too aware of the crimes of his past, and the actions in his present were the only things that could absolve him of them. They'd never be absolved all the way, but part of the way would have to do for now.

'Stay close,' he said to Megan, Bits alongside him, as they reached the bottom of the stairs. 'We're getting out of here.'

'Don't have to sell me on that one,' said Megan.

They strode through the centre of the casino, aiming for the corridor they'd first walked down, the living punters – and dead spirits with them – watching with distracted interest.

They reached the corridor.

Joe tightened his fists and set his jaw, then went to work.

Megan had to admit: Joe was kind of kick-ass.

It was like he was a blur of justice, his glimmering form surging here and there, plucking the pasty, naked living scumbags from the dank, dingy rooms and dumping them outside, the men screaming in protest, those who tried to fight back receiving broken noses and fists of fury for their trouble. He herded them like cattle into the service lift, the attendant fleeing his post when he saw the look on Joe's face.

'I ever see any of you fuckers again, I'll kill you. Understand?'
They did.

He shoved the final straggler – a portly pensioner with his trousers round his ankles – into the lift, then sent it up to the ground floor.

'Mint, that,' said Bits with a smirk. 'Let the dirty fuckers explain to the commuters outside why they're naked.'

'He's like Jesus in a trench coat,' said Megan. 'Turfing the moneylenders out of the temple.'

They followed him back down the corridor, watching as he yanked the doors fully open. As well as a mangy, stained mattress in the corner, Megan saw that each room contained a small metal box. Joe took a boot to each one, the subliminal hum that was coming from the rooms dying as he did so.

Carefully, gently he gathered the women together. 'You're free to go,' he said. 'I'm sorry about what was done to you. I'm going to try my best to see that it never happens again.'

And he meant it.

Hans had parked his car behind a church, of all places. The Marienkirche was the sort of Gothic throwback that gave cathedrals a vainglorious name, all sweeping spires and ornate knaves, the TV Tower they'd just come from looming over it. The street was deserted.

Fifty yards away from Hans's Mercedes, on the opposite side of the road, two dead men and one living woman were attempting to break into one black Skoda.

'Can't see why we can't just jack the Mercedes, man,' said Bits. '*Proper* car, that.'

'Because when Hans comes back to it, we're going to tail him,' said Joe. 'If we're actually *in* the car, that might give the game away a bit.'

'Still not mad on this plan,' said Bits.

'Hold that negativity,' said Joe.

He passed seamlessly through the Skoda's driver-side door, sliding into the seat then reaching across and flicking up the passenger lock. Megan checked to see she wasn't being watched – she wasn't – then opened the door, slipping into the seat, Bits taking his place in the back.

'Problem with nicking this car is that I can be seen,' said Megan. 'You guys can't.'

'If you're serious about finding out about your past, this is our best play,' said Joe. 'Hans will come back to get his car. When he does, we follow him. Where he'll head to will have your answers.'

'How do you know?' said Megan.

'Because he works for Lucia, and she can see the dead, just like you. She's weaponised it somehow. Uses the dead for profit. She'll know about your grandad, or she'll know someone who does. Can't say I'm crazy about leading you into the danger that'll bring, though.'

'She doesn't need any help walking into danger, believe me,' muttered Bits.

'It's worth the risk,' said Megan. 'I need to know why I can see the dead. Why the Generation Killer targeted me. Who my parents are, and why they abandoned me. Bits promised that you'd help me.'

Bits nodded at Joe in the rear-view mirror. 'She helped me find you, we help her find out what she needs to know. That was the deal.'

'You don't have to sell me,' said Joe. 'I've got unfinished business with Lucia myself.'

Megan crouched down low in her seat. 'Hans is coming.'

Joe saw she was right, and copied her slouch.

'Risky, this, mate,' said Bits. 'What's to stop him calling Lucia and telling her you've gone rogue?'

'He won't,' said Joe. 'He'll want to deal with me before she finds out. I know him. Trust me.'

Hans got into the car and gunned it into life.

Joe turned to Megan. 'We might want to swap seats, or any onlookers are going to see a car driving itself. Even in this city, that'll raise eyebrows.'

Wherever they were headed, it was west.

They'd left the centre of Berlin behind them, giving Hans a good ten cars' length, Joe calling out if he felt they were getting too close.

'Any of this look familiar to you?' said Megan, gazing out at the streets of suburbia blurring past them.

'Honestly, no,' said Joe. 'Don't read too much into that, though; until recently, I struggled to remember my own name.'

'What changed?' said Bits.

Joe reached out, tapping the car stereo. A talk show boomed on, the conversation conducted in indecipherable German. He frowned, hitting the scan button. The radio's digital frequency readout whirled, alighting on a station called RADIO ON. Darkly minimal techno seeped from the speakers.

'This changed,' he said. 'Music.'

He caught Bits's gaze in the rear-view mirror. 'You remember what Elias told us? About the research he'd done with music and the dead?'

Bits nodded. 'At the nightclub in Manchester.'

'Right,' said Joe. 'He'd discovered that by using music – particularly music that meant something to the spirits – he could help them claw back memories, in much the same way that dementia patients use music in their therapy.'

'And they say serial killers are all bad,' said Bits.

'I remind you, this is the bloke who kidnapped me, then tried to inject me with a fatal dose of radiation,' said Megan.

'It was the music,' said Joe, trying to wrestle back control of the conversation. 'It helped me remember. As long as I hear music every half an hour or so – something simple and beat-heavy, like this techno crap – I can remember who I am, and what it is I'm trying to do. Remember stuff in the past, too.'

'You don't need the pills?' said Megan.

Joe shook his head. 'Natural beats synthetic every time.'

'Leave you for a couple of months and you go all homeo-pathic on me.' Bits leaned forward. 'Where've you *been*, man? What happened to you in the storm drain? Searched it high and low. Couldn't find you or Elias.'

'Careful,' said Joe, tapping on the windscreen. 'You're going too fast.'

Megan swore under her breath, but nevertheless eased her foot onto the brake, slowing the car and allowing the Mercedes to recede into the distance.

Satisfied, Joe continued.

'Until a few hours ago, my past was a smeary window I couldn't see through. Even now, with the music, it's fragments that I can't completely trust. I remember taking a tumble down the storm drain. I ended up in Salford, of all places, and I wasn't alone. Elias was still alive, and trying to haul himself out of the water.'

'Not an easy thing to do when you've only got one arm,' said Megan.

'Easier when you've got help. Lucia must have tracked him somehow, to be able to find him at that specific spot.'

'So she was there to rescue him?' said Megan.

'That's what I assumed,' said Joe. 'Until she shot him in the face.'

'Fuck.'

'The rest's just a bunch of indistinct dreams. I remember

being at their base of operations. I'm as helpless as a baby, and twice as impressionable. They tell me I'm dead, that I work for the Dying Squad; basically, they feed me enough half-truths so that I believe the false whole one.'

'You didn't have any doubts?' said Megan.

'See it from my point of view. I'm amnesia-riddled and desperate; if I don't believe them, who *do* I believe? I'm police, I know that in my gut, and they give me a case: catch the Spook dealer. A girl dies, and it's easy to park my doubts, because I want to catch the fucker who sold her the drugs. Then Hans's methods get more brutal and I start to have doubts, about him and me, because the brutality brings out a side of me that isn't alien to me, but my true self.

'It was music that saved me. The more I heard, the more I could claw back my memories. They weren't always memories I wanted, but it's the bad ones that tell you you're on the right track.' Joe stared grimly ahead. 'I kept this from Hans, because the more I remembered, the less I trusted him.'

'Pretty sure he doesn't trust you either, mate,' said Bits. 'Considering you just eye-raked and headbutted him.'

Joe glanced down. 'I've done things I'm not proud of. Things that would have got me thrown into hell if the Xylophone Man was still stomping around the place.'

'That's true of all of us,' said Megan. 'You didn't have to free those women. You made the right decision when it would have been easier to make the wrong. Reckon that counts for something.'

'She's right, man,' said Bits. 'No point fretting about a past that was mis-sold to you. All we can do is the right thing in the present moment. Reckon that should be enough to keep us both out of hell.'

Joe hoped his partner was right.

'He's slowing down,' said Megan.

388

A massive, half-crumbling structure came into view on the horizon.

Teufelsberg – Devil's Hill – was what happened when you repurposed the rubble and embers of the Second World War into something practical.

For twenty-two years, eight hundred trucks a day transported the detritus of the Allied bombing and piled it into a vast mound. The purpose of this operation – other than removing the concrete wounds of the war – was to give the American and British military forces somewhere to build a state-of-the-art spy station. *Its* purpose was to act as an early-warning system against the burgeoning Soviet threat, listening in as Uncle Joe chattered to his East German brethren.

When the Cold War ended, so did the station's purpose, and so it was abandoned, falling into graffiti-drenched rack and ruin. It attracted the odd urban explorer, the occasional group of teenagers who wanted somewhere to make out and scare themselves silly, but mostly it was abandoned to the weeds and the wilderness.

'Can't believe this place is just half an hour away from the city,' said Megan, peering through the windscreen at the fractured towers that still stood proud and tall. They were crumbling, naked in places, but the golf-ball-like white bubbles at the peak remained intact. 'It's like it's from another time and place altogether.'

'It is,' said Joe. 'It's from a Germany that doesn't exist any more. Sort of the perfect place to have a research lab that experiments on ghosts. Hiding in plain sight.'

'You know how to get in, I'm assuming,' said Megan. 'Otherwise, it's just hiding.'

'No, but Hans does. Look.'

★

Hans had to confess he was a little disappointed.

For all the distaste he had for working with a spirit like Lazarus, he was grudgingly admiring of the man's talents. He'd been like a bloodhound when tracking down the Spook dealer. Would probably have found him, too, if Hans hadn't been suckered in by Megan. That had been a rookie error. He'd let pride and his hatred of Lazarus cloud his judgement, and it had almost cost him everything.

Certainly it had cost him his implants. Or resulted in them being damaged, anyway; his vision was jittery, sketchy. It remained to be seen whether it would affect his ability to see spirits.

He was praying it wouldn't. He was due some good fortune.

Certainly he'd got it when Megan had decided to tail him. She'd not done a bad job of it, but Hans had spent the best years of his life tracking – and evading – bad actors in some of the hottest military spots on the planet. She had placed herself – and, he assumed, Joe – right at the entrance to the lion's den.

All Hans needed to do was open the cage door and let them walk through it.

When it came to crossing the bridge, Lucia had never quite conquered her nerves. To have bent the laws of science in the way they had was enormous, history-mangling. It was wise to remember that, and just how dangerous the act was.

It was worth the risk, though, because Hanna had been right about Lucia's intentions. Instilling Hanna as Warden of the Pen would be beneficial to her, but it wasn't just second-hand power she was after.

It was protection.

Her childhood had been one of brutality. Experimentation. Then she'd been taken to Russia and it had become one of survival.

She'd had to do unspeakable things to ensure that survival. Killed many men and women. She didn't regret it, but nor did she expect judgement on her to be forgiving.

She was headed to the Pit. It was nailed on. And God help her, she was going to do whatever she could to avoid that fate.

The bridge came into sight, the tunnel that led to it instantly seeming more claustrophobic. It always reminded Lucia of the tunnel you'd walk down before boarding an aeroplane, holding that same tingle of anticipation.

'The closer I get, the less impressive it looks.'

Lucia turned to Hanna, managing, for the fiftieth time, not to flinch at the creepiness of her home-made mask. 'Looks can be deceiving. You should know that better than anyone.'

'What's that?' said Hanna, nodding at the chunky plastic-moulded suitcase in Lucia's hand.

Lucia smiled. 'A gift for an old acquaintance. A gift for you, too, because it's going to help ease your ascension to the throne.'

They stopped, the gold-foil doorway thirty feet or so away, the square block of light spilling from it.

'It's difficult to believe that doorway leads anywhere,' said Hanna.

'It leads home. Are you ready to return?'

'I'm ready to rule,' Hanna said.

So am I, thought Lucia.

They walked towards the light.

The entrance to Wraith's facility, like everything hidden, was easy to find if you knew where to look. It was a hundred feet or so to the left of the main communications tower, in a concrete underpass that had long ago relinquished control to graffiti and tumbleweed. If you stared – and you really had to stare very hard – you would have seen the faintest outline of a doorway set into the underpass's concrete skin. The CCTV camera you would never see; it was pin-head small, its lens looking like nothing more than a smudge.

Joe knew it was there, though. Knew a microphone was there too, similarly small, similarly hidden away.

He'd spoken loudly enough for it to pick up his voice, explained that he had two prisoners in custody, like this was a regular lock-up and he was a regular copper. They should have opened up by now. There should have been a subliminal buzz and the scraping of a door. Instead, they were being forced to stand there and wait.

It's because Hans isn't with me. Probably started ringing his phone the moment they saw me here alone. No part of this plan involved them refusing to let me in.

A buzzing sounded.

The door began to open.

Chapter 30

Berlin, two hours ago

Hotel Control is easy to find again. This is still my city, one I have known, in one form or another, all my life. It never changes, not really. It's always been full of back-stabbers and degenerates. The people here will use and abuse you as they see fit. That's the mistake I've made all these years: doing the right thing has always landed me in the wrong place.

That changes tonight.

Once I reach the hotel, it's a simple matter to retrace my steps up to Colonel's room. It will be important for him to see me. Perhaps I'll force-feed him some of the Spook he is so intent on selling. His face will be priceless. It's many decades since he gazed upon me. I intend to haunt the fiend. Do a great deal more to him, for his betrayal of Flames and his principles.

I believed in him. What a mistake, to believe in someone who believes in nothing. It's one I've made many times over the years. I won't make it again.

Normally, I would take the stairs up to the penthouse. Even though I can't be seen, it's the easiest way to keep a low profile. Why court attention? My anger is such, though, that I call the lift, delighting in pushing every one of the buttons, much to the consternation and surprise of the hotel guests. A small transgression, perhaps, but a delicious one. From little acorns, and all that.

Music vibrates from Colonel's room. The painted mural of the rock star smiles at me. I take it as a welcoming omen, one that tells me I am on the right path. It is time for Colonel to pay. I will be an avenging angel. For that reason alone, it won't be murder.

I stop when I get to the door. Music bleeds through it.

I pass into the suite. It's even more dishevelled than it was before. The empty bottles and overflowing ashtrays are still here – have grown in number, in fact – but Colonel isn't. It's strange, because there appear to be signs of a struggle. Perhaps he has been wrestling with his demons.

There's a peculiar sound, too. An odd mewling. It gets louder as I walk through the living-room area, towards the bedroom. It sounds almost like a dying animal. Colonel doesn't strike me as an animal lover. The only thing people like that love is themselves.

Someone has beaten me to it.

Colonel sits on the bed, kitten-weak hands on his neck, trying to staunch the flow of blood that leaks from it. His hands can't disguise the thick line that has been scored across his throat.

There is a slogan daubed on the wall. An old punk declaration.

Colonel's eyes see me. I flatter myself they bulge a little larger.

'Jacob,' he gasps.

Only now, at the end, does he see.

His pupils roll white.

A toilet flushes.

We're not alone.

The bathroom to my right. Somebody's in it.

I don't know why I dive behind the bed. The chances of whoever it is that's killed Colonel being able to see me are infinitesimal. It's an instinct honed over decades of danger and peril.

I peek over the top of the duvet. A hooded figure exits the bathroom. I can't see their face. I can see their robes, though. Black. Of the cloth, but not. A flash of red around the neck. I've seen their like before.

Deacon Voigt. These are the robes of his order.

He moves his head slightly, revealing a mane of grey hair.

There is little doubt.

It's Voigt who has murdered Colonel.

I allow the deacon thirty seconds' head start before slipping out from behind the bed and following him.

He moves quickly, not casting the briefest of glances back towards the rock star he has just slain. What could possibly have been his motivation for such an act? Drugs? A petty trifle to commit murder over. But then what murder is ever committed over anything greater than triviality? Did I myself not intend to commit it from an oversaturated desire for revenge for my decades-dead sister? Colonel wronged me, but he wronged Flames more. He abandoned his principles, but he didn't deserve to die for that fact. No one deserves murder. Not even the darkest of souls.

Would I have done it if I'd have got there thirty minutes earlier? Would I have taken Colonel's life, unseen and malevolent?

I tell myself I wouldn't have.

I follow Deacon Voigt into the night.

★

I'm fortunate that Berlin's underground system hasn't gone the way of its soul. It is mercifully unchanged, and allows me to trace my way back to the deacon's church. Doubly important, because the deacon managed to lose me somehow. Whether this is deliberate or accidental, I cannot be sure; the only thing I am sure of is that he slipped from my sight.

Why I follow him, I am less sure. Am I planning to confront him about Colonel's murder? He will deny it, presumably. He's lied to me so many times in the past, it will be as easy as breathing to him.

It's the search for the truth that drives me. The need to know the *why* of it. I flatter myself that this would raise a wry smile from those I was to have led in the Pen. Their Dying Squad, who seek to wrong rights and uphold justice. I want my own justice. The justice of truth.

It is a long time since I've been amongst so many people. The lateness of the hour has not thinned the herd. They're packed into subway carriages, on their way to their homes or the next party. Imagine such normality. The luxury of it. I've never known its like. People unencumbered by destiny and duty. People tasked with doing nothing more than living their lives. I suppose I should envy them, but it's difficult to miss what I never had.

I think I see the deacon several times before I get to the church. He is not alone in wearing black garb. It's all anyone in this city seems to wear.

I approach the church slowly. It's like old times. I am reminded of a joke that Director Matthews told me once. 'Nostalgia isn't what it used to be.' At least, I believe it was a joke. It was often difficult to tell with Matthews.

I don't know why I am drawn, magnetically, back to the church. There is nothing to say that that's where the deacon will flee. It is what my gut tells me, though, and I have learned to trust such base emotions. They're not tainted by experience or prejudice. If the deacon isn't present, perhaps some of his followers will be. I can eavesdrop. Observe. Perhaps discover what he has been up to.

I pass through the church's front entrance.

I see that there are two Deacon Voigts.

One kneels in front of the altar with its gaudy glowing cross, his hands stretched out beseechingly, begging.

The other stands with a gun in his hand, aimed at the one who kneels. It's like they're photocopies of each other.

Neither sees me. I can't hear what they say.

The deacon with the gun fires.

The other folds in on himself.

Creeping forward, I see the living deacon wipe down his gun, then place it in the hand of the other, adjusting his body slightly.

He straightens up and walks over to the wall of the vestry a few feet away, then takes out a can of spray paint and begins daubing something on the wall.

I walk forward carefully, grateful for the soundlessness of my feet.

I cast the quickest of looks at the deacon on the floor. There is little doubt that he's dead; his scattered brains speak to that.

Who, then, is this second deacon?

He finishes writing.

TOO MUCH FUTURE has been daubed onto the wall.

'You can stop skulking in the shadows,' the second deacon says, turning to me.

The disguise is remarkable.

I've known the deacon for decades, and on first glance, even I think that this is him.

The beard is the same. The pallor of the skin. The way he holds himself, even. It's a look that's supposed to be viewed from a distance. It is not a look to be viewed by a dead spirit who knew the man well.

It's his eyes that betray him.

The real deacon's eyes are grey and green. They're unique.

These eyes I know just as well, but they don't belong to the deacon.

They belong to the man who liberated me from the Nazis.

A man who then went on to betray me and sell me to the highest bidder.

They belong to Director Isiah Matthews.

For a second, it looks like my old CIA handler is about to deny it's him. His body stiffens, his fists clench. Then he seems to realise the futility of such an act. I'm not a policeman; I'm merely a stranded spirit with no home to go to.

'Jacob,' he says. 'It's good to see you again.'

'I don't understand,' I say, because I don't. 'Why kill the deacon? Why murder Colonel? What did they do to you?'

'You've been around for a long time, Jacob. Almost as long as me. Why would you assume these men had done something to me?'

'You killed them for sport?'

'That's the worst reason for anyone to kill.'

Silence.

I break it.

'You sold me into slavery.'

'I merely transferred the deeds,' said Matthews, his smile fading. 'It's one of the few things I feel guilty about, if that makes any difference.'

'I won't absolve you of that guilt, if that's what you're after.'

'Nor would I expect you to,' he replies.

I feel a strange stirring amid the horror and shock of these revelations. It's like it's been hard-baked into me. It's curiosity. A need to know the truth.

'What happened to you after you sold me to the Germans?'

Matthews looks at the lifeless body of Deacon Voigt, bleeding at the altar. It's a look almost of tenderness. 'I'll tell you everything. I owe you that. Not here, though.'

He begins to tear off the deacon costume he's been wearing, stuffing it into a plain black backpack, and the effect is shocking; it's like he shrinks in front of my eyes, becoming an aged photocopy of the man I knew almost fifty years ago.

This doesn't make sense. Matthews doesn't make sense. Why did he disguise himself as the deacon?

This confusion I feel doesn't mean I underestimate how dangerous he is. He must be in his eighties, but he's murdered men far younger. I would do well to bear that in mind, especially when his history of betrayal is considered.

We walk.

We don't talk. I assume this is because Matthews doesn't want to draw attention to himself. Talking to thin air tends to bring inquisitorial glances, even in this city. He keeps his head down and his strides long. It's discombobulating to be with him once again, after all these years. Strange to be with him full stop. Is he racked with guilt about the murders he's just committed? How can he bear to live with himself?

He slows his pace, then looks both behind and in front of him. It's an action so quick, it's as if it doesn't happen at all. There's no one around.

Keeping his head down, he sidles down an alley. The ground is uneven, potholed. Dog dirt carpets the mottled concrete. It is difficult to see what he has come down here for.

Ah.

There is a building that buttresses the alley, one with an open window. With a grace belying his age, Matthews reaches for the windowsill and pulls himself up. He only strains a little. It is not, I'd wager, the first time he's done it.

Old spies never quite lose their instincts for deception, that's what I begin to realise about Matthews. He moves silently as he drops down into a dimly lit corridor, his subsequent footsteps almost as soundless as mine. He's so slight, so ghostly, it's as if he's not there at all, like he's left this realm and ventured to the next.

The doors in the corridor all have large letter-box-shaped windows. I peer through them as I follow Matthews, and quickly realise something: all the occupants are elderly.

'Why have you brought me here?' I hiss at him.

He doesn't reply, instead heading for the stairs, stopping at the foot of them and looking upwards. Clearly, he's heard something I've missed; he takes a step backwards, then plunges into the gloom, contorting himself into a recess. Within seconds, I see why: some sort of nightwatchman descends, a butchered tune on his lips.

He walks past, blind to me, sporadically looking through the windows in the doors.

Matthews sticks his head out as the watchman rounds the corner.

'Normally I wouldn't care about being caught out of my room,' he whispers, 'but there's nothing normal about tonight. Come, it's this way.'

The room isn't what I expect, but then nothing with Matthews ever is. The other rooms I peeked in at were functional, sterile things. Matthews' is positively bohemian. A record player spins in the corner, jazz leaking from it. Flowers stand in a vase in the corner. A tasteful-looking lamp casts the room in a heavenly glow. It feels like a home rather than a prison.

He pulls out a chair from the small desk in the corner and places it opposite his armchair, which he slips gratefully into.

'This is to be my confession, I suppose,' he says. 'I think that deserves a Scotch, don't you?'

I say nothing as he reaches down, bringing a bottle out from underneath the armchair, and a tumbler, too. He fills it with a healthy measure, returns the bottle under the chair, then takes a sip, closing his eyes gratefully.

'What do you know of love, Jacob?'

This is not a question I expected.

'I know the love I had for my family,' I say. 'I don't know whether it's possible for the dead to truly love. Not really.'

He takes another sip. 'Not just the dead. I always thought myself a freak, not because of my ability to see the dead, but because I found it impossible to love anyone but myself. That was, until I met Ralf Voigt.'

I frown. 'You loved the deacon? I just saw you murder him.'

Matthews smiles sadly. 'You've been on this earth long enough to know those things aren't mutually exclusive. There's a razor-thin line between love and hate. Thinner than most people are willing to admit.'

'This is to be a justification of murder, then.'

'It's to be nothing more than the truth, as seamy and unkempt as that is.'

He reaches into his jacket and withdraws a packet of cigarettes. He taps one out, and a match appears from nowhere, almost as if it's a magic trick. He strikes it, birthing the flame into life, inhaling deeply.

'Those things will kill you,' I tell him.

He laughs. 'Fingers crossed.'

He considers me. 'After I betrayed you, I began my new life

in East Germany. It wasn't what I expected. If I'd been in the West, things would have been easier. Freer. It was the communists who had bought my loyalty, though, so I had to make the best of it. I received a palatial apartment, a driver, everything a good defector could want. I struggled with the constriction of it all, though. I've never been much good with being told what to do. It doesn't agree with me.'

'The army wasn't the best choice for you, then.'

'I was conscripted,' he says. 'Then co-opted, because of my abilities. Choice never really came into it. It did when I made my decision to defect to East Germany. The problem with people like me is we get antsy. And I did.'

He takes in another lungful of smoke. 'I retreated into the shadows, and that was where I met the good deacon. We became lovers. It *was* about love, for me. I was older than him, but that didn't seem to matter. Not to me, anyway. A man of the cloth would have normally baulked at the riskiness of our relationship, but Ralf already operated on the edges of society; religion was a barely tolerated minority concern in communist Germany. We were happy together.'

'So happy that you murdered him.'

Matthews places the cigarette in a pale blue ashtray, then picks up his glass of Scotch, swirling its contents. 'Voigt lost his faith. In us, at least. Our ability to see the dead was something that never really bonded us. It should have brought us closer, but it became a dirty, shameful secret between us. That was partly my fault. I hated how it defined me. Then, the Wall fell, and we met another who shared our gift. Though Lucia's was grafted onto her rather than naturally obtained.'

'You know Lucia?'

He nodded. 'One of the most brilliant people I've ever met, and certainly the most ruthless. Lucia isn't who you think she is, Jacob.'

'I'm aware of what Lucia is. She betrayed me in the same way you all did.'

'She's good at that.'

'How did she betray you?'

'We went into business together.'

This isn't possible. I would have seen him at the research facility.

I tell him this.

He smiles. 'You wouldn't. I would have liked to have seen you very much, but Lucia was always protective of her pet science project. Ignoring the fact that it was I who brought you to Berlin in the first place. I made sure you were well treated over the years, though. Lucia has a habit of tossing aside her playthings after she's finished with them. I made sure she kept you in good condition. Then you tried to venture to the Pen, and I was unable to protect you any longer.'

'The Pen is my birthright.'

'You'll get no argument from me there. Soon after you attempted to pass over the bridge, Lucia ended our business relationship. She had what she needed from me. I'd spent decades working with her, helping build up Wraith as an organisation. She locked me out of the boardroom. Gave me some laughable honorary title. I was finished.'

'Where was the deacon in all this?' I ask, and it's as if I've slapped Matthews across the face. He goes for another slug of Scotch, then realises there's none left and sets the glass aside.

'Ralf never trusted Lucia. Rightly, as it turned out. She wasn't the cause of our relationship ending, though. Ralf changed. The destruction of the Wall had been the focus of his life; when he achieved it, he suffered a crisis of faith that had little to do with religion. His had always been a life on the edges: he ran drugs from East to West, did you know that?'

'When?' I ask.

'Before the Wall fell. To start with, his aims were noble; he channelled the money back into humanitarian causes in the East. Revolutionary ones, too. Then, after the Wall came down, he simply did it because he liked the money. Such a slide is never precipitous; it is a slow, mission-creep descent. His elevation to drug kingpin had one benefit, though: it showed me how I could have my revenge upon Lucia.'

'I feared this was a story that would be bathed in revenge.'

Matthews laughs. 'What stories aren't? The Bible is soaked in them.'

He leans back, getting comfortable. He's enjoying this, despite his protestations and tone of contrariness.

'I hadn't spoken to Ralf for a long time. I'd heard the rumours, though, of his descent into criminality. I thought of the drug I'd developed with Lucia that allowed the living to see the dead.'

I frown. 'What do you know of Spook?'

'As much as any man alive; I spent the best part of two decades developing it. That, and Lucia's other toys and trinkets. I saw how I could use it to hurt her. I still had friends in Wraith, if little influence. I learned that you were being transported to a more secure facility, along with a consignment of Spook. I offered Ralf a business opportunity, and he took it. He hijacked the van and liberated you.'

'The deacon used me,' I say, anger rising. 'Just like you all used me.'

Matthews nods. 'That wasn't part of the deal. My cut from the Spook sales was a means of supporting myself. A retirement home is a wonderful cover, but it's an expensive one. Needless to say, I never saw a penny from that Spook. Voigt betrayed me.'

'That's what the murders were about?' I ask, failing to keep the disappointment out of my voice. 'A drug deal gone wrong?'

'They were about betrayal,' Matthews says, leaning forward. 'They were about our years together meaning nothing. They were about me rotting away in this place while he lorded it as the angel of Berlin, feted for his decency and generosity.'

This is beginning to make a sick sort of sense.

'It was all about sullying the deacon's name. Scorching his reputation to the ground.'

Matthews' smirk disappears. 'I won't deny it wasn't a delicious by-product. Spycraft – the art of disguise – never really leaves you. Colonel had never wronged me, but he was a useful idiot. Murdering him dressed as the good deacon forged a connection between the two of them. I made sure to reveal just enough of myself to the CCTV cameras to be identifiable. Then I killed the deacon in his own church and passed it off as suicide. I didn't want the police looking too closely at his dealings, because they would lead back to me. I left just enough information on his computer to frame the whole thing as Voigt finally taking revenge for Colonel's defection all those years ago.'

'That's what the writing was about at the hotel room,' I say. 'The church, too. Old punk slogans from the past, making people think it was an idealist taking his revenge.'

Matthews seems to age before my eyes. Anyone who says confession is good for the soul has clearly never witnessed it.

'I loved him,' he says, 'but it was never enough. I was never enough.'

He looks at me intently. 'Have I disappointed you, Jacob? This is what we are, as a species. We love, we fuck, we betray, we are cast low. It has always been this way.'

He's right, of course. I've seen it time and again, over the decades.

A plan forms in my head.

★

As I walk towards the nursing home's entrance, I see the telltale glimmer of the dead.

I copy Matthews from before, ducking underneath the stairwell. It affords me a good view of the reception area. A man in a trench coat operates a device there. As I suspected, he's dead; his skin shimmers in the moonlight. Interesting that one of our kind knows how to use the equipment of the soil. Apparently he obtains the information he's looking for, as he leaves the reception area and walks up the stairs over my head, heading for the floor I've just left.

Some instinct tells me he is on my side, but I quell it. I don't have time to talk to him.

I have had enough of the brutality of man. His betrayal. His pettiness.

It's time to change my fate.

It's time to go home.

Chapter 31

'I love what you've done with the place.'

Lucia felt the hulking monstrosity alongside her bristle and fidget, his anger barely restrained.

'I haven't done anything,' said Uriel, his words bassy and wet. 'It's the girl. She's riled the Dispossessed up. Got them to riot.'

'I don't make many mistakes, but underestimating Daisy-May was one of them,' Lucia replied. 'I should have killed her when I had the chance.'

'You assume you could have done. If she could strip me of my wings, what chance did you have?'

They stood at the brow of a hill, looking down upon a tableau of destruction. Fires raged in the blackened factories, charcoal smoke billowing next to licks of flame. The lines of Dispossessed outside them were gone; instead, they had massed hundreds of feet away, forming a horseshoe shape around the main compound. Thirty or so fallen angels guarded it, their wings flapping.

'I don't see the Warden,' said Hanna, shielding her eyes with a curved hand, scanning the army of Dispossessed.

'She'll be there,' said Lucia. 'She always is. You see why I needed you now, Hanna.'

Uriel grimaced at the half-masked white-haired girl in front of him. 'We don't need any more children interfering in the actions of grown-ups.'

Hanna laughed, looking the monstrously sized angel up and down, taking in his ill-fitting skin suit. 'I'm not the one who's playing dress-up. What are you supposed to be, exactly?'

Uriel took a step towards her, his red maw of a mouth snarling, his chiselled white teeth flashing.

Lucia raised an arm. 'There's no need for unpleasantness, Uriel. I come bearing gifts.' She nodded towards the suitcase at her feet.

Uriel sneered. 'What could you possibly have that would interest me?'

Lucia leaned down, punching in a code on the case's recessed keypad.

A whirring sounded as the case opened like a concertina.

Two sharp arcs of metal were inside, connected to what looked like a metal harness. The quickest of glances would have made you think they were wings.

Uriel looked at her with contempt. 'Is this supposed to be some sort of joke? Would you mock me now, Lucia?'

Lucia smiled. 'I'm liberating you. Pick them up.'

Still scowling, Uriel reached down, grasping the metal harness in his clawed hand and pulling it from the case. Almost immediately, the harness – and the two sleek slivers of metal attached to it – began to grow, the mechanics inside it grinding and grumbling. As Uriel held it at arm's length, the wings dipped into the dirt of the Pen floor.

'Well?' said Lucia. 'Aren't you going to try them on?'

Patience had never been one of Daisy-May's virtues.

She was more of an act-first-repent-later sort of girl. So it almost hurt her, making the army of Dispossessed wait. The compound was right there in front of them. Remus had made the decision to erect a gaudy, ridiculous statue of himself on the roof (one with a whacking great spear, hilariously), which was worthy of revolution by itself. There were thirty or so fallen angels guarding the compound, but would they really hold the line when the chips were down? It was difficult to believe they cared much for Remus. They cared for their freedom, though, and the fact that they'd been let back into the Pen. Daisy-May threatened that, which was why she hadn't given the signal to attack yet.

She wanted to get a good look at them. Stare them right in the eyes and see how much they actually meant it.

There was the chance, too, that she was about to walk the thousands of souls behind her into a trap. Their deaths would be on her hands.

'You hold, Warden. Why?'

Daisy-May didn't turn to the Judge. Instead, she continued to stare out at the squadron of fallen angels above her.

'When I give the order to charge, that's it. It's going to mean obliteration for a shitload of the Dispossessed behind me.'

'They knew what they were getting into. We all did.'

'Doesn't mean the decision to attack's any easier to give. Wish there was a way that didn't involve wholesale fucking slaughter.'

'You're too indecisive,' spat Oma Jankie. 'You must give the order to attack *now*.'

'*You* must shut your fucking trap,' Daisy-May snapped back.

She frowned, pointing towards the sky. 'What's that?'

A dot had appeared on the horizon, growing larger by the second. As it got closer, Daisy-May realised it was an angel unlike the others. Light reflected off its metallic wings, and the speed at which it was travelling was far greater than she'd seen from the rest. Its skin was different, too. It was pink. Ill-fitting.

'I killed this fucker.'

'It seems unaware,' the Judge replied.

Two flashes of light erupted from the angel's wings.

Two black dots hung in the sky for a few seconds, then began screaming towards them.

They looked awfully like missiles.

Better to be lucky than good: that was what Hans's old drill sergeant always used to say. Tried to claim the phrase as his own, when it was actually Napoleon who had coined it.

The little French bastard had been right, because as Hans stood in Wraith's main control room, looking at the bank of CCTV monitors (and he *could* just about look, despite the glitchiness of his vision and the haze of pain – Lazarus's thumbs had done quite the number on his implants), he realised he was just about the luckiest man alive. Not only had Joe and his ragamuffin partner walked Megan right up to the front door, they also weren't alone.

A couple of hundred yards away, emerging from the bushes, was a boy. One who glimmered in the way of the dead.

One who was dressed in a Hitler Youth uniform.

Jacob.

You came home.

The more Joe saw of Wraith's headquarters, the more memories of the place came back.

The walls were bleached white, like heaven had reinvented itself as an Apple store. Lab-coated people did important things, secretly. The place positively thrummed with invention and innovation. It wasn't like other research labs, though. There'd never been anywhere quite like Wreath's main hub of operation. He was pretty sure of that.

I've been here before. When I was so amnesia-riddled it didn't matter, because Hans and Lucia knew I'd forget it minutes after I'd seen it.

Take the five glass-walled rooms in front of him. To the living souls that walked past them, they were empty, stripped of furnishings and life. Each had a cot in the corner and a subliminal, twang-your-teeth hum, but that was about it.

If you were dead, though – which Joe most assuredly was – they were anything but empty. Each contained a spirit, souls that had once been alive but now weren't. Some of these were distressed, struggling to come to terms with their state of being. They hammered on the walls of their glass prison to no avail, raging against the injustice of it all.

When you considered the five rooms behind him, though, Joe was of the opinion that the spirits were the lucky ones.

'They're alive,' said Megan. 'They don't glimmer. Why have they trapped the living here?'

'Call this living?' said Bits. ''Cos I don't.'

Joe didn't, either.

The living souls' cells were quite different to those of the spirits. All of them enjoyed flat-screen TVs, comfortable beds, plush couches and a sense of lazy decadence. What riches had been promised to tempt them in? Perhaps they were just desperate. That was what desperation did to a person: it made you strangle doubts before they had a chance to take hold.

This place wasn't a homeless shelter, or a refuge. It was a lab, and the rats in it looked half starved.

It was a mistake bringing Megan here. A major one.

'Thought the shit back at the casino was bad,' said Bits. 'This is next-level.' He turned to Joe. 'We have to stop this, man. Free these people, then raze the place to the ground, brick by brick.'

'You sure you want to know about your past?' Joe asked Megan. 'Seeing all this, you might not like the answers to the questions you have.'

'I still need those answers,' said Megan. 'I won't have any peace until I do.'

Joe nodded. 'Then let's get them for you, quickly.'

I'd never seen Wraith's research facility from the outside before. That's true of so many of the foul dungeons I've been kept in over the years. At least Himmler allowed me to see the castle he enslaved me in. Lucia never did me that courtesy.

Not that it's particularly impressive. If you didn't know about the hive of industry that throbbed beneath it, you would dismiss the place as decrepit and abandoned. This is, I suppose, the point.

The technique Lucia – and all my other jailers over the years – employed to imprison me hasn't been used on the outside of the structure. Why would it? They want to keep spirits from getting out, not from getting in.

As I slip soundlessly through the recessed concrete doorway, I tread lightly and carefully. There are those here who would do me harm. Most here, in truth, would gladly do so.

As I venture deeper into the facility, the surroundings become more familiar. It was rare that I was allowed the opportunity to wander here, but the industrial nature of the corridors strikes a chord. There's something else, too. A tingle in the air, a charge that promises things to me. Like the bridge to take me to the Pen. I just need to evade detection till I reach it.

I offer up a prayer to the Almighty. I'm not someone who keeps a tally of debts owed, but I'm of the opinion that his assistance in my cause is long overdue.

Jacob may have been ancient, but it seemed to Hans that he was unable to shake his childish naïvety. The boy was clearly under the impression that he hadn't been noticed, merrily strolling as he was into the research facility's inner sanctum. That was fine.

Better than fine, in fact, when you considered that Lazarus and his motley crew were on a collision course with him. All Hans had to do was allow them access to the high-security area, and they'd be trapped like bluebottles in a jar.

Once they were – and as long as his juddering, glitchy vision would allow it – it would be time to squash them.

Daisy-May kidded herself for all of three seconds that the two black dots in the sky weren't missiles.

They hadn't been enough to worry her; all she needed to do was use that telekinetic mind trick of hers, send them right back at the freaky angel with the cyborg metal wings and that was that. Two birds, one rocket-powered stone.

Problem was, the mind trick wasn't working. No matter how vividly she imagined the missiles veering off course and ploughing into Uriel, they kept on coming towards her.

They've been adapted somehow. Upgraded to be resistant.

She thrust her hand out for a final time, straining.

Nothing.

The missiles dipped.

They'd miss her and the rest of the front line, but the Dispossessed packed in behind wouldn't be so lucky.

'Fall back,' she bellowed, as loudly as her teenage lungs would allow. 'Fall *back*.'

A whine filled the air as the Dispossessed did as they were told, jostling, heaving and straining backwards. Panic flooded the ranks as they realised what was speeding towards them. Daisy-May watched helplessly as the missiles dipped further, overshooting her position then ploughing into the bodies several hundred feet behind.

The aftershock lifted her and those around her clean off their feet, scalding them with heat and petrol fumes then dumping them into the dirt. She shook her head clear and looked backwards, instantly regretting it. Clumps of bodies lay in piles, browning almost immediately. Hundreds of limbs had been torn asunder. Wails and screams filled the air. The Judge and Oma Jankie lay several feet away from her, stirring slightly.

This is on me, thought Daisy-May. I've led them to a slaughter.

'Girl.'

The voice rang out loud and true, reverberating around what had become a battlefield.

Daisy-May looked up to see Uriel. Where before there had been tar-black wings was now a pair of mighty steel ones, gleaming fiercely under the grumbling Pen sky.

She clenched her fists, her eyes burning. 'I obviously didn't kick your arse hard enough last time.'

Uriel began to laugh, his metal wings beating the air steadily. 'I will end you, child. I will make you suffer first, though.'

'Already suffering, listening to your babble.'

His red maw contorted itself into a smile. 'Time to die.'

Hanna had to admit it: she was impressed.

She'd known about Daisy-May before, of course: they'd competed for the Dispossessed's loyalty in the Pen. But whereas Hanna had had to rely on the language of the dead to keep that loyalty, Daisy-May hadn't needed such tricks. She'd led simply by being herself. And there she was now, a frail rag doll of a thing when compared with that monster in the sky, utterly undaunted, ready to fight. How Hanna could have used her on the soil. She would have made a fine number two.

'Come,' said Lucia. 'We have business to attend to inside the compound. There's a back entrance, away from all this unpleasantness.'

'What about Daisy-May?' said Hanna. 'If I'm to become Warden, she needs to abdicate.'

Lucia smiled. 'Not if she's dead. Which in a few short moments she will be.'

Hanna nodded, but waited a few seconds to watch nonetheless. She felt a certain kinship with the girl. She'd had the enormity of leadership thrust upon her, and had then been betrayed by those alongside her. She deserved better.

She deserves what she's going to get, Oma Jankie's voice said. *I've brought her to you. If Uriel fails, you'll need to finish the job.*

The monster in the sky screamed and began diving towards Daisy-May.

Hanna turned away.

It seemed unlikely that Uriel would fail. There was nothing to be done now. Daisy-May's reign would soon be over, and hers would begin.

That was simply the way of it.

'Kill it, child,' said the Judge.

'Smite it from the sky,' Oma Jankie weighed in.

'I'm trying,' Daisy-May said, her hand outstretched, her mind visualising the creature's metallic wings ripped from its back. 'It's fucking hard to smite.'

Because it was; in the same way that the missiles Uriel had launched had been impervious to her mind manipulation, so too was Uriel himself. He was powering towards her, that sick look on his face, and all of a sudden, she felt every inch the teenager she actually was.

When it came down to it, she was a sixteen-year-old shit-kicker from Nottingham, not an afterlife demigod.

'Surrender is an option,' said Oma Jankie. 'There's no shame in it.'

'No sense in it, either,' said Daisy-May. ''Cos the minute I do, that winged fucker will slaughter every last one of us.'

Fire flashed from Uriel's steel wings.

Machine guns, Daisy-May thought. The bastard's got machine guns.

Bullets thudded into the mass of Dispossessed behind her, spinning their bodies like tops.

I have to end this now.

She stepped forward, her arms up.

Uriel hung in mid-air, a smile scarred on his face

'All right, you big twat,' said Daisy-May. 'I surrender.'

Getting to the lab's restricted area was easier than it should have been.

Joe found easy hard to trust.

They stood in one of the laboratories, racks of computer servers surrounding them, red and blue lights blinking, streams of coloured wires leaking from the black towers.

Joe reached into his pocket and removed a small plastic case, handing it to Megan.

She looked at it doubtfully. 'What is this?'

'One of Lucia's little toys.'

'Looks like something you'd get out of a cracker,' said Bits, as he watched the thin sliver of metal curl and wriggle. 'A shit one.'

'What does it do?' asked Megan.

Joe told her. 'Any info they have on you, this device will make it happen. I've seen it in action.'

Megan gingerly picked up the wiggling sliver and fed it into the back of one of the servers. The machine chuntered, like it resented being cajoled into action.

'What do I do now?'

'Ask it what you want.'

Just as she was about to do exactly that, Joe felt a presence behind him.

So, apparently, did Bits; they both whipped around at the same time.

A boy was standing in the doorway.

These people claim to mean me no harm. After a lifetime and an afterlife of betrayal, that's difficult to believe somehow.

'I know you,' the shorter of the two men says. His accent is sharp, like there are razor blades embedded in it. His tone is not unfriendly, though. He's dead, like me. 'I definitely know you, lad. Where from?'

'I've never seen you before,' I reply.

I've seen the other man, though. The one in the trench coat. He was at the nursing home, arriving as I left.

The ratty-looking man clicks his fingers. 'Saw you in a photo.' He turns to the living woman. 'That Julius wanker had a photo of this lad at his gaff. He was jumping around on stage with a punk band. Had that same Nazi Youth outfit on.'

The man I saw at the nursing home looks at me curiously.

'My name's Joe Lazarus,' he says. 'I've got a feeling you're the boy I've been looking for.'

I ask him what he means.

'Every step of my investigation seemed to involve this mythical boy spirit. It's you, isn't it?'

I've never been described as mythical before. I suppose I am.

I don't want to talk to these men. I'm sick of being lied to. Betrayed. I'm of a mind to simply walk away. Ignore them.

But walk where?

There is nothing else to take from me. What have I got to lose by talking to them?

I tell them my name, of how I was destined to be Warden of the Pen, a destiny that was wrestled away from me by the Nazis.

When they don't blink at this revelation, I feel confident enough to continue.

I tell them of how I have been bought and sold over the

417

decades, how I was saved and betrayed by Lucia and Deacon Voigt. How they were responsible for the supply of Spook that has flooded Berlin's streets. How Director Matthews took his revenge on the deacon. It sounds incredible, this story that I tell, yet it lightens me somehow, salves my soul.

Confession does have its benefits, apparently.

'Mad story, that,' said Bits.

It was. A real head-spinner, when you considered that the dead boy in front of them should by rights be their boss, the Warden of the Pen himself. Joe had to admit he felt a degree of anger. While he'd been chasing his tail all over Berlin, a kid had solved the Spook case for him. And Joe had been in Matthews' room. He'd been taken in by the elderly con man, beguiled by the half-truths that had been whispered to him.

Maybe he shouldn't feel too bad. If what Jacob said was true, he'd been born about thirty years before Joe. That was a lot of life experience to call on.

The Warden of the Pen in waiting. It was hard to believe. What did it mean for Daisy-May?

'You got out of here once,' said Joe. 'What made you come back?'

'There's a bridge,' Jacob said, 'one that will take me to the Pen.'

Joe frowned. 'That's impossible.'

'Why?'

They turned to Megan.

'After everything you've seen in the last few weeks,' she said, 'is a bridge to the afterlife really the most outlandish?'

'She's got a point,' said Bits. 'Feels like all bets are off. Know what I mean?'

'Unfortunately, I do,' said Joe.

And in fact, he'd seen it. The woman who didn't glimmer had crossed over it when leaving the Pen and returning to the soil. Slit the throat of a Dispossessed called Zed, right in front of him.

Which meant they could cross it the other way.

He looked at Jacob. 'This bridge: do you know where it is?'

'All too well.'

He turned to Bits. 'You ready to go home?'

'That's what we're calling the Pen, is it?' said Bits.

'I suppose we are.'

'Sounds good, then.'

Joe looked at the bank of monitors to his left. He remembered the cages containing the spirits he'd seen earlier.

A plan formed.

He told Megan what he wanted her to do.

She sighed. 'Will this ever end?'

'For you, it ends here. Whatever happened to you in the past – whatever the reason is for that barcode on your hand – it'll be contained on these servers. The Ghost in the Machine will help you find your truth. Your peace.'

Bits smirked. 'Missed your inspirational talks.' He jabbed a thumb at Megan. 'Had to put up with this one's sarkiness. Proper millennial, her.'

Megan rolled her eyes. 'He didn't know what a millennial was. Thought it was something to do with *Star Wars*.'

Silence between them.

Megan broke first. 'Never thanked you, for rescuing me back in Manchester.'

'And you were right not to,' Joe replied. 'Don't get paid in thanks when you're Dying Squad.'

'Don't get paid at all,' muttered Bits.

'What would you spend it on if we did?' said Joe. 'Spirits?'

Bits's face wrinkled. 'Proper dad joke, that.'

Megan smiled at Bits. 'I never thanked you, either. You saved my life in that psycho drug dealer's lab. All I did was bitch about you possessing me.'

'Reckon that bitching was legit. Must have been mega creepy, having the likes of me stuffed inside you.'

Megan smirked at him. 'Of all the people I'd like to be possessed by, you're at least . . . I don't know, a *hundredth* on the list.'

'High fucking praise.'

'We should go,' said Jacob. 'I do not know how much longer the bridge will be open for.'

The boy was right.

They gave Megan a final wave, then rounded the corner, slipping out of sight.

As Hans watched Lazarus, Jacob and the other one run down the corridor, he knew he was taking a risk.

It was a calculated one.

The security here was tight. If that trio of freaks did manage to find their way to the bridge, there was a mob of armed technicians waiting to cut them down. With any luck, they'd do so without the need to involve Lucia.

Megan, on the other hand, was a living, breathing blot on his copybook, one he was going to have the opportunity to wipe clean.

Creeping towards the server room, he resolved to do just that.

Chapter 32

Daisy-May stood with her arms aloft in surrender, several feet in front of Oma Jankie and the Judge, the ranks of Dispossessed jostling behind them.

Uriel hovered above, his metallic wings rippling, a look of triumph on his face.

'You're making a mistake, Warden,' the Judge called out. 'This beast will not accept your surrender.'

'Nonsense,' Oma Jankie replied. 'There is no disgrace in negotiating terms. Why, I am even prepared to do so on your behalf.'

'You're not negotiating a fucking sausage,' said Daisy-May. 'I want you where I can see you.'

She tuned out Oma Jankie's reply, keeping her eyes on Uriel and her mind on something else.

The fallen angel beat his newly sutured wings, gliding downwards.

'What's wrong, girl? Have your powers deserted you?'

'Powers are just fine,' said Daisy-May, her eyelids fluttering slightly. 'Guessing me not being able to split you in two's due to those fancy metal wings of yours?'

Uriel landed just a foot or so away from her, the Pen floor kicking up as his hooved feet ground into it. 'A present from the woman who doesn't glimmer.'

'I've not been living under a rock,' Daisy-May replied. 'You can use her name.'

He flashed his white spear teeth. 'You've met Lucia before, of course.'

'Yep. Just one of the many pricks that have tried to kill me lately. Bit emasculating, isn't it, having her fit you out with new wings? Sort of like having your mum choose your clothes for you when you're forty.'

The fallen angel's grin turned into a scowl.

'And that fake skin you wear, mate. You're over seven feet tall; only person that's mistaking you for human is my Grandma June, and she's half senile and all the way dead. Give it up.'

Uriel flexed his wings again, the metal sighing in response, then thrust out an arm, wrapping his fist around Daisy-May's T-shirt and lifting her clean off the ground.

'Enough,' he said, in that gutter-full-of-grit way of his. 'I'll make it quick.'

Good, thought Daisy-May, as the beast's hand closed around her throat.

Me too.

Joe stood with Bits and Jacob, separated from the bridge by a transparent security door, the technicians on the other side oblivious to them. Light seeped from the gold-foil doorway, reflecting off the white plastic of the bridge itself.

'That's it?' said Bits. 'Don't even look finished, man.'

'Science doesn't always play by the rules in your head,' said Jacob. 'I'm the living proof of that.'

Joe had to agree with Bits. The bridge looked painfully inadequate, like a prop from a bad film. How could it possibly take them home?

Jacob seemed to sense his doubts.

'The bridge works. Lucia has used it many times. I myself

have crossed it once before. It will return us to the Pen.' He pointed to the technicians. They were resolutely undistracted. 'That is, if your friend has done what was asked of her. I see no sign of it.'

Joe shifted on his feet. Neither did he.

Come on, Megan.

What are you doing?

The Ghost in the Machine was a hell of a toy. Megan could see them selling like crazy at Christmas.

All she'd had to do was command the cell doors to open, and hey presto, they had. She had to assume there'd been some sort of containment field that had lifted when that had happened, because the spirits that had been trapped inside were distrustful of the door opening at first, tentatively sticking out a limb here and a head there. It was only when they realised pain wasn't following such an act that they gained confidence and scampered from their prisons.

Which was her good deed for the day done, and hopefully they'd provide a distraction while Joe and Bits made it over the bridge.

Now it was her turn.

The server room was a strange beast, half technological hub, half supply room, with a rack of cattle prods like the one Hans had tortured Joe with back at the casino, but it was the computer tower that Megan's attention was fixed on.

She slipped the Ghost in the Machine out of its plastic case, and dropped it into the tower's CD tray.

The tray closed, slowly.

'Show me all files related to Megan Veins.'

The operating system thought about it.

Then it complied.

★

Uriel became watery in front of Daisy-May's eyes, his hand tightening on her throat. She was in no doubt that he could snap her neck with a flick of his wrist, but was grateful for the monster's sadistic streak; he wanted to prolong her agony, savour every last second of her eyes bulging and the life leaving her body.

It was what gave her a chance.

The wings he'd been gifted by Lucia acted as some sort of force field against her powers. Those powers were still there, though; she could feel them bubbling in the trough of her stomach. All she needed to do was tap into them, then direct them somewhere else.

Towards the big-ass statue of Remus that sat on the roof of the compound, for instance.

It had begun to strain and creak, and she was grateful for Uriel's bloodlust, because he hadn't noticed. He was too busy strangling her.

She didn't feel her windpipe being crushed. Instead, she'd retreated into the sanctuary of her mind. The scene there didn't look that different. Uriel was there, and he'd still got her by the throat. The heroic statue of Remus clutching a spear was the main difference. In her mind, that statue was being ripped free of its moorings, floating like a proper old-school matinee ghost, then plunging down on top of Uriel, the spear impaling him right through the middle.

She'd never had much of an imagination when she'd been breathing, and in truth, she didn't need much of one now. She just needed to visualise this one body-splitting act.

There was a scream.

She felt the pressure on her throat slacken.

The ground rushed up to meet her arse.

Daisy-May blinked, back in the real world.

Uriel staggered, staring down in outrage at the stone javelin that had found itself thrust through his stomach. The wing harness lay slashed and crumpled at his feet.

'Looks painful,' said Daisy-May, her voice strained and cracked. 'Let me help you pull it out.'

She swiped downwards.

Uriel screamed again.

The spear sliced the fallen angel in half, the two sides of him falling at opposite angles.

Daisy-May looked upwards as the remaining creatures moved into an attack formation. Or what she assumed was an attack formation; her experience of facing down a sky full of demons was pretty limited. Better to err on the side of caution. It was unlikely they wanted to discuss crochet techniques.

She raised her hand and risked a look behind her. Oma Jankie had disappeared.

The Dispossessed were still there, though. They'd been shot at and half blown to hell, but they were still there.

The Judge, too.

My people, thought Daisy-May.

She dropped her hand.

She screamed, 'Attack!'

'It seems you've got yourself into something of a pickle, Remus.'

Remus grimaced as he looked up at the monitor. It showed thousands of Dispossessed surging forward, the fallen angels swooping and surging above them, several of the beasts already felled due to the sheer number of the embattled half-souls.

'If your science experiment had worked, we wouldn't be having this problem,' he said. 'You swore those wings would make Uriel unbeatable.'

'There's nothing wrong with the technology,' said Lucia. 'Only the creature I entrusted it to. The Warden is still just one person. She can be stopped.'

'And the thousands of cattle that so slavishly follow her? How are you proposing to stop them, exactly?'

'That was your department,' said Lucia. 'They were broken-spirited and beaten, that's what you told me. Yet here they are, fighting a war.'

As she stood in the compound's control room, surrounded by a wall of screens and inquisitive, questioning eyes, Hanna realised she'd never actually been inside the concrete building before. She'd led a platoon of Dispossessed to the gates (and been fired upon for her trouble), but she'd never made it this far. If things had gone to plan – if she'd been allowed to fulfil her birthright – she'd have been Warden here, commanding every last soul in the room. As it was, she was just a tool to be used, then discarded.

That wasn't going to work for her.

It was time to see whether the language of the dead still did.

'Do you have any sort of amplification system?' she asked. 'Any way I can talk to the Dispossessed?'

Remus scowled at her. 'I don't want you talking to anyone. The last time you were here, you almost brought about the end of existence.'

Hanna smiled, her hand-made mask crinkling as she did so. 'We all have our off days.'

'Why have you brought her here?' Remus asked Lucia. 'It was difficult enough to get rid of her the last time.'

'I've brought her here because she's capable of something that we're not: she speaks the language of the dead. That will be rather useful, will it not?'

'I can make the Dispossessed stand down,' said Hanna. 'I just need my voice to be able to reach them. Before, I had months living amongst them, time to plant the seed and nurture it. Now, I need something a little louder and more immediate.'

Remus glowered, but didn't contradict her.

426

And nor should you, thought Lucia. Hanna's the secret weapon you didn't believe it possible to possess. She's your saviour.

'We have a speaker system, yes, though little reason to use it,' said Remus. 'One of the Duchess's follies.'

'This amplification,' Hanna said. 'You can operate it?'

He nodded. 'As can my team.'

She smiled. 'Good.'

She turned to Lucia and thrust a formless hand into her chest.

Lucia frowned. 'What are you doing?'

Hanna willed her hand to solidify as it closed around Lucia's heart, calcifying as it did so, squeezing the pulsing, clammy organ.

Lucia opened her mouth in surprise.

Blood began to seep from it.

Good, thought Oma Jankie, her voice bouncing around Hanna's head. *Good.*

Hanna withdrew her hand.

Lucia tumbled to the floor.

The white-haired girl turned to Remus, who stood gawping, slack-jawed.

'Wh-why?' he stammered.

'Because her heart wasn't in it, and she'd outlived her usefulness,' said Hanna. 'If you don't want to outlive yours, show me how to speak to the Dispossessed.'

'What about the Warden?'

'Daisy-May's as dead as the rest of them. She's already proved herself vulnerable to the language of the dead. She'll follow what I say to the letter, and thank me for it.'

The door is open.

The bridge is in sight.

The spirits from the cells are streaming towards it. Megan found a way to release them, clearly.

427

Lazarus turns to me. 'We have to go now, while the technicians are distracted.'

I nod. I'm so close now to the Pen. I believe I can smell the bleach-like odour it emits from here.

'Thanks for coming to find me,' Lazarus says to his partner. 'For giving a shit.'

Bits shrugs. 'Thanks for giving me a reason to.'

Lazarus turns to me. 'Are you ready, Jacob?'

I tell him that I am.

He smiles. 'Then the last one to the Pen buys the beers.'

Megan's eyes devoured the information, her brain cursing at not being able to absorb it quicker. She'd been part of a programme run by her grandfather. One that experimented on the living so that they could see the dead. Dormant cancers engineered to trick the body into a sort of twilight between living and dying enabled the ability.

Some of it she'd suspected. Some of it she'd been told by the Generation Killer. None of it told her who her parents had been, or whether they were alive or dead.

The file on her had led to others, though. Grainy video footage of Nazi research into the dead, research that had been co-opted by the Americans. Collaborations between the purgatorial realm known as the Pen and various governments of the world. An agreement that seemed to bridge different political philosophies, embracing both capitalism and communism. All of it involving people like herself, rats to be tested on and eventually culled.

The world needs to hear about this, thought Megan. It's not right. Any of it.

Her fingers started dancing over the keyboard. The world *would* hear about it.

She knew it was a risk, the time she was taking to forward

this ream of information into the digital heavens, but it was one worth taking.

Newsroom email addresses were plucked at random, messages with dozens of documents fired over to them. Some might dismiss it as the work of a crank, but not all of them would. Hanna and her actions in New Tokyo would see to that.

Finally she stepped away from the keyboard, knowing that to linger here would place her in even more danger.

Then that danger found her.

Hans had never taken much pleasure in the business of killing.

Murder was messy. It always made his job harder.

On this occasion, though, he intended to enjoy it.

He had nothing against Megan personally. He had plenty against freaks like Lazarus, though. He'd made him look foolish, and worse, incompetent. That was bad for his employment prospects as well as his ego, so as he wrapped his hands around Megan's throat, he enjoyed the slightest rush of pleasure. Any friend of Lazarus was a sworn enemy of his.

He'd forgotten what it was like, that shocked look in their eyes as they struggled to comprehend what was happening to them.

He wasn't ashamed to say he liked the power of it, because the last twenty-four hours had contrived to make him feel power*less*.

This was more like it.

They managed to make it halfway up the bridge's steps before they were spotted.

It was better than Joe had dared hope. They'd been helped by the influx of freed spirits, the technicians fiddling with the bridge's apparatus surprised by a jailbreak of that type.

Surprised, yet not unprepared. As they reached the bridge proper, sulphur scorched the air, white light exploding several feet in front of them. Joe looked down to see one of the technicians with a bulky weapon in his hands.

Like Elias used in Manchester. He called it a bolt cutter. One of those bolts hits us, that's exactly what it'll do.

Crack.

The sound was like someone had taken a bullwhip to the air.

Crack.

Crack.

More of the technicians were firing now.

It's like we've wandered into a firing squad, thought Joe. Why isn't anything ever easy? Or at least not fatally hard.

'Don't stop,' he called to the others, aiming straight for the doorway of light.

Two more bolts sizzled, exploding just half a foot in front of him.

He heard a yell from behind and risked a look backwards.

Bits had fallen.

With death so close, Megan realised she'd never wanted to live more.

It was a life she'd filled with art and music and travel and forward motion. It was impossible to dwell on a past she couldn't remember, and she didn't plan for a future she couldn't predict. She took risks and embraced her freakery, throwing a protective arm around the dead. She'd never found peace, though. Until she'd found out about her past, that had always seemed out of reach.

Now that she had, she found it didn't change much. To live would simply be enough.

Ironic that realisation had come now, at the moment of her death.

She'd tried to wriggle free of Hans, but he was too strong. Too big.

430

She kicked out, her left foot connecting with the rack of cattle prods, the thin black weapons spilling noisily onto the floor.

She reached out, fingernails scratching the cold metallic surface of one of the prods.

Please, she thought.

Please.

I don't want to die.

I'm so close now. So close to the Pen.

A bedraggled platoon of spirits surrounds me. Some are picked off by the bolts of fire unleashed by the technicians below, but others make it through, into the light.

I can still get there.

The air is pregnant with sulphur.

Three more spirits pass through the door.

A fourth is vaporised on the brink.

That won't be me.

I'm so close.

So close.

Bits stumbles, then falls. Instinctively I reach down for his arm, pulling him to his feet.

He smiles at me. It's a look of naked gratitude, one that makes me feel attuned to the world and its innate goodness. He carries on running.

Lazarus is ahead of him.

They both reach out a hand for me.

This is what it means to be liked. To help and be helped.

To belong.

As I fold my hand around Lazarus's, a sea of warmth drenches me. In my many years of life and death, I've never felt anything like it before.

I look down, and realise there's a hole in my chest.

I hold up my hand, and frown as it begins to dissolve in front of me.

I am coming undone.

I walk forward. I will not be stopped. I will make it to the Pen.

Molten flame erupts on my right leg.

My feet are disappearing.

I am disappearing.

I was so close.

'Go,' I shout to my new friends. 'Go.'

Bits pulls Lazarus through the doorway.

Another bolt whizzes past my head. It hits the doorway of light.

The doorway screams in response. It didn't want to be hit. It wasn't designed to be hit.

Neither was I.

It explodes.

There's very little of me left.

Where will I go after this?

What happens after you die for a second time?

Hans didn't need his optical implants to kill Megan. That was fortunate, as they'd become much worse. It wasn't just that he was struggling to see spirits; he was struggling to see the living soul he was strangling to death, too. She was a foggy, blurry, wriggling mess.

After he'd killed her – and her thrashings were getting mercifully less wild – he'd ask one of the techs to take a look at the implants. He wouldn't pretend this whole thing had gone smoothly, but if the action on the monitors was anything to go by, Lazarus would be toast by now, vaporised by a bolt cutter.

Then it might be time to cut and run. Head back to South Africa for a couple of months, lie low. There'd be other

432

opportunities for a man with his skill set. Maybe he'd concentrate on working with the living for a while. You knew where you stood with them.

An alarm continued to sound somewhere.

The whole thing was going to hell.

He squeezed Megan's neck tighter.

He'd take care of her, and then he'd take care of himself.

As Megan's vision began to dim – and for the second time, she had the sensation she was leaving her body – her right hand finally closed around the cattle prod.

Her fingers searched desperately for the 'on' switch.

They found it. A whine filled the air.

'What the fuck?' said Hans.

With every last ounce of her strength, she jerked the prod upwards and felt it connect with the South African's face.

Hans screamed, and God help her, she'd never heard such a sweet sound. The pressure on her neck disappeared, and although it was a blessed relief, she knew she didn't have time to recover. Instead, she convulsed upwards, jabbing the prod into Hans's side, ripping another scream from him and dropping him onto his back.

She should get out. Run while she had the chance.

The cattle prod crackled in her hand.

Fuck *that*.

She wielded it like a bullwhip, lashing him again and again, each scream making the pain in her throat more tolerable.

Only when he'd stopped moving did Megan cast the weapon aside and start to run.

Chapter 33

Joe and Bits stood at the top of a ridge, a scene of wanton de-struction laid out in front of them. It was a long time since either of them had been in the Pen, and a great deal had changed.

'Where the fuck is everyone?' said Bits.

'Hopefully not in those burning buildings,' said Joe.

'We go away for five minutes, and the place falls apart.'

'It was already falling apart.'

'Not this badly.'

'One thing's for sure: no clip-clopping back over that bridge,' said Joe. 'The boom that thing gave off, every fucker on the soil will have heard it.' He lowered his head. 'Jacob didn't make it.'

'Lad stopped to help me up,' said Bits. 'He'd have made it if he hadn't. Doesn't seem right, if even half the stuff he said he'd been through is true. Doesn't seem fair.'

'Life never is. Neither's death.'

Bits looked at his partner expectantly. 'So, what do we do now?'

'We go to the compound,' Joe replied, 'and find out exactly what Daisy-May's been up to since we've been away.'

What Daisy-May had been up to was fighting a gutter war against a squadron of devils that used to be angels.

Winning that war, too, judging by the number of corpses on the floor.

She'd been responsible for her fair share of those corpses, but the Dispossessed had more than stepped up. They'd worked together, becoming with each passing moment a well-oiled machine, standing on each other's shoulders to form towers of humanity that snatched the fallen angels from the sky then plummeted down with them into the filth of the Pen floor, ripping and tearing at their bodies.

We're going to win, thought Daisy-May. This is going to be over soon, and we're going to win.

A scream of static sounded, scoring itself onto the air.

A siren, the sort you'd hear as part of an early-warning system.

A voice boomed out. The words it spoke made no sense, but the tone, the voice itself, she knew. Where from?

The fighting around her slowed. The Dispossessed looked confused. Distracted. They craned their heads upwards, listening to the voice on the air.

Some sort of PA system, thought Daisy-May. It's coming from the compound.

Oh shit.

Dah–dah–*duh*.

Dah–dah–*duh*.

I know that voice. I know that language, too, even though I can't understand it.

I heard it during the trials, in fake Tokyo.

The trial I failed.

It's the language of the dead, spoken by that white-haired bitch who almost brought the whole of existence crashing down.

The Dispossessed had stopped.

Each and every one of them was looking at her.

It wasn't a friendly look.

A whine started in Daisy-May's head as Hanna's voice continued to ring out.

Dah–dah–*duh*.

Dah–dah–*duh*.

It was similar to the chant she'd heard during the trials, but spoken with ten times the conviction. The words seemed to fill every inch of her.

And the thing was, the more she listened, the more those words were beginning to make sense.

She raised her head to the sky and closed her eyes.

She needed to hear this.

'Why not have them tear her to pieces?' said Remus, staring at the display monitors. The Dispossessed had been brought to a standstill, as had their leader.

'I don't want her torn to pieces,' said Hanna. 'She'll be an able number two. A puppet figurehead.'

She took pleasure in the nervousness of Remus's swallow.

'What's to become of me, then?'

'I need you to witness the inauguration. After that, perhaps I'll keep you around as a pet.'

Hanna knew she could have had the Dispossessed attack Daisy-May, but knew too that the current Warden's powers were considerable; there was nothing to say she couldn't have fought them off. Besides, she needed Daisy-May to abdicate to her. Only then would there be a proper transference of power. Only then would she be able to claim her birthright.

No, better to let the recording of her voice play on a loop, keeping them hypnotised and docile. Daisy-May would be similarly enraptured, and then she'd do whatever Hanna told her.

It was all coming together at last.

★

As Daisy-May listened to the rhythmic, seductive repetition of the chant, her eyelids twitched, images flashing back and forth beneath them.

Her grandma.

Her Nottingham home.

Ryan.

Joe.

The Duchess.

The louder the chanting became, though, the muddier these images became. And wasn't that a good thing? There was comfort in forgetting these people, because in various ways they'd brought her nothing but pain and suffering. The chant – Hanna behind it – gave her the opportunity to be part of something bigger.

She wouldn't have to make decisions any more. She needed to merely follow.

God, that sounded good.

Dah–dah–*duh*.

Dah–dah–*duh*.

Mabel's face appeared then, with that familiar grumpy smirk. Her words sounded. The last ones she'd spoken to her.

Remember who you are. There'll be tests – voices – that'll make you doubt yourself. Block 'em out.

Dah–dah–*duh*.

Dah–dah–*duh*.

Maybe she didn't want to block them out.

You're Daisy-May, the bad-ass council-estate girl who became ruler of a realm. Remember that.

Dah–dah–*duh*.

Dah–dah–*duh*.

Maybe she didn't want to remember that. What had remembering ever done, except cause her pain?

I'm going to rest now. Thank you, Mabel. For everything.

When it comes to you, Daisy-May, Mabel replied, *everything always felt like nothing at all.*

The words stung.

Daisy-May flexed her fists, welcoming the pain of nails on palms.

Her eyes opened.

The chant continued. It sounded so good.

Felt even better.

Her subjects were waiting for her.

Hanna smiled generously as she exited the compound's front entrance. The last time she'd been here, her sister had fired upon her, dousing her with a liquid that should have wiped her mind clean. It hadn't, because the Duchess had made it her life's work to underestimate her. Now, she was walking out as Warden in waiting.

Thousands of Dispossessed had massed in front of the compound, dazed expressions on their faces, Hanna's pre-recorded voice still echoing all around. In time, she wouldn't need it, but it was important she re-seed her consciousness and will amongst them. The Dispossessed had changed since she was last here. Grown more intelligent. More wilful. Free will was fine up to a point, but allow it to run *too* free and it was like any weed; it strangled the life out of everything else.

She smiled – with no little amount of relief – when she saw Daisy-May. Like the others, her head was raised, a look of rapture on her face as she listened to the language of the dead. Hanna had to admit, she'd been concerned the Warden would be immune to it, despite her failing the trial, but the girl was as transfixed as the rest of them.

Soon she'd be relieved of the role of Warden. It was perhaps best to then remove her from the equation altogether, despite what she'd said to Remus. Daisy-May had already proved more than capable of fomenting unrest and revolution amongst the Dispossessed; it would be a concern that she'd do so again. A number two that used to be a number one was maths that made no sense.

Hanna looked up. Five of the remaining fallen angels were hovering warily, distrustful, seemingly, of the Dispossessed's cessation of hostilities. They were immune to the language of the dead – indeed, it was a tongue they'd helped invent. It had been a mistake by Remus, allowing them back into the Pen, and one she'd correct when she took over the mantle of Warden.

Still, first things first.

'Kneel,' she called out, gesturing downwards with her hand.

The Dispossessed obeyed.

Daisy-May followed suit.

Hanna walked towards her, glorying in the thousands of eyes upon her, energised by that sense of destiny. There it was – the pin on Daisy-May's black leather jacket. Such a small, insignificant thing, considering the authority it brought with it. This guttersnipe wasn't worthy of it, no matter how much respect Hanna had for her. Rachel had been insane to grant her so much power.

'Give me your hand, Daisy-May.'

Daisy-May obeyed, holding Hanna's hand daintily, like she was visiting royalty.

'Look at me.'

The Warden did so, a dazed look upon her face.

'You've caused us all a great deal of trouble,' said Hanna. 'You've caused a great many deaths, too. Your Duchess died because of you, did you know that?'

Daisy-May shook her head blankly.

'I only wanted to be left alone, yet you and my sister weren't able to do that. Isn't that right?'

Daisy-May nodded dumbly.

'I can't hear you,' said Hanna. 'I asked you whether I was right.'

'Yes, you're right,' said Daisy-May, her voice a monotone.

'Yes, you're right, *ma'am*.'

'Yes, you're right, ma'am.'

Hanna nodded, apparently satisfied. 'That's better. It's important to maintain standards, Daisy-May.'

She turned, beckoning to Remus.

The old man walked forward.

'We're ready to begin.'

Remus nodded. 'Raise your hand,' he said to Daisy-May.

Daisy-May looked at Hanna, who nodded permission.

'Repeat after me,' said Remus. 'I, Daisy-May Braithwaite . . .'

'I, Daisy-May Braithwaite,' she said, a slur in her words.

'Anointed Warden of the Pen.'

'Anointed Warden of the Pen.'

'Hereby renounce that title and bestow it upon Hanna Jankie.'

'Hereby renounce that title,' parroted Daisy-May, 'and bestow it upon Hanna Jankie.'

Hanna smiled. She couldn't help it.

'Now,' she said. 'All that remains is for you to pin the badge onto my chest, and the ceremony will be complete.'

Daisy-May nodded, reaching for her jacket.

Hanna closed her eyes. She needed to savour this moment, to run her tongue around it and drink down every last drop. She'd waited so long. Endured so much.

She felt Daisy-May's hand press against her chest.

She looked down.

Her smile fell off.

'What the hell is this?'

Hanna stared incredulously at the label that had been stuck

440

onto the front of her smock, the one that stated, in messy felt tip: *I DRINK PISS*.

Daisy-May winked at her.

'Dirty cow,' she said.

Playing dumb was difficult when you were smart. Playing befuddled was even trickier; push it too far, and you descended into am-dram zombie mode, slurring your words like a car had just driven over your head.

She'd been tempted. Ready to give up. Mabel's words had hit like a fist, though. She'd given up everything so that Daisy-May could return to the Pen. What was that sacrifice for if she'd just handed over her free will to Hanna?

She looked at the speakers recessed into the compound's roof and waved a hand. Feedback squealed as metal mangled, the barely visible speakers folding in on themselves.

Hanna's recorded voice stopped. The white-haired girl took a step backwards.

'It's impossible,' she said. 'No one can resist the language of the Dead.'

'I've been pissing on impossible from day one,' Daisy-May replied.

'I demand you renounce your title to me.'

Daisy-May gave her the finger. 'Demand this.'

Hanna looked around her wildly, settling on the fallen angels who circled above. 'Kill her.'

The creatures looked from Daisy-May to the dozens of their fallen comrades on the ground. Then they turned, and with a mighty beat of their wings, flew higher into the sky, away from the people down below.

'Looking short on allies there, duck,' said Daisy-May. 'Still got Remus left, I suppose.'

She glanced around. Her former number two had disappeared.

'Just you, then.'

Hanna took another step back. She closed her eyes and began chanting.

The Dispossessed around Daisy-May began to stir.

She's trying to rile them up against me, thought Daisy-May. As long as she can walk and talk, she's going to be a danger.

She sighed. She didn't want to do this. She was no killer.

She was the Warden, though, and these people were her responsibility.

They were people Hanna had abused and used. That made her angry.

She felt molten rage surge in her veins. It powered her. It would allow her to do incredible things if she let it.

She wouldn't.

There was another way.

Daisy-May stuck out a hand.

Hanna snapped rigid.

'What are you doing?' she said, fear etched on her face for the first time.

Daisy-May blinked, and Hanna's mouth opened, a gargled scream escaping from it.

'What I should have done a long time ago,' said Daisy-May. 'Shutting you the fuck up.'

She pulled back with her hand, and the sound of muscle tearing meshed with Hanna screaming.

As she thrust her hand forward again, something flew clean into it.

She looked down in disgust at Hanna's tongue, then tossed it over her shoulder.

'Try that language-of-the-dead shit now.'

Hanna gurgled and choked, her words smashing against the rocks.

'Not so easy without a tongue, is it? I should let the

442

Dispossessed tear you apart. It's what you deserve for controlling and using them. For what you did to the Duchess, too, and all the people you killed on the soil. Not my call, though, and not the way we do it in the Dying Squad. So I'm going to take you into custody and wait and see what the big man says.'

Daisy-May turned away from Hanna and started walking towards the compound entrance.

'I'm not an executioner, I'm just a shit-kicker from Nottingham who tries to do the right thing,' she called out. 'You got a problem with any of that, just gargle.'

The compound had changed a lot.

Remus, it seemed, had a gaudier sense of style than his sackcloth-and-ashes vibe suggested. The efficient aesthetic of the command centre had been replaced by an Ancient Rome vibe. That fitted, Daisy-May supposed; Remus was so ancient, that was probably his era. She'd need to do something about him. Send a team to pick him up from wherever he was hiding. Lucia would provide no such problem; her cooling corpse spoke to that.

It felt a lifetime ago since she'd left here to look for the missing children. Daisy-May didn't know what came next, but she hoped it involved solitude, and maybe old episodes of *Friends*.

She noticed the twitchiness of her colleagues as she strode around the control room. Maybe they thought of themselves as collaborators. Maybe they were. They had to follow someone, though, and Remus would have led them to believe she was dead. She'd put their minds at ease, sooner rather than later. She'd need them. Judging by the screens, there were loads of officers left on the soil, Squad members stranded in the living world, where Remus had effectively abandoned them. She'd need to bring them home. They had work to do.

She hadn't seen Joe on the screens. That was her first thing to dig into, when she'd caught her breath.

Daisy-May retreated to her office. It was a simple place, thread-bare to the point of famine.

No one had cleaned out the bin she'd been sick in, which was *pretty* annoying.

'Is Hanna in the cells?'

She looked up to see Oma Jankie standing in the doorway, her hands behind her back, like she was leaning down to in-spect an antique.

'Yep.'

'I heard you took her tongue.'

'I did,' said Daisy-May. 'You got a problem with that?'

Oma Jankie shook her head. 'Wise of you. She's dangerous.'

'Not a massive fan of your granddaughters, are you?'

'Not when they disappoint me, no.'

'Lost sight of you on the battlefield. Seemed to scarper pretty quick.'

'A battlefield is no place for one as ancient as me.'

'You're the most dangerous person in any room,' said Daisy-May.

'You flatter me.'

'Wasn't really what I was going for.' Daisy-May looked at her wearily. 'What can I do you for?'

'I've had Remus taken into custody,' said Oma Jankie.

Daisy-May leaned forward. 'Really?'

'Of course. He's a danger to every single person in the Pen.'

Smiling, Daisy-May got to her feet. 'Yes, he is. Thanks. Maybe had you pegged wrong after all.'

'I'll take you to him,' said Oma Jankie. 'I imagine you would like a word.'

'I want a lot more than that,' said Daisy-May.

She followed Oma Jankie out into the corridor, knowing that she was going to have to do something about the old woman, find some role for her. She was too disruptive a presence to be allowed to wander the corridors of power freely. Still, she'd shown her loyalty by apprehending Remus. Perhaps there was hope for her yet.

She frowned as a sharp pain flared at the back of her neck.

She put a hand to it. She'd been stung by something.

Her body turned to jelly and she slumped to the floor.

She tried to speak.

She couldn't.

Remus was standing over her, a syringe in his hand.

He tossed it away and crouched down over her.

'You've ruined everything, you silly little girl. Everything I've helped build.'

Daisy-May looked to the left – her eyes were the only thing she could still move – and saw Oma Jankie watching.

'She won't help you,' said Remus. 'She knows you're an aberration that must be corrected.'

'Correct her, then,' said Oma Jankie. 'Quickly.'

Daisy-May felt Remus's hands close around her throat.

How many times can a girl get strangled in one day? she thought. Twice is just fucking careless.

She tried to visualise throwing Remus across the room, but nothing happened.

He seemed to read her mind. 'A sedative that dulls your powers,' he said, increasing the pressure on her throat.

'No,' Daisy-May gasped.

'Who will stop me?' said Remus, deranged zeal in his eyes.

The world began to fade.

'Who?' Remus said again. 'Who?'

'Me.'

Daisy-May's eyes opened.

Her mouth smiled.

Joey.

Joe threw a right hook straight into Remus's face. The pressure on her neck faded as the old man cried out, staggering backwards.

Bits was to the left of him, Oma Jankie large in his gun sights.

Joe hauled Remus to his feet, pinning his arm behind his back then slamming him against the wall. 'Everything all right, guv?'

'Fucking peachy,' croaked Daisy-May. 'What kept you?'

Epilogue

Manchester had put her glad rags on, and she didn't give a damn who knew it.

The city shimmered and glimmered in front of Megan, hundreds of people lining its streets, life force spilling from them, sequins, glitter and gold reflecting off the sun's punchy rays. Pride was as close to a celebration of life that Megan had ever seen, and all the more glorious for it.

She raised her camera, firing off a series of shots, the composition studied, the spontaneity empowering. She'd made a career out of photographing the dead, curated Easter eggs for those who shared her ability. Now, she didn't care to share her gift with those people. She'd spent enough time dealing in the business of the dead and the past. Her next exhibition would celebrate life, and the future.

She'd changed things at the compound. She'd shared the secrets of the experiments on the living, bust open the myth of the afterlife. There was no denying it now. What Hanna had done in Tokyo had wedged open the door, and Megan had proceeded to drive a tank through it. She didn't know whether that was a good thing, but she truly believed it was a necessary one. No more secrets.

She didn't know how the knowledge she'd released would

reshape the world. To tell the truth, she didn't much care, either.

Music blasted from the procession as the people danced, and Megan lowered her camera.

Smiling, she melted into the crowd, pressed in by love and happiness, by peace and joy, all thoughts of a past she'd never known forgotten.

Life was good.

Life was for living.

Hanna hadn't found time to miss her tongue yet, because she had nothing to say to Remus. How she wished her cellmate shared that sentiment. The silly old fool never shut up, blathering on endlessly about revenge he'd take, and how everyone had betrayed him. If only Daisy-May had ripped her ears off, instead of her tongue, she wouldn't have been forced to listen to him.

And then there was Oma Jankie.

She'd prayed she'd never have to see her grandmother's craggy, whiskered face again, yet here she was, glowering away in the corner like there wasn't enough disappointment in the world to sum up her feelings towards her granddaughter.

Some plan. The language of the dead had failed her. She should have known better than to trust the senile old hag.

At least she didn't have Oma Jankie's voice in her head any more. Why would she bother when she could simply call across the room?

Hanna closed her eyes. It didn't feel like there was very much left of her. Half her head was gone. Her tongue was gone. Her plans to rule the Pen were gone. And now she had the ignominy of being locked up in one of the holding cells.

Still, at least it wasn't hell.

A rumbling sounded, far away.

Hanna froze.

'What's that?' said Remus, looking behind him.

Hanna squeezed her fists. It wasn't possible.

'No,' said Oma Jankie. 'No, no, no.'

I killed you, Hanna thought. Drove a piece of metal right through your heart.

Thunder, louder this time, a bass growl that seemed to vibrate through her body.

A crack of light appeared in the cell.

'What devilry is this?' said Remus, scrabbling backwards, away from the light.

A hand appeared in the light slash.

A man followed that hand.

He wore a suit so well cut it was as if God himself had tailored it.

A hat sat jauntily on the top of his head.

A guitar was slung around his back. An old acoustic thing.

'How you folks doing today?' he asked, raising the hat in greeting and offering them a broad smile, a cigarette dangling from the corner of his mouth.

Hanna wouldn't have replied even if she could. She knew what this man represented. *Who* he represented.

His accent was thick with the American South. His face smiled when his eyes did anything but.

'Name's Robert Johnson,' he said, returning the hat to his head. 'I've been sent to collect you people. Don't s'pose I need to explain who I'm collecting you for, or where that fella resides. None of us are children here; we know the deals we made, and who we made them with.'

'I made no deal,' Remus said, indignation crawling all over his face.

'Broke one, though,' said Johnson. 'Supposed to be working for the Lord, yet all you cared about was working for yourself.

449

Consequences for those sorts of decisions. Repercussions, too.'

'I don't answer to you,' said Remus.

'Girl in the corner knows what's what,' said Johnson, winking. 'Cat might have her tongue – hell, that puss clean ate it down – but her mind's working just fine. You know what's coming, don't you, Hanna? You gonna fight me, despite that?'

Hanna shook her head.

There'd be another day. Another chance. Another fight, and one she might be able to win.

Johnson swung the guitar around, then began picking at the strings. 'Wrote this song a long time ago. Always like to play it at times like this.'

He closed his eyes and began to sing.

I got to keep movin', I got to keep movin',
Blues fallin' down like hail, blues fallin' down like hail,
Hmm-mmm, blues fallin' down like hail, blues fallin' down like hail,
And the days keeps on worryin' me.

He opened his eyes, and looked from Hanna to Remus to Oma Jankie, the playing getting faster, his fingers on the strings a blur.

'There's a *hellhound* on my trail, *hellhound* on my trail . . .'

Thunder rumbled. Hanna felt her body go rigid.

She began floating towards Johnson.

'Hellhound on my trail . . .'

Whiteness engulfed her.

In her head, she screamed.

Whoever said trains were the only way to travel was a cretin. That, or they'd never travelled first class on a plane before.

It was a long time since (former) Director Isiah Matthews had been on a plane himself, and those last few occasions had been on military charter flights, which tended to skimp on the customer service somewhat. No such problem today: the 13.45 from Berlin to Panama was shaping up nicely in that department, thank you very much. There'd been champagne as he'd boarded (a very respectable Drappier Grande Sendrée), and a seat that was more of a bed. A flat-screen, too, for him to watch a film on later.

There was also a delicious young man, one seat over. They'd exchanged a couple of glances, and half a smile. Forty years his junior, at least, but that had never stopped him before. You didn't lose your charm with age, just your looks, and he'd kept hold of his better than most. He'd go over, say hello in a couple of moments. One didn't want to look too keen. They had the first-class section to themselves, by the look of it.

Matthews closed his eyes and settled back into his seat. It had been quite the week. So strange to have seen Jacob again. To be interrogated by Lazarus, that Dying Squad lackey, too. He didn't like people knowing he'd murdered Colonel and Ralf Voigt, but there wasn't a great deal either of them could do about it; spirits were hardly people, after all. It wasn't the perfect crime, but it was pretty close. People always said money was never worth falling out over. That might be true, but it was *always* worth killing over. So was revenge.

He opened his eyes, checking his Cartier Santos wristwatch. Frustrating that the plane hadn't taken off yet. Money could buy you vintage champagne, but not punctuality, apparently.

'Excuse me, sir.'

Matthews turned to see that the young man he'd spied earlier was standing above him. This time, he didn't look quite so friendly.

'Yes?' Matthews said, flashing his best Errol Flynn smile.

He noticed movement out of the corner of his eye. Two sky marshals, trying not to look armed.

'Can you confirm you are Isiah Theodore Matthews?'

This wasn't good. This wasn't good at all.

'I can,' said Matthews, 'but you clearly know that anyway.'

The man nodded, then turned to the two marshals. 'Please take Mr Matthews into custody.'

Matthews shifted in his seat. 'This is outrageous. On what charge?'

'The charge of treason, sir,' said the man, a small smile on his lips. 'That's for starters. The German authorities will want to have a word with you too, I shouldn't wonder, about a series of murders. They'll have to wait their turn, though.'

Matthews looked left and right.

'You could try and make a run for it,' said the man. 'Save the American taxpayer a lot of money.'

He considered it for a second, then slumped back in his seat. 'Aren't you supposed to read me my rights?'

The man leaned in. 'If it was up to me, I'd have this plane take off, shoot you in the kneecaps, then throw you out over the Atlantic Ocean. Traitors like you deserve little else.'

Matthews shook his head. 'How did you know where to find me?'

As one of the marshals slapped a pair of handcuffs on him, the man smiled.

'A little ghost told us.'

Everything changes, Joe thought, and everything stays the same.

It wasn't so long ago that it was him and Daisy-May down there in the main control room, running an eye over their rookie Dispossessed recruits. The Nottingham girl he'd had a hand in killing had plucked him from hell and tasked him with training the next band of Dying Squad officers – had eventually partnered him with one, too – and now it was Bits

452

who was down there, giving the same sort of faux-inspirational speech he himself had given all those months ago.

'Jealous?'

Joe smiled.

'Just thinking what a tough job Bits has, whipping that lot into shape.'

'You managed it,' said Daisy-May, perching next to him on the desk, 'and you're *shit*.'

'Cheers,' said Joe. 'Loyal as anything, Bits. Didn't give up on me even when I disappeared.'

'You're loyal enough,' said Daisy-May. 'Came back for me, didn't you?'

'That was just lucky timing.'

'That's all timing ever needs to be.'

They sat in silence for a moment, watching as Chestnut broke ranks to make a finger-wagging point. From this distance – and through the glass observation window – it was difficult to see what that point was, exactly, but there was little doubt that it was both animated and passionate.

'Wouldn't fancy training Chestnut,' said Daisy-May. 'Right gob on her.'

'That doesn't sound like anyone I've ever met,' said Joe, with half a smile.

'I'm the height of restraint, mate. Barely know I'm in the room.'

'They can hear you in hell,' said Joe. 'Probably half the punishment of being there.'

She jumped to her feet. 'You ready?'

'Yeah,' he replied. 'I'm just not sure what it is I'm supposed to be ready for.'

Joe tried to find a description for the place they'd walked to that wasn't *underground cavern*. He couldn't.

453

Whatever this place was, he'd never been here before. It was underneath the Dying Squad compound itself; judging by the three-minute rickety lift ride, deep underneath it. The air was different down here, not as chlorine-heavy, and the setting was spectacular; like so much of the Pen, it seemed designed to show how utterly insignificant you were, so colossal was its scale. The lift had spat them out into a cathedral of rock, the vast mountain wall facing them appearing to have had a small railway track stitched onto it. That track, Joe noted, started just a few feet away from them. An old mining cart sat on the rails.

'What is this place?'

'This is one of those hidden-away places they tell you about when you become the big dog,' Daisy-May replied. 'Admittedly, I've only *just* been told about it.'

Joe looked around him wonderingly. 'Looks like a labour yard for building heaven.'

'Not quite,' said Daisy-May, 'but you're on the right lines. We park our arses in that cart and it'll take us to the soil.'

Joe frowned. 'What?'

'Used to be the only way to travel there until the Gloop became a thing,' said Daisy-May. 'Don't need a mask or any of that shit. You just sit back and enjoy the ride.'

Joe shook his head. 'You couldn't have told us this before? Bits and I almost got eaten the last time we went through the Gloop. You should see the horrific shit that's in there now.'

'Like I said, I only just found out about it,' said Daisy-May. 'Think it's a rarely used, need-to-know thing. Like, it shouldn't be easy making this journey, otherwise going to the soil'd be like piling onto a Ryanair flight: every fucking spirit'd be doing it.'

'Why do we need to go to the soil at all?' he said. 'I just left that party. Never thought I'd say this, but I could really use a bit of Pen time. Recharge the batteries.'

'It's not a case, if that's what you're thinking,' said Daisy-May. 'It's something else.'

'Very mysterious.'

'Very ignorant. Got no more idea of where we're heading than you do. All I have is an order: we're to get onto that cart and see where it takes us.'

Joe looked at it thoughtfully. 'You don't think . . .'

'. . . that it's going to take us to heaven, or whatever they're calling it this week?' Daisy-May smiled sadly. 'No, mate, I don't. We couldn't be that lucky. Or that good. This is destined for the soil; I can smell it on the wheels. Why it's taking us there, well, we'll find that out soon enough.'

As soon at their arses hit the cold bucket seats, the cart began to move. Joe had feared it'd be roller-coaster fast (it had the appearance of something out of an Indiana Jones theme-park ride), but the pace as it proceeded up the gentle incline was Sunday-driver sedate.

'Wanted to talk to you about the lad in Berlin.'

Daisy-May's voice snapped his attention back. 'Can't get enough of talking about my failures,' he said.

'Not sure how you failed.'

'Jacob was on the periphery of every lead I had about the Spook dealer,' said Joe, tapping his fingers against the cart's metal skin as it climbed higher and higher. 'If I'd found him earlier, I could have brought Matthews to justice.'

'That's what's bugging you? I wouldn't worry about Matthews. I've got that situation in hand.'

Joe looked at her. 'Yeah?'

'Yeah. The lad? Turns out he has quite a backstory. Every word he told you was true, 'cos when I got the order for this meeting, I got the down-low on him, too. Jacob Block was supposed to be the Warden after the Duchess. Would have

455

been if he hadn't been trapped on the soil by the Nazis and a whole host of other wasters. Poor lad was pawed and pawned over every minute of his life. His death, as well.'

'What would have happened to him?' said Joe. 'After he got hit on the bridge?'

'I don't know,' said Daisy-May. 'For his sake, I hope he didn't end up in Oblivion.'

They glanced at each other as the cart came to a stop.

Joe looked down, his stomach lurching. They were high. Very high.

Might have spoken too soon on that whole theme-park thing, he thought.

The cart began to drop.

Daisy-May screamed with sheer, rip-it-up pleasure. Hers had been a life and death of challenges and hardship, but just occasionally, it tossed you a moment of white-hot joy, too. The faster the cart plunged downwards, the bigger the blob of light grew at the bottom of the track. It had started as a pinprick to begin with, so small she'd assumed she'd imagined it. The closer they got, the more it looked like a doorway.

The wind tugged at her hair, whipping at her skin.

Never been on a roller coaster before, she thought. And you know what? It's not shit.

She laughed as Joe screamed.

They plunged into the light.

The cart didn't so much as come to a measured stop as tip them both out, arse over tit. It was like there was a blockage on the track that had flipped the humble carriage clean in the air. That was what it felt like to Joe, anyway, as he tumbled hard onto the ground. He was left flat on his back and looking up at a sky of clear blue.

He sat up, dusting himself down. There was no sign of the cart. Daisy-May, though, he could see clearly enough; she sat a few feet away, tousling her green hair.

Joe looked around him. The place was familiar.

'Not this shithole again,' said Daisy-May. 'Whole world of places to visit, and we keep getting sent to a Lincolnshire graveyard.'

Joe got to his feet, assessing the scene. This was where he'd been buried. The graveyard was deserted, save for a robin sitting on a gravestone a few feet away, and a gardener clad in green overalls. The man's hair was long (pinned up in a style Joe could only describe as a man bun), and he was crouching in front of a gravestone, digging away at a clump of weeds that were threatening to overgrow it.

'So what do we do now?' Joe asked.

Daisy-May shrugged her shoulders. 'This is as much as I was told. Didn't even know we'd be travelling back to your old stomping ground.'

She closed her eyes and angled her face towards the sun. 'Missed the soil, have to admit. Missed daylight, anyway, and people not trying to overthrow me.'

'Well, watch out for that gardener,' said Joe, nodding towards him. 'He looks like he's got revolution in his eyes.'

The gardener turned, smiling, looking right at him. 'Not really my style, man. I'm a lover, not a fighter.'

'You can see us?' said Daisy-May, staring at him.

'I can,' said the man. 'Hustle on over here, so I can do it properly.'

Joe put the gardener at around thirty years old, but honestly, it was difficult to tell, so unkempt and hipster was his beard. He was deeply tanned – he clearly spent a great deal of his life outside – and one look at his hands revealed that working with them was what he spent most of his day doing. He had a smile that said he knew the secrets of the universe and would gladly share them if you'd just ask.

His accent was American. West Coast, if Joe was pushed.

'What's your name?' asked Daisy-May.

'Names, man,' the gardener replied. 'Who's got time for them? They're like a chain round your neck.'

'Always found they're useful for knowing who I'm talking to,' said Joe.

The man laughed. 'I know yours. Joe Lazarus. Made quite the impression in the short time you've been around.' He pointed at Daisy-May. 'And this queen? Daisy-May. So amazing, they named you twice.'

'That's *who* we are,' said Daisy-May, hands on her hips. '*Why* are we here?'

The man clicked his fingers. 'Straight to business. Give a guy a hand first, would you? Just need to clear this headstone. Damn shame, the way these things get.'

Joe and Daisy-May walked over, Joe stopping dead when he read the inscription. 'This is *my* headstone.'

'That it is,' said the gardener, pulling Japanese knotweed from the base of the stone.

'Doesn't look like you've OD'ed on visitors to it,' said Daisy-May.

The gardener pulled the last piece of vegetation away, then stood up, nodding, seemingly satisfied.

'That's what being a treacherous drug dealer gets you, I suppose,' said Joe. 'Heavily limits the floral arrangements.'

'There's not even a message on it,' said Daisy-May. 'Just your name, and when you lived and died.'

'What else is there when it comes down to it?' said Joe. 'I'm lucky to get that much.'

'See, Joe, that's personal growth that lights me up inside, it really does,' said the gardener. 'We've been impressed upstairs by the things you've done. You put others first and yourself last. That's a hell of a thing, and a hell of a change. Kind of dug your whole Jesus-in-the-temple vibe, too, when you were freeing those poor women. Very cool.'

'Where's "upstairs"?' said Joe.

'Shit,' said Daisy-May. 'You're from the Next Place, aren't you? From heaven itself.'

The gardener smiled. 'Always the smartest person in the room, DM.'

'Smartest mouth, maybe,' said Joe. 'That true, though? You're really from the Next Place?'

'That I am, Joseph,' said the gardener. 'And I come bearing gifts. Gifts don't come much better than when they're delivered from heaven. It's sort of a gold-plated seal of approval.'

Joe and Daisy-May exchanged a look.

'We've made it to the Next Place?' said Joe.

The gardener shifted on his feet. 'One of you has.'

Daisy-May's heart began to race.

It can't be me, she thought.

The gardener turned to Joe. 'Need to level with you, man: it's not you. I made a case for you, but you're not quite there yet. Got a path for you, though. It's a winding one, but the Next Place is at the end of it.'

'Will I still be Dying Squad?' asked Joe.

'You never stop being Dying Squad,' the gardener said, smiling. 'Am I right, Daisy-May?'

'Fucking A,' the girl replied.

'It's a special department, though,' the gardener said. 'You'll be working on the soil, with a living partner. That was something we did a lot of, back in the day, and the idea's picked up traction again. That Japanese cop, Hatoyama, showed it could work. He's a cool cat, by the way; you'll meet him one day.'

'Will I still be working out of the Pen?' said Joe.

The gardener shook his head. 'We need you on the ground quicker than that. You and your music trick showed us there's a better way of doing things.'

He reached into his overall, withdrawing a second-generation iPod. Its white plastic shell was reassuringly grubby. 'This'll mean you can have a top-up whenever you need it. Keep that memory good and sharp.'

Joe took the device, noting the white headphones that had been wrapped around it. 'When do I start?'

The gardener smiled apologetically. 'No time like the present, right? We don't really do R&R. Least, not until we get to the Next Place. Spook's everywhere now, and that chemical isn't going away. Going to be lots of consequences to that – it'll be your job to deal with them. More besides.'

He nodded at the iPod. 'Oh, and check out the nineties playlist I put on there. Pure Britpop heaven, man. We've tried to pick out tracks that mean something to you. They seem to work the best.'

Joe slipped the device into his coat pocket.

The gardener turned to Daisy-May. 'Which brings me to you, DM. It's time to hang up the crown. We're calling you in.'

'Why?' said Daisy-May.

'Seen a lot of people over the years, and not one has deserved to go to the house in the sky more than you. The old man requested it personally. You've done several lifetimes' worth of good deeds.'

'The old man?' said Daisy-May. 'You mean . . .'

'We don't do names,' said the gardener, smiling. 'Let's leave it at that.'

'What about the Pen?' said Daisy-May. 'I'm, like, the *boss* there.'

'Got a replacement for you. It's all in hand. You don't need to worry about a thing.'

Daisy-May stood there considering. 'So this is it?'

The gardener nodded.

'Well fuck me.' She jabbed a thumb towards Joe. 'Will I ever see this clown again?'

'That's kind of up to him, isn't it? I'll give you a couple of minutes to say your goodbyes.'

The gardener strolled away, whistling a tune. 'Oh Happy Day', if Joe wasn't much mistaken.

'Not big on goodbyes,' said Joe, sticking his hands in his pockets.

'That's like saying "I hate hospitals". It's obvious, man.'

'Giving me shit right to the end,' he said with a smile.

'You can take it, Joey.'

'It's Joe.'

Daisy-May sprang at him, folding him in a hug.

Joe stiffened, then returned it.

'Thanks for coming back to save me,' said Daisy-May.

'We're not close to being even,' said Joe, 'but you're welcome.'

They broke apart, Joe frowning.

'Is that a tear,' said Daisy-May with a delighted squeal. 'Is the baddest drug dealer this side of Boston actually crying for little old me?'

'Hay fever,' said Joe gruffly. 'We're in the countryside, in case you'd forgotten. Now fuck off. You've got a cloud to catch.'

Daisy-May went to say something, then thought better of it. She nodded, and walked over to the gardener.

The cart had appeared next to Joe, magically turned the right way up and back on the tracks. He looked at it quizzically.

'That'll take you where you need to go,' said the gardener. 'Good luck, man.'

'How will I know when it's my turn?' said Joe.

'You'll know,' replied the gardener.

Joe gave Daisy-May a final wave, then hopped into the cart.

It shuffled forward, then just like that, he was gone.

'Now it's our turn,' said the gardener.

'Got a favour to ask,' said Daisy-May. 'A wrong that needs righting.'

'My favourite type,' said the gardener. 'Shoot.'

'There's a friend of mine. She's trapped where she shouldn't be. It's plain wrong. Any chance you could get her out?'

The gardener smiled. 'Sister, I'm *literally* Jesus. If I can't spring the occasional miracle, then what's the point of me?'

The last thing I remember is pain.

That's gone now. There's just a corridor of light that seems to go on for ever but doesn't. Red and black cauldron skies are visible in the distance. I've seen their like before, on the bridge.

I'm walking towards the Pen.

There's a woman there waiting for me. I've seen her before, too. A long time ago. She came to collect me when I died at the hands of the Nazis. I never forget a face, but her name is more difficult.

I step out of the corridor of light, and find the old woman is appraising me.

'You remember me, lad?'

I nod, though I say that her name is less clear to me.

'Mabel,' she says, 'and seeing as you're going to be the new Warden, they reckon it's a good idea for me to show you what's what. How does that sound?'

I tell her it sounds wonderful, and she mumbles something about remembering how I always did sound like I had a broom shoved up my arse.

I think this is a joke.

We walk together past streams of smiling souls, and I think of my sister and my parents, hoping that they know, somehow, that I am finally here.

That I am finally home.

Acknowledgements

Writing this trilogy wouldn't have been possible without these behind-the-scenes stars, so a massive thank you to Harry Illingworth for taking a chance on *The Dying Squad*, and on me. Rachel Winterbottom of Gollancz was our first recruit; she's also an editing ninja, and a ton of fun to work with. Thanks to Brendan Durkin for keeping the whole thing running in Rachel's absence. A special shout-out to Jenna Petts, publicist-extraordinaire, who went above and beyond time and time again, and was an absolute pleasure to work with.

Throughout the trilogy Dan Woodall, the Simcox brothers and Christa Larwood have been great beta-readers and even better friends. My dad was there throughout with positive vibes and tons of support, which I hugely appreciate.

Goldsboro Books is the best bookshop in the world, and not just because they produced special edition copies of the books and hosted a kick-ass launch for them. Thanks to everyone there for their hard work and support.

Kirsty Eyre is the ultimate partner in writing and in life, and is never afraid to call me out on my bullshit. It's no exaggeration to say these books wouldn't exist without me having met her, and without our two sons keeping me well and truly grounded.

Finally, thanks to everyone that's bought and supported these books, it's meant everything. As a great man once said, I don't know where I'm going from here, but I promise it won't be boring . . .

Credits

Adam Simcox and Gollancz would like to thank everyone at Orion who worked on the publication of *The Ungrateful Dead* in the UK.

Editorial
Brendan Durkin
Áine Feeney

Copy editor
Jane Selley

Proof reader
Patrick McConnell

Audio
Paul Stark
Jake Alderson

Contracts
Anne Goddard
Paul Bulos

Design
Rachael Lancaster
Tomas Almeida
Joanna Ridley
Nick May

Editorial Management
Charlie Panayiotou
Jane Hughes

Finance
Jennifer Muchan
Jasdip Nandra
Sue Baker

Marketing
Brittany Sankey

Production
Paul Hussey

Publicity
Jenna Petts

Operations
Jo Jacobs
Sharon Willis
Lisa Pryde

Sales
Jen Wilson
Esther Waters
Victoria Laws
Rachael Hum
Ellie Kyrke-Smith
Frances Doyle
Georgina Cutler